For Amy Griswold and Sally Malcolm,
the rest of the Legacy team.

STARGATE ATLANTIS™

THIRD PATH

Book eight of the LEGACY series

MELISSA SCOTT & JO GRAHAM

FANDEMONIUM BOOKS

FAN DE MON IUM

An original publication of Fandemonium Ltd, produced under license from MGM Consumer Products.

Fandemonium Books
United Kingdom
Visit our website: www.stargatenovels.com

STARGATE ATLANTIS™

METRO-GOLDWYN-MAYER Presents
STARGATE ATLANTIS™
JOE FLANIGAN RACHEL LUTTRELL JASON MOMOA JEWEL STAITE
ROBERT PICARDO and DAVID HEWLETT as Dr. McKay
Executive Producers BRAD WRIGHT & ROBERT C. COOPER
Created by BRAD WRIGHT & ROBERT C. COOPER

MGM

Print ISBN: 978-1-905586-70-7 Ebook ISBN: 978-1-80070-007-9

CHAPTER ONE

"DAMN IT, McKay." John Sheppard urged the damaged puddle jumper to its best speed, ignoring the warnings flashing across his control boards. In the distance, he could see McKay's puddle jumper, and beyond it the greater bulk of the Vanir ship that they were chasing. His own main propulsion unit was damaged, yes, but everything else was holding together, and there was no way McKay could stop the Vanir ship from escaping without some help. And the Vanir had to be stopped: not only had Ronon been caught up in their transport beam, but Elizabeth Weir had been taken with him. Elizabeth... He had given her up for dead three years ago, endured her return in a Replicator's body, and thought he'd come to terms with losing her. When Rodney had come back from his suicide mission claiming to have been saved by an Ascended version of Elizabeth, John had been skeptical, but there had been enough evidence to make it worth pursuing. And then... He checked his altitude, urging the puddle jumper to gain height as the ground grew rougher beneath them, rolling hills turning to steeper foot-hills. And then, against all odds, they'd found her — as he would have expected, she'd found them, worked the problem, gotten herself to Sateda. He'd seen her, spoken with her just long enough to be sure it was in some meaningful sense Elizabeth Weir, and then the Vanir had appeared out of nowhere to snatch her away. He didn't know why they wanted her — didn't care — but he was going to get her back.

In the distance, he saw a flash of light, and the puddle jumper reported that McKay had fired more drones. John checked the auto-repair circuits, and asked for more speed. The puddle jumper tried to answer, shuddering under him, but warnings flared across his displays.

"All right, all right," he said, and let the puddle jumper settle back into optimum flight. McKay had to hold them, had to stop them from leaving the atmosphere. "You can do it, Rodney," he said, under his breath. "Just hold them for me, that's all you have to do —"

There was another flash in the sky, and a smudge that might have been smoke, quickly whipped away by wind. The puddle jumper reported that the other craft had slowed, that Sheppard was starting to gain on them. "Come on, Rodney—"

A third flash, and he checked the telemetry, frowning at the sudden deceleration. "Rodney..."

"No!" McKay's voice was suddenly sharp in his earpiece. "No, no, no—"

"What?" John checked his boards again. The Vanir ship had slowed still further, and was losing altitude fast. "Jumper two, what's your status?"

"They're going to crash," McKay said.

John swore, but one look at the warnings already flickering on the displays told him he was pushing the jumper to its limits. At least the sensors had a good lock on McKay's jumper; there would be no trouble finding the crash. "Stay with them," he said, and turned his attention to the controls.

It wasn't long before he saw the plume of black smoke rising from the slopes ahead of him, but it seemed to take hours before he could bring the jumper down beside McKay's machine. McKay was already out, of course, poking at the twisted metal of the Vanir ship, and as soon as the jumper's door opened he waved and shouted.

"Come on, Sheppard! We've got to find them!"

"Hang on," John said. McKay already had one first aid kit, he was pleased to see; he grabbed the second as he left the jumper, and then stopped, studying the wreck.

"Come on!" McKay turned back toward the ship, but John caught his arm.

"Wait!" He scanned the wreck, biting his lip as he took in the extent of the damage. The smoke had cleared—presumably fire suppression systems had done their work—but the forward quarter of the ship was buried deep in the rocky ground. Buried and crumpled, he amended, wincing. Nothing in that section could possibly have survived. If Ronon and Elizabeth had been in the control section—He shoved that thought away. "How much do you know about Asgard ships?"

"What?" McKay blinked, shook his head. "I've read papers, why?

How does that matter?"

"Do you know where they'd keep prisoners?"

McKay blinked again. "No. We haven't exactly spent a lot of time as prisoners of the Asgard, considering that they were kind of our allies."

"What about when you and Jackson were taken prisoner?"

"Stasis pods," McKay said. "They didn't let us out until we got to the planet."

John bit his lip again. Stasis pods needed power and, from the look of the ship, it would be running on back-ups if there was any power at all. Surely stasis pods would have failsafes, he told himself, and looked back at McKay. "Let's go."

A side hatch had broken open in the crash, and John climbed carefully through the jagged gap, trying not to burn himself on the hot metal. He found himself in a narrow corridor, lit only by the light from the torn hull, and he played the light from his P90 around the area as McKay clambered in after him.

"Maintenance corridor, I think," McKay said, after a moment. "Try to your right."

John moved carefully forward, hunching his shoulders as the ceiling sagged toward him, but a few yards along, he found a hatch. It was unlocked, the mechanism still moving smoothly, and he pushed it open, P90 at the ready. There was more light beyond the hatch, pale but definite, and McKay gave a gasp of relief.

"All right. They've got emergency power, at least."

"That's a mixed blessing," John said.

"It's good if we want to find Elizabeth alive. And Ronon." McKay paused. "Of course, yes, it may mean that there are also some Vanir around, which, no, that's not so great."

"Yeah." John turned slowly. They'd come out into what was obviously a main corridor, a weak band of emergency lighting glowing along the center of the ceiling. The walls were smooth, gray, unmarked, the deck only a little darker, though toward the ship's bow the ceiling was cracked and caved in, spilling a tangle of cables.

"There's a hatch back here," McKay said. "Hang on — I've got it."

John turned, keeping his P90 ready. "Anything?"

"No sign of Vanir." McKay peered cautiously through the opening. "No sign of anything, but I think — yeah, if we go this way, we should hit a central corridor. That should be the most efficient way to search."

"Good enough," John said.

The central corridor lay about thirty feet along, wider and taller than any of the other corridors they'd seen so far. More compartments opened off of it, some doors jarred open, some still sealed, and a string of lights in the ceiling flashed alternately blue and orange, adding weird shadows to the emergency lighting.

"Forward?" John said, after a moment, and McKay nodded.

"Checking the compartments as we go."

"I'll cover you," John said.

The first two compartments were already open, doors fully retracted into the bulkheads. Both contained only a few pieces of furniture that seemed to be attached to the deck and bulkheads, and they moved on quickly. The next door was jammed halfway open, but it was enough to see that it held more of the same gray furniture. There was a scattering of something that looked like they might be DVDs on the deck, if DVDs were matte purple triangles. McKay gave them a covetous look, but John pushed him on.

"We can come back for those."

The rest of the compartments were empty, too, though their doors were jammed and cracked and the deck underfoot was starting to make ominous snapping sounds. "We must be getting close to the control room," John said, and adjusted his grip on the P90.

"Yes. Not that I think there's going to be anything left that'll be of use to us —" McKay stopped abruptly, grimacing in disgust. "Ugh, do you smell that?"

"Yeah." It was coming from the bulkhead just ahead of them, an ugly mix of hot metal and ash and an acrid, electric scent underlain with something sickly and vaguely sweet. John made himself try the hatch, and wasn't surprised when it jammed. He slung his P90 out of the way and tried again, using both hands, and this time the heavy metal slid sideways a few inches, releasing another wave of the smell.

"Oh, that's not nice," McKay said.

John didn't bother to answer, but adjusted his P90 so that he could shine its light into the gap. He caught a glimpse of twisted metal and a few thin curls of smoke, and what looked like a Vanir hand protruding from between two fallen beams. It looked surprisingly vulnerable dangling there, and he looked away, tasting bile.

"Ok, nothing there we can do anything about."

"Are you sure?" McKay began, pushing past to look for himself, and stopped abruptly. "Oh."

"Yeah," John said again. If Elizabeth and Ronon had been in the control room, they were definitely dead, sliced to pieces and crushed by the weight of metal. But there was no reason to think they were there, he told himself. The rest of the ship was intact, and McKay and Jackson had been put into stasis.

"That's an Asgard hand," McKay said. He looked a little green, but had himself well under control. "Well, a Vanir's, anyway. Not human."

"We keep looking," John said, and knew he sounded grim.

They made their way back down the main corridor. Once they passed the cross corridor where they'd come in, they began searching the compartments, but most of them were the same nearly-empty spaces they'd seen before. One had been hung with viewscreens, a ring circling nearly the entire compartment just below the ceiling, but all of them were cracked, and one was just an empty frame, with a spill of something acid-yellow down the compartment wall.

"Let's not touch that," John said, and for once McKay nodded.

The next compartment looked as though it might have been some sort of lab, though the screens of the workstations were also shattered, and all the loose material had been flung violently against the forward bulkhead.

"This has to be a good sign," McKay said. "Right? Things are in a lot better shape back here."

It was true, but John didn't dare let himself hope. "Stasis pods. Can you find them?"

"If you can find me a working console, yes."

John nodded. "Let's go, then."

The next two compartments were much the same, all the equipment destroyed, but when John glanced into the third, he caught his breath. There was a lot less trash on the floor, and no broken equipment; instead, the consoles looked intact and at least one of the screens was dark but undamaged. He put his shoulder to the door and pushed it back. "McKay! Take a look at this."

He stopped, so suddenly that McKay collided with him. The consoles were mostly intact, all right, and on the floor between the two rows of control boards lay an unconscious Vanir.

"What — oh." McKay sounded just as shocked as John felt, and John shook himself back to business.

"See if you can figure out what this all is, and if it's safe to get it working. I'm going to take a look at this guy."

"Or whatever," McKay said, and turned his attention to the nearest console.

John went to one knee beside the Vanir. He'd forgotten how small the Asgard were, just about three feet tall, gray and skinny with wrinkled skin and oversized heads. This one's eyes were closed, which made it look even more fragile. John felt carefully along the thin neck, wondering if this was where you found its pulse. He felt nothing, but as he moved his hand away, he thought he felt the ghost of its breath against his wrist. He froze, and a long moment later it came again, the faintest touch of air on his skin.

"I think this one's alive," he said, "but it's not looking good."

"I've found the stasis pods," McKay said. "Damn it, I can't operate them from here — something seems to be wrong with the remote controls."

"Then we'll go to them," John said. He pulled one of the Mylar blankets from his first aid kit and tucked it around the unconscious Vanir, not daring to do anything more. Once they'd freed Elizabeth and Ronon, someone on Atlantis would probably be able to tell them the best way to treat a Vanir.

McKay led them down a side corridor, past compartments that showed even less damage than before, and John allowed himself to hope that they might find the stasis pods similarly undamaged.

"Here," McKay said, and shoved at a stubborn door. John put his shoulder to it as well, and it slid back to reveal a narrow room dominated by a row of translucent cylinders. Three were empty, their lights all out; the remaining two showed a steady pattern of blue at top and bottom.

"Elizabeth and Ronon?" It was impossible to be sure through the clouded glass, but certainly the one on the left was big enough to be Ronon.

"Uh-huh." McKay was already busy at the nearest console. "Ok, they have power, and plenty of it — looks like there's a separate back-up source for this whole system, probably some sort of battery. Life signs check out, so we should be — Oh."

"Rodney..."

McKay looked up, his face stricken. "The main computer is dead. I can't find any preprogrammed routine to get them out of here."

"Ok, that's not good." John looked at the pods, wondering how long this battery would last, and made himself look back at McKay. "Can you figure out how to do it?"

"Well, probably — I mean, yes, of course, I can, but we're talking bringing a human being out of Asgard-induced stasis without any help from the computers or an instruction manual. I can't even read most of what the screens are telling me. So, yes, I can probably deduce which things do what, eventually, but I'd really like not to experiment on friends. On Elizabeth." McKay took a breath. "Which means, and I can't believe I'm saying this — Dr. Jackson is likely to know more about how to get them out safely. He's had more experience with the Asgard."

John considered the question, but he knew McKay was right. The sooner they got Ronon and Elizabeth out, the better, and there was the injured Vanir to consider — he knew he personally had a few questions he wanted to ask that being. "All right. I'm going to take your jumper back to the Stargate and pick up the rest of the team. It's going to take me about an hour to get there and back. Will you be all right that long?"

Will they be all right, he meant, and McKay seemed to pick up the real question. "This battery-like object should last several days, so that's all right. But the sooner the better, Sheppard."

"Right," John said, and turned away.

Teyla Emmagen stood in the center of the new Satedan gate square, trying to concentrate on the discussion between Ushan Cai, Margin Bri, the woman Cai had introduced as his head scavenger, and Daniel Jackson. At least, at the moment it was staying within the bounds of what she would consider a discussion, and it was important to keep it there, but her eyes kept straying to the horizon beyond the Stargate. John and Rodney had taken off in pursuit of the Vanir ship, and so far they had heard nothing. If they had lost the ship, John would have radioed, she told herself, for the hundredth time. If they had rescued Ronon and Elizabeth, they would have radioed. So they were still somewhere in between, still chasing or still trying to break the others free. Or they were dead, of course, but she would not let herself think of that possibility. Instead, she fixed her smile more firmly on her face, and forced herself to pay attention.

"So are these trade goods contaminated or not?" Cai demanded. A couple of his men had already pulled the newly arrived supplies into a shed and were now stripped naked under the nearest pump, hosing themselves down.

"We don't know," Jackson said. "This is a precaution. I think it's a smart precaution, because if this bug is as bad as it sounded, you don't want it loose here. Even if you don't use a lot of petroleum-based plastics, it would mean you couldn't trade with us, or with anyone else who did, and eventually you're going to want to get to that level of technology—"

"We've gone to a lot of trouble to salvage things that we can't replace," Bri said, grimly. "I think we have to assume the worst."

"We will, I hope, have more information for you from Atlantis," Teyla interjected. "Both as to whether this material was exposed and how best to deal with the underlying problem." She hoped that was true: neither Major Lorne nor Dr. Zelenka had sounded anything but harried when they'd reported the problem. Contamination between worlds was not common — the Stargates themselves destroyed many commonly dangerous micro-organisms as people passed between worlds — but it was not unknown. There were terrible stories of diseases carried from one world to another, of gate addresses that had had to be forbidden, the worlds shut off for months or years until the disease burned itself out and left them more empty than the most ferocious Culling. And then there was the nightmare that was Banissar, which had simply vanished, its

Stargate no longer functioning. Seventy years later, a Traveler ship had landed, looking to trade, only to find everyone dead. The people of Banissar had removed crystals from their DHD to keep anyone from dialing in — or escaping to carry the plague — and had left written warnings sealed in multiple containers. The Travelers had fled as soon as they had understood what had happened, but even seventy years later the disease was present, and the Traveler ship had broadcast its warning and then driven itself into a sun rather than spread it further. And that was something else she didn't want to think about, any more than she wanted to think about the empty sky.

"It probably couldn't hurt to disinfect anyone who handled the boxes," Jackson was saying. "I mean, more than just washing them down, though that's a good start. If you have any sort of medical disinfectant, something for surgery or things like that?"

Cai looked at Bri, who shrugged. "We found some, yes — it was one of the things I was looking for. But there's so little. I really don't want to waste it."

"Perhaps cleaning fluid?" Teyla said. "Of course there is plenty to spare on Atlantis, but that does not help you here."

"Not so much," Cai said, with the flicker of a smile.

"Industrial cleaners aren't easily come by, either," Bri said. "What we've got is good lye soap." She looked at the men still under the pump, rubbing soap in their hair. "That kills most things, it's just hard on the skin."

Something moved in the sky beyond the Stargate, a dark fleck against the blue, its motion unlike any bird. Teyla's breath caught, and the others turned to see.

"That's one of the jumpers," Jackson said, and Teyla's radio crackled.

"— Teyla. Come in, Teyla."

Teyla touched her earpiece. "I hear you, Colonel Sheppard."

"Good news. We stopped the Vanir ship, and Elizabeth and Ronon are both alive. But they're in stasis pods, and Rodney says he thinks Dr. Jackson has a better chance of opening them safely than he does."

Teyla felt her eyebrows rise at that. "Very well."

"We've also got one injured Vanir on our hands, and no first aid kit. Contact Atlantis and see if they can send someone through to help it."

"I will do that," Teyla said. "But, Colonel, we do not yet know if the gate room has been cleared."

"I know. Do what you can. Sheppard out."

"They are alive," she said, to the others, and even Bri cracked a smile.

"That's good to hear," Cai said, and shook his head. "To lose your friend so soon after you'd found her —"

"She's a tough one," Bri agreed. "Smart. I'm sorry she wasn't one of ours."

"Thank you," Teyla said, and took a deep breath. "If you'll excuse us, Dr. Jackson and I need to arrange some things before Colonel Sheppard gets here." She took Jackson's elbow and walked him away before anyone could protest.

"So what does Sheppard want us to do?" he asked, when they were more or less out of earshot.

"Dr. McKay says Elizabeth and Ronon are in Vanir stasis pods, which he is reluctant to open."

"That's got to be a first time." Jackson waved a hand. "Sorry, go on."

"He seems to think you have more experience with such devices," Teyla said. "Also, one of the Vanir has survived, but is injured, and John would like us to bring a medic from the city."

"I don't think that's going to happen."

"No. Not unless they have made much more progress on this eater-of-plastics. But we must ask."

It didn't take long to make contact with Atlantis and relay John's request, but Teyla could hear the worry behind Lorne's careful answer.

"I can send someone through, but we haven't knocked down the contamination problem. I'm reluctant to do that unless it's absolutely necessary. You said Dr. Weir and Ronon are all right?"

"They are in stasis pods, and seem unharmed," Teyla answered. "Though Dr. McKay has requested Dr. Jackson's help in opening them."

"I think what Dr. McKay probably meant is that I should collect any information you've got on Asgard stasis devices," Jackson interrupted. "I've had some — contact — with the devices, but I'm not by any means an expert."

"Copy that," Lorne said, after a moment. "I've got Dr. Ando searching the databases right now."

"I see that sending Dr. Beckett would be unwise," Teyla said. "Perhaps you could also send us any information you have on Asgard physiology?"

"Can do," Lorne answered. There was a long silence, and Teyla turned, shading her eyes again to track the approaching jumper. It was much closer now, only a few minutes away, the familiar boxy shape dark against the bright sky.

"At least Elizabeth and Ronon are ok," Jackson said. "If we can help the Vanir, that's great, but they're our first priority."

"Yes." Teyla nodded. "But I for one would like to ask that Vanir a few questions. There are many things it could tell us that we might find helpful."

"You know, if I had to pick one word for the Vanir, 'helpful' wouldn't be it."

Teyla smiled in spite of herself. "That's true, your previous experiences with them have not been pleasant."

"I liked the Asgard," Jackson said, abruptly serious. "They really liked Jack — General O'Neill — which shows a certain amount of good taste, and they did try to help us, for some definitions of 'help,' anyway."

"And yet they destroyed themselves," Teyla said. It was something the other Lanteans didn't like to talk about, and she had never heard the full story.

Jackson nodded. "They were dying off as a species. They had ceased to reproduce sexually, and millennia of cloning had degraded their genetic material past the point where even they could repair it. They didn't want to linger like that, dying slowly and in pain, and they didn't want to risk their knowledge falling into the hands of people who'd make bad use of it. They gave us, us Tau'ri, a library computer containing — well, I don't know if it's all their knowledge, but it was everything they were willing to trust us with, anyway. And then they blew up their planet. No more Asgard, no more Asgard technology, gone, just like that." He shrugged. "Or so we thought. Except that some of them seem to have made it to the Pegasus Galaxy, and they weren't planning on going quietly. Whatever they're up to, it's probably got something to do with preserving their species."

"Yes, I see." Teyla turned to look for the jumper, not sure she could hide her feelings. Surely it would have been better for the Asgard to fight, to protect what they had — and that, she thought, was surely Osprey's blood speaking. But it was also Athosian. How many times had they been Culled to the bone, and brought themselves back as a people? Perhaps it was simply the way things were in Pegasus, as opposed to the Milky Way.

"Teyla, Dr. Jackson." Lorne's voice crackled through the radio. "We've got your files ready to transmit."

Jackson's fingers moved on his laptop, and he nodded.

"Go ahead, Major," Teyla said. That was good: they would waste no time on the ground this way.

"Hang on," Jackson said. "Major, this — there's hardly anything there."

"It's what we've got," Lorne answered. "You know they don't give us access to that fancy library, that's all on a need-to-know basis."

"Well, at the moment, we really need to know it," Jackson said.

"Sorry, Dr. Jackson. You have everything we do."

"Thank you, Major," Teyla said, smoothly. "We will contact you as soon as we know anything more."

It wasn't a long flight back to where the Vanir ship had crashed. Daniel used that time to brace himself on the bench seat behind Teyla and Sheppard and read and re-read the material Lorne had sent to his laptop. At least there were some notes on Asgard stasis devices, and specifically on the controls, though he thought he could have handled that for himself. The memory of Jack on Thor's ship, held in failing stasis while he used the knowledge of the Ancient database to try to figure out some way to stop the Replicators, rose unbidden in his mind, and he shoved it away. That had all worked out in the end; no point in thinking about it now. The main thing was to get their people out of stasis and find out if they'd guessed right about the Vanir's plan to repair their damaged DNA by steal-

ing genetic material from the Ascended Asgard who had helped
Elizabeth to ascend in the first place. It was the only thing that made
sense. And it wasn't all that surprising that someone had come to
Elizabeth's rescue, just as Oma Desala had come to his all those
years ago. It seemed to be something the successfully Ascended
were prone to doing, no matter what the rules were supposed to
prevent. And no matter whether it was truly wise or not. Daniel
grimaced at the memory of Oma locked forever in combat with
Anubis. Everything he tried to do on this mission seemed to lead
back to something else he didn't particularly want to think about.

Right, he told himself. Asgard first aid. Unfortunately, that file
was painfully short, and dominated by a crude drawing indicating
little more than gross anatomy. The note said it had been done in
Area 51, and Daniel decided he didn't really want to know any of
the details. What they really needed was a doctor, somebody who
could turn those notes into something like treatment.

He looked up, feeling the jumper pitch down toward landing,
and for the first time saw the Vanir ship where it had arrowed into
the hillside. "Wow, that's — final."

Sheppard shot him an unreadable glance. "We couldn't exactly
let them get away, could we?"

"No, but I would have thought you might have done a bit less
damage, you know, brought it down gently or something."

"I'll keep that in mind for next time," Sheppard said, and brought
the jumper to a stop beside its twin. "Let's go."

He led them into the bowels of the wrecked ship, Teyla at his
back, heading, Daniel was glad to see, for the stern. The emergency
lighting was still working, casting faint shadows — another good
sign, he thought, and hoped there would be enough power left to
open the stasis pods.

The system on this ship had diverged from the ones Thor used.
He hid his immediate worry, and made himself look over the consoles carefully, identifying each of the control systems. They were
all there, just laid out in a different order: no surprise, really, if
the Vanir had diverged from the Milky Way's Asgard thousands
of years ago.

"Well?" Sheppard demanded.

"What?"

"Can you open them?"

Daniel looked at the controls again. "Yes. Yes, if there's enough power left to run the circuits. But McKay can tell you that better than I can."

"There's plenty of power," McKay snapped. "As much as you could possibly want."

"Ok, then." Daniel took a breath and pressed the sequence of buttons. The lights flickered and the deck shuddered as though the ship was trying to bring a second power source online.

"I thought you said there was enough power," Sheppard said.

"There was." McKay's hands flew over a second set of controls. "Ok, yes. There is. We should be fine—"

A chime sounded, two-toned and urgent, and the lights at the head of each pod went from blue to purple.

"Jackson..." Sheppard clutched his P90 as though shooting something might help.

"It's ok," Daniel said, and hoped he sounded more confident than he felt. "That's what it's supposed to do."

The chime stopped, and all the lights went out.

Sheppard swore and swung his P90, the light attached to the barrel flicking from pod to pod and then settling on McKay's console. "McKay..."

"On it." McKay's hands were moving with purpose, pale in the sharp light. "Ok. Ok, I think we've—yes. Got it."

The emergency lights flicked back on, and in the same moment the lids of the stasis pods began to slide open. Teyla darted past him to reach for Elizabeth's groping hand, and a moment later Ronon dragged himself to a sitting position.

"This sucks."

"It's a lot better than it could be," McKay said, and offered a hand to steady him as he climbed out. A shower of sparks fountained from the pod, and everyone flinched.

"Are you all right?" Sheppard asked, and Ronon nodded.

"Yeah."

"The pods aren't," McKay said, fiddling with the controls. "That one's definitely out of commission, and—oh, no, no, no, the other one's gone too. So much for using them on the Vanir."

Sheppard acknowledged that with a look, but his focus was on the rescued. "Elizabeth?"

She nodded. "I'm unhurt. Though that wasn't the most pleasant thing that's ever happened to me." She looked around. "We're on the Asgard ship?"

"Rodney shot it down," Sheppard said. "Unfortunately, the control room was destroyed, and that killed most of the crew. We've got one survivor, but he's in a bad way."

"I've got some notes on Asgard physiology," Daniel offered, "but they're not much."

Elizabeth nodded decisively. "Lead the way."

"This way," McKay said, after only the briefest of pauses.

Someone — Sheppard, Daniel suspected — had wrapped the injured Vanir in one of the Mylar blankets from the first aid kits. Elizabeth went to her knees beside the body and, after a moment, Daniel joined her, turning his tablet so that she could see the illustration. Her eyebrows lifted.

"That's it?"

"That's all we've got." Daniel shrugged. "Maybe there's more back at the SGC, but this is what they have on Atlantis."

Elizabeth folded back the blanket, cocking her head to one side as she studied the Vanir's still form. Lying there, it looked even more fragile than the Milky Way Asgard, the enormous eyes closed and the skinny limbs sprawling. Elizabeth checked for a pulse, then felt carefully along the arms and legs, and finally, delicately, over the enormous dome of its head. She was careful not to move its neck, her hands quick and competent, and Daniel remembered that she had come to the SGC from medical NGOs. Apparently she'd spent enough time in the field to learn more than the basics of first aid.

"He's alive," Elizabeth said, sitting back on her heels. "Or she. And I don't see any obviously life-threatening injuries. But I do feel what I think is a skull fracture, and that means we need to get him to a doctor as quickly as possible. Better still, bring the doctor here to stabilize him."

Sheppard bit his lip. "We've a bit of a problem there, Dr. Weir."

"The creature that eats plastic is still on Atlantis," Teyla said, "and the gate room is still contaminated. Major Lorne is rightly unwilling to risk spreading the disease here."

"He still needs a doctor," Elizabeth said. "This is a severe head injury. If he were human, I'd say he was already in a coma, and I have no idea what that would mean for a being that has this much brain."

"Is there anyone back at the main settlement?" Sheppard looked at Teyla. "Have they managed to recruit any doctors yet?"

"Not that I am aware of," Teyla said. "There have been some nurses who have visited, but their skills are greatly in demand elsewhere."

"They were willing to take me as an assistant," Elizabeth said, "so I'd say they didn't have anyone better."

"Not the Genii," Ronon said.

"They sort of owe us over that Sora person," Daniel said, but the others ignored him.

"What about the Travelers?" Teyla asked. "I have heard that some of their ships have salvaged medical devices."

"Dekaas," Elizabeth said. She pushed herself to her feet. "I told you, he treated me when I was with the Travelers. He had... some experience treating other species besides humans. If we can't get someone from Atlantis, he might be able to help."

"The Wraith worshipper," Ronon said, grimly, and Daniel winced. That had not been one of his better moments.

"You remember, we also met Dekaas," Teyla said, to Sheppard. "While we were searching for Elizabeth. Apparently he had been on one of the Wraith hives, but he has been accepted among the Travelers for many years now. If we knew where to find him —"

"They were going to a rendezvous," Ronon said, reluctantly. "After Manaria."

"Do you remember where?" Teyla asked.

Ronon nodded. "Hirard."

Daniel knew he looked blank, and the same uncertainty showed on Sheppard's and McKay's and Weir's faces.

"I also know Hirard," Teyla said. "There was once a great star port there, though I thought it was picked clean long ago. John, if we take a jumper now, we may be able to find Dekaas and bring him back here. That would be better than nothing, especially if Major Lorne has not yet lifted the quarantine."

Sheppard nodded. "All right. Teyla, you're in charge. Rodney can fly you there —"

"Let me go," Elizabeth said. "Dekaas is likely to listen to me."

"We need you here to keep an eye on the Vanir," Sheppard said.

Elizabeth glanced down at the motionless body, a flicker of pity crossing her face. "There's nothing more I can do — nothing more any of us can do, not without better tools and more knowledge. But I think Dekaas will trust me."

"All right," Sheppard said again. "Go."

Evan Lorne scanned the gate room, for the moment ignoring the flickering screens and the mumble of worried voices. The city was in lockdown, the sections where equipment had been affected sealed off, and so far there were no more reports of trouble outside the sealed areas. If one of those areas hadn't been the gate room, he could almost fool himself into thinking he had things under control. Except, of course, for the way that the SGC-issue laptops had been carefully unplugged from their usual interface points in the control panels, and had been set aside where the technicians could keep an eye on them. Everything they'd turned up so far suggested that this was in fact some sort of microorganism that broke down petroleum-based plastics, brought from the proposed alpha site, and that the contamination could be carried from object to object. The team that had worked to set up the alpha site had passed through the gate room more than once, carrying contaminated gear, and therefore they had to assume that the gate room itself was contaminated.

The supply room in Tower B was also contaminated, as well as one of the landing pads where they'd set up test equipment before they'd realized what was going on. A hazmat team was supposed to be decontaminating that pad, but there was no guarantee that their usual procedures would be effective — Lorne reined in that thought sharply. They had to assume that the procedures would work, or they had nothing.

"Major Lorne." Airman Salawi looked up from her board. "Dr. Lynn would like a word."

At least the Ancient installation was made primarily of silicates and metal. Atlantis itself would probably be all right, as would the puddle jumpers that had taken personnel to the alpha site. Lorne leaned over the microphone. "Yes, doctor?"

"I have your translation." Lynn sounded embarrassed. "I'm afraid it's as we feared."

"Danger, something here eats plastic?" Lorne kicked the edge of the console, thinking he should be kicking himself. The first team through the Stargate had reported an inscription carved into a set of rocks near the gate. It hadn't been in Ancient or any of the other known alphabets, and he hadn't pushed for a translation.

"Warning, site contaminated with *alflageolis*," Lynn said. "We don't yet have a translation for '*alflageolis*' but Dr. Hagebeck and Dr. Beckett think it's the type of microorganism. '*Ageo*' is related to other words for petroleum products, *alfla* is one of a number of compounds generally indicating destructiveness, and '*-lis*' is a marker for biological activity. In this case, going by related words, we think it indicates a bacterium."

"That's —" Lorne swallowed his first response. "That's potentially helpful."

"I have my team going through the databases," Lynn said, "but from the style of the writing I'd say there's a good chance this inscription post-dates Ancient occupation of that area."

Which meant there wouldn't be any handy home remedy in the database, Lorne thought. Lovely. "But you think we're dealing with bacteria?"

"The word is similar in its formation to most other bacteria catalogued in the system," Lynn said. "Dr. Hagebeck thinks she may be able to make a guess at some of the other elements — she's working directly with Dr. Beckett now."

"Thanks, Doc. Let me know if you turn up anything else." Lorne kicked the edge of the console again. It's progress, he told himself, and straightened as Radek Zelenka came to join him.

"Did I hear Dr. Lynn say we are dealing with a bacteria?"

"That's what he thinks at the moment," Lorne said. "Carson's working on it."

"If it is a bacteria, perhaps we can fine-tune our decontamination procedures."

"Maybe." Before Lorne could say anything more, there was a splat from the end console, and one of the airmen swore. "Nelsen?"

"Sorry, Major." The airman picked up what was left of his travel mug. The entire bottom of the plastic cup had melted, spilling lukewarm coffee across the console and floor.

"Decon," Lorne said, and Nelsen carried the mug across to the makeshift safe disposal station. At least they hoped it was safe, Lorne amended. It was really a solid metal canister from the kitchen with several quarts of the strongest disinfecting solution in the city. Hopefully it would be strong enough to kill this *"alflageolis"* and if they kept disinfecting everything that showed signs of infection... Maybe that would stop the contamination. Maybe. Nelsen came back with a wad of paper towels and began mopping up the spilled coffee. He started to toss the wet towels in the nearest wastebasket, but stopped himself in time, and added them to the canister instead. That was the only thing that was going to work, Lorne thought. Disinfect everything and make sure there's no more contact. Then we get the Stargate open and find out what's happening with Elizabeth.

"Major Lorne," Salawi said. "Dr. Beckett would like to talk to you and Dr. Zelenka."

Lorne looked at Zelenka, and saw his own worry reflected in the scientist's expression. "Put him through to the conference room, please, Airman."

The conference room seemed weirdly empty without the usual collection of laptops and coffee mugs, just the boxy display in the center of the table — original to Atlantis, not something they'd installed, so it ought to keep working — and Lorne dropped into the nearest chair, grateful that it, too, was mostly metal and Atlantis resins, and stretched out his leg. He'd broken it in a fight with the Wraith, and even now it still stiffened up if he stood too long.

"Dr. Beckett? I'm here with Dr. Zelenka."

"Major." Beckett's voice was taut with stress. "I wanted to give you an update on this possible bacterium."

"Go ahead." If Lorne had been alone, he would have crossed his fingers, hoping for a good answer.

"We've been able to make a provisional identification, thanks to Dr. Lynn and his team, though so far we haven't turned up any information in the Ancient database. We have determined that *aflageolis* preferentially attacks and digests petroleum-based plastics, which is kind of good news, in the sense that almost all of the Ancient technology is metal, silicone, or crystal. Atlantis itself should be unharmed."

"But?"

"But most of our equipment — including, I regret to say, most of our hazmat gear — is either made of or contains crucial parts made of petroleum-based plastics. And *alflageolis* attacks those substances voraciously."

"Is there any good news?" Zelenka muttered.

"Some," Beckett said. "First of all, it doesn't seem to affect human beings directly. Both the team at the alpha site and several supply personnel were exposed for longer than the equipment that has already fallen apart, but none of them show any signs of injury or illness."

"You're still keeping an eye on them, right?" Lorne asked.

"I have the supply staff in quarantine down here," Beckett said, "but I really think it's an unnecessary precaution. I'll hold them another twenty-four hours to be certain, though."

"Good idea," Lorne said.

"We've also been able to isolate samples of *alflageolis* — which we are handling under extreme safety protocol in an entirely Ancient lab — and I can confirm that it is a bacterium. We're hoping that further study will lead us to a way to eliminate it." Beckett paused. "There is just one other thing I'm worried about. Looking at the cell structure, I — it seems as though it might not be a naturally-occuring organism."

Lorne looked at Zelenka, whose eyebrows had risen in shock. "Are you telling me this is something the Ancients created?"

"I'm saying it's possible that someone created it," Beckett answered. "For what it's worth, I don't think it was the Ancients, or we'd have found something useful in the database. But there are other cultures in Pegasus that have, or had, the capability to manipulate bacteria this way."

"The Wraith," Zelenka said.

"Also the Genii, the Satedans before the Wraith attacked, the Hoffans…" Beckett's pause was almost imperceptible. "Michael."

"Do you think it's Wraith?" Lorne asked.

"I can't even be sure it's engineered," Beckett said. "Much less tell who might have done it. But I thought you should know it was a possibility."

"Right." And if it was a weapon… Lorne shook his head. "Thanks, Dr. Beckett. Is there anything else we should be doing to keep this thing contained?"

"I don't have anything new to suggest. We'll be running some more tests that may let us tweak the decontamination fluid soon. I take it the standard issue gels still aren't doing anything?"

"Not noticeably," Lorne said.

"Aye, I expected that. I'll let you know as soon as we have something."

"Thanks," Lorne said again, and Beckett cut the connection.

"Well," Zelenka said, after a moment. "That is… interesting."

"About *alflageolis* being non-natural?"

Zelenka nodded. "Tell me, Major, what sort of planet would you pick to test a weapon like that?"

Lorne grimaced. "A desert. With a Stargate that was a long way from anything. And, yeah, if something went wrong, I'd put up a big sign to tell everybody to stay away. But that's not actually proof of anything."

"It is not." Zelenka nodded again. "But it cannot be ignored."

"No." Lorne sighed. "But there's nothing we can do until we have more information."

CHAPTER TWO

IT WAS the height of the dry season on the planet the humans called Sabras, and the air tasted like flames. The Ring of the Ancestors rose from its platform in the center of a barren plain, only a few clumps of scrub sprouting from the cracked red soil. There were trees in the middle distance, though, and from the shape of their leaves and the way they stood in a straggling line, Guide guessed they lined a watercourse of some sort. They were perhaps a quarter-hour's walk at a comfortable pace, though nothing was comfortable on this world at this season. It was a pity they could not have waited for nightfall, but Alabaster was right. To come by day not only expressed good intentions toward the humans who were now part of their hunting ground, but affirmed their power to come and go as they pleased. That was worth a certain amount of discomfort. Guide took a shallow breath that still seared his throat, his eyes slitted tight against the noonday sun, and looked at the nearest blade.

The village?

Just downstream. The blade's mental touch was a bleak wind in the heart of winter, weirdly refreshing in the dry heat. He pointed, his eyes blank green in the scorching light. *Just beyond those trees.*

Let us go. Guide turned as he spoke, feeling the others fall into place at his back. They were three blades and twice as many drones, more than enough to deal with the Sabrasa villagers, and for a moment he wished there was a chance that the Wolf had remained. He would give a great deal to make that one pay for his crimes. Three times in the last year the Wolf had attacked, each time killing Wraith and leaving others to take the consequences. On Dhalo, he and his men had come at tribute time, killing the blades who had come to collect the human tribute, and Queen Death had demanded a hundred-fold tribute in payment. It had been tribute time on Halpsar, too, and much the same pattern of attack. Queen Sky had depopulated the town, and taken the survivors into her feeding pens: she was young and her hive was starving after having spent too much time avoiding Queen Death, but he

could not help feeling that it was a poor solution. And on Sabras...
On Sabras, all he knew was that the Wolf had attacked clevermen
bringing back volunteers who had taken the retrovirus. The rest
he would find out shortly.

The human village was in a sheltered hollow where the little river
widened to a shallow pool. The air held more moisture under the
trees' shade, and the leaves rustled in a gentle breeze. The village
itself was little more than a collection of a dozen wood-and-fab-
ric huts, their sides rolled up in the day's heat to allow the air to
circulate. Most of the humans were huddled behind them, only a
woman and two men facing them in the center of the open space
between the rows of huts. The clevermen's bodies rested at their
feet, and Guide bared his teeth in anger.

The woman saw, and went to her knees. "Lord, we beg your par-
don! We had no part in this, we swear it!"

The men went to their knees as well, and even some of the people hiding between the huts copied them. Guide stopped well out of
reach, looking down at the bodies. They were both men of his own
faction, Rise and Riverstone, and grief and anger stabbed through
his chest. He should not have sent them alone, not without blades
to defend them, though from the marks on their bodies the Wolf
had once again used superior firepower to overwhelm their ability
to heal themselves. That was another hallmark of the Wolf's attack,
and one more reason he had to be destroyed.

"Tell me what happened," he said aloud. "I will listen."

The woman stretched out her hands. "These came to us two
moons past, and told us of the treaty. There was fever in the village
then, Lord, and many of us were ill. All of our children, or we would
not have agreed so quickly! But we did so, and they treated us, and
saved the children — a dozen live, who would be on the pyres long
since. So when they said they must take some of those who volunteered away with them to further their tests, those agreed, and went.
These said they would return our people at the second new moon,
and so they did. But two nights before, travelers came through the
Ring, carrying one of their number in a sling. They said they had
heard that the Wraith had made a bargain here, and one of them
was badly hurt. They said they were prepared to trade their lives

for his, and so we let them wait with us. And then, when your people came, the travelers attacked them and they died."

"And you did nothing to stop them?" Guide tilted his head.

"Lord, what could we do? The travelers had Genii rifles and Wraith weapons. We have spears and hunting knives."

"Where did they come from?"

The woman blinked in surprise. "They were Travelers, Lord. I do not know their ship."

Travelers. Not ordinary strangers traveling between world, but the people who called themselves Travelers. That was a connection Guide had not heard before. It made sense, though. If the Wolf had allies among the Travelers, it would explain why he vanished for long periods, only to turn up on a world far distant from the site of his last attack.

Do you believe her? That was Winterheart, who was senior, but Guide could feel Avalanche mirroring the same question.

It is plausible enough. It could explain many things. Guide considered, staring down at the woman who knelt beside the clevermen's bodies. "Stand up."

She rose to her feet, straight-backed, afraid but determined not to show it more than she must.

"Did you take the retrovirus?"

"Yes, Lord. But I am the woman of this village, I could not leave my people."

"So." Guide walked slowly around the bodies, circling the woman and the kneeling men until he came to stand directly in front of the woman. "And you swear that what you've told me is the truth?"

"I do."

"Let us put it to the test." Guide lifted his feeding hand, saw her eyes go wide. "I can tell if you lie to me, and if you do I will see this village wiped from the face of Sabras. I ask again, is what you have told me true?"

She took a shaken breath, but stood firm. "It is truth."

Guide reached for her, sinking his claws into the flesh of her chest. He could taste her fear, her strength, the retrovirus coursing in her blood, could taste grief and terror and confusion — and, beneath it all, the truth of her memories. He released her, and she staggered back a step, the marks of claws and handmouth bloody on her skin.

"She speaks the truth," he said aloud, so that the entire village could hear. "Take our people back to the Ring, bear them home in honor. I will remain, and hear more details from all of you. I intend to bring down the Wolf once and for all."

I will stay with you, Winterheart said, and Guide nodded.

Yes. Two minds are better than one.

The jumper emerged from the Stargate onto an enormous paved surface, an area currently occupied by at least four Traveler ships. Five, Rodney corrected, checking the jumper's sensors, and hastily activated the communications unit. "Hello, Traveler ships! Lantean jumper here —"

"Allow me, Rodney," Teyla said, and a woman's voice spoke from the console.

"We see that. Is that you, Sheppard? This was supposed to be a private get-together."

"It is Teyla Emmagen," Teyla answered. "And also Dr. McKay. I apologize for the intrusion, but the matter is urgent."

"Teyla. And Dr. McKay."

Was it just me, Rodney wondered, or did she sound disappointed?

"Larrin here. You can park to the right of the small blue ship. And then we can talk."

Rodney brought the jumper down into the spot Larrin had indicated, rather pleased with himself for the precision of the landing, and looked over his shoulder. "Everyone ready?"

"They are waiting for us," Teyla said, and Rodney lowered the rear door.

They walked down into heat and the smell of dust and hot metal. Rodney flinched, wishing he'd brought a hat and sunscreen, and Elizabeth pulled the collar of her shirt up over her nose and mouth for a moment, coughing, until she could settle herself. Teyla — as usual — seemed undisturbed, walking a little ahead to offer both hands to the Traveler leader.

"Larrin. A pleasure."

"Likewise," Larrin answered, looking past her. "So, there's Dr. McKay, but who's she?"

"That is our missing person," Teyla answered. "Her name is Elizabeth, and we are deeply grateful to you for having helped her."

"Glad to be of service," Larrin answered, but her eyes were wary. And well they should be, Rodney thought. When Teyla starts talking about how she owes you — you should be extra careful, that's all. "But I'm not sure I understand why you're back here."

"We would like to borrow one of your doctors," Teyla answered. "Elizabeth worked with him to earn her passage. I believe he can help us with some further questions."

Rodney blinked, and felt Teyla's voice in the back of his mind. *Let us not mention contamination until we absolutely have to.*

Right. Rodney forced a smile. "Right."

"Which one?" Larrin asked.

"Dekaas, his name was."

"On *Durant*." Larrin nodded. "I'll tell the captain to let you on board."

"We'd like to take him back to Sateda with us," Teyla said. "We have an injured alien that he may be able to help us treat."

"I don't see why we should let you walk off with one of our doctors," Larrin said. "They don't exactly grow on trees."

"We would bring him back as soon as possible," Teyla answered. "And while he was gone, I would be willing to leave one of our largest aid kits as partial payment."

It'll come back empty! Rodney protested silently, and felt Teyla's amusement in answer.

Yes. And we have plenty more. Right now we need Dekaas.

"It's true that we have a couple of other doctors at the gathering right now," Larrin said. "And maybe use of your equipment would help make up for not having him around for a while. But you'd need to bring him back as soon as you were done with him."

"I do not think this will take too very long," Teyla said. Rodney felt the shadow of sorrow cross her mind. "Either he will be able to help or he will not."

"Right." Larrin eyed them for a moment longer, not visibly persuaded. Rodney could feel the sun beating down on the back of his neck, his skin reddening by the second. A breath of wind lifted the fine dust that covered the paving, and Elizabeth smothered a cough.

Teyla waited, still smiling, and Larrin sighed, reaching for the radio she wore at her hip. "Give me a minute. *Durant*!"

She stepped back as she spoke, not quite out of earshot, but far enough that Rodney could only hear fragments of the conversation. "— take Dekaas with them... Yes, I know... Yes, fair enough." She lowered the radio, frowning, and rejoined them. "All right. We won't object to him going with you, but the decision is up to him." She looked at Elizabeth. "I expect you know where you're going?"

"I know *Durant*," Elizabeth answered with a smile of her own, and Larrin nodded.

"Go on, then. And give my love to Colonel Sheppard."

"Thank you." Elizabeth nodded in turn, and started toward the larger of the two ships parked opposite the jumper. Even by Traveler standards, it looked a bit battered, its hull a discouraging shade of rust, stains trailing from several of the access ports. It bore the marks of energy weapons, too, most of them older, and the ladder that led to the main hatch rattled alarmingly under Rodney's weight.

A teenaged girl was waiting just inside the hatch, her dark hair braided tightly against her skull. She was dressed in the same random mix of styles that all the Travelers seemed to affect, but there was a heavy energy weapon strapped at her waist, and Rodney didn't doubt that she knew how to use it. Her attention was all on Elizabeth, however.

"Wow, so you're really Lantean? Who'd have guessed that?"

"I certainly didn't," Elizabeth said, with a smile. "Cara, this is Teyla Emmagen and Dr. Rodney McKay."

Cara nodded politely, but turned back to Elizabeth immediately. "Did you remember anything else?"

Elizabeth shook her head. "A few things. Not as much as I would like. Is Dekaas in the infirmary?"

"Yes." Cara's eyes fell. "Sorry. Didn't mean to be nosy."

"It's all right," Elizabeth said — and meant it, Rodney thought. "This way."

She led them through a series of shabby corridors, following, Rodney realized, a green line painted on the deck. It ended at an open door, through which Rodney could see the corner of an examining table and a wall of closed cabinets. There was no sign of this Dekaas, and he saw Elizabeth frown.

"Dekaas?"

An inner door slid open, and a gray-haired man appeared, drying his hands on a towel which he promptly discarded into a sealed container. "Elizabeth. I see your people found you."

"They did." She smiled at that, an unexpected, beautiful expression, and Rodney caught himself smiling with her. Dekaas smiled, too, though it was more restrained.

"I'm glad for you." He nodded to Teyla. "Teyla. I don't know this other."

"Rodney McKay," Teyla said. "Also of Atlantis."

"Larrin said you needed help with an injured alien." Dekaas lowered his voice so that he was barely breathing the word. "Wraith?"

"No." Teyla shook her head. "I will be honest with you, it is highly unlikely that you have ever seen such a being. Even the Lanteans know little of them, and they are more common in their galaxy than in ours."

"Then why not get a Lantean doctor?" Dekaas tipped his head to one side in a weirdly familiar gesture. Wraith, Rodney thought, even as Dekaas corrected himself. "They're far better trained than I am, never mind being more familiar with these aliens."

"We can't," Elizabeth said. Teyla gave her a swift, sidelong glance, but did not protest. "I can't give you any more details than that, but I give you my word it's true."

Dekaas looked from her to Teyla. "You're still worried that she's a Replicator."

"It has not been satisfactorily disproven," Teyla answered.

"And you'd let this alien die because of that?"

"We cannot risk all our people's lives to save someone who is almost certain to die himself, but we cannot leave him untreated, either," Teyla said. She paused. "But if you have records of your proof—"

Dekaas sighed heavily. "And I'm wasting time. Right, I'll come. Larrin said we get the use of one of your aid kits while I'm gone."

Teyla dipped her head. "That is correct."

"Right." Dekaas gave the infirmary a sweeping glance. "All right.

I need to pull together a kit — which will include the proof I have that Elizabeth's as human as anyone — and get someone to cover while I'm gone. Give me fifteen, twenty minutes."

"Of course," Teyla said. "We will return to the jumper and collect the aid kit for your people."

Rodney tapped his fingers nervously on the puddle jumper's console, his worry no secret from Teyla, who sat beside him in the co-pilot's seat. *Dekaas is coming,* she said mentally. *You know he said it would take him a little while to pack up his medical equipment, and there is little use in bringing a doctor with us if we do not give him time to bring the things he will need.*

Rodney grimaced, but his hands stopped moving. *I don't like this,* he replied. *How do we even know he's on the up and up?*

We do not, Teyla said. *But he is our only alternative at the moment. Besides,* she said, casting a sideways glance at him, *Elizabeth thinks well of him.*

And that was an entirely different pool of rolling emotions, worry and regret and relief all at once.

You are usually happier to be proved right, Teyla observed. *After all, you are the one who insisted that Elizabeth was alive, and here she is. She is sitting right behind us.*

Rodney met her eyes, his thought involuntary. *If she's really Elizabeth.* He got to his feet. "I'm going to get Dekaas to hurry," he said aloud, scrambling around the rear seats and exiting the puddle jumper.

Teyla sighed. *It will do no good!* she thought after him. *He is already hurrying.* There was no reply.

Elizabeth leaned forward from the seat behind the pilot's, her arms crossed around her middle. "Same old Rodney."

"In some ways," Teyla said. Of course Elizabeth was not aware of the silent conversation. She knew nothing of Rodney's experiences with the Wraith, or of how they had left him with the residual Wraith telepathy that allowed him to speak privately with her.

"What's the date?"

Teyla looked around.

"The date," Elizabeth said firmly. "What day is it?"

"According to the reckoning of your people, today is February 24, 2010," Teyla replied.

Elizabeth sat back in her seat, nodding slowly. "February 24, 2010. The last things I remember were in June, 2007. Not quite three years."

"Yes," Teyla said. "That was when we lost you to the Asurans. You truly do not remember anything since then?"

"Not until a few weeks ago," Elizabeth said. "When I was on Mazatla." Her frown deepened. "I have no idea what happened between."

"A great many things," Teyla said ruefully. There were so many things Elizabeth had missed. The war between the Wraith and the Asurans. Atlantis' return to Earth. The war against Queen Death. She did not even know that Torren existed. "I do not know where to begin."

"It's going to take a lot of catching up," Elizabeth said. She took a deep breath. "Who's in charge in Atlantis?"

"Colonel Sheppard is temporarily in charge. While the IOA considers a replacement for Richard Woolsey."

"Woolsey?" Elizabeth's voice went up a tone. "Woolsey was in charge in Atlantis?"

"He did a very good job," Teyla said, obscurely defensive of him. He was not at all a bad man, and he had become a good leader. "After Colonel Carter."

"And Carter is where?"

"In command of the cruiser *General Hammond*," Teyla said. "But perhaps we should not talk of these things. I am not certain that the colonel would approve of telling you of our command structure until Dr. Beckett has examined you."

To her relief, Elizabeth did not argue. "Of course," she said. "It's wise to be prudent. Don't tell me anything that makes you uncomfortable." Which of course was a point in her favor. Someone programmed by the Replicators or others to find out information would push harder. There was a silence, and then Elizabeth said, "So how are you?"

"I am well," Teyla said, and was surprised to discover in that moment how much she meant it. She had made her peace with the Gift and her Wraith heritage. She had at last untangled her relationship with Kanaan and found a place where they could parent Torren together without conflict. And she was happy in her friends, in her family, in all those she loved. For the first time in many years she could truly say that things were well.

"That's good," Elizabeth said, and her keen eyes were warm.

Teyla smiled. "Perhaps you do not remember all you said to me when you were Ascended, but I do, and I thank you for it."

"I don't have any idea."

"I know." Teyla glanced out the forward window of the jumper, remembering Elizabeth's presence in her dreams. Dream-Elizabeth — Ascended Elizabeth — had helped her find a way to reconcile the two parts of her heritage, and for that she would always be grateful. There was still no sign of Rodney and Dekaas returning. She hoped Rodney would not annoy the man to the point where he would not help them.

"Maybe I should go get Dekaas," Elizabeth said. "Rodney can be…"

"Yes." Teyla nodded. "Though he has changed as well in the time you have been gone. Perhaps more than is apparent on the outside."

"It's not just his hair?"

"No." She smiled.

"It's a little disconcerting. It looks like Michael."

"Yes," Teyla said shortly.

"Do we know what ever happened to him?"]

"I killed him," Teyla said. She could not regret that, not for one moment. Of all those she had killed, Michael was the one whose death she regretted least.

"Ah." Elizabeth leaned back in her seat. "I have missed some things around here."

And how to explain that tangle, her long captivity in late pregnancy, the birth of her son? How to even begin to speak of those, the worst days of her life? She had not yet spoken of them to anyone, even John who already knew or could guess the worst of it.

"You will have much to catch up on," Teyla said, her eyes on the distance beyond the puddle jumper's window. "Dr. Jackson said that he was confused by all that had transpired, and he was only gone a year, not nearly three."

"My mother." Elizabeth's voice was suddenly flat, and Teyla

twisted around in the seat to look at her. Elizabeth's hands were clenched. "They must have told her that I was dead."

"I expect so," Teyla said.

"I can't even imagine how that hurt her."

Teyla reached back over the seat, taking Elizabeth's cold hands in hers. "Now you will have something of great joy to tell her. That is what you must think of. The unexpected joy."

Elizabeth's eyes searched her face, taut muscles relaxing. "You're right," she said. "We all have to look to the future."

There was nothing to do but wait. Well, wait and stare at the weird creature the Lanteans called either Vanir or Asgard, but Ronon didn't think that got them any further. What little he knew about the Vanir, he didn't like: they'd invaded Atlantis, kidnapped McKay — and Jackson, who'd been visiting at the time — and nearly gotten everyone killed by the Wraith as a side effect. No, he didn't like the Vanir at all. Though they seemed to have an unreasonable fondness for Jackson. The archeologist was studying the writing on a panel between two darkened consoles, his hands stuffed in his pockets as though to remind him not to touch. Every time they'd had to deal with the Vanir, Jackson had been involved, even though he'd barely managed to get to the Pegasus Galaxy.

"Hey, Jackson. Why do the Vanir like you so much?"

"What?" Jackson turned away from the wall, looking genuinely startled. "No, it's Jack they like, not me. General O'Neill, that is. And anyway, that doesn't matter anymore, because these aren't our Asgard."

"Every time you come to Atlantis, these guys show up."

"That's not quite accurate. That first time, they were after yet another of Janus's unfinished devices —"

"Everybody's favorite," Sheppard said.

"Yes, well, we've had to deal with him more than you have."

"Yeah, but we've had some real delights. The Attero device was about as bad as it gets." Sheppard rested one hip on the nearest console, folding his arms on the stock of his P90.

"Agreed," Jackson said. "And that was what the Vanir were after that time. It had nothing to do with me or McKay, it was just bad luck that he accidentally activated it. This time, it seems as though they're looking for people who have ascended and — voluntarily or not, been un-ascended. Which, yes, would include me, but their real interest seems to be in Elizabeth. Which makes some sense if she was indeed aided to ascend by an Ascended Asgard."

"I'm still trying to get my head around that one," Sheppard said. "I thought only the Ancients could ascend."

"We don't know that," Jackson answered. "What we thought we knew was that only Ancients *had* ascended, plus one or two humans who didn't exactly manage to make it stick. Not to mention at least one Goa'uld. But there's a hell of a lot we don't know about the whole process."

"There's what we figured out that time McKay got himself zapped by the ascension machine," Ronon said.

"Which still doesn't add up to very much," Jackson answered. "Since McKay didn't manage to retain any of the information he was supposed to have learned in the process."

"What's your problem with McKay?" Ronon asked. He'd been wondering that for a while, but there'd never been any chance to ask.

Jackson turned sharply away from the wall. "I don't have a problem with him. He's — a very intelligent man and apparently has been very useful on Atlantis."

"See? You're doing it again." Ronon carefully didn't look at Sheppard.

"Doing —" Jackson darted a wounded look at Sheppard, but seemed to get no help there. He pushed his glasses to a better position, choosing his words with visible care. "McKay wasn't precisely easy to work with back at the SGC. He gave Sam — Colonel Carter — a really hard time, he was abusive to his subordinates — in fact, he was generally just an ass. Now, from the way everyone acts around him here, he's clearly gotten better, at least enough for you to put up with his behavior, but he hasn't exactly let it go when he's around me. He's still trying to get me to argue with him about our salaries, for God's sake. And whether archeology is a real science."

"You have to let it roll off you," Sheppard said.

Jackson showed teeth in an almost Wraith-like smile. "I am tired of cutting Rodney McKay slack he hasn't earned."

"He's earned it," Ronon said. He saw Jackson take a deep breath, and let it out, the tension draining from his shoulders.

"Yeah, so I hear."

There was a little silence, and then Sheppard said, "You know, Ronon's got a point about these rogue Asgard only showing up when you're around."

He had that little smile that meant it was at least partly a joke, and Jackson gave him a sidelong glance. "Except that from what Elizabeth said, it was an Ascended Asgard who rescued her, and who presumably un-ascended her after she broke all the rules by rescuing McKay — which, by the way, I am taking as an indication that he's definitely changed for the better."

"He was willing to die to save all of us," Ronon said. He still didn't understand why the Lanteans felt they had to pretend that hadn't happened, or to treat it as either a joke or something that didn't actually matter. On Sateda, at least, they had words to describe heroes, and they weren't afraid to use them.

"I know." Jackson's face changed, as though he understood some of the things Ronon was thinking. "Yeah, I know." He shrugged. "But, back to the Asgard. From everything we've seen, they're looking for Ancient ascension technology, and I think they want to use it to force this Ascended Asgard — who from Elizabeth's description has to be from before they started screwing around with their DNA — to un-ascend so that they can take genetic samples and use them to recreate their species."

"Can they actually do that?" Sheppard asked.

"Probably." Jackson spread his hands. "We never did figure out if there were any limits to what they could do, except that they couldn't keep cloning themselves. Everything else — maybe they couldn't do it, or maybe they just didn't think they should? They didn't want to share too much of their technology with us lesser races."

Ronon looked back at the creature lying helpless under the Mylar blanket, its enormous eyes closed. It looked uncomfortably tiny, no larger than a child, every bone thin and sharp beneath the gray skin. It was hard to believe that such a thing could be as wise as the Ancestors, as advanced as the Wraith — but then, he reminded himself, the Ancestors had been far from perfect, too.

The top of the hill was bare of everything but the fine pale grass that seemed to be ubiquitous on PGX-239. Atlantis botanist Nick Parrish stopped, hands on hips, and turned slowly to survey the scene, considering how to prioritize the various pieces of his mission. To the northwest, back the way they'd come, he could see the Stargate sitting in the center of another clearing, DHD set back at the usual distance: nothing odd there, except that there was no sign of non-insect life, and usually when they found an uninhabited planet, the reasons were pretty clear, like hostile wildlife or immense deserts. To the north and northeast, the hill sloped away to more of the low-lying forest that surrounded the Stargate, twisted conifers that grew in tangles that ranged from waist-high to almost as tall as he was. The bark was jagged, fissured, and he hadn't wanted to risk trying to push through it, not when there were more promising targets to the southeast.

He shaded his eyes, peering down the steeper slope to the vegetation that rose from what looked like the banks of a dry stream. PGX-239 had a particularly long day/night cycle, nearly fifty hours from one dawn to the next, and the sun was hot enough to cause most shallow water to evaporate. It was beating down on his shoulders now, scorching his neck in spite of his broad-brimmed hat, and his shirt clung damply to his back. He tugged the cloth free, and pulled out his binoculars, focusing on the stream line. The plants that rose on the opposite bank were succulents, with thick, fleshy leaves clearly intended to store moisture through the long hot day; he was willing to bet that the outer skin was thick enough to protect the moisture-retaining tissue from freezing through the long night. They were large, though, bigger than any similar plant he'd seen in Pegasus or in the Milky Way, notched ovals nearly as long as his arm along their central axis. They seemed to grow singly, surrounding what looked like a central bud or pod that was set deep within the foliage.

He put down the binoculars and turned back to the west, wincing at the brilliant sunlight. One of the planet's fist-sized flying insects bumbled past him, double wings making a palpable breeze; a shadow flickered above him and he looked up to see something like an enormous dragonfly, easily half a meter long from bulging eyes to skinny tail. There was another stand of succulents along the western edge of the clearing, running into and blending with the line of conifers. Not very far into the conifers, he thought he saw a gap, and lifted the binoculars again. Yes, there was a ragged clearing several meters into the stand of trees. It looked like the aftermath of a brush fire — yes, he thought, almost certainly so. The ground was gray with old ash, and a few charred branches still poked up out of the rubble.

"Interesting," he said, and lowered the binoculars as Gina Hunt came scrambling up the hill.

"We've got the preliminary samples you wanted, boss, and Doctor — sorry, Captain Aulich's got her instruments just about set up. What's next?"

"I want a look at those succulents by the stream bed," Parrish answered. "Why don't you take the corporal and get some samples of the conifers?"

Hunt grimaced. "Thanks a lot."

"Be grateful they don't have thorns."

"They might as well," Hunt said, shading her eyes to scan the clearing's western edge. "That bark's almost as nasty. Is that a break there?" She raised her own binoculars.

"It looked to me as though there'd been a brush fire," Parrish said. "I was thinking it might be possible to cut through there."

"Maybe." Hunt slid her binoculars back into their case. "Ok, Sammy and I will take on the conifers."

She started down the hill and Parrish touched his radio. "Sergeant Joseph."

The sergeant looked up from the meteorological equipment she had hauled to an open space next to the DHD, and touched her own radio. "Sir?"

"If Captain Aulich can spare you, I'd like to take a look at the succulents on the other side of this hill." They were under strict orders not to allow anyone, even the team leader, to head off on his or her own, and Joseph nodded.

"Just about done here, sir. Can you give me ten?"

"Absolutely." Parrish sank to his haunches, not sorry of a few minutes just to survey this new world. In the distance, the horizon was blurred in haze, the sky pale behind thin sweeps of cloud. All the colors seemed to be blurred as well, from the dusty brown of the conifers and the gray-green leaves of the succulents to the pale yellow-green grass. He touched it idly, and then more purposefully: the strands were thicker and tougher than he had expected, and there were some old brown marks on some of the stalks, rather like scorch marks. In fact, there were small circular gaps in the growth patterns, and all the stalks around the gaps showed those marks —

There was a flash of light from the western edge of the clearing, and the sharp snap of an energy weapon. Parrish threw himself flat on the ground, scrambling to draw his pistol, and crawled forward on knees and elbows to get a better look. Hunt and Corporal Samara were prone, caught in the open without cover; even as Parrish watched, Joseph rose from behind the meteorological equipment and fired a burst from her P90. There were more flashes in answer, short blue-white bolts lancing out from among the succulents. One struck a conifer branch, which bloomed into flame; more went into the air or into the ground, mercifully nowhere near Hunt and Samara. More shots came from behind him; he wormed around, pistol ready, but there was no sign of movement beyond the dry stream. The open ground and the slope of the hill were utterly empty.

The Stargate lit, its energy ballooning out before it stabilized, and Parrish touched his radio. "Atlantis, this is Dr. Parrish. We're coming through."

"Negative, Doctor," Banks said, her voice tight. "Atlantis is under quarantine, divert to Sateda or PVX-993."

"We're under attack," Aulich said, crouching in the shelter of the DHD, her own P90 at the ready.

"Are you in imminent danger?" That was Lorne, and Parrish rose slowly to his knees, ready to drop again at the first sign of an attack. Nothing happened, and he swiveled cautiously. There were no more shots and nothing moved.

"Hang on," he said, generally. "I'm not — this may be a natural phenomenon."

"Are you —?" Aulich bit back what was likely to have been an impolitic remark. "Someone's shooting at us, Doc."

"I don't think so." Parrish paused. "Hunt, Samara, see if you can get back to the DHD."

Even at a distance Samara looked doubtful, but Hunt pushed herself up onto hands and knees and scrabbled backward. Nothing happened, and Aulich said, "Sammy."

Samara did the same, still without drawing fire, collapsed into the shelter of the meteorological equipment.

"Dr. Parrish," Lorne said. "What's going on?"

"I'm not completely sure," Parrish answered. "We saw bolts of energy — like shots — but there's no sign of any attacker, no sign of any people at all except us. And the bolts don't seem to have been directed at any of us; it's more as though they were a response to some other stimulus."

"Ok," Lorne said. "We've got a problem here at the moment — we've picked up a bacteria that eats plastic — and we're closing down gate travel until we can get it under control. I'm not letting anyone back through the Atlantis gate unless their lives are in danger, and if you do, you'll be quarantined here with us. Do you need to come through?"

"Hang on," Parrish said again. He stood up, bracing himself to drop if he'd gotten it horribly wrong. When nothing happened, he holstered his pistol and dragged out the binoculars again, surveying the empty ground. "I don't see a thing. Anyone picking up anything different?"

There was a generally negative murmur in answer, and Parrish scowled. "Somebody fire a shot."

He saw Samara and Aulich exchange glances, and then Aulich said, "Go ahead, Sammy."

Samara flipped the P90 off automatic, and pointed the muzzle high. He fired twice, arcing the shots well away into the mixed underbrush, and a moment later there was another flash of energy further away from the clearing, the bolts clearly not aimed at anything in particular.

"Captain?" Parrish said.

Aulich pulled herself to her feet. "Ok, that's one of the weirder things I've seen. I think you're right, Doctor."

"I think we're all right for now, Major," Parrish said. "It seems to be — natural, and not directed at us. We'll evacuate to Sateda if we have any further problems."

"Roger that," Lorne said, and sounded relieved. "We'll let you know as soon as the problem is under control."

"Excuse me, Major," Aulich said. "I think Dr. Parrish is right, but just in case — is there any chance we could get a few more Marines here?"

"We can't risk this spreading, Captain," Lorne said. "But if there's anyone to spare who's already off-world, I'll send them your way. Atlantis out."

"Well, that's not very helpful," Hunt said.

Parrish came cautiously down the hill. "What do you mean?"

"Most of the teams currently off-world are civilian," Aulich answered. She had re-slung her P90, but she was still watching the vegetation warily. "Not a lot of back-up available."

"Let's hope we don't need it, then," Parrish said. "All right, people, let's see if we can figure out what was letting off those energy bolts. But — carefully, please."

CHAPTER THREE

GENERAL Jack O'Neill stuck his head around the corner of the door to Richard Woolsey's new office in Homeworld Security. "Knock, knock," he said.

"Come in," Woolsey said.

O'Neill grimaced. "You're supposed to say 'who's there?'"

"I can already see you," Woolsey replied perplexedly.

"That's beside the point." O'Neill came in and sat down in one of the two visitor chairs, lounging back in the seat.

"Why is that beside the point?" Woolsey asked. "Why would I ask who was there when I can already see that it's you?"

"It's a joke," O'Neill said. "Never mind." He looked around the bare office. "I thought I'd stop by and see how you were settling in. Nice office. Very beige. Taupe."

"It doesn't have Atlantis' view, no," Woolsey said, feeling unaccountably irritated by that. "But it's a perfectly nice office. Was there something you wanted to talk to me about?"

O'Neill shrugged. "Sure. Would you say that the Satedans are our allies? Are American allies?"

Woolsey considered. "Well, not in the strictest meaning of the word, no. There are no treaties ratified by Congress as only members of the Select Committee know that Sateda exists. So in that sense, we are not party to a formal treaty of alliance." He held up a hand as O'Neill started to speak. "However, that's often the case with unrecognized governments, sympathetic factions, friendly leaders, that sort of thing."

"Ah yes," O'Neill said. "That sort of thing. Contras. Militias."

"Er," Woolsey said. "There is some considerable diplomatic latitude for friendly yet unrecognized governments, which I would say Sateda certainly is. Certainly friendly. And we have provided them aid, which is often a hallmark of an unofficial…" He broke off. O'Neill appeared to be checking his teeth with his tongue.

"Aid," the general said. "We do give lots of aid to friendly yet unrecognized governments. Medicine. Generators. Surface to air missiles."

"I'm not aware that we've given the Satedans surface to air missiles," Woolsey said. Not that it was impossible. Sheppard might have handed over a MANPAD quietly, or some other missile system. If that's what this was about...

"Civilian advisors?"

"We often have civilian advisors with friendly factions, yes," Woolsey said. "After all, American civilians are free to work wherever they want as long as no laws are broken. Certainly there are plenty of NGOs who are active in troubled zones, and there are always individuals..." He broke off. "Exactly who are we talking about here?"

"I'm just considering a notion," O'Neill said. "If a retired Air Force officer were to take a job flying civilian aircraft for a 'friendly faction'..." He made air quotes to emphasize the words. "That would be pretty much 100 per cent kosher and A-OK, right?"

"You're not talking about a security firm, are you?" Woolsey asked sharply.

"I'm talking about an individual working on Sateda as a commercial pilot. Is there a problem with that?"

"I can't think so, no." Woolsey frowned. "Leaving aside the question as to how such an individual would get to Sateda, since the Air Force is controlling gate travel and space on the ships is limited."

"If some kind of arrangement were made," O'Neill said. "You know. As a gesture of friendship to a friendly faction. Colonel Caldwell could make room for one more warm body."

"Who are we talking about?" Woolsey asked. "This isn't hypothetical. You have someone in mind."

"Lt. Colonel Melissa Hocken — she's in command of *Daedalus's* 302 wing, just in case you've forgotten — is planning to retire as soon as her twenty years are up. She's entertaining an offer to be a commercial pilot on Sateda. It seems that the Satedans want to purchase a couple of light planes to help them reestablish contact with settlements that are some distance from their Stargate. Hocken's interested in working for them. Medical flights, supplies, and of course being a flight instructor."

Woolsey looked at O'Neill keenly. "What's your interest in this?"

"The precedent." O'Neill shrugged. "Where one goes, many

shall follow. That which is done may not be undone. One good turn leads to another."

Sometimes he wanted to strangle O'Neill, especially when he wouldn't stop making light of something eminently serious. "If Hocken can stay in Pegasus, then anyone can," Woolsey said.

"That would be the issue."

"And you want her to stay."

"I do." O'Neill sat up straight in his chair, humor falling away. "It's going to happen. I'd like some control over who sets the precedents and how."

"You mean not somebody going AWOL."

"That has occurred to me," O'Neill said.

"But you think the IOA won't like it."

The general shrugged. "I think the IOA will want to control it. And I'd rather…"

"Normalize?" Woolsey raised an eyebrow.

"How is it different than going off to work in South America or the former Soviet Republics?"

"Other than being on another planet?" Woolsey took a deep breath. "Your argument is that it's not?"

"My argument is that it shouldn't be. And I'd rather cross that bridge with Hocken and Sateda than later with somebody else. She's an exemplary officer, and many, many Air Force retirees have taken jobs flying commercially all over the world. If we say it's no different than if she were flying in the Balkans or Guatemala…"

"You're thinking about Sheppard," Woolsey said.

"I never said a word about Sheppard." O'Neill leaned back in his chair. "As far as I know, Sheppard is staying in. There's nothing to say about Sheppard."

Woolsey twitched. "But there will be someday."

"I don't believe in borrowing trouble." O'Neill got up. "The question is about Hocken. Yes? No?"

"I don't see any problem with Colonel Hocken working for the Satedans," Woolsey said slowly. "Nor do I see any reason why the IOA should micromanage that. The decisions of individuals are of course up to them."

"I thought you might see it that way." O'Neill gave him a jaunty smile and headed out of the office whistling.

What have I gotten myself into? Richard Woolsey wondered.

It didn't take as long as Rodney had expected for Dekaas to collect what equipment he had and to transfer the aid kit to the Travelers. Even so, as he dialed the Stargate for Sateda, Rodney couldn't help being aware that nearly three hours had passed since they'd left the injured Vanir. They'd done the best they could, and Sheppard would be doing everything he could to keep the Vanir alive, but — that wasn't much, and it had been a long wait. They had to find out why the Vanir wanted Elizabeth if they were going to keep her safe, and he wasn't about to let anything happen to her, not after everything they'd been through. And there was no knowing how good a doctor Dekaas really was. Admittedly, the Wraith knew a lot about human biology, but there was always the question of how much Dekaas's Wraith — captor? teacher? — had chosen to share with him. Rodney made himself focus on the controls, closing his mind tightly. Dekaas probably felt as ambivalent about Seeker as Rodney did about Dust and Ember, the two Wraith who had been both his closest friends and assistants and the agents maintaining his transformation into a Wraith.

The jumper emerged from the Stargate into the capital's main square, and Teyla reached for the radio.

"Mr. Cai. This is Teyla. Is there any word from Colonel Sheppard?"

"Nothing," a voice answered promptly. Not Cai himself, Rodney thought, but otherwise didn't recognize the voice. "And nothing more from Atlantis. No sign of problems here, though."

"That is good news," Teyla said. "We are proceeding directly to the wreck. Teyla out."

As fast as you can, please, Rodney, she added silently, and Rodney obeyed.

Even pushing the jumper to its best speed, it seemed to take forever before the wreck came into view. The last wisps of smoke had vanished and now there was just the heap of twisted metal, burrowed into the mountainside. It was late afternoon now, and the sun was retreating up the slopes, leaving what was left of the ship in shadow. Rodney brought the jumper down next to its fellow, aware that Dekaas was staring past him at the view screen.

"What sort of ship is that? I've never seen anything like it."

"It belongs to a people we call the Asgard," Elizabeth said. "Or perhaps the Vanir — two related peoples, one in our galaxy, one in yours."

Dekaas was still staring at the wreck as Rodney lowered the rear ramp. "Who shot them down?"

Rodney gave him a sharp look. "Who said they were shot down?"

"I can see engine damage from here," Dekaas answered. "I've been with the Travelers for decades, I can recognize the aftermath of a firefight as well as anyone. Did you shoot it down?"

"Well —"

"Then why do you want me to save one of their crew?" Dekaas demanded. "What are you trying to get from them?"

"We want information," Teyla began, and Dekaas shook his head. "I won't be party to torture."

"No one is torturing anyone," Teyla said.

"I shot it down," Rodney said, "And you know what, I'm not at all sorry about it, because they were trying to kidnap Elizabeth and Ronon. But now that we've done it, I'd really like to know why they were trying to kidnap them, and the only person who can tell us that is the guy inside. Who, you know, may be dead by now."

Dekaas lifted his hands. "All right," he said, and followed Teyla into the wreckage without further complaint. Elizabeth followed, and Rodney brought up the rear.

As far as he could tell, nothing had changed since they'd left, and he allowed himself a sigh of relief. The Vanir was still lying silent and motionless on a stretcher from the jumper, wrapped in one of the Mylar blankets from the first aid kit; Ronon was sitting on the floor with his back against one of the consoles — giving him a clear field of fire at the doorway, Rodney noted — and Sheppard was leaning on a console while Jackson studied something inscribed on a wall panel.

"John," Teyla said. "This is Dekaas, the doctor of whom I told you. Dekaas, this is Lieutenant Colonel Sheppard."

"Dekaas," Sheppard said. "Thanks for being willing to help out here. That's your patient."

"Colonel," Dekaas said, warily, but he went to one knee beside the stretcher. "I have never seen such a person before. You called him an Asgard?"

"Or Vanir," Sheppard said.

Dekaas folded the blanket back carefully. "You said there was a head injury, Elizabeth?" He ran his hands lightly down the Asgard's limbs, pressed gently along what would have been its stomach without eliciting a response, then cupped the oversized skull.

"Yes," Elizabeth answered, "over its left ear. I think I feel a fracture there."

"Ah. Yes. I think you're right. That's not good." Dekaas sat back on his heels. "And as far as you know, this is what they normally look like?"

"Pretty much," Sheppard said.

"They're all sort of putty-colored," Rodney said, in spite of himself, "and nobody can tell them apart except maybe what's-her-name, the engineer with the hiccups."

"Jack could," Jackson said. He held out his tablet, and Dekaas took it warily. "This is all the information we have about the Asgard. It's not much —"

"And I don't read Lantean," Dekaas said. He looked from the drawing to the motionless figure in frustration.

"I'll translate," Jackson said.

There was nothing Rodney could do to help that an actual doctor — well, a Wraith-trained medic — wouldn't do better and there was still the ship to think about. "Sheppard. Did you think to look for an infirmary on board?"

Sheppard stared at him. "Wow, no, we never thought of that, Rodney, no wonder they call you a genius! Of course we did. It looks like it was forward, just behind the control center. Everything's smashed, not even the emergency power is getting through."

"Why would they put it there?"

"How would I know?

"I should take a look." Rodney pushed himself away, Sheppard's voice trailing after him.

"You do that, McKay."

The infirmary wasn't hard to find, but, depressingly, Sheppard was right. There had been what looked like treatment beds or pods, but they were snapped from their bases and crumpled against the forward bulkhead. All the consoles were dark, the emergency lights dead, and when he tried to trace the circuitry, it ended into a splatted hunk of slag. Ok, he thought, we're not going to get any help here. Let's hope Dekaas really does know what he's doing. He started back toward the rest of the team.

Elizabeth watched closely while Dekaas examined the Vanir, wordlessly handing him things from his kit when he asked for them, as his expression grew more and more grim. At last Dekaas stood up. "I don't know what I can do for him that you haven't already done," he said.

"You're the doctor," John began.

"Oh come on!" Rodney expostulated. "Surely you can do something! Don't give me this there's nothing you can do."

Dekaas squared his shoulders. "I don't even know where his organs are or what his vital signs are supposed to be! You hand me someone of a species I've never seen before who has catastrophic injuries and what do you think I'm going to do? Just wave my hands over him and heal him?"

John stepped between them. "Ok," he said, running his hand through his hair. "Ok, what would you need to have a chance?"

Dekaas shook his head. "Some idea what the baseline vitals for his species are. Some diagnostic equipment designed for his species. Not to mention little things like an operating theater." He gestured around the wrecked Vanir ship. "If this was his ship, doesn't it have first aid equipment at least?"

"If it did, it was destroyed in the crash," Teyla said. "Much of the front of the ship burned and is completely destroyed."

Dekaas shook his head. "I don't know what to tell you. Without anything designed for him, I don't see what I can do for him. I think the palliative care you've been giving him is the best we can do."

"Seriously?" Rodney began, his shrill tone masking concern. And he was concerned, Elizabeth thought. He didn't want to watch this injured Vanir die while they had no idea how to help him. It wasn't in Rodney's makeup to accept death.

"Rodney, why don't you look around and see if you can salvage anything," John said. "Maybe try to get into the ship's computer system and get some information on this guy's physiology."

"I can't do that when the actual data storage is a pile of slag," Rodney retorted.

"Well maybe there's a backup system," John said. "You don't know until you look."

Dekaas appeared troubled. Elizabeth put one hand on his elbow and steered him away from the quarreling gate team. "I'm sorry to have asked you to come here so fruitlessly," she said.

"I wish I could do something for him," Dekaas said. He looked back at the Vanir lying beneath a blanket on one of the jumper's stretchers. "As a doctor, that's the worst part – failing a patient."

"You can't blame yourself," Elizabeth said. "If you've never even seen his kind before, how could you know what to do? A completely unfamiliar race…"

"I've never seen his kind before, no." Dekaas glanced around the wrecked Vanir ship. "But I feel like I've seen something like this. This kind of architecture, this kind of writing…" He shook his head.

Elizabeth dropped her voice. "When you were with the Wraith?"

"No. After that." Dekaas ran his hand over the battered bulkhead, Asgard lettering still visible around the door frame. "Lettering like this."

"Where?"

"There's a deserted world the Travelers use," he said. "Nobody else comes there. It's a fairly bleak world with a thin atmosphere and it's mostly ocean, but there's one set of caves that used to be some kind of installation. They use it for a supply depot."

"And it had writing like this?" Elizabeth tried to suppress the excitement in her voice.

"On some of the walls. There's some broken machinery – nothing works but the power supply. Some of the Travelers have figured out how to jack into the power supply to run lights and heaters. But somebody who knew more about it might be able to tell what some of the other equipment was or what it's supposed to do." Dekaas looked rueful. "We don't read this language."

"But Daniel Jackson does," Elizabeth said. She looked over his shoulder. "Daniel! Come over here a moment."

Daniel came, followed closely by John. "What's up?"

"It may be nothing," Elizabeth said, "but Dekaas knows of what might be an abandoned Vanir installation. He says there's some broken machinery and a power supply that still works."

"A power supply?" John said.

"What kind of machinery?" Daniel asked.

"I don't know," Dekaas said. "I was telling Elizabeth that we don't read this language."

"If I could get a look at it…" Daniel began.

"…there might be a database," John said. "Or if we're lucky some of the equipment is medical. Maybe even one of those healing pods they had back in the Milky Way. We should take this guy there and see."

Dekaas held up a hand. "The patient is barely stable. If we start trying to carry him around, he may die."

"If the damned stasis pods hadn't failed when we released Elizabeth and Ronon," Rodney began, and shook his head, scowling. "But they did."

John frowned. "And if we don't get him some treatment, he'll probably die. That's where we were before. If I were him," he jerked a thumb at the unconscious Vanir, "I'd rather try to get to something that might help than just lie here and hope for the best."

"I think that's right," Elizabeth said. "We can't help him anymore here. Let's take him to the facility Dekaas knows about and see if there is anything there that can help him. It's the best shot we've got."

"Elizabeth," Dekaas said. "There are no guarantees. I don't know if any of the equipment is medical or if it can be operated even by someone who reads the language."

"Understood," Elizabeth said. "Colonel, let's get our patient ready for transport."

There was a long moment of silence, everyone looking at her. She had forgotten she wasn't in charge, wasn't Dr. Weir in command in Atlantis. This was John's show, not hers.

Then Teyla smiled. "What are we waiting for?"

"Let's go," John said.

Ember rested his off hand lightly on the frame of the long window, staring out into the deepening twilight. It was at this hour that Atlantis felt least hostile to him, most willing to tolerate his presence, and he could not help admiring its beauty, its towers of glass and metal wreathed in light. It was not alive, or at least it was not grown from living tissue, as a hive was, but in some sense, at least, he began to believe it lived. And he was one of the few Wraith, perhaps the only Wraith, to have seen this view without being a prisoner condemned to death. He was here, in fact, as something like an ally, to help the Lanteans in their search for Asgard sites, in exchange for the chance to examine what was found. He had walked freely into the towers, and would walk freely out again. It was a strange and alien thought, and neither he nor the city knew what to do with it.

Not that he was unescorted, of course. There was a Marine guard at his door, and others would follow him if he asked to leave his quarters, though it had been made clear to him that there was some disturbance that had interrupted the search for Asgard sites. Some sort of contamination brought through the Stargate, he guessed, from the things that were being done and the things that were not said. That argued unusual carelessness on the Lanteans' part, though they seemed confident in their ability to bring things under control again.

He hoped it would be soon. His feeding hand twinged, the handmouth opening and closing involuntarily, and an image of the Marine at the door rose unbidden in his mind. He was full-fleshed, young and strong and full of life — and that was a thought that should not be pursued. Ember bared his teeth in a silent snarl, turning away from the window. He was hungry, and growing hungrier; were he on the hive, he would have fed a day ago, but here... Teyla had promised that there would be volunteers who would let him feed, but that was not an option, not unless he was truly starving.

He glanced around his pair of rooms, so different from his comfortable quarters on Alabaster's hive. It was all so open, so bright;

in the day, the sun filled the larger room like water even after he had opaqued the windows to their fullest degree. The smaller room, clearly intended as sleeping space, was mercifully less bright, but it was still terribly open. He had taken the mattress from the bed and used it and the blankets and pillows to create something more nest-like in one corner, but it was still hard to fall asleep, surrounded by so much air. He missed the rhythms of the hive, the pulse of its functions just at the edge of hearing. Atlantis breathed, long soft sighs that were sometimes even strong enough to ruffle his hair, but there was no blood in it.

The Lanteans had left him access to their communications system, or perhaps they had simply not chosen to disable the Ancient device that rested on one of the tables, and he eyed it thoughtfully. It had been more than a day since he had last spoken with anyone other than his escort. Perhaps it was time to remind them of his existence, and to find out what was going on.

He touched the code they had given him, remembering the formulae the Lanteans used. It still seemed strange that they could not recognize each other's voices. "It is I, Ember. I wish to speak to Dr. Zelenka if he is free." And that, he thought, was a clever touch: Zelenka was a master of sciences physical; if the emergency was contamination, it should not be he who was dealing with it.

There was a moment of silence, and then a female voice answered. "Banks here. Dr. Zelenka will be with you in just a moment."

Ember lifted an eyebrow at the machine, knowing it transmitted only sound. "Very well."

It was some time before Zelenka called, long enough for the last of the sunlight to have vanished from the city's towers. The first strands of the aurora rose in the north, pale green against the purple sky, flickering behind the towers, and he was watching them coil slowly up from the horizon when the machine chimed again.

"Ember. Zelenka here. Look, I'm sorry we've been neglecting you, but we've been a bit busy."

Ember tilted his head to one side. Was that a note of fear he heard in the human's voice? And surely those were other human voices in the background, the words not distinguishable, but the tone sharp and alarmed. "You are in trouble."

"Everything is under control."

"I don't wish to add to your troubles, but if this is a question of biological contamination —"

"Who told you that?" That was a different voice, the blade who was the Consort Sheppard's right hand.

"No one," Ember said. "I guessed it from the patterns of activity. And if that is your problem, I am a master of sciences biological. I may be able to help you."

"I don't know," Lorne began, and Zelenka interrupted.

"He has a point, you know."

"And I am also here and affected by — whatever this is." Ember couldn't keep his voice from rising slightly.

"Yes, that had also occurred to me," Zelenka said. "Wait. I will contact Dr. Beckett."

The machine switched off before Ember could respond. He bared teeth at it, for the first time feeling a thread of fear work its way down the ridges of his spine. He had not really thought that the Lanteans could be so careless as to let some organism loose in their precious city, and yet it was beginning to sound as though that was exactly what had happened. And if that were the case... He shook himself. The odds were that anything that affected the Lanteans would not affect the Wraith, or at least not in the same way. He should be able to survive, though he could not in conscience use the Stargate if he had also been contaminated, and Guide would not want to risk bringing him back to the hive until they were sure he was free of any contagion. But if the humans died... For a bleak moment, he could see that future, trapped alone in the empty city, starving, stalking empty halls beneath the flames of the aurora. It would not come to that, he told himself. Guide would find a way to rescue him.

A second chime sounded, and the door slid open to reveal not only a pair of Marines but a slender woman with dark hair cut short and blunt at her shoulders. "Ember." She managed the word almost without a stumble, though her body language was distinctly wary. "I'm Dr. Wu. Dr. Zelenka says you've volunteered to help us analyze this bacteria?"

"I would be glad to be of assistance," Ember answered, and knew he sounded equally wary.

"Good. Well. If you'd come with us, then?" She waved vaguely toward the corridor.

Ember followed her through the maze of Atlantis's corridors, very aware of the Marines at his back. They both carried guns slung across their chests, and in his current state either one of them could do enough damage to overwhelm his ability to heal. His feeding hand twinged again, and he wished passionately that he could feed. The taller of the Marines was strong and hearty; Dr. Wu shone with the inner fire of one who lived for the mind. He could almost feel their life force flowing into him, and he had to close his feeding hand tight to hide the sudden gaping of his handmouth.

"Dr. Beckett," Wu said, as the laboratory door opened for her. "I've brought the Wraith — the Wraith scientist."

"Good." The man to whom she had spoken did not look up from his microscope, but typed one-handed on a laptop that sat beside him. He straightened then, checked the screen, and finally looked up, meeting Wu's eyes with a smile. "Thank you, Marie. Corporal, you won't be needed."

"Major Lorne's orders, sir," the taller man said. "We'll just wait right here by the door, I promise we won't be in your way. In fact, if you'd like, I'll send Patterson for some fresh coffee."

Beckett seemed to relax at that. "Aye, that would be helpful. And a tea for me, if you would."

"Right away, Doc," the smaller Marine said, and disappeared down the corridor.

"So you're Ember," Beckett said, coming out from behind his workstation, and Ember nodded once.

"And you are Dr. Beckett." There was something odd about him, something off in the flavor of his life-force, and Ember frowned abruptly. "A clone?"

Beckett scowled. "Aye. Though that's a fairly personal question."

"I'm sorry." Ember cocked his head. "It's just I didn't think the Lanteans — you — were capable —" He stopped, knowing he'd said too much, and Beckett sighed.

"Actually, it was done by Michael. And I'm not at all sure I want to talk about it."

"Michael," Ember repeated. The renegade his own people knew as Lastlight. It was an ill-omened name, a cleverman both brilliant and deranged, damaged beyond hope by both the Lantean attempts to transform him and by the rejection of his own queen. "I am sorry."

"Well. It's all right." Beckett paused, a wry smile curving the corners of his mouth. "Though I'm curious to know how you could tell."

"Clones feel different," Ember said, startled. "Your life-force. It's — thicker. Shorter? No." He shook his head, tracing a shape in the air with his off hand. "A cord, not a river?"

"Interesting." Beckett's annoyance had faded, replaced by curiosity. "Have you ever encountered the Asgard?"

"Not personally. The hive on which I was born fought them over several of our feeding grounds, but I'm a cleverman, not a blade. Why?"

"I wondered what they felt like. They've cloned themselves so many times they've wrecked their base DNA." Beckett shook his head. "But that's not important at the moment, though I'd like to talk to you a bit more about this when things calm down. Right now, we've got more important things to worry about."

"Perhaps you could tell me what has happened?" Ember moved closer to the workstation, careful not to go too fast, and Beckett nodded.

"We picked up an unknown bacterium on a planet we were hoping to use as — well, never mind for what, it's not important. The main thing is, it destroys petroleum-based plastics, and we can't seem to find an effective decontamination procedure."

"Have you isolated the organism?" Ember asked.

"Yes." Beckett swung a screen so that he could see it more clearly. "It's not in any of our databases, and there are structures that make me think it's not a naturally-occurring organism."

Ember frowned at the image, considering the shapes. Lantean characters filled a smaller window — results of their analysis, he guessed, but he couldn't read enough of the symbols for it to be helpful — and he pushed it aside. Beckett was right, the original bacterium had certainly been artificially created, though it had bred with other strains to produce this variant. "This is your model? May I work with it?"

Beckett waved his hands. "Be my guest."

Ember frowned at the keyboard, orienting himself, then began removing the unfamiliar pieces of the structure. It didn't take long for the new pattern to emerge, and he allowed himself a sigh of relief. "I know what this is, this part of it."

"Aye?" Beckett leaned over his shoulder.

"It's a —" Ember groped for a word, shaking his head. "It's one of our tools, a common one, we use it to dissolve certain compounds after we've created pathways within an organic structure. We prefer petroleum-based plastics for laying out vascular systems, they don't interact with the hive itself — but perhaps that's better not spoken of, either. My point is, I know what this is. Or at least what it started out as. We should be able to deactivate it."

"Let's not hang about, then," Beckett said. "Tell me what you need."

John brought the jumper to a gentle landing in the square beside Sateda's Stargate, glancing over his shoulder to make sure that the Vanir was still all right. It still lay unmoving on the stretcher, great eyes closed, but Dekaas nodded.

"Still breathing."

"All right." John glanced at his controls, seeing the second jumper still a good twenty minutes away. Rodney was pushing the damaged engine as much as he dared, but it still couldn't make full speed. "As soon as McKay gets here, we'll head for this planet. In the meantime, I'm going to check in with Atlantis."

He lowered the back ramp as he spoke, and clambered out. Neither Dekaas nor Elizabeth said anything, and Jackson was still busy with his tablet, running through the Asgard files one more time as though it might turn up something new.

Unsurprisingly, Cai came out to meet him, and John put on his best smile. "Cai! Any news?"

"No sign of the contamination having reached us here," Cai answered, "though we're going to continue to keep those supplies separate until Atlantis tells us they're clean."

"Yeah, I was hoping they might have managed that by now."

"Not so far as we've heard," Cai said. "If you want to talk to them — help yourself."

"Thanks." John crossed to the building where they had set up the radio system — Ronon snickered every time he looked at the place, said it had been one of the raunchiest bars in the city — to find one of Atlantis's technicians reading a battered paperback. She sat up hastily as he entered, and John gave what he hoped was a disarming smile. "Hey — Dr. Parker, isn't it?"

"Yes, sir."

She looked and sounded about twelve, which made John feel suddenly old. "Any news from Atlantis?"

"Nothing since Teyla returned," Parker said. "Shall I raise them for you?"

"Thanks."

John waited while she dialed the Stargate and then made contact with the gate room.

"Lorne here. Everything all right there, Colonel? Teyla said you'd gotten the doctor you needed."

"We're fine," John said. "What's your status?"

As he had expected, there was the slightest of pauses. "We're still trying to get the contamination under control. We have it mostly contained, and Dr. Beckett thinks he has a possible counter-agent." Lorne paused again. "He thought that the bacterium might be artificially created, so he's got the Wraith, Ember, working on it with him."

Great, John thought. One more thing we're going to owe Guide. It wasn't helpful to actually say it, though, and he settled for, "Is this a Wraith weapon?"

"Apparently not. Beckett says it's more like a tool that's apparently gotten loose and maybe mutated or maybe interbred with some local bacteria. Ember seems to think he can get it under control pretty easily, though."

"That's good news."

"Yes, sir."

There was something in his tone that made John hesitate. "What's the bad news?"

"Dr. Parrish and his team — they were investigating PGX-239 — they reported a discharge of energy bolts near the Stargate.

Dr. Parrish says it wasn't actually aimed at them, and there's still no sign of any life bigger than the insects, but Captain Aulich asked if we had any available back-up. Trouble is, we don't have that many Marines off-world right now, and most of them are needed where they are."

"Are you saying something shot at them?"

"Dr. Parrish says not, sir. He says he thinks it's a natural phenomenon. I've told him to divert to Sateda or PVX-993 if that judgement changes, those are the safest options we've got right now."

"All right."

"Is there any chance you could spare them Ronon and one of the Marines on Sateda?" Lorne asked. "I don't want to pull all our guys off of Sateda, given how many civilians we've got there at the moment, but Ronon would make a big difference. And he knows this galaxy."

He'd hate not having Ronon with them, particularly if the Vanir were involved, but if something was shooting at the botany team… There were never enough men, and the ones you had were never where you needed them. "I'll send Ronon."

"Thank you, Colonel."

John bit his lip, knowing there was a question Lorne carefully wasn't asking. By rights, he ought to return to Atlantis, but that was putting himself into quarantine, and right now there didn't seem to be any reason to do that, especially if Beckett was right and they were about to get the problem fixed. "All right, Major, carry on. We've got a line on a possible Vanir installation — an abandoned one — so we're going to take our patient there to see if we can't save him. We need to find out what they wanted from Elizabeth, and there's no way we can get anything from him in this condition." He glanced out the window, seeing Rodney's jumper making its final approach, and recited the new gate address. "We'll check in again once we're there."

"Very good, sir," Lorne said, and John motioned for Parker to cut the channel.

Ronon was waiting in the main square, talking to a hard-faced, gold-skinned woman whose complexion had the weathered look that John was beginning to associate with Satedan scavengers. Ronon looked up at John's approach, patted the woman on her shoulder, and came to join him, saying, "We're going now?"

"Change of plans," John said. "I need you to back up one of the other teams."

"Trouble?" Ronon didn't seem to move, but his posture tightened somehow.

"We're not sure. Dr. Parrish took a botany team to PGX-239 and apparently there's something there that shoots energy bolts. Parrish says he doesn't think it's actually shooting at them, but they wanted back-up just in case. Lorne can't send any Marines off Atlantis — obviously — and we don't have enough people already off-world. So I want to send you."

Ronon looked down at him with narrowed eyes. "You're not trying to get rid of me, are you, Sheppard?"

"You're the last person I want to lose from this mission," John said. "But you're the best man I've got."

There was a little silence, and then Ronon nodded slowly. "All right. PGX-239?"

"Yeah." John gripped his shoulder. "Thanks, buddy."

Rodney and Teyla had already joined Elizabeth in the undamaged jumper, and John settled himself into the pilot's seat, Rodney at his side. Dekaas recited the address again and John punched it in, then waited while the Stargate lit and opened.

"Still ok back there, Doc?" he asked.

"As far as I can tell," Dekaas answered, his voice grim.

The tone said more than the words, and John bit his lip. "Right. We're on our way."

CHAPTER FOUR

THEY CAME out of the Stargate over a rocky, broken land that might have held ruins, though it was impossible to tell as quickly as they moved and as dark as it was, a sort of purply twilight with a sky studded with stars. Daniel craned his neck over the seat in front of him, over Teyla's shoulder as she sat in the shotgun seat. "It's night."

Behind him in the back with the injured Vanir on his stretcher, Dekaas replied, "It's always like this. This planet is a long way from its sun."

"Though clearly not so far that there isn't liquid water," Rodney said as the jumper soared over the verge of a dark sea, sharp cliffs and little islands outlined by the white foam of breaking waves.

"Not that far, no," Dekaas said equitably. "The climate isn't bad except for the polar regions. There are some plants that can handle this little light and some sea life too. But the Travelers have never settled this world for obvious reasons."

"There must be subsurface heating," Rodney said. "An active core—"

"It's definitely too dark for agriculture," Daniel said.

"Yes," Dekaas said. "As I said, we've just used it as a depot."

"Ok," John said from the pilot's seat. "Where is this place?"

Dekaas came forward, standing between the rows of seats. "I've never come here from the Stargate. I've always arrived on a Traveler ship from orbit. It's in the temperate zone of the southern hemisphere, the largest island in an archipelago that curves west."

"I can find it from that," John said, the jumper obediently creating a heads-up display map of the planet at his thought. Seas and islands filled in.

"It's mostly water," Daniel said.

"93 per cent," John said, glancing up at the display. "Not too bad. There." He pointed. "Is that the archipelago you mean, Dekaas?"

"That looks right."

"Ok, folks," John said. "About twenty minutes flight time. Is there a good place to park the jumper?"

"There's a landing field the Travelers use," Dekaas affirmed. "It should be more than large enough."

"Great."

Daniel glanced out the window at the dark waves, now featureless beneath the flawless, starred sky. How many worlds like this were there, worlds that were marginally inhabitable but weren't because there were so many places that were better? Most people on Earth still wondered if there were other planets capable of supporting human life. How would they even begin to deal with the truth – that there were so many that the humans who were there ahead of them couldn't be bothered with most of them? It was an embarrassment of riches. Most people on Earth – well, if the truth about the Stargate program was ever believed, it would throw society into a crisis. The biggest argument against revelation was the consequence. It would be loosing a bear into a crowded marketplace, starting an unimaginable chain of events that could topple governments, economic systems, religions, entire ways of life. No wonder everyone so far had preferred to keep the secret, to pass the responsibility for revelation along for another year or two – everyone except a few people here and there who thought no further than the revelation itself. Daniel certainly hadn't started out a fan of military secrets, but the Stargate was a secret he was willing to take to his grave if necessary. He'd seen too many ruins of civilizations torn apart by an unforeseen crisis. He wasn't going to be the person to precipitate one.

Elizabeth turned around in the seat next to him, glancing back toward Dekaas. "How is our friend doing?"

"He's holding on," Dekaas said. "Respiration is weak but steady. I think he's comatose. I can't tell you how much brain damage there is. Even if we find equipment, it may be too late."

"Understood," Elizabeth said.

"Let's hope we're not too late," Daniel said.

"We're coming up on the island," John said, and Daniel shifted to see it coming up in the front window, a darker mass against the sea limned by the white of breakers that gleamed more brightly than they ought to.

"Bioluminesence?" Daniel asked.

"That seems reasonable," Elizabeth replied. Her face had lost some
of the tension that had marked it as she returned to the familiar
routines and familiar people she had known before. It took time
to come back, as Daniel knew. But the best thing for it was people
– and the missions you'd cared about before.

John Sheppard put the jumper down gently on a wide flat place
just below the crest of the island. It was open on three sides, the
fourth being a rocky pinnacle that crowned the island.

"That's where the entrance is," Dekaas said.

"I see it," John said easily, and as he brought the jumper to a halt
Daniel did too. There were what appeared to be four bay doors that
covered a break in the cliff, but now they were all jammed open.

"Definitely Vanir," Daniel said. "They're the only ones we know
of who typically construct doors as four-part irises. Other races
tend to either have one or two moving planes that open to either
side as the Ancients did, or up and down as the Wraith do. The
Goa'uld appropriated technology as they found it, thereby creating an eclectic…"

"Can we save the lecture on doors?" Rodney snapped. "We all
know what a door is."

"I'm just saying that those doors look Asgard."

"That's great," John said. "Now let's go see what we can find.
"Teyla, Rodney, and Daniel, you're with me. Elizabeth, would you
mind staying with Dekaas and our patient until we check the place
out? No reason to haul him all over until we know what we've got."

"Absolutely," Elizabeth said. "Good luck."

"Thanks," John said, and opened the rear hatch of the jumper.

Ronon watched the puddle jumper vanish through the Stargate.
The wormhole winked out behind it and he allowed himself a sigh.
If this — thing — on PGX-239 turned out to be nothing, he was
going to be annoyed. He'd been looking forward to seeing what
they could find out from the Vanir.

"Dex?" That was Cai, coming across the gate square to join him.
"You're not going with Sheppard and the others?"

"One of the exploration teams reported a problem. Sheppard
wanted me to check it out."

"Do you want help?"

Ronon considered the question. Sheppard hadn't told him to take anyone else — hadn't told him not to, either. Given that the Lanteans only had a couple of Marines currently on Sateda along with half a dozen civilians, he was inclined not to take them. They'd just had a lesson about how crazy random outsiders like Sora could be, and Sateda was starting to make itself a target again, if not for the Wraith, assuming they kept their promises, then for other aggressive human cultures. Nobody trusted the Genii further than they could throw them. Cai could probably spare a couple of the scavengers, all of whom were well used to fighting, but from what Sheppard had said, Parrish didn't think whatever was going on was an active attack. And Parrish's judgment was usually pretty good. He shook his head. "Thanks, but I think we're all right. I don't want to take your people away from their work."

Cai relaxed a little, and Ronon was glad he'd thought to add the explanation. The last thing he wanted to do was to insult Ushan Cai. "What about supplies? I notice they didn't leave you any."

"That I'll take," Ronon said, gratefully. He'd probably end up with a couple of Lantean energy bars anyway, but he'd missed the dried meat and vegetable leathers that had been Sateda's military rations. Well, along with the canned meals, but he'd bet no one was sorry they couldn't make those any more. "Thanks."

"Bri!" Cai waved at the scavenger. "Can you round up a few day's rations for Dex?"

"Atlantis will pay you back," Ronon said, and Cai nodded.

"We'll take it, particularly those MREs. We're starting to explore outside the city, it's nice to have something that light to pack with us."

"Bri told me you just found some people from — Escavera, was it?"

"Yes. There are half a dozen families up there, hiding out near the mines." Cai grinned. "And I'll bet there are more out there. The Wraith can't have Culled every single farm. If we can just get that light aircraft Hocken was talking about…"

"Her word's good," Ronon said. She was Sheppard's friend, and he'd gotten to like her as well as to respect her.

Cai nodded. "I want her to come here. Someone not just to fly for us, but to train a new group of pilots —" He stopped, his smile wry. "And we could use you, too. But I've said that before."

"Yeah." Ronon looked away, past the Stargate to the mended buildings. Not much, compared to a lot of other worlds — not much at all, compared to Atlantis — but more than any of them had ever imagined would be possible. "There's — there are still some things I need to do. Stuff I need to take care of." Things he needed to forget, but he didn't need to say that, not to another survivor. "But, yeah, eventually."

"You'll always be welcome," Cai said. He looked over his shoulder, nodding as he saw Bri returning with one of the vine-woven carriers.

"Three days' rations," she said, holding it out, and Ronon took it gratefully.

"Thanks," he said, and hoped it would cover both parts of the conversation.

One of Cai's gate guards dialed PGX-239 — it was a good thing he didn't recognize everyone anymore, Ronon told himself, it meant that the settlement was growing — and Ronon touched his radio. "Dr. Parrish. It's Ronon Dex."

There was a pause, and then Parrish answered, his voice crackling in Ronon's earpiece. "Ronon?"

"Yeah. Sheppard said you needed backup."

"Yes. Yes, we could probably use the help." Parrish sounded more than a bit worn, and Ronon wondered what exactly was going on. "Come on through."

"Roger." Ronon loosened his energy pistol in its holster and slung the ration-carrier over his shoulder, then took a deep breath and walked up into the shimmering blue of the wormhole.

He emerged in what looked like the planet's mid-afternoon, the pinpoint sun halfway down the western sky, shadows lengthening. There was no sign of habitation other than the Stargate, just a low hill rising to his left and a tangle of low-growing vegetation surrounding the open space that held the Stargate. Someone had set up a stack of equipment in the clearing beyond the DHD, but there were no tents in sight. He glanced at the sky again, hoping they'd either brought shelter or were planning to evacuate to somewhere like Sateda after it got dark, and Parrish came forward to meet him, holding out his hand.

"Ronon. Thanks for coming."

Ronon nodded. "Want to fill me in on what's going on?"

Parrish gave a sharp smile, showing teeth. "That's an interesting question. Something on this planet shoots bolts of energy, but as far as we can tell, there's no intelligent life here — no life at all any bigger than those insects."

Ronon ducked as a flight of half a dozen multi-winged creatures the size of his thumb darted past his face. "But something is shooting — at you, or just shooting?"

"Just shooting, we think," Parrish answered. "But it's — disconcerting."

The rest of the team had moved to join them, two Marines, a white-blonde Air Force captain, and another scientist, her gray-streaked hair pulled back in a tight bun.

"Dr. Parrish is right," the captain said. "Sorry, I'm Isabella Aulich. Meteorology."

Ronon nodded, grateful that he didn't have to worry about reading her name tape. He was getting better at Lantean writing, but it still took him more time than he liked to admit. "Tell me what happened."

"We can show you," Parrish said, with another of his sharp smiles. "Sammy, would you do the honors?"

"Yes, sir!" The corporal — Ronon remembered his actual name was Samara — unslung his weapon and took a few steps to the side. He snapped the machine off automatic and fired a couple of shots into the air. An instant later, a bolt of light shot out of the underbrush, followed by three more at increasing intervals. None of them came anywhere near the clearing, and Ronon slid his energy pistol back into its holster.

"What's the trigger, the shot or the noise?"

"That's an excellent question," Parrish said. "I think it's the sound, because Sammy's shots have to be hitting further away from us than the source of those bolts. Dr. Hunt agrees."

The other scientist nodded.

"What is it? Some device of the Ancestors?" That was a thoroughly unpleasant thought, and Ronon couldn't hide a grimace.

"God, I hope not," Parrish said, and the sergeant gave an involuntary grunt of agreement.

"It could be, though," Aulich said, wiping her sweat-damped hair off her forehead. "We've seen weirder."

"Damn straight," the sergeant said. She was a short, broad-shouldered woman with dark skin and hair braided close to her scalp. Ronon squinted at her name tape, and made out the word "Joseph."

"We've been a little wary of looking too closely," Parrish said, "but there's no sign of any non-vegetal infrastructure beneath either the conifers or the succulents, nor is there a visible power source."

"In other words, no guns?" Ronon asked.

"Pretty much," Hunt said.

Ronon looked around the clearing. Everything was quiet now, nothing moving in the underbrush. A few of the big insects swung in lazy circles over the twisted plants with the jagged bark, but there was nothing else in sight, not even a cloud in the pale sky. "What do you want to do, Doc? You can always pull back to Sateda, come back another day when Atlantis is open."

Parrish spread his hands. "I'd like to stay. Whatever this is, it doesn't seem that interested in actually shooting at us, and I'd like to know whether this is some man-made device or if it's a natural phenomenon. We've got another, what, eight, nine hours before dark?"

"Nine hours, forty-one minutes," Aulich said. "It'll be twilight for a couple of hours before that, though." She paused. "I'd like to stay, too. I'm getting some unusual readings from my equipment, and I'd like to try to lock them down."

"I agree," Hunt said.

The two Marines exchanged glances, and then Joseph gave Ronon an almost imperceptible shrug. He knew what that meant — it was their job to stay, and so they'd stay — and nodded back.

"I think we kind of over-reacted," Parrish said, his voice apologetic. "But —"

"It looked like something was shooting at you," Ronon said. For a minute, he wanted to yell at them — wanted to have gone with Sheppard and the others, where there almost certainly was real danger, but stopped himself, knowing it was pointless. "Ok, Doc, what's the plan?"

"It looked to me as though most of the shots — energy bolts, whatever — were coming from among the inner rank of succulents,"

Parrish said. "Dr. Hunt?"

She nodded. "I — yes, I'd agree, and maybe on a line running straight back from the gate?"

Ronon squinted, then pointed toward a particularly juicy-looking plant that stood about a hand's-breadth above its neighbors. One thing for being a Runner, it taught you to locate the source of fire quickly and accurately. "At least one shot came from there."

Parrish sighted along the same line, and nodded. "All right. Let's take a look."

"A careful look," Ronon said, and Parrish grinned.

"Always."

Ember frowned at the screen, squinting as he tried to make sense of the Lanteans' unfamiliar notation. There was the odd spiked shape that represented the Wraith solvent, the various receptor sites turned to red and orange as Beckett added the model of the neutralizer. And there were the numbers that spelled out the success rate: about eighty-five percent completely blocked, which was lower than he would have expected.

"Not bad for a first try," Beckett said.

Ember's feeding hand twitched, another sharp reminder that he had not fed in days. "I think we can adjust the —" He tried again to think of a verbal translation that would convey the way that the molecule flashed hot as it joined with its target — its unique quality — but again the problem defeated him, and instead he touched the screen. "This, here. If we increase its presence by 0.08 percent, I think we will improve the rate of uptake, and thus the ultimate success rate."

"That's not so much of a change," Beckett said.

"No, and too much will only spoil things," Ember answered. He reached for the keyboard, and stopped as he felt the Marines at the door shift and startle. "If I may?"

"Go ahead, let's try it."

Beckett stepped out of the way, and Ember began entering the new parameters. Once again, he wished for his own lab, the familiar tactile interface that let him feel how the new compound would come together, but he put that thought aside. He was on Atlantis; he

would have to work with the Lanteans' tools, no matter how strange.
He checked the results, then touched keys to restart the simulation.
The image flickered crazily for a few seconds, then steadied to the
new result: more than 95 per cent of the receptor sites showed red,
and the rest glowed deep orange.

"That looks good," Beckett said, moving closer again.

"I would like to do better," Ember said. "Perhaps a touch more
of this?" He touched another symbol.

Beckett gave him a sidelong glance. "Are you seriously thinking
you can get one hundred percent response?"

"It would be best if we did," Ember answered. "Otherwise some
will still be effective, and if those survive to breed, you will have
the same problem all over again."

"You're right, of course, but we need to take action now." Beckett
studied the screen, pursing his lips. "It'll be close to 96 per cent
effective, which is damn good, and the remaining bacteria will be
severely weakened. Even if they can affect plastics, they're going to
be a lot less efficient about it — they're going to lack a strong copy
of the plastic-dissolving enzyme."

Ember rubbed his fingers together. If he could just touch the
model, turn it and feel it — He put the thought aside. "That's so.
And an effective quarantine should eliminate the rest."

"Let's try it, then." Beckett turned toward his console.

It took some hours to persuade the Lanteans' equipment to produce even a meager amount of the compound, long enough that
Beckett had to return to his quarters to sleep, and the last of the
manufacture had to be completed under the supervision of a nervous technician. The result was dead matter, not the living organism that Ember would have preferred to use, but it seemed to do its
job well enough, at least in simulation, and Ember looked up from
his screen as Beckett reappeared.

"Doctor. I think we're ready to try this."

"Don't you ever sleep?" Beckett settled himself at the station
next to Ember's, squinting slightly as he pulled up the final analysis on his own screen.

"Not quite as you do." Ember suppressed the thought of hiber-
nation, decades, even a century or two of stasis, held secure in the

hive's embrace. That was not what the human had meant. "Certainly not as often."

"That was true with Michael," Beckett said quietly. "He worked all hours, kept going until the job was done, mostly, and then he'd crash. Do you tell me that's a Wraith pattern?"

Ember tipped his head to one side. "We are capable of sustained effort, yes. Though most clevermen learn that it can be counter-productive to push themselves too hard, particularly if there is any shortage of food—"

He stopped, aware that his own hunger had led him into an unguarded statement, and Beckett gave him an unreadable glance.

"Aye. And how hungry are you, I wonder?"

"I do not need to feed for some time yet," Ember said, stiffly. His feeding hand throbbed, but he closed his fingers over the hand-mouth. "Let us proceed."

Radek stared at the test bench he and Dr. Sindye had improvised in one of the smaller rooms which were still inside the quarantine line. At least Sindye was a chemist, the only one who'd been unlucky enough to be in the gate room when the quarantine was imposed. They really needed a biologist, Radek thought, or perhaps a botanist, but he and Sindye would have to do. Unless, of course, things got markedly worse, in which case they'd need every scientist in the city working on the problem. He picked up the sealed cylinder that had been passed through the quarantine—literally rolled across the corridor that marked the boundary—and turned it carefully in his hand.

"So this is the compound?"

Sindye didn't look up from her microscope. "Yes. Dr. Beckett says that it was nearly 96 per cent effective in simulation, so it's time to try it on the actual bacteria."

"Which we have no equipment capable of isolating."

"No, but we do have exposed equipment and unexposed plastic." Sindye straightened. She was very tall and thin, with close-cropped graying hair, her borrowed lab coat very white against her dark skin. It was too short, and the sleeves rode up to expose several centimeters of wrist. A risk, Radek thought, but there was nothing they could do about it. "And a couple of nice metal boxes to put them in. I think that's our best protocol."

Radek nodded. "A test and a control, yes?"

"That's the plan." Sindye reached for her radio. "Dr. Beckett. We're ready to begin the test. I have two metal containers of identical volume, a contaminated object which I have cut in half—"

"You weren't able to isolate the actual bacteria?" Beckett interrupted.

"I can see it and identify it under the microscope," Sindye said, patiently, "but I have no way to collect a separate sample. Dr. Zelenka and I think it would be more accurate simply to use the item in question."

"What is it?"

"A travel mug," Radek said. He refrained from mentioning that it was a souvenir of an important sports event—something to do with American football, he thought—and that Spec. Kirkpatrick had been very unhappy to sacrifice it.

"I'm worried about contamination," Beckett said. "Food particles, that sort of thing."

"It was well rinsed before the problem started," Sindye said. "At the moment, we're just seeing the first signs of erosion along the rim."

"If it doesn't work, we can revisit the question," a second voice said, and it was a moment before Radek recognized it as Ember's. "For now, though—"

"Aye, best to get on with it," Beckett agreed.

"All right," Sindye said. "I have the travel mug, one half for each box, and some uncontaminated plastic. And I have the compound you sent. My thought was to place it and the uncontaminated plastic in one box, and just uncontaminated plastic in the other, make sure the plastic was well and truly covered with the compound, and then add the halves of the travel mug."

"Simple and elegant," Radek said, half under his breath, and she grinned.

"That'll work," Beckett said.

"Then we're starting now." Sindye used a pair of metal tongs to move the pieces of plastic into each of the boxes. "Dr. Zelenka, if you'll do the honors?"

"Of course." Radek unscrewed the lid of the cylinder and poured about 250 milliliters of clear liquid over one piece of plastic. It looked like plain water, though as he used the tongs to swish the plastic through box, he caught of whiff of spoiled apples.

Sindye grimaced as well. "That's kind of nasty."

"Yes." Radek looked at the box, now awash in the liquid. "Do you think that's enough?"

"As good as it's going to be," Sindye answered. "I'm adding the contaminated material." She suited her actions to the words, using a second pair of tongs to place each half of the travel mug into a separate box. "And now —"

"And now we wait," Radek agreed.

She pulled a stool away from the bench, brought it to one side so that she could rest her back against the wall. "So this is supposed to be a Wraith tool, huh?"

"That is what Ember said. Or at least that it may have begun as such."

"I mean, I more or less understand what he's doing, what they're doing, using bacteria and viruses like wrenches and hammers, only on a cellular level." Sindye shook her head. "It's very weird."

Radek nodded, and found a stool for himself. "An entire science based on manipulating living tissue rather than inorganic materials the way we do. It is hard to get one's mind around it sometimes."

"Yeah." Sindye rested her head against the wall and gave him a wry smile. "It doesn't help that Ember — every single Wraith — creeps me out. No, that's not fair. They terrify me."

"Have you taken the retrovirus?" Radek tipped his head to one side, not sure why he felt as though he ought to defend Ember. The Wraith had saved his life, thrown him clear of falling debris in the chaotic last battle against Queen Death, and had been badly injured himself. Radek had let him feed in order to save his life, and still wasn't sure how he felt about the bond Ember claimed it had made between them.

"Yes. Though there are times I think maybe I shouldn't have — the idea of being caught on a hiveship permanently is really unpleasant."

"Yes." That was Ronon's argument, of course, and not at all unreasonable. And yet — "I think of it as giving me a chance to escape, or to be rescued."

"I suppose." The idea seemed to relax her slightly.

"Ember is not a bad person," Radek said, and Sindye gave him a sideways look.

"If you say so."

And that was about as much as he ought to say, Radek thought. "How long do we wait?"

Sindye glanced at her watch. "It's been taking about ninety minutes for us to see any signs of degradation."

Radek sighed, and shifted to a more comfortable position. "So we wait some more."

The time seemed to crawl by. No matter what topic either of them introduced, from the unavailability of certain movies on Atlantis's intranet to recent work on Sateda to who supplied the Marines' poker school with moonshine, everything turned back to the Wraith, and to the mysterious bacterium that currently cut them off from the rest of the galaxy.

"And if we had simply read the sign that was standing there…" Radek broke off, knowing he was being unfair, and to his surprise Sindye gave a wry smile.

"Well, considering how rare it is for any Ancient label to say anything useful, I suppose I can't entirely blame them."

Radek smiled himself, looking around the room. Sure enough, the lettering around the door read 'caution — door closes quickly,'while the decorative band around the worktable actually repeated 'do not remove' a dozen times. "That is true. And we will know better next time."

"If there is a next time." Sindye shook her head. "I'm surprised stuff like this doesn't happen more often — biological materials coming through the Stargate to contaminate a new world. Or chemicals, for that matter."

"The Stargate removes most contamination," Radek said. "Or at least that has always been true so far."

"Yeah, but how does it know? That's one of the things I was working on before I got tapped for Atlantis, and now that it might actually be relevant, I realize we don't have the faintest idea."

"The Ancients did it," Radek said, his voice dry.

"And when was the last time the Ancients left us something that worked the way they said it would?"

"Not in my time with the SGC," Radek said. "I wonder if the Stargate — or whatever part of it that looks for contaminants — didn't recognize this because it was Wraith?"

"It's possible," Sindye said. "Do you think Ember has come up with an answer?"

"I think he is going to try his best," Radek answered, "because if he doesn't, he is trapped here with us." And that was an ugly thought, one Wraith in a community of humans, some of whom, at least, had taken the retrovirus. He shook the thought aside. "I think it is time."

"Yeah." Sindye slid off her stool. "Let's see what we've got."

Radek followed her to the worktable and peered over her shoulder into the first box. The travel mug was nearly half gone, and the previously untouched plastic was starting to get a chewed look along its edges. "This is the control?" he began, then realized that the plastic was wet.

"This was the test." Sindye looked stricken, then shook herself. "Let's see the control."

It, too, held a deteriorating travel mug and a chewed-looking piece of plastic. In fact, Radek thought, it was very nearly identical to the test. "This is not good."

"No." Sindye groped for the tongs, then retrieved both pieces of plastic, laying them side by side on the tabletop. "I don't — the compound didn't do a bit of good."

"No." Radek reached for his radio. "Dr. Beckett. We have some bad news."

"Looks like a landing bay." John shone the light from his P90 around the empty space. There were faded markings on the floor, lines that might have demarcated parking areas for various craft or marked some areas off for maintenance or passengers – it was impossible to tell. Or maybe the Travelers had put them there, blocking off areas for various ships to use. One way or another, the chamber's use was obvious.

"Those look like Traveler packing crates in the corner," Rodney said. "Probably it's some stuff they left."

"That could be," Teyla said. She had ranged ahead a little bit, toward the set of doors to the left. There was another, identical set to the right. Going that way first made as much sense as the other.

Daniel Jackson squinted up at the ceiling far above. "Is there power?"

The lights went on with sudden, dazzling brightness. Rodney looked smug from where he stood at a panel at the hangar door. "Amazingly, if you use the light switch, it works."

"Thanks, McKay," John said. He'd gotten used to Ancient installations where the lights went on for him. It actually hadn't occurred to him to look for a manual control beside the door.

"Ok," Daniel said. "That's a good sign. If there's power, there might be equipment intact."

"Remember," Teyla said. "The Travelers use this as a waystation. They have probably removed anything that was obviously useful."

"Let's have a look," John said. "Rodney, you go with Daniel and take the right door. Teyla and I'll take left."

"Do you think we ought to split up?" Rodney asked.

"Yes, I think we ought to split up." John turned around and stared at him. "There's not some big green monster here or the Travelers would have found it. And remember? We've got a patient dying in the jumper? We need to search this place quickly. Why are you arguing about everything all of a sudden?" Though the answer to that was obvious – Jackson. He and Rodney had problems that went back to years ago at the SGC, and every time Jackson set foot in Atlantis, Rodney got weirdly territorial.

"Why don't I switch with Teyla?"

"Why don't you go do what I asked you to?" John said. "You and I are the ones with the ATA gene. It doesn't make sense to have us in the same party."

"But this isn't…"

"Rodney!"

"Fine. I'm going." Rodney spun on his heel and headed for the other door. "We'll go find the secret hidden machinery that kills people."

"If there was secret hidden machinery that kills people, it would already have killed the Travelers," Daniel said as they went out of earshot. "Not that I'm saying there may not be something there, but if you avoid turning it on —"

"Jesus." John shook his head.

Teyla looked vaguely amused. "You gave me Daniel Jackson before. He is just as bad around Rodney as Rodney is around him."

"I'm going to kill them both," John said.

"The thought has crossed my mind," Teyla said with a smile. And that made it better. It always did. She had his back with no drama.

"Let's see if we can find anything useful," John said.

Of course what they found was a warren of rooms used by the Travelers and not exactly put back the way they found it. "Take only photographs and leave only memories," John said as he surveyed a large room full of debris – papers and tatters of cloth, empty food containers and burned out electrical components and what looked like one frayed sock.

"I have found the latrine," Teyla said from the doorway of a smaller room. "Or at least that is its function now."

"Great." Those looked like plastic wrappers from MREs. When did the Travelers get their MREs? "Let's try down here," John said, opening the next door into a dimly lit corridor. Most of these chambers seemed to be on emergency power, every fourth fixture lit. They could see well enough. There were two more rooms along the hall that looked like they'd been occupied, and a door at the end that stubbornly stayed closed when John tried to open it.

"It is not like the others," Teyla said, running her hand over the elaborately inscribed Vanir letters around the top and sides of the door. "They do not have this." She traced them down the side. "I wonder if it says keep out or if these are directions."

"Or the name of the room," John said. He opened his radio. "Jackson? I need you to come down to our location. We need a door read."

"Say again?" Jackson's voice was tinny.

"We've found a door with inscriptions," John said. "We need you to read them."

"On my way."

It took a few moments for the other party to arrive, Rodney in the lead.

"Did you find anything interesting?" Teyla asked.

Rodney shook his head. "Stuff the Travelers used. Rooms full of trash and useless junk. How about you?"

"We found much the same thing. And then this." She nodded at the door.

Daniel was already examining it. "Ok, this inscription is pretty typical. It says, 'Authorized Personnel Only. Do Not Enter. Not a User Entry.'"

"Not a user entry?" John said.

"I suppose not a client entry would be more exact," Daniel said. "Or not a customer entry."

"So this is the back door, the employees only entrance? To what?"

"I don't know," Daniel said. He stood back, his hands on his hips. "But it doesn't look like the Travelers have opened it."

"I don't see any way to open it," Teyla said. "Did it respond to Vanir speech? Or to their genetic pattern?"

"Maybe it had to be opened from the inside," John said.

"These kinds of doors…" Daniel wandered back down the hall away from the door.

"What?" Rodney said.

"…generally had to be opened from some distance. Ah ha!" Daniel pointed to a line of letters at waist height and twenty feet back. "It says 'press for attendant.' So we press here and…" He pressed a section of wall and waited.

"It's like those hospital doors," John said. "Going into an ICU or something. You buzz the nurses' stand and then wait for them to open the doors from inside. So there should be a manual override, right?"

"There should be," Daniel said. "So let's look for it."

"I don't think we have to look very far," Rodney said triumphantly. "It's right here by the door. See?" He turned a piece of the carved panel outward at knee level so that it was a lever that pressed down. "Turn and pump. The doors slide right open." He put his foot on it and stepped hard. The doors slid open an inch.

"I am very glad that you are both so experienced with doors,"

Teyla said with a smile. "It is always useful to travel with many experts on Vanir doors. You are both irreplaceable."

John tried hard not to laugh.

Rodney pumped and slowly the doors ground open until a space about a meter wide appeared between them. "That's good," John said, shining the light from his P90 through them. "Let's take a look." There were shapes, surfaces. They were dust covered, but the room wasn't empty. He stepped inside.

Daniel followed almost on his heels. "There's the switch," Daniel said, reaching to a panel at hip height beside the door. "And there." Light came up from recessed fixtures in the ceiling and along the walls, an amber glow that grew rapidly to the brightness of sunlight. There was a low desk with a single seat behind it, a triangle with the seat in the middle, giving it access to three sides where amber letters scrolled down across the surface of the desk.

"Bingo," Rodney said, making a beeline for the terminal. "I think we've got something."

"What is this?" Teyla asked. On one side of the room was a large tube, clear at one end and dark metal elsewhere. Through the clear surface could be seen a padded interior. "It looks like the chambers on the ship."

"I agree," Daniel said. "And we've certainly seen Asgard stasis chambers before." He bent over Rodney's shoulder, weirdly folded into the short desk, peering at the amber letters.

"What have we got here?" John asked. "Control center? Power supply?"

Daniel pushed his glasses up on his nose. "Better than that. I think – if I'm reading all this correctly – this is a field medical station. And it looks like it has power and might be working."

"Then let's get our patient down here," John said, keying on his radio.

Daniel looked around. "We need to run a diagnostic. This equipment hasn't been used in hundreds of years and…"

"The guy's dying," John said. "What could happen? It could kill him? We don't have time to run a bunch of tests on it first. Elizabeth? Do you hear me?"

Daniel's eyebrows rose but he didn't argue.

"Elizabeth?"

There was no answer.

"We're probably too far underground," Rodney said. "Radio, remember? Not mysterious Ancient device."

"We will go and get them," Teyla said. "After all, they cannot carry the stretcher and all the equipment alone."

"Yeah," John said. "Daniel, you and Rodney stay here and do what you're going to do to get that thing working. You have until we get back to run tests if you want. We'll go get the patient."

It was twenty minutes before the injured Vanir was closed into the regeneration chamber, Dekaas bending over the control panels with Daniel translating and Rodney adjusting power levels. John shook his head, looking down at the small, still form in the coffin like box. The Vanir looked nothing like human children, but...

"We have done what we can do," Teyla said quietly. "And that is all we can do."

"Yeah." He took a deep breath. "I wish I could win them all."

"I know." Teyla put her hand on his arm. "But there is nothing more we can do at the moment."

Dekaas looked up at her words. "It's going to be a while. It looks like the regeneration chamber goes through several cycles. It's in the diagnostic cycle now. It has three cycles after this, so..."

"Don't ask me," Rodney said. "A couple of hours at least. Maybe longer."

"If you do not mind," Teyla said, "I would like to investigate this installation further. Perhaps there are other machines that would be useful."

"That's a good idea," John said. "We could do that."

"We'll stay with Dekaas and monitor the patient," Daniel said.

"Sounds like a plan," John said. Anything was better than sitting around watching the regeneration tube do its work.

The installation was bigger than it looked. Forty minutes later John and Teyla had found more mazes of corridors and empty rooms beyond the medical center. As yet another door led to yet another corridor, John shook his head. "This place is enormous. I wonder what they built it for."

"I cannot even guess," Teyla said. She looked up at him sideways. "But I thought you would prefer to explore it rather than watch the medical equipment."

"You've got that right." He paused, glancing down two identical corridors.

"Someone you cared about?"

As usual Teyla was too perceptive. John shrugged. "My mom. She died a while ago. But she had a lot of procedures. I don't know."

"Ah." She waited, not saying anything.

He glanced off down the corridor, the silence heavy around him until it seemed easier to fill it. "My mom thought there was some kind of higher purpose to everything, that things happen for a reason. I don't know if that's true or not."

"I think that it is," Teyla said.

"I don't like to think it is. I think the reason people suffer is because shit happens. You know? It just does and mostly it's nobody's fault. Or it's some big global thing and nobody can really do anything about it."

"Like Cullings."

"No." John frowned. "Cullings don't just happen. And they can be stopped."

"If you know about them ahead of time and you have the technology or you have the diplomatic relations or you have the weapons," Teyla said. "But most people do not have those things. Cullings simply happen. They are a thing we endure."

"But it's not that they can't be stopped. It's just that a lot of people can't stop them."

"That is my point," Teyla said. "To the inhabitants of a world that would have been Culled, we are the eyes and hands of the Ancestors."

John looked at her. "So you're saying there are no higher powers?"

"I am saying that I believe they work through us."

He took a deep breath, feeling something loosen inexplicably in his chest. "That's what my mom said. She said we all have a purpose and I hadn't found mine yet."

"And have you now?" Teyla's eyes were knowing.

"Yeah," John said. He looked ahead at a pair of double doors at the end of the corridor, trying to lighten it up. "And you never know what you're going to find right around the corner. There might be something amazing behind those doors."

"Or another empty room," Teyla said with a smile.

"Maybe." John pressed the plate to open it, then reached inside for the light plate beside the door. Then he stopped, staring at what rested inside.

"Perhaps I was mistaken," Teyla said.

It was a Vanir ship. The sleek lines of its hull meant it could be nothing else. It was small, perhaps only twice the size of a puddle jumper, but far more lethal in appearance, a wedge of dark gray steel with no markings whatsoever on it and no windows or ports either, just a smooth turret that rose midships like the conning tower on a submarine.

"Wow," John said.

"I wonder why it was left here."

John walked around it carefully, though there was nothing to suggest it was powered up. No cables attached it to anything in the bay – and it was a bay. Above, maybe forty feet up, there was an irising hatch more than big enough for the ship. Which meant it was expected to takeoff in hover mode. He ducked underneath it, looking for some kind of emitters or jets. Other than some large, darker circles in the metal, almost like the burners on a flat surface stove, there was no sign of anything.

"I'm wondering why the Travelers didn't find it," John said.

"Perhaps they could not get through the doors as we did," Teyla said. "They did not have someone who could read Asgard."

John nodded, his eyes on the ship. "And there are a lot of empty rooms to discourage looking any further." Cautiously, he reached up and touched one sleek fin, the metal cold and smooth under his hand, almost oiled to the touch. "But whatever happens with the injured Vanir, this is a find for Atlantis. Maybe one of the most important finds we've made in the Pegasus galaxy. The Asgard gave us a lot of technology, but they refused to give us warship specs."

"Why is that?"

John glanced at her over his shoulder. "Because they were afraid of what we'd do with it."

Elizabeth sat with Dekaas watching the unconscious Vanir in the regeneration tube while Daniel and Rodney bickered over something on the screen at the control station. "Do they do that all the time?" Dekaas asked bemusedly.

Elizabeth considered. "Yes," she said.

He shook his head. "They must need a strong…leader to keep them on track."

"They do." Elizabeth dropped her voice. "You nearly said queen, didn't you?"

Dekaas shrugged apologetically. "I suppose. Old habit."

"I understand," Elizabeth said. Rodney and Daniel were arguing, oblivious to anything she and Dekaas discussed. "How long were you among the Wraith?"

For a moment she thought he wouldn't answer, and then he shook his head again. "Long years," he said. "More than a century."

"But you can't be more than sixty," Elizabeth said. "And I would guess closer to fifty!"

"Appearances can be deceiving," Dekaas said.

She lowered her voice still further. "How old are you, Dekaas?"

"I don't know precisely." His eyes avoided hers, scanning instead the immobile form in the regeneration tube. "Somewhere around three hundred."

"Three hundred years old? That's…"

"Impossible?" Dekaas looked up, a slight smile on his face. "I assure you that it isn't. During the time I was with the hive, they hibernated twice. So did I. Each time we spent several decades in stasis. And the rest of the time – I told you that I was a favored pet. I have lived through nearly a hundred and fifty years of linear time outside of stasis."

Things clicked into place, pieces fitting together. "So in addition to healing physical injuries or critical diseases, the Wraith can also undo the effects of natural aging?"

Dekaas nodded. "To a certain extent. The Gift can be used to repair natural wear and tear on the organs, to clear blockages and tumors, and to repair degeneration. Not infinitely, of course, and there are some conditions that humans are subject to which the Gift cannot wholly restore, but for most people the Gift can grant a lifespan of several centuries."

Elizabeth sat back, her hands on her knees, her mind whirling. "Do you realize how many people would want to know that?"

"That's why the Gift is a secret," Dekaas said. "Only the most trusted Worshippers know that it can be used this way."

"Why are you telling me?"

"I think you will need to know." Dekaas glanced across the room at the arguing scientists. "Things have changed. I think you'll need all the information you can get."

Elizabeth took a deep breath. "Is that why when you left the hive you didn't return to your own people?"

"Who of my people would have been left after nearly three hundred years? Certainly no one I knew. The hive had become my family."

"But you said you were treated as a pet."

"Is your dog part of the family?" Dekaas smiled again. "Lots of people say their dog is. If you could ask the dog, what do you think he'd say?"

"I don't know," Elizabeth said. "I like to think a dog who is well treated is happy."

He looked away. "Well, that's your answer, isn't it? The hive was my family, complicated as that seems. I mourned their deaths and the loss of my home. And I have not had one since."

"What about the Travelers?"

Dekaas shrugged. "I've found useful work there. But it's not home. I don't think there is a place I can go home to now."

Elizabeth put her hand on his arm. "Could you return to another hive? I know the one you were on is gone, but are there others?"

For a moment hope flared in his eyes, but he looked away. "I don't know," he said. "There were not many like Seeker." He busied himself checking the unchanging data. "And what I told you..."

"I won't mention it unless I need to," Elizabeth said. "I understand it's dangerous."

"All knowledge is dangerous."

"Yes." She considered for a moment. "One question. Could a Wraith be compelled to give the Gift in that fashion against his will?"

"No," Dekaas said. "I don't believe so. But if he were threatened with death if he did not? Yes, of course he would." He held up one hand. "But understand, Elizabeth, that the Gift isn't free. Life given to one person is taken from another. Life force is finite."

"In other words, thirty years given to me…"

"Is thirty years taken from someone else," Dekaas finished. "Or more likely, someone else is drunk dry, the rest of their natural life consumed, and then some portion of that is fed to you."

"To you."

"Yes." Dekaas looked away. "My longevity is at the expense of others."

"Vampire," Elizabeth said. He glanced at her curiously, and she continued. "Our culture has stories about those who are effectively immortal, living by drinking the blood of others and thereby extending their lives."

"Then I suppose you could call me a vampire," Dekaas said. He bent over the screens again with his gentle physician's hands. She didn't ask if he'd taken the Gift willingly. It was obvious he had.

CHAPTER FIVE

PARRISH picked his way cautiously along what seemed to be either a dry streambed or a stretch of ground that suited neither the conifers nor the succulents. On most other planets, he would have called it the track of some medium-sized animal, but nothing on PGX-239 seemed large enough to create a path like this.

"I thought you said there wasn't any animal life here," Ronon said behind him, and Parrish jumped. It still startled him that such a big man could move so quietly.

"There isn't. Or at least not that we've seen so far. There are insects, and possibly a land-dwelling crustacean, but we haven't seen anything big enough to leave a track this size."

"That would be a pretty big bug," Ronon said.

This time, Parrish did glance over his shoulder and thought he surprised a glint of humor in the Satedan's face. "Bigger than I'd like to deal with," he said. "With my luck, it would be poisonous."

"Or shoot lightning," Ronon said.

"That's an unpleasant thought." Parrish straightened cautiously, surveying the ground to either side. The conifers were a tangled mess, the jagged bark as dangerous as thorns, but you could get a decent look at the ground in between the plants. There was nothing hiding there, only one of the football-sized woodlice rooting in the dirt at the base a conifer stem. Its segmented carapace provided excellent protection against the bark. To the other side, the succulents' heavy leaves completely obscured the ground and cast deep shadows over even the few open spaces. Just about anything could be hidden beneath those leaves. Could an insect have produced the bolts of energy they'd seen? On balance, it wasn't impossible. There were plenty of examples even on Earth of animals producing intense electric currents; there was no reason a complex insect couldn't use similar methods to produce a spark. Though what it would use such a bolt for... "It's possible, though. In fact, that might explain why it looks unaimed — if it's some sort of purely defensive reflex?"

"Maybe." Ronon shaded his eyes, scanning the succulents. "I

think that's where that shot came from – under that thing in the center there, that pod?"

Parrish looked where he was pointing, found the pod — a rounded shape a little darker than the leaves that surrounded it — and lifted his binoculars to see if he could make out anything in the dirt around it. His view was blocked by the spreading leaves, thick and fleshy and mottled green, deep pine-green shading into the near-black of an avocado's skin. There were no signs of damage on the leaves, neither the lacy tracery where an insect had nibbled, nor the pale lines that betrayed a boring insect. If anything, the plant looked… satisfied and well-fed. And that was a ridiculous fantasy —

He stopped himself abruptly. If there was one thing he'd learned during his five years in the Pegasus Galaxy, it was that nothing should be discounted as too fantastic. "Have you ever seen anything like these plants?"

Ronon shook his head.

Parrish sighed, and lowered his binoculars to see if there was any way through the overlapping leaves of the smaller plants to get to the one with the visible pod. Were there other pods as well? Yes, a few — it looked as though about one in four or five of the succulents had grown a central pod, while the others had only a much smaller, lighter green lump. Pollinator and pollinated? He should definitely take samples of both types.

If he could just figure out how to get in there without having to hack his way in with a machete. He raised the binoculars again, searching for some path between the heavy leaves, but his attention was drawn inexorably to the central pod. It really did look sleek and healthy, the pebbled skin unscarred, unmarked in any way. Or was it? He adjusted the magnification, and thought he could make out a small depression on the very top of the pod. It was smaller than the palm of his hand, and shallow, though the plant's shifting color made it hard to tell what he was seeing. And… he let his focus drop lower, down the sides of the pod. Was that a crack in the sleek surface?

"You know," Ronon said, "I have seen something that's a little bit like this. But it was a lot smaller."

"Oh?"

"Not on Sateda," Ronon said, as though that was important. "A place called Dengar. There were Wraith Worshippers there. And there was a plant in the swamps that ate insects. It smelled like rotten meat, and when enough flies gathered, it would open up its flower and release a gas that stunned the flies. They'd fall out of the sky into the bud and it would eat them." He paused. "I guess it's not all that like this one."

"Or maybe it is," Parrish said. "If a carnivorous plant were hunting insects the size of the ones here—"

"You think the plant is shooting at you?" Ronon gave him a doubtful look.

"I think the plants might be shooting," Parrish corrected. "Notice that we don't see any of the big insects hovering over the succulents. I didn't think anything of it—not their proper food source, other predators might be lurking, there could be a dozen reasons. But if the succulents are carnivorous, that would be an excellent reason to stay away." He touched his radio. "Dr. Hunt! Are there any insects in your section?"

There was a brief pause, and when she answered Hunt sounded puzzled. "A few of those big pillbugs. Not that I think it's actually an insect, any more than a pillbug is. One of the giant ladybugs. I can see a couple of the big flying things, the ones that look like dragonflies, but they're over in the conifers."

"Confirmation," Parrish said.

"Dr. Parrish?" Hunt said. She sounded nervous, and Parrish grinned at Ronon.

"Want to test it?"

"What are you thinking?"

"Well, if it hunts insects…" Parrish stooped, scrabbling on the ground until he found one of the hard, fist-sized cones dropped by the nearest conifer. "If it hunts flying insects, and I throw this over it—that ought to trigger it, wouldn't you think?"

"I think we're standing too close," Ronon said, backing quickly down the path.

He was probably right. Parrish retreated after him, activating his radio. "I have a theory about the source of the energy bolts that I want to test, and I need everyone to move well away from the patches of succulents — back to the Stargate and the DHD ought to be far enough."

"You think something among the plants is the source?" Hunt asked. She and Samara were already moving toward the Stargate, where Aulich and Joseph waited by their equipment.

"I think the plants are the source," Parrish answered.

"But —" Hunt stopped, audibly reconsidering her protest. "Ok. How to you want to test it?"

"I think they've evolved to hunt the flying insects," Parrish said. "I'm going to throw something over what I think might be a sense organ, and see what happens. That's why I want everyone back out of range."

"Roger that," Hunt answered.

"I didn't think plants had organs," Ronon said. He'd reached the edge of the greenery, and was waiting, eyeing the succulents thoughtfully.

"Some do." Parrish juggled the cone, trying to judge the best line and whether or not he could actually throw anything that far, and Ronon plucked it out of the air.

"You want it thrown so that it passes over that central pod, right?"

"Right."

"Ok." Ronon weighed the cone for a moment. "Heads up!" He cocked his arm and threw. The cone arched up into the white sky, rising over the bed of succulents. Blue fire blasted up from the ground, the bolt close enough to make Parrish's skin tingle, and he flung himself to the ground. Ronon hit the dirt beside him as three, four more bolts blasted into the sky. Parrish lifted his head in time to see a fifth bolt strike the flying cone, which burst into a ball of fire. Beneath it, a pod stretched skyward for a moment, two halves gaping wide, then seemed to sense the falling flames, and snapped shut again. The smoking fragments bounced off its hide and disappeared among the leaves.

"Everyone all right?" Ronon asked, pushing himself to his feet, and there was a chorus of agreement. "Doc?"

Parrish nodded, and accepted the hand Ronon held out to him. "Yes. I'm all right - didn't expect that, exactly."

"Let's not try that again," Ronon said.

"I think I've proved the point." Parrish realized his hands were shaking, and stuffed them in his pockets. "I probably should have thought. If a bullet triggered them, the reaction to something more insect-like would be — more dramatic."

"So all those pods are capable of shooting at us," Ronon said.

"Um. Probably?" Parrish squinted at the mass of plants, trying to figure out which ones had fired. "Though of course there's the question of whether they need a recharge period —"

"We're not testing that right now," Ronon said firmly. "Let's move back to the Stargate."

There was something in his tone that brooked no argument. "Yes," Parrish said, and followed meekly.

They gathered around the DHD, everyone looking a bit shaken by the sudden display of vegetable firepower. Everyone except Ronon, that is, Parrish thought, who looked concerned but not particularly surprised.

"Might as well eat," Ronon said, after a moment, and they sorted out rations. Parrish busied himself heating his chili, and traded his candy for Hunt's Pop-Tart. The others were swapping bits and pieces, too, though he noticed that Ronon didn't offer to share any of his Satedan rations. From the look of them, Parrish didn't blame him at all.

"Right," Ronon said, after everyone had had a chance to get their meals heated. "So what you've discovered here is pod-plants that shoot energy bolts at people."

Everyone looked at Parrish, who sighed. "That pretty much sums it up, yes."

"Any word on whether Atlantis is open again?" Ronon looked at Joseph, who shook her head.

"No, sir. We haven't heard anything new."

"Check that, would you?"

"Yes, sir." Joseph rose gracefully and dialed the gate. The wormhole whooshed out and stabilized, and Parrish could hear her going through the check-in procedures. It didn't take long, and he wasn't surprised when she returned shaking her head. "Sorry, sir. Atlantis is still under quarantine. They're sounding a bit stressed, too, if you take my meaning."

"Lovely," Aulich said, not quite under her breath.

Ronon just nodded. "All right. The question is, is there any reason to stay here instead of going back to Sateda?"

Parrish hesitated. He supposed they ought to withdraw with the information they had before one of the plants actually aimed in their direction, but this was, as far as he knew, an entirely unique situation. "I'd like to investigate further — cautiously! Very cautiously! But these plants might have useful applications later on."

Hunt nodded. "If we take every care not to trigger them - I'd very much like some tissue samples before we leave."

"And I'm getting some odd readings, meteorologically speaking," Aulich said. "I'd like to finish this sampling run."

Ronon tipped his head to one side. "What makes you so sure the plants won't start shooting at us?"

"They're clearly triggered by something passing over the central pod," Parrish said. "Possibly just by the change in light, or maybe by sound waves, or possibly by change in air currents, but regardless of the mechanism, the triggering object needs to pass directly over the sense organ on top of the pod. The bolts went straight up last time, or at a slight angle off the vertical, again calculated to bring down something flying over the plant. As long as we don't trip that sensor, I think we'll be all right."

Ronon nodded again. "All right. But I want us off world before it gets dark."

"That shouldn't be a problem," Aulich said. "That gives us about eight hours. A little less."

And that should be plenty of time, Parrish thought, tucking the last of the MRE wrappers back into its bag. Plenty of time to get the samples Hunt wanted and plenty of time for Atlantis to deal with its problems. Surely.

Twenty or so more minutes passed. Elizabeth had opened a package of granola bars that Rodney had brought with him, trying to remember the last time she'd eaten, when suddenly the regeneration tube lights dimmed and brightened, dimmed and brightened.

In an instant, Daniel was beside it. "I think that's what they do when they're ending the cycle," he said.

"How would you know that?" Rodney asked. "It might mean anything."

"Because when Thor healed Jack the time he'd been stuck in stasis because of the Ancient head-sucky device, that's what it did right before the cycle ended," Daniel replied.

"Oh please. Is head-sucky device a technical term?"

"Cut it out, Rodney," Elizabeth said, putting the granola bar down and joining the others beside the tube. "We haven't seen one of these devices before and he has."

The lights brightened and then dimmed again, and the transparent faceplate over the tube began to retract. Inside, the Vanir stirred. Its grayish lids opened and then its eyes widened.

"We mean you no harm," Elizabeth said quickly.

"Unlike you, who meant her all kinds of harm when you kidnapped her," Rodney said. He spread his hands as Elizabeth looked around at him. "Just saying. He kidnapped you. That wasn't exactly friendly."

"And now you have kidnapped me," the Vanir said. It sat up, looking for a moment disoriented as it glanced around the room. Or at least Elizabeth assumed that was what its expression meant. The Asgard didn't show facial expressions in the same way humans did, in her very limited experience, so it was a guess.

"We rescued you from your crashed ship," Daniel said diplomatically, sitting down on the end of the regeneration tube to be more or less face to face, a move Elizabeth inwardly applauded.

"After you caused the crash in the first place."

"After you kidnapped me," Elizabeth said, her mouth firming into a hard smile. "So I don't think you have the high moral ground here. I'd like to know why you did that. If there was information you wanted, you could have started by asking me."

"Why would you tell me the truth?" the Vanir asked as though that were the most obvious thing in the world. Perhaps it was, in his culture. No, Elizabeth thought, these were not at all the Asgard of the Milky Way. They had an entirely different set of assumptions, for all that they appeared to be the same race.

"If you had simply asked me, I would have considered it," Elizabeth said. "It is to our advantage to open diplomatic relations and be on good terms with our neighbors."

The Vanir looked at her like she was crazy. "You would give me information for nothing?"

"Perhaps we could have worked out a trade that would benefit us both," Elizabeth said. "Information for information."

At that it seemed to relax a little, perhaps because she had suggested something that made sense.

"On the other hand," Daniel said, calmly adjusting his glasses, "we don't usually deal with kidnappers. We might make an exception, but we would expect you to answer our questions truthfully first." An unspoken 'or' hung at the end of his sentence. After all, Elizabeth thought, the Vanir consider us barbarians who aren't worth negotiating with.

There was a long moment, during which Dekaas was the only one who moved, coming a little closer.

The Vanir took a breath. "What is this place? I do not know this facility. Where are my shipmates?"

"You answer our questions first," Elizabeth said. It was worth gambling on a guess. "We already know you wanted to kidnap me because I used to be Ascended. So why don't you tell us your name and let's talk?"

The Vanir remained stock still for a moment, disconcerting, as humans always move in small ways even when they're trying to be still. Elizabeth waited.

"Very well," it said at last. "You may call me Dis. And as to why we wanted you – you do know that not very many individuals unascend, don't you?"

"We do," Daniel said. "But it's entirely possible." He didn't add that he'd done it too, which was probably a wise move. He glanced at Elizabeth and she nodded imperceptibly. "And we know you may have a device to assist someone to unascend."

"We have a device to force someone to unascend," Dis said.

"Which is pretty shitty, if you ask me," Rodney said.

Dekaas frowned.

Dis's voice was tranquil. "We believe it will work. But what we do not know is if it will be harmless to the subject. If unascension causes damage, that would be problematic for us. We wished to examine a female individual who had unascended and determine whether there was genetic damage as a result."

"Why a female?" Rodney asked.

At the same moment Daniel said, "Because ova are not renewable."

"Every female is born with the full complement of eggs she will produce in her lifetime," Dekaas said. "Unlike males, whose genetic material renews in a matter of days or weeks."

Dis inclined his or her head. "Just so."

"Ran," Elizabeth said. A picture was beginning to form in her mind, a terrible idea. "You want to force Ran to unascend because she Ascended before your species did itself irrevocable genetic damage through generations of cloning."

"She is a female who at the time of her Ascension carried a nearly full complement of undamaged ova," Dis said. "Thousands of undamaged ova, each with a unique and unduplicated mix of genes. Each one, crossed with our damaged material, has the potential to grow into a unique individual, uncloned and completely original."

"You want to make her unascend so that you can harvest her eggs?" Rodney sounded indignant. "Seriously? That is the most sick and twisted…"

"However, as far as we know, she is the only female of our species to ascend, so we must take no chances that we will cause damage with the device or through unascension itself."

"So you wanted to examine my eggs and see if they were damaged," Elizabeth said. "Without bothering to ask."

"It is necessary. We regret the loss, but we are prepared to do what we must."

"That sounds like you were intending an autopsy," Daniel said.

"Of course. We need to have full access to the ovarian structures as well as the ova themselves. If there were partial damage, we might be able to determine the cause and prevent it. After all, the future of our species is at stake."

Elizabeth stood up. "Forgive me if I don't have a lot of sympathy."

Daniel shook his head. "The Asgard of the Milky Way faced the same choice, and they chose to die out rather than do something like this."

"That may have been their choice, but it is not ours," Dis said calmly. "We do not choose extinction. Nor would you, were you in our situation."

"To violate every right that Ran has?" Daniel asked.

"The rights of one person or of an entire race? I think the answer is clear," Dis said. "It is regrettable that we must interfere with Ran's choice, but the good of our entire species outweighs that. I do not intend to let my people perish."

"At what cost?" Daniel demanded. "If you begin by forcing Ran to unascend, taking her eggs without her consent—"

"Later generations can judge us harshly. While they owe us their existence," Dis said. "I am sure they will claim the moral high ground. But if we do not do this, there will be no future generations."

John walked around the Vanir ship again, then stopped, gazing upward at the bay doors in the ceiling. "It looks like there are ramps that go up along the wall there. See what looks like a solid rail there?"

"It makes sense that they would have a way of reaching the doors and maintaining them," Teyla agreed. "Perhaps we should see if we can get the doors open, or at least see if they are operable."

"Yeah." They started up the ramp, which wound around the docking bay. It was only three or four stories, but the ramp was fairly steep and the rail, which must have been shoulder high on an Asgard, was only hip high or so on a human, not actually enough to keep a human from falling.

Teyla shook her head as they went around the third loop. "My people have never even heard of the Vanir. They stand apart from the other peoples of this galaxy."

"You may be lucky," John said.

"Very likely."

They reached the top of the ramp, which ended in a wider space just below and to the side of the doors. There was a control panel and a hatch. John ran his hand over the surface. "No power," he said.

"Perhaps it is not activated."

"Or there's a short in the system somewhere between here and the medical center down there. Or it's not connected to the emergency power down there." John shook his head. "Rodney can reroute it. We'll get him up here in a little bit. Meanwhile…" He glanced

at the hatch. The round knob set low in it looked like it belonged
on a submarine. "Want to bet that's the manual override to get the
hatch open?"

"I will not take that bet." Teyla smiled.

The knob turned smoothly and the hatch folded inward, showing a round tunnel about five feet high sloping gently upward to a
second hatch about fifty feet along. John grimaced. "Short people."

"I am sure to a Vanir the tunnel is spacious," Teyla said.

"Yeah well. Not to me." John bent over as he climbed, shining
his flashlight ahead. The hatch at the other end seemed the same,
though it was stiffer to turn and the door stuck when he first pushed
on it. It opened a crack and he put his shoulder to it, Teyla behind
him. The door gave.

It opened on a rocky outcropping. Just below, maybe three or
four feet, were the closed bay doors set under a lip of overhang-
ing rock which made the entire thing invisible from below. On the
other side, the rocks dropped away down to the landing field where
their puddle jumper sat.

It was no longer alone. Two Traveler ships also rested on the field,
and a third one was making a slow descent, its sides streaked black
and its maneuvering jets firing unevenly. Cautiously it settled onto
its landing gear. A makeshift hull patch on its side showed how it
had been temporarily repaired in deep vacuum.

"Looks like they took some fire," John said as Teyla joined him.

"Yes." Teyla frowned. "Is that not the ship captained by the trader
Lesko? The one we asked about Elizabeth?"

John nodded. "I think so. That's bad. Let's get down there and
talk to them. We need to find out what happened."

There was a path that wound down from the overhang, and he
and Teyla descended as quickly as possible. It was already deep
night, and the lights from the Traveler ships didn't shine far up the
slopes. Before they were all the way down they were noticed, and
three Travelers came toward them, including the captain, Lesko.

"Hi there," John called, holding up an empty hand.

"Hello," Teyla said with a trader's smile on her face.

Lesko nodded. "Lanteans. We saw your ship. We wondered
where you were."

"We needed to use the shelter for an injured person," Teyla said. "There was no one here when we arrived. I hope we have not trespassed."

John gave her a sideways look which he hoped conveyed that they weren't going to say that this installation and everything in it belonged to the Travelers, including the Asgard ship. Teyla kept right on smiling.

"No, no, of course not," Lesko said. "This is an open world. We wondered when we saw your ship who was here and why."

"As soon as it is safe to move our injured, we will be gone," Teyla said.

"No rush." Lesko looked back over his shoulder at the ships. Ramps were down now, some of the Travelers emerging to look over the damage to the exteriors.

"What happened to you guys?" John asked with forced casualness. Teyla shot him a look as if to say, I was coming to that.

"We ran into a few problems." Lesko said. "Some repairs. *Osir* and *Mirilies* are mostly just helping out."

"We will be no trouble to your repairs," Teyla said.

"And we've got no problem with your medical mission." Lesko gave them a distracted nod and strode away to join a group that was clustered beneath his ship, looking up at the hastily patched hull.

John waited until he was out of earshot. "What do you make of that?"

"He has more important things to do," Teyla said. "He only wanted to be sure that we would not interfere."

"Why would we do that?"

Teyla shook her head. "I don't know. But I believe he is concealing something."

John glanced at the ships again. "Look at that pattern of damage."

"Wraith."

"The Travelers aren't party to our treaty," John said. "And I'll bet you any money they're not in a hurry to be."

Teyla nodded. "And they are worried that we will tell the Wraith where they are."

"Not our fight," John said. "Let's go back to the puddle jumper and radio Rodney. We need to see if our guest is awake and if we can get out of here."

John gave them a sideways look which he hoped conveyed that

Ronon found a rock halfway up the low hill and settled himself there. From that vantage point, he could see everyone in the party, and, more importantly, could cover them all with his own energy pistol. Not that he really expected anything to start shooting at them, now that Parrish had identified the source of the energy bolts, but there was no point in taking any chances. Samara was sitting on one of the empty instrument cases at the foot of the Stargate, P90 on his lap as he took a careful swallow from his canteen, while Aulich and Joseph monitored their equipment, Aulich with a tablet in her hand. Parrish and Hunt were working their way along the edge of the patch of succulents, careful not to let their shadows fall anywhere near the central pods. Watching Samara drink reminded Ronon that he was thirsty, but he didn't unsling his own water bottle. If they were stuck here for any length of time, they would need to find a water supply — maybe the stream bed that Parrish had talked about, over on the other side of the hill. A lot of times if you dug in the center of the channel, you'd find water a hand's-breadth below the surface. Trouble was, the Lantean rations required a lot of water to make them palatable, more than you could easily get from a simple seep like that. All in all, he thought, it might be better to head back to Sateda as soon as the scientists had finished their exploration. There was plenty of room, and Cai would be happy to take them in.

Parrish and Hunt had found a way to get in among the succulents, crouching low to avoid casting shadows. Parrish drew a small knife and sliced carefully at the edge of the nearest leaf, cutting out a small triangle of tissue. Ronon held his breath, but nothing happened: apparently the leaves weren't sensitive to touch. Hunt did the same, taking a sample from a smaller leaf, and then went to one knee to reach beneath the leaves. The big pod rustled alarmingly, and Ronon straightened.

"Hunt!"

A bolt of lightning cracked from the pod. Parrish flung himself sideways, flattening Hunt beneath him, and the entire bank of plants erupted, energy bolts rising into the sky and lashing across the clearing. Aulich and Joseph dropped to the ground, and Samara rolled sideways, coming up with his P90 pointing at the mass of plants. Ronon's gun was in his hand as he dropped and rolled, but he didn't return fire. There was nothing to shoot: every blast of energy was coming from a plant.

"Lie still!" Parrish yelled, his voice muffled. "Everybody, lie still!"

Ronon froze, his skin itching with the desire to move. The air stank of ozone, but the worst of the barrage seemed to have ended. A few more shots sounded, but they were in the distance, and moving away. He made himself wait, then cautiously lifted his head. Nothing happened, and he rose to one knee. "Everyone all right?"

There were scorched marks on the hillside and in the ground of the clearing, but the equipment seemed untouched.

"Ok here," Samara answered, and Joseph echoed him.

"All right," Aulich called. She sounded a little breathless, but that was to be expected.

"Dr. Hunt?" Ronon rose to his feet, ready to flatten himself again, but nothing happened. "Dr. Parrish?"

"We're all right." That was Parrish, though he wasn't moving just yet. "I just have to —" He gave a complicated wriggle, and rose to his knees in the space between two of the plants. "Ok, ease back —"

Hunt pushed herself cautiously to hands and knees, moving as though she was balancing on glass, and finally backed away so that she was crouching next to Parrish. "That was too damn close."

"What happened?" Ronon scanned the ground around them, looking for anything that could have set the plants off. Surely they hadn't cast a shadow, they'd been being careful.

"I think —" Hunt's voice was shaking, and she stopped to take a careful breath. "Yes. These things send out runners that apparently also act as triggers."

"And it changes the aim of the shots," Parrish said. He was holding his upper arm in a way Ronon didn't like.

"All right. Come on out of there —"

"Yes," Parrish said. "But — carefully, Gina."

Hunt made a noise that was almost a giggle. "Oh, yes, very carefully."

Ronon came down the hill to meet them, frowning. "Parrish. You're hurt."

Parrish gave a wincing smile. "It just nicked me."

"You've always wanted to say that," Hunt said.

Aulich grabbed the first aid kit and came to join them. Parrish took his hand away from his arm, revealing ripped and melted fabric, and a bright red mark along the outside of his upper arm. "It's really not bad," he said, and managed not to flinch when Aulich ripped the fabric further to expose the burn.

It wasn't that bad, Ronon saw with relief, and holstered his energy pistol. "You got your samples?"

Hunt nodded. "We did. At least, I still have mine."

"So do I," Parrish said, indignantly. "I don't drop samples just because some plant is shooting at me."

"He's right," Aulich said, unwrapping a field dressing. "It's going to hurt, but it's nothing serious."

Ronon nodded his thanks.

Parrish said, "Ow. Do you have to do that?"

"Yes." Aulich finished attaching the dressing and stepped back.

"All right," Ronon said. "I think we've gotten enough information for now. Captain, how close are you to finishing your tests?"

Aulich glanced at the nearest screen. "Less than twenty minutes. Then we're done."

"Good," Ronon said. "Once you're finished, shut it down, and we're heading back to Sateda. Unless Atlantis has fixed its problems." He braced himself for a protest, but none came. Parrish nodded instead, looking faintly sheepish, and Aulich looked at her screen again.

"I agree. I'm getting some... unusual... readings."

"Unusual how?" Ronon asked, and Joseph interrupted them.

"Sir. Captain. We've got a problem."

Ronon turned to see a scorch mark cutting across the upper left quadrant of the DHD. A thin coil of smoke rose from under one scorched symbol and drifted away into the air. Aulich swore, and both Samara and Hunt looked stricken. Ronon kept his voice calm with an effort of will. "How bad is it?"

"Don't know, sir." Joseph went to one knee, reaching into her pocket for her toolkit.

"Find out," Ronon said, and hoped she would have an answer.

Rodney sat on the edge of one of the Vanir consoles, kicking his feet against the pedestal in the vague hope that it might annoy the Vanir. Dis seemed impervious, both to provocation and to any arguments that either Jackson or Elizabeth could muster. It sat on the edge of one of the lightly padded tables, blinking slightly; it allowed Dekaas to run his hands over the site of the skull fracture, but proclaimed itself entirely healed.

"I'm not sure that's actually true," Dekaas said, narrowing his eyes. "Admittedly, I don't know what your vital signs should be, but they are considerably weaker than I would expect."

"Our technology is capable of repairing far worse damage," Dis said. "I feel... well enough."

"That's assuming the stasis pod is fully functional," Jackson said. "And, you know, it would kind of surprise me if it were in perfect shape after who knows how many hundred — thousand? — years. I wouldn't push matters if I were you."

"Is that meant as a threat?" Dis inquired, its voice mild, and Elizabeth shook her head.

"Not at all. It's a simple statement of fact."

Dis started to rise, blinked hard, and sat down again. "Perhaps there is something in what you say."

"No kidding," Rodney said. Before he could say anything more, his radio buzzed, and he put his hand to his ear. "McKay here."

"Rodney." Sheppard's voice was perfectly clear, the transmission unaffected by the metal surrounding them. "We've got company."

"Oh?"

"Travelers — one of them's the same ship you got Dekaas from, Teyla says. The *Durant*. Plus two more, *Osir* and *Mirilies*. It looks like they've been in a firefight, maybe with the Wraith, but they're not talking about it. Where do you stand with the Vanir?"

"It's conscious, but still weak." Rodney paused, considering what he could say that wouldn't give too much away. "Our guess about what it wanted was pretty much spot on, but at the moment it's not in any position to do anything about it."

"Good. Keep it that way." Sheppard paused. "Look, keep every-body out of sight for now. We don't want the Travelers making any claims to the parts of the installation they don't know about."

"We closed all the doors behind us," Rodney said. "And there's really not much else they could use."

"Actually..."

"Oh, God, Sheppard, what did you find?"

"How would you like one Vanir scout craft, apparently in per-fect condition?"

"Seriously?" Rodney heard his voice rise, and cleared his throat. "Ok. That's – different."

"Yeah." Sheppard paused, clearly marshaling his thoughts. "It's up a couple of levels, in what was probably a docking bay that over-looks the landing field. The power was off in the area when Teyla and I found it, and then we saw the Travelers landing before we had a chance to look over the scout. If things are secure where you are, I want you to head up there and see if you can get the power back on. I'd like the chance to be able to open that hangar door if things get dicey. And then if there's time, take a look at the scout."

A Vanir scout, apparently intact and in perfect condition. Yeah, he could get it working; he'd had enough experience with Asgard technology to feel sure of that. And that meant Sheppard could fly it, or maybe he could even fly it himself if he had to. And there was always the chance – a pretty good chance, he'd bet – that the Vanir had left some things installed that the Asgard hadn't wanted to trust humans with. That would definitely come in handy, even if they were sort of at peace with the Wraith these days. "Yes. Absolutely."

"If it's safe to leave the Vanir," Sheppard says. "Security first."

"Yes, of course. Do you think I'm stupid?"

"I think you want that ship," Sheppard said.

"Not that badly." Rodney paused. "I'll make sure."

"Right. Sheppard out."

Everyone was looking at him, of course, even Dis, enormous black eyes focused and intent. Rodney cleared his throat again. "Ah, that was Sheppard. We have visitors."

"What sort of visitors?" Jackson asked.

"Travelers. Which I suppose we might have expected, given that this is a Traveler base – oh, and it's *Durant* and a couple of others. *Osir*, he said, and *Mirilies*." Rodney stopped, watching Elizabeth's face. "What?"

"Why are they here now?" she asked. She looked at Dekaas. "I understood they were going to be at the rendezvous for some time."

"So did I," Dekaas said, grimly. "In fact, I wouldn't mind asking them that myself."

"Ah. I don't think that would be such a good idea," Rodney began.

Dekaas lifted an eyebrow. "So should I consider myself –"

Elizabeth laid a hand on his arm. "No. You're not a prisoner or a hostage or anything like that. I presume Colonel Sheppard is concerned about Dis."

"Yes," Rodney said. "Exactly."

"And about this installation," Dekaas said. "You don't want it to fall under Traveler control. Because – didn't you say this device could be used on humans as well as Vanir?"

"The Asgard used it on Jack – General O'Neill," Jackson said. "Of course, that was to reverse something that the Ancients, or at least an Ancient device, had done to him, so that doesn't prove it could or couldn't cure more ordinary problems."

"The installation belongs to the Vanir," Elizabeth said. "We came here to save Dis's life." She gave the Vanir a hard stare. "And we have a number of things to discuss with Dis's people, which may or may not include further use of this base."

"I do not think that will be negotiable," Dis said.

"Be that as it may," Jackson began, and Rodney waved his hands.

"Whatever! Look, go ahead and talk all you like, but I've got other things I need to do."

"Such as?" Jackson lifted his eyebrows.

"Sheppard asked me to see if I could get the power on in another part of the installation. He thought we might need it." And that was perfectly true, even if it wasn't the whole story.

"So you're just going to leave us here with Dis," Jackson said.

"I'm going to assume you know what you're doing," Rodney snapped.

"I think we can handle this," Elizabeth said.

Rodney backed away, glad to leave this in Elizabeth's hands — and, all right, maybe that was premature, but it was just as important to see if the Vanir scout was in fact operational. If they needed a back door, or another bargaining chip, it was perfect, and if they could take possession of it... Well, Atlantis always needed more ships. Even if that one couldn't be brought back to Earth. They could still use it in Pegasus, and it was bound to be better than anything the Wraith had. Just in case that agreement fell through.

Up a couple of levels, Sheppard had said, and back toward the entrance. Rodney found the docking bay after only two wrong turns, and caught his breath as he worked the door open. It was a Vanir scout, all right. It looked pretty much identical to an Asgard scout, and Rodney was willing to bet that the technology would be just about identical, too. He played his flashlight over the hull, and found where the hatch should be, but it was, unsurprisingly, sealed tight. He needed light: Sheppard was right, the first step was to get the power up and running in this part of the installation.

He let the light play across the walls, and found a set of consoles that formed a triangle against one wall. All the readouts were dead, but the pattern was familiar from work at the SGC, and he found the access panel and pried it loose. And there it was, the neat five-pronged bar that had been removed from its clips. He fitted the prongs into their sockets and snapped the bar's other end into the clip. For a moment nothing happened and he shook his head.

"It's never that simple—"

A pattern of lights flashed on the nearest console, was copied by the other two. Screens lit, data moving sluggishly across their depths, and one by one a string of lights sprang to life, running from one side of the hangar to the other.

"Except when it is." Rodney allowed himself a moment to savor the success, then turned his attention to the controls. Yes, there was the screen that controlled the hangar doors, both the set that led back into the complex and the larger four-part clamshell of the overhead doors. The rest looked as though they were supply and maintenance systems, and Rodney paged through the latter, looking for a way to open the scout's hatch. He found it eventually, and worked the controls. Lights flashed, and there was a grinding noise, and then finally the hatch opened, a ramp extending jerkily from the hull. Rodney waited until it was grounded and he was sure the systems were stabilized, then headed for the ship.

The air inside was stale and smelled of something that seemed vaguely familiar. He sniffed again, sniffed harder, and abruptly remembered the smell of the Vanir installation where he and Jackson had been held prisoner. He made a face, and hoped he wasn't going to end up electrocuted or destroying Stargates this time. The ship seemed just as empty as the rest of the installation, though, thin lines of tubing providing what he guessed was emergency lighting, and he made his way cautiously into the main corridor. Engineering or control room first? He flipped a mental coin. He'd try the control room.

All the interior hatches were shut tight, and the deck and walls were coated with some sort of the gray polymer-like material that damped all sound. The control room hatch, however, stood open, and he caught his breath at the sight. Everything in the compartment was swathed in layers of thick, cobwebby material, sheet after sheet of the stuff wrapped around each console and crew station, protecting the delicate instruments. Rodney touched the nearest piece with a cautious finger, ready to jump back if his guess was wrong and this was some weird natural phenomenon, spiders or caterpillars or something even worse lurking in the webs. But there was nothing. The material was dry and slightly stiff, as though it had frozen in that position.

"Mothballed," he said aloud, and could barely suppress his glee. He reached for the radio, then stopped himself. Better see what was in the engine room before he called Sheppard.

CHAPTER SIX

"I DON'T understand," Ember said. His fingers moved delicately over the controls, reviewing their work. "It should have worked — the simulation was perfect."

"Aye, but we've missed something, clearly." Beckett rubbed his chin unhappily. "Dr. Sindye, there was no change at all between the first test and the second?"

"The results were identical." The picture in the screen changed from the Lantean's dark face to four squares of plastic, all of them eroded by the *aflageolis*. "The only difference is that this pair has been exposed longer."

"So we're back to square one," Beckett said.

"Thank you, Dr. Beckett, Dr. Zelenka," Sindye said. "We'll look at the results and see what more we can do."

"We must start over," Ember said. They had missed something obvious — he had missed something obvious, he whose specialty this was. The Lanteans could in some sense be excused for their failure, but he should see it. "From an untouched sample."

"I agree." Becket sounded profoundly tired. "Well, we should have plenty of that to go around."

"I fear so." Ember studied the screen again. The pattern of degradation was different from the pattern that resulted from the solvent: perhaps that was significant, or perhaps not. His feeding hand throbbed, and he rubbed it against his coat, wishing he were on the hive. Then he could just go and feed, let the life-force rush into him, sating his hunger — He realized that he had closed his eyes, and shook himself back to the moment. There was no time to waste daydreaming. "I would like to examine a sample myself, from the start." He saw Beckett frown, and added carefully, "I think you should do the same. Perhaps our different techniques will give us some new information."

Beckett relaxed slightly. "Aye, that makes sense."

"Dr. Beckett. Do you have a minute?"

The voice from the speaker should have been familiar, but it took Ember a moment to identify it: Lorne, the blade who was the

Consort's right hand.

"I do." Beckett seated himself beside the console, resting one elbow on the work surface.

"Any progress?"

Beckett shook his head as though Lorne could see. "The first compound had no discernible effect. We're starting over, Major."

"That's — not good news," Lorne said.

Beckett looked annoyed. "No, but it's the best I've got. And the sooner you let us get back to work —"

"Sorry, Doc, that's not what I meant." Lorne paused. "We're seeing new infections, and an increased rate of destruction in those new infections."

"Has it crossed the quarantine line?" Beckett asked sharply.

"Not yet. And before you say it, we've doubled all the precautions. At the moment, we're not allowing anything to enter the quarantine zone."

"How long can you keep that up?" Beckett asked.

"We've got emergency rations in the jumper bay, we'll dole those out for now. But I'm hoping you can come up with something that's even partly effective before things get any worse."

"We're working on it," Beckett said.

"Wait," Ember said. "This new bacteria — we should have a sample."

"It's not safe," Lorne said.

Ember ignored him, focusing on Beckett. "If the *alflageolis* has mutated, and it sounds as though it has, we will need to see the newest strain in order to stop it."

"You're right," Beckett said. "He's right, Major, much as I hate to admit it. If we bring a biohazard box, can you pass it back out to us?"

"Are you sure that's a good idea, Doc?"

"No," Beckett said. "But I don't have any better ones."

"I would like to go with your people to collect it," Ember said. He didn't know quite what he was looking for, only that he would feel more certain of his research if he had the sample under his eye from the beginning.

Beckett shrugged. "If you want. I'll have to send a couple of Marines with you, though."

"I have no objections," Ember answered.

In the end, they sent not just Marines but a pair of younger doctors, both carrying heavy decontamination equipment. They had not bothered with the enveloping suits, made as they were of a petroleum-based material, but they each carried tanks of different disinfectants and a high-powered sprayer. Either the disinfectant would work, Beckett had said, or the spray itself would wash off any contamination, and Ember thought he was probably right.

They emerged from the Ancients' transport system a floor below the planned transfer point. It would be a much longer return trip, as they'd be avoiding the transfer chambers for fear of spreading the contamination, but he tried not to think about that, or about how... tasty... the older of the Marines felt as he marched behind them. No, his main concern had to be to ensure that all the protocols were followed, and that he had as good a sample of this new mutation as possible.

The transfer point was a corridor two floors below the transport chamber that served the main tower. Doors opened almost directly across from each other, and the corridor was narrow enough that it would be possible to use a hooked metal pole to push the biohazard box across the gap. The older of the two doctors, a lanky woman who had cropped her hair almost as short as the Marines', checked the box a final time, then touched her earpiece.

"Dr. Sindye, Dr. Zelenka. We're in place. Ready when you are."

"We are ready, too, Dr. Harris," Zelenka answered. "You can open your door."

Harris worked the controls, and the door slid back to reveal Zelenka and Sindye standing in the opposite doorway. The younger doctor held up the biohazard box, and then set it carefully on the floor just inside the door. He used the pole to push it out into the corridor, and then all the way across. Sindye retrieved it, and stepped back out of the doorway.

"Dr. Beckett wanted me to ask again if anyone was showing any physical symptom," Harris said.

"Not so far," Zelenka answered. His mouth quirked into a familiar wry smile. "None of us have implants or the like that might be affected, and it seems uninterested in human flesh."

"Let's hope it stays that way," Harris said.

Zelenka nodded vigorously. "Yes, indeed."

Ember shifted impatiently, and Zelenka looked at him.

"Ember. You are well?"

If anyone knew what it meant for him to go hungry, it was Zelenka, who had shared his life-force before. Ember bent his head, embarrassed. "Yes. I am well." For now, he thought, but would not speak that weakness aloud.

"Ready," Sindye said, reappearing at Zelenka's shoulder. She held up the biohazard box, once again tightly sealed, then slid it gently out into the corridor. The younger doctor hooked it, and Harris picked up the first of the disinfectants. She sprayed it thoroughly on all four sides, then switched to the second tank and repeated the procedure. When she was finished, she nodded to the younger doctor, who brought it all the way in and then quickly zipped it into what Beckett had promised was a secure carrier.

"Let us know what you find as soon as you can," Zelenka called. "The degradation has accelerated considerably."

"As soon as we know anything," Ember said, and Harris gave him a startled glance.

"Absolutely."

It seemed to take forever to return to the medical lab, and another age to transfer the new samples — a ragged square of thick white plastic, a cup that had collapsed into itself — into a containment unit. Ember paced the length of the lab and back again, his teeth closed firmly over any injunction to hurry, and at last Beckett looked up from his screen.

"All right. All's secure, and it looks as though we have good samples. You said you wanted one to examine yourself?"

"Yes." Ember slowed his movement, feeling the Marines come to attention behind him. "Thank you."

"Two sets of eyes are better than one," Beckett answered. "You're right about that."

"Let us hope so." Ember took his place on the opposite side of the containment unit, cocking his head as he identified the various tools. Yes, there was the microscope platform, and the screen that allowed him to visualize and manipulate the images, and the secondary screen that let him perform any other necessary calculations. The remote operating tools were awkwardly shaped, and he worked his fingers into the gloves, flexing his hands cautiously. The rasp of the material against his handmouth was unpleasantly distracting, but he forced himself to ignore it, moving his fingers until he was sure he could use the tools without damaging the containment unit.

Beckett was ahead of him, of course, practiced hands already scraping an invisible film from the nearest piece of plastic. Ember found his own broad-bladed knife and did the same, transferring a thin curl of plastic to the microscope's platform. The first slice looked well-populated, but he cut a second, and then a third, before he worked his hands free and turned his attention to the screen.

Most of the cells looked like the ones he had seen in the first sample, the familiar, utilitarian solvent, and he adjusted the magnification, looking for any anomalies. Dispiritingly, it looked normal, and he slid his hands back into the controls to transfer some of them to the mass spectrometer for further analysis, then returned his attention to the screen. All of the samples looked the same, even at the highest magnification, and he wished again for his familiar toolset. If only he could touch the solvent, sieve its DNA for mutations, feel the changes — He shoved that thought aside as pointless, and added a sample to the Lantean DNA sequencer.

It would take some time for that machine to finish its work, and he turned his attention to the other, less familiar bacteria that seemed to accompany the solvent. He had not looked closely at them before, so convinced had he been that the solvent was the problem, and now he wondered if that was his mistake. They seemed to be a variant of a common strain of airborne bacteria, harmless to Wraith and their ships, occasionally a vector of disease for humans; he didn't think he'd seen this particular variety before, but there were thousands of related organisms. Even so, he picked it apart, working at the highest available magnification, cataloguing its features in detail. If it had interbred with the solvent, its characteristics might be more important than they seemed.

And then he saw it, the odd hook at the tip of several of the spikes sticking out of the cell wall. Surely not, he thought. Surely that was just damage, some peculiarity of that cell — but, no, there it was again, and again. He pulled away from the screen, looking for the rack of familiar stains that he would have used in his own lab to identify various organisms, but the Lantean system had strange gaps in it. He hissed in annoyance and fear, and got himself under control.

"Dr. Beckett. Do you have any —?" He stopped, unable to find a word for the thing he saw and felt, and reached for the nearest laptop. He called up one of the modeling programs and quickly entered the codes to produce an approximation of his tester. "I need this compound. Do you have any?"

Beckett squinted to see across the containment unit, his hands still encased in the heavy gloves. "No. I don't even know what that is."

"It's a stain. We use it to test for the presence of a certain virus, a bacteriophage."

"I expect Dr. Wu can make you some, if it's important."

"It's vital." Ember kept his tone steady with an effort. For once he was grateful that he was not among his own kind: it would be all but impossible to hide what he was thinking. "I need to be sure that we are not dealing with this virus."

"You might have thought of that before," Beckett said.

"I had no reason to consider it," Ember snapped. "It's not something we let anywhere near our toolkits."

"Dr. Wu," Beckett said, and the dark-haired woman came over to the console to study Ember's screen. "See what you can do about making up a batch of that."

"Of course." She gave Ember what might have been a fleeting smile. "Twenty minutes."

"Thank you," Ember managed, though he wanted to shout at her to hurry.

"Do you want to tell me what you're looking for?" Beckett asked.

"I would like to be sure first," Ember said. "There is no point in worrying before we are sure."

"I'm worried already," Beckett said.

"I am mostly concerned to eliminate the possibility," Ember said, and almost believed it himself.

Wu was better than her word, turning away from her lab bench in slightly less than fifteen minutes. She held up a small glass tube, displaying a cloudy liquid that rose maybe a thumb's width up the side of the glass. "Is this enough?"

"Yes." Ember started to take it from her, then realized that he didn't know how to get it into the containment. "Ah. Could you —?"

"Oh." Wu blushed pink, a reaction Ember had never been able to interpret. "Right. Just a second."

She took back the vial and fiddled with the containment unit for what seemed like an unreasonable amount of time, but finally she straightened.

"There. You should have full access to it, in dispenser 7."

"Thank you." Ember fitted his hands into the gloves again, hissing at the pressure on his feeding hand. He found the correct tool and dispenser and carefully transferred a small amount of the stain to the microscope's platform. For a long moment, nothing happened, and he allowed himself a sigh of pure relief. But then he saw it, the faintest shift in color from the ordinary clear fluid to a blue as pale as ice, and he hissed again.

"Problem?" Beckett asked, his voice very controlled.

"I can't tell." Ember added a bit more of the stain, but there was no further reaction. If it was there, there was only a minuscule amount, and that gave them a chance. "How long will it take your equipment to read the DNA from these samples?"

"Another few hours," Beckett said. "I think you should tell me what you're worrying about."

"There is a bacteriophage that is very aggressive, very effective at colonizing bacteria," Ember said. "It is, so far, fairly rare and reasonably fragile, in its natural state. But when it does find a host, it is much harder to kill, and it enhances the effect of the bacteria it infects — if this is what happened, it explains why our solvent is so much more virulent." He looked at the screen again. "The stain has barely reacted, though. It may — I hope it is — a false positive."

"And if it's accurate?"

"Then we are indeed in serious trouble." Ember bared teeth in a mirthless grin. "We have fought this virus before. It is extremely persistent — I have known of hives that have been infected that have had to be destroyed. But surely this is not it."

"Does this thing have a name?" Beckett was already reaching for his radio.

Ember hissed. "We called it the 'little replicator.' Because it reproduced nearly as fast."

"Lovely."

"There is worse," Ember said. "It reproduces quickly, it is genetically unstable, and when it mutates — it can become dangerous to living tissue."

"To humans?" Beckett paused. "Dangerous how?"

"And also to Wraith," Ember said. "In us, it causes a fatal infection of the lungs, one that spreads so quickly that even our ability to heal cannot keep up with it. I don't know the effect in humans."

"Probably similar," Beckett said, grimly. "What are the chances of it mutating to that form?"

"Eighty percent. But perhaps we will be fortunate," Ember said, and wished he could believe it himself.

The hive *Just Fortune* came smoothly out of hyperspace and into orbit above the planet, placing itself between the distant pinpoint of the sun and the ocean-covered surface. Guide waited while the sensors probed, building a picture of the world to fill their displays, and in the queen's chair Alabaster shifted to look up at him.

This world does not seem particularly hospitable to humans.

Looking at the readouts, Guide had to agree. The surface was almost entirely water, and this far from the sun, the scattered landmassses lay in perpetual twilight. The Stargate stood at the edge of one of the larger islands, and there were lines and masses of rock nearby that suggested purposeful placement. *No hive I know of has used this as a base,* he said thoughtfully.

Bonewhite? Alabaster asked.

The Hivemaster lifted his head. *Nor I. Perhaps Night's lineage? They often sought planet-bound sanctuaries.*

He looked at the man at the sensor station as he spoke, and the blade dipped his head. He was a relative newcomer, his mental voice a bright banner tossed on a strong wind, and had come to them from a hive of Night.

Had our people used this world, I would have said so. His tone was deferential. *I do not believe it was ever one of ours.*

It is known to the Travelers, Guide said.

You are very certain they will be here, Alabaster said.

It is the known stopping point closest to where the ships escaped to hyperspace, Guide answered. *And we did at least some damage.* Not enough, he added inwardly, closing his mind tight to keep his daughter or any other from hearing his doubts. It had taken them longer than he had liked to identify Traveler ships that might have worked with the Wolf, though they had gotten lucky in tracking the one called *Durant*. They'd been less lucky to find it in company with two others, and the Travelers had worked together well enough to hold them at a distance that allowed all three to successfully make the transition to hyperspace.

The cruiser *Thrice Bold* winked into existence beside them, and a new screen lit to show her commander's face. "My Queen. There was no sign of them on Ulliga."

"Then we will keep searching here," Alabaster answered, leaning back comfortably against the well-grown supports. *Put us into a search orbit, Guide.*

Guide suppressed a snarl, and focused his attention on his controls, easing the hive into a new pattern that would allow the scanners to reach one hundred percent of the planet's surface in the shortest possible time. For the first orbit, the screens showed nothing but sea and sky, both fertile in potential, but largely empty of life. That was unsurprising, as far from the sun as this world lay, and he wondered why the Ancients had bothered with it at all. Had the sun been brighter when the Ring was set in place, or had there been resources to exploit, now exhausted?

There! Banner pointed a claw at the main display.

Guide eased the hive into a turn that brought the signals into closer focus. Yes, three ships showed vivid against the cool ground, their hulls still warm from reentry, their engines glowing brighter still. *More detail.*

Yes, Commander. Banner adjusted his controls, and the image shifted, losing the brilliance of the false colors, but taking on subtler detail. The ships stood on a plateau, a flattened spot on the largest of a series of islands that trailed away in the direction counter to the planet's rotation, three ships — and was that a fourth? If so, it was much smaller, the details blurred by the bigger ships around it. A tender or a lifeboat, Guide thought, deployed for repairs or for shelter. Nothing to worry about. His attention sharpened as a secondary scan drew new lines through the scene.

That is not a natural clearing.

No, Banner answered, his fingers busy on his controls. *I am scanning for metals and for formed stone. This is an artificial surface, probably intended as a landing area, and there are more artificial cavities inside the hill.*

An Ancient installation? Alabaster's tone was still serene, but Guide knew her attention had sharpened. Ancient installations meant mystery weapons, drones and beam weapons and who knew what else. Although if this were defended only by Travelers… He put that thought aside. Time enough to consider that once they had dealt with the Wolf.

I'm not — I don't think so? Banner worked his controls again, his head cocked to one side. *The materials are similar, but the construction is very different. I don't recognize this style.*

Defenses? Weapon sites? Bonewhite leaned over Banner's shoulder.

None. There are pits that might have been outlying cannon stations — no, probably not, there are no connections to the main installation.

Then what are they? Guide demanded. He could see the pits himself how, six spaced evenly to cover the landing area: surely any sane commander would have placed weapons there, to cover both anyone landing and to protect the entrance to the underground installation.

They may have been weapons once, Banner said, his tone carefully deferential, *but there's nothing there now.*

Except the Travelers, Alabaster said. *And they are grounded and damaged, at our mercy. We can put an end to this Wolf once and for all.* She rose to her feet. *Bring us in over the field, Guide, and contact their captain. We can at least offer them that much grace.*

Guide brought *Just Fortune* around onto a looping course that kept the curve of the planet between them and the Travelers' sensors until the last possible moment. He doubted they were in any condition to escape, but there was no point in taking chances. *Thrice Bold* mirrored the movement, coming in over the pole, and the two ships took up station directly above the field.

Any sign of activity? Weapons activation? Guide asked.

Nothing, Commander, Bonewhite answered, and Guide allowed himself a sigh of relief. Mysterious installations, even ones that had not been built by the Ancestors, had an unfortunate tendency to turn out to have sharp teeth.

Do they see us? Alabaster asked.

No active scans, Lady, Banner answered. *We're well within range of any passive monitors.*

Alabaster leaned back in her chair, visibly considering. *Contact them,* she said abruptly. *We have them trapped. Let's see if we can end this without further damage.*

Yes, Lady. Bonewhite worked his controls. *I have the frequency they used in battle. It should reach their commanders.*

Good, thank you. Alabaster straightened abruptly, the ease vanishing from her pose, her face hardening into a cold mask. For an instant, she looked painfully like her mother, in the last days of their hive, and Guide had to look away to master himself.

"Traveler ships," she said aloud. "We know you have aboard the assassin called the Wolf. Surrender him to us, and you will come to no harm."

There was a long silence, the open channel hissing faintly, a high note just at the edge of hearing. Alabaster sighed. *They are receiving us?*

This is their common channel, Bonewhite answered. *It is possible that their receivers have been damaged, of course —*

Hardly likely on all three of them, Guide said.

Indeed not. Bonewhite ducked his head in agreement.

"Traveler ships," Alabaster said again. "I know you can hear me. We would prefer only to take the Wolf, but if you persist in ignoring us, we will simply destroy you and your ships from orbit. It is your choice."

Again there was nothing but silence. Guide glanced sideways, but Alabaster's expression made it clear that she would not welcome any comment.

"Very well," she said. "We will attack—"

"Wait!" That was a human voice, a man's, high and sharp with fear. "Wait, wait, it's taken us a minute to fix our transmitter, that's all."

Guide rolled his eyes, and felt the same disbelief fill the control room.

We do not need to believe them in this, Alabaster said, her tone tinged with amusement. "Then you have heard what I said. Surrender the Wolf, and we will let the rest of you go free."

"How can we believe you?" That was a different voice, and the first voice cut in quickly.

"But we don't have him! Is that why you attacked us? You've made a mistake, the Wolf isn't with us—"

Guide saw Alabaster look to him, and spoke aloud. "We tracked him to your ship, and he had not left it when you lifted from your last trading stop. Don't toy with us."

"I swear! We don't have him! He's not with us, nor would we let him on board." The speaker drew a ragged breath. "He's a danger to everyone, and we have our families with us. We're not stupid, we wouldn't risk them. Not for him."

"Liar," Alabaster said, dispassionately. "We're wasting time, Commander."

"If that is so," Guide said, "if the Wolf is not hiding among your people, allow us to search your ships."

"Why should we trust you on our ships?" the man demanded. "For all we know, this could all be an excuse to put trackers on board, so you can hunt us down at your leisure later. No, Commander, you can bomb us all."

"That can be arranged," Alabaster said.

"Bring all your people out of the ships," Guide said. "Line them up on the pavement or bring them into that installation that we can see from here, but empty your ships. We will scan them, and if they are empty and the Wolf is not among you, then we will let you go."

"Wait a minute, now." A new voice broke in on the circuit, a voice that was painfully familiar, and at the same moment a new image appeared on the sensor display, warning glyphs flashing red around it.

Lantean jumper! Banner cried. *Where—*

Cloaked, Bonewhite said, grimly. *Commander, it's readying drones.*

Guide bared teeth in a snarl of pure frustration. "Sheppard. What are you doing here?"

"Exploration, curiosity, you know. The usual." Sheppard's voice hardened. "But since we are here—how about we all sit down and discuss this like civilized people?"

Guide growled aloud, ready to refuse and damn the consequences, but beside him Alabaster laughed.

"Colonel Sheppard. How—interesting—to find you here as well! By all means, let us talk. But I remind you, we have an agreement. By it, the Wolf is ours."

"That's still up for discussion," Sheppard said, "especially seeing as under that same agreement you shouldn't be chasing these people."

"We will land," Alabaster said, and rose to her feet. She nodded to Bonewhite. *End the transmission.*

The Hivemaster obeyed, though Guide could feel the worry rising from him. He said what they were all feeling: *My Queen, you must not go—*

But of course I must. Her tone was calm, not even angry. *I will brook no argument. Guide, you will accompany me, and Hasten—choose another handful of blades as you will.*

And drones, Bonewhite said, greatly daring.

And drones, yes. Alabaster nodded. *Now, come.*

Guide stood frozen, furious and unexpectedly afraid. The queen should not risk herself, not unnecessarily, not against humans and most especially not against Sheppard—

Alabaster touched his wrist, the gentle press of skin against skin carrying her message. *Father. I am the queen.*

So Snow had looked, at the height of her glory. Guide bowed his head. *As the queen commands.*

John shut down the jumper's communications system and reached for his radio. "Rodney"

There was a moment of silence before McKay answered, sounding slightly breathless. "You know, I'd get a lot more done if people didn't keep interrupting me."

"Where are you?"

"At the Vanir ship. Trying to see if it's in fact space-worthy, since, as you so rightly pointed out –"

"McKay. We've got Wraith in orbit."

"Ok. That's not good."

"No kidding." John took a deep breath. "It's Guide, which may or may not turn out to be helpful. I want you to get back to Daniel and Elizabeth and keep them and Dis out of sight. They already know about Dekaas, but see if you can't persuade him to stay with his patient for a little longer."

"On my way," McKay said. "Do we know what Guide wants, except maybe a free meal?"

"He claims the Traveler ships that just landed are sheltering the Wolf – you know, the guy who'd supposedly been killing Wraith all over the galaxy."

"That's just great," McKay said. "Do we know if they actually are?"

"They say they're not, but — that's what I'm about to go ask. Sheppard out." John hooked his P90 back onto its neck strap, and silently told the jumper to go to a ready/wait mode. He looked at Teyla. "What do we know about this Wolf?"

Teyla tilted her head, her eyebrows rising. "Not as much as we should, it seems."

John grunted in agreement. "I thought somebody'd decided he wasn't real, just a Rambo figure people made up to make them feel better about the agreement with the Wraith."

"Rambo?" Teyla began, then shook her head. "Oh, yes, never mind. I believe the anthropologists have been arguing about the Wolf since first we heard the stories. But Dr. Lynn does not believe he is a myth."

"Guide sure doesn't think so," John said, and headed down the ramp out of the jumper. "*Durant*! Lesko! I want to talk to you."

Durant's captain was already halfway down the ramp, and there were signs of hasty movement on the other ships. John ignored them, coming to a stop beside the ship just as Lesko's boots touched the ground. Teyla planted herself at his shoulder, her expression unnervingly serene.

"Colonel!" Lesko spread his hands in a gesture that was probably supposed to express bewilderment. "I'm just glad you were here to hear that. We need your help."

"They'll be landing in minutes," John said. "Do you have the Wolf on board?"

"No!" Lesko shook his head vigorously. "No, of course not, would we risk our families like that? They've picked on entirely the wrong ships."

The other two captains had joined them, a stocky, graying woman and a skinny red-head who walked with a limp. "Completely the wrong people," the woman said, and Lesko waved a hand. "Tallisk. And Yoran."

"Why don't you tell us what happened?" Teyla asked, with dangerous calm.

"As you know, we were holding a meeting of a number of our ships," Lesko began.

"You were there," the red-head, Yoran, said, and Lesko glared at him, but Yoran ignored him. "As a matter of fact, you took *Durant's* doctor—"

"Yoran!" Tallisk said, and the younger man subsided reluctantly.

"As you know, we had arranged a rendezvous, for trade among ourselves and to balance out crews and so on," Lesko said again. "We had just completed the last exchanges and the ships were ready to lift when we were attacked by a Wraith cruiser. We managed to hold it off until we could all get off planet, but then the hiveship showed up. We played tag with it until we could all make the jump to hyperspace, planning to meet up here and fix the damage. And now they've followed us."

John carefully didn't look at Teyla. Lesko was leaving out a few things, he thought, maybe quite a few important things. "Why did they think you were hiding the Wolf?"

"How would we know?" That was Tallisk, her arms crossed on her chest. "The Wraith don't generally tell us what they're thinking."

"Yet in this case they have hailed you," Teyla said, "and offered you the chance to turn over the Wolf in exchange for your lives." She lifted a hand. "I am certainly not saying that you should do so, but I am asking if they offered that bargain in the first place."

Lesko licked his lips. "They did, yes. But we don't have the Wolf! We wouldn't give him shelter, we're not stupid. And when we told them that, they attacked us. So of course we ran."

"You didn't try to persuade them?" John asked.

Tallisk glared at him. "They're Wraith. What proof could we offer that wouldn't leave us vulnerable?"

"We have made an agreement with the Wraith," Teyla said. "And so far they have abided by it."

"We haven't made any agreement," Yoran said.

"But you benefit as much as anyone from us getting rid of Queen Death," John said. "Whatever else you think about it, not having the Wraith hunting down every stray human is good for everybody."

"And that is a matter we can discuss later," Teyla said. "The Wraith — this Wraith, Guide — is coming now, and wants an answer. We are willing to stand with you, stand between you, as far as we can, but first we must know two things. Do you want our help? And do you in fact have the Wolf?"

Lesko licked his lips. "Of course we want your help. We've been friends before, if not quite allies, and frankly if there's anything you can do to keep this from ending with all of us drained dry, we'd appreciate it. So say we all, right?" He looked hard at the other captains, and Yoran dipped his head.

"Yeah."

"I don't see that we have a choice," Tallisk said. "Yes."

"You did not answer my second question," Teyla said.

"But I have," Lesko protested.

Teyla waited.

"No, we are not sheltering the Wolf!" Lesko said.

"And these other captains?" Teyla's voice was implacable.

"Neither are they," Lesko said.

John could hear a faint, high whine, not as shrill as a Dart but just as piercing, and tilted his head back to look for lights against the darkness. There were none, but he thought he saw a dark shape move across the stars. "They're on their way."

The others turned to look as well, and they stood in silence as the shape swelled, blocking out more and more of the sky, until at last a Wraith scout dropped slowly into the lights of the landing field.

It settled at a respectful distance — also a distance that would let it use its cannons to best advantage, John thought — and he heard noises from the Traveler ships that suggested their weapons were being brought to bear.

"Whoa, hang on —"

Teyla had that faintly abstracted look that suggested she was talking to the Wraith. "It's all right, John. Though Captain Lesko would be well advised not to offer further provocation."

"No, no," Lesko said. "None intended."

"Only if they shoot first," Yoran murmured.

A hatch opened in the side of the scout, and a short ramp reached for the pavement. A moment later, Alabaster appeared, Guide hovering protectively at her shoulder, a blade and a handful of drones behind them. Alabaster started toward them, Guide matching her step for step; the blade and his drones followed them to the foot of the ramp and stopped there, stunners ready. Teyla squared her shoulders and took a step forward.

"Alabaster. We appreciate your willingness to discuss this further."

"There is very little to discuss," Alabaster answered. "We will have the Wolf. He has murdered too many of our people, and will continue to kill without thought or even clear intention, save to bring us death. I will not allow you to stand in my way, allies though we have been."

"We don't have the Wolf," Lesko said, without conviction. Both Yoran and Tallisk looked pale in the field lights: John guessed it was the first time they'd been this close to a Wraith without having to fight for their lives, and he eyed them cautiously, looking for signs that either of them was about to draw a weapon. Tallisk still had her arms crossed tight across her chest as though she was cold, and Yoran's hands were clenched at his sides. About as good as he was likely to get, John thought, and rested one hand on the butt of his P90.

Teyla met Alabaster's stare with a smile. "As you hear, Captain Lesko says the Wolf is not among his people. Is it not possible that you are mistaken?"

"We tracked him to the rendezvous with the Traveler ships," Guide said. "He arrived, and did not leave. Therefore, he is on one of these ships."

"Is it not possible that he left through the Stargate?" Teyla asked. "It is difficult to monitor gate travel from any distance."

Guide showed teeth at that, but Alabaster said calmly, "It is possible, but we deem it to be highly unlikely. What we have learned, from the peoples of the worlds where the Wolf has struck, is that he comes with the Travelers. He claims to be a Traveler. It is most likely, therefore, that he left with them, and is here now."

"If he told the truth about being a Traveler," Teyla said. "To claim that kinship endangers his people no less than hiding among them. Captain Lesko is right, a man who loves his kin would not place them in harm's way."

Guide growled. "A wounded wolf returns to his pack, and does not count the cost."

"We do not speak of animals," Teyla said, her voice suddenly steel, "but of humans."

"You speak as though the Wolf were rational," Guide countered. "I see no sign of that."

Alabaster lifted her head. "We can debate this until the seas rise to sweep us away, but there is a simple answer to the problem. Allow us to search these ships. We will take only the Wolf, and if he is not here, we will let the others go free."

"Absolutely not," Yoran said, and Tallisk unfolded her arms long enough to lay a hand on his shoulder.

"We can't let you do that," Lesko said. "What if this is all just an excuse to sabotage us? Or put trackers on our ships? I can't let Wraith onto my ship. It would be madness."

Guide growled again, and Alabaster said, "What, then, would you suggest?"

Lesko paused. "I'd be willing to bring my people out in groups, let you see that the Wolf isn't among them."

"That is what we suggested before," Alabaster said. "Have your people leave the ships, and if we do not find the Wolf among them, and the ship scans as empty, we would let you go."

"I'm not leaving my ships empty and my people unprotected," Lesko retorted. "Suppose you had Darts waiting, huh? You could just scoop up everyone and that would be the end of us."

"Let us not be hasty," Teyla said. "We have a point of agreement, I believe. Captain Lesko, you are willing to prove that the Wolf is not among your crews, are you not?"

Lesko gave her an uncertain glance. "Yes. Well, if we can—"

Teyla ignored him, focusing on Alabaster. "And that is what you require, yes? Proof that the Wolf is not among them. So. Let us each step apart a little, and consider some way to meet these reasonable objections."

Her voice was steel again. For a second, the decision balanced on a knife-edge, and then John saw both Lesko and Alabaster concede. The Wraith Queen dipped her head gracefully.

"We will consider." She took Guide's sleeve and drew him back out of earshot. From the look on Guide's face, he was shouting mental objections, but Alabaster's expression remained serene.

"Yeah. Yeah, ok," Lesko said. He jerked his head toward the foot of *Durant's* ramp, and the others followed him, Yoran already protesting.

John touched Teyla's arm, drawing her back a few paces as well. "Ok, well, that's progress."

"It is something," she said. "I am not entirely sure what."

John lowered his voice. "Lesko. Do you believe him?"

Teyla sighed. "He is hiding something. Certainly I think he knows more of the Wolf than he admits. But surely he is not so much of a fool that he would lie to us now, when he knows he must be found out."

But he would. John bit his lip, remembering Afghanistan. Lesko would lie because he didn't trust them any more than he trusted the Wraith, and in the long term, that was likely to get them all killed. "Let's hope so."

Elizabeth looked up sharply as Rodney burst through the door. Dekaas shot to his feet and Daniel had his pistol half drawn before he realized who it was.

"What the hell?"

"What's wrong?" Elizabeth said, riding over Daniel's protest.

Dis straightened. "Perhaps my people have come."

Rodney stopped, breathing hard. "No. No, they haven't, and

frankly, I'm not expecting them to, considering that there can't be very many of you left, and you just lost — how many was it? — when your ship crashed."

Dis blinked again, and Elizabeth frowned. They hadn't gotten anywhere with the Vanir, but she was sure it wouldn't help to remind Dis that they'd caused the deaths of its compatriots. "Rodney."

"Sorry." Rodney shook himself. "Look, it's a little — the Wraith are here. They were chasing the Traveler ships, that's where they got all the damage, and now Guide's here to finish them off."

"Elizabeth." Dekaas reached for the jacket he'd shed in the relative warmth of the infirmary. "I must go. Guide at least knows who I am —"

"Wait," Elizabeth said. "I thought you said the Wraith weren't trying to hunt down the Travelers, that there was some kind of deal with them?"

"Guide thinks they're hiding that guy, the Wolf, the one who's been killing Wraith," Rodney said. "He says they have to hand him over, or he'll destroy the ships on the ground. But of course they don't have him."

"Who said they don't have him?" Elizabeth felt a familiar chill settle into the pit of her stomach. This was something she'd seen before, the showdown between two equally angry, equally desperate sides.

"Um, their captain? I think that's what Sheppard said."

"Elizabeth," Dekaas said again, and his voice was full of pain.

"I know." She straightened, and Daniel gave her a worried look.

"You know something about this."

"Yes." Elizabeth took a deep breath, marshaling her thoughts. "*Osir* may not have the Wolf on board now, but they have in the past. And they also have his wife and son."

Daniel swore under his breath. "That's really not good."

"No," Elizabeth said. "I'm going to talk to Colonel Sheppard."

"Wait, wait, wait," Rodney said. "Hold on. Sheppard told me to keep everyone here, out of sight."

"He has to know this," Elizabeth said. She smiled. "You can't stop me, Rodney. I'm going."

"I'll go with you," Dekaas said.

"No," Elizabeth said. She put her hand on his arm. "Let me hold you in reserve, for your connection with the Wraith. If you come with me now, it's likely that your past will be revealed, and you'll lose your home. If it's necessary, yes, I will call on you. But not now."

"I'll come if you need me," Dekaas said, but let his jacket fall. Elizabeth could guess at his feelings, torn between relief and regret, but she put them aside.

She retraced their path through the empty corridors and out into the installation's main room, careful to close the door behind her. Beyond the main entrance, lights blazed on the landing field, and she could see shadows moving against the pavement. Three Traveler ships stood toward one side of the field, a group huddled at the foot of *Durant's* ramp, and a Wraith cruiser dominated the other side. The Wraith she knew as Todd stood behind a scarlet-haired queen, drones and a warrior ranked behind him. Sheppard and Teyla stood a little apart from the others, their backs to the entrance. Elizabeth took a deep breath.

"Colonel Sheppard!"

For a moment, she thought he hadn't heard, but then his head turned slowly, a reasonable facsimile of a casual glance. She saw him frown, and say something, and Teyla turned, too. Her eyebrows rose, and then she beckoned. Elizabeth straightened her shoulders, and came to join them as though she still had all the right in the world to do just that.

"I thought I told McKay to keep everybody inside," Sheppard said.

"There's something you need to know," Elizabeth answered. "Rodney said Todd was here because of the Wolf. Is that true?"

"Guide," Sheppard said, absently.

Elizabeth blinked, and Teyla said, "His name is Guide, the one you called Todd. But, yes, he and Alabaster are here because they claim the Wolf is aboard one of these ships."

"He may well be," Elizabeth said bluntly. She kept her shoulder turned to the Wraith, just in case their hearing was as enhanced as their night vision, or they had learned to read human faces. "He has been in the past. And when I was on *Osir*, before I joined *Durant*, his wife and son were there."

"Damn it." Sheppard didn't raise his voice, but his hands tightened on the stock of his P90. "I knew they were bullshitting us."

"John," Teyla said. She kept her expression placid, though her eyes were wary. "You did not see him yourself?"

"No." Elizabeth shook her head. "I heard of him, that's all. But I met his wife — she was assigned to keep an eye on me while we were in transit."

Teyla pursed her lips. "This changes matters."

"No kidding." Sheppard looked as though he wanted to hit something, and Elizabeth couldn't entirely blame him. "They got us to stick our necks out, and the whole time they had this Wolf guy — Lesko knew they had him."

"John," Teyla said again. "He may not have known. It occurs to me now that Captain Lesko made all the promises, but the other two did not. We must talk to Captain Lesko at once."

"Oh, yeah," Sheppard said.

"And you will let me do the talking," Teyla said firmly. "Me and Dr. Weir."

She turned on her heel and started toward the group at the base of *Durant*'s ramp. Elizabeth fell into step behind her, and Sheppard grimaced, but followed.

"Captain Lesko," Teyla said. "You have not been honest with us."

Elizabeth saw Lesko's face change as he recognized her, and at his side the stocky woman lifted her head. "The Forgetting Woman! She's Lantean?"

"You said she was Satedan," the red-headed Traveler said.

"She is the woman we were looking for," Teyla said, "as indeed Captain Lesko knew. And she has told us enough to make us certain that you have lied to us."

"We didn't lie," Lesko said. "Shaded the truth, maybe — but these are Wraith!"

"You told me that none of you were sheltering the Wolf," Teyla said. "And that is not true."

It was pure bluff, Elizabeth thought, but effective nonetheless. She saw the three captains exchange uneasy looks, saw the moment it worked and Lesko exhaled a long sigh. "We can't give him up. You have to understand that. He has family among us now."

"So you were just going to leave us hanging out there," Sheppard said.

"Colonel Sheppard is right," Teyla said. "How did you expect to conceal him from the Wraith?"

"We have ways," Tallisk began, but Lesko interrupted her.

"We were working on that. And, no, we didn't really have any good ideas, but let me tell you now, we're not handing him over."

"And so you would sacrifice all your people, the people of three ships, to protect him?" Teyla asked.

"He's one of us. We don't give up our own." Lesko matched her stare for stare. "And you'd just stand by and let the Wraith murder us all?"

"There is very little we could do to stop them, should they chose to act," Teyla retorted.

"They're your allies!" Tallisk said.

"We fought together against a mutual enemy," Teyla said.

"One who would have been just as happy to destroy your people," Sheppard said. "Queen Death wasn't planning on leaving any humans alive outside her control."

"They'd've starved to death if they'd tried that," Yoran said.

"Just so," Teyla said, "except that they planned then to move to another galaxy, and conquer new feeding grounds there." Her voice hardened. "And that is why we fought alongside Alabaster and her fellow queens, to prevent a fate far worse for all of us, human and Wraith. And, yes, the price of that was that we agreed to let the Wraith take certain parts of the galaxy unmolested, in return for them granting us the same freedom."

"We weren't part of that deal," Lesko said.

"We've been trying to get you in on it," Sheppard said, "only Larrin's been dodging us. And now I think I know why."

This was going nowhere, and taking too long. Elizabeth glanced sideways, and saw without surprise that the Wraith were watching with interest, and even as she watched, Todd — Guide — put his hand on the queen's sleeve and stalked forward.

"Enough wasting time," he called. "Have you come to your senses?"

Sheppard turned quickly, putting himself between the Wraith and the other humans, that familiar uneasy smile spreading across his face. "We're just talking here —"

Guide stopped abruptly, his eyes widening as they fixed on

Elizabeth's face. "Surely—"

Elizabeth gave him her best cool smile, seeing Sheppard's finger resting on the P90's safety.

"They told us you were dead," Guide said, after a moment, and looked at Teyla. "Your first queen has returned?"

"It is complicated," Teyla said, "but, yes, in essence, it is so."

"Reports of my death were... exaggerated," Elizabeth said. This was no time for clever quotations. "And I have — my people have found me." If Guide was going to treat her as though she were a Wraith queen, it would be just as well to act like one.

Guide slanted a look at Teyla. "Two queens in one hive is always an awkward thing. Or so it is among my people."

"It is much less so for us," Teyla said. "Or have you not noticed?"

"Be that as it may," Guide said, "and I am glad to welcome your return on behalf of my queen, this has no bearing on the problem at hand. We are here for the Wolf, and the Wolf we will have, or we will destroy these ships as they stand."

"That could only be construed as an irreparable breach of relations," Elizabeth said.

Guide smiled. "Perhaps we should take that risk. After all, who can tell what story would come home to Atlantis from so far away?"

Especially if we didn't survive either, Elizabeth thought. The threat was clear. She was glad the others had stayed behind in the Vanir installation. If worst came to worst, Rodney would see that Atlantis was warned.

"Guide!" That was the Wraith queen, striding across the cracked pavement. Her hair was brilliant scarlet, bright as fresh blood, and she wore an ankle-length leather vest over a white dress that was a sharp contrast to the pale green of her skin. Her eyes were as green as Guide's, the sensor pits bracketing her nose sharply defined in the field lights. "What is this?"

Guide turned, bowing slightly. "It seems the Lanteans' first queen is now returned to them."

"Oh?" The queen tipped her head to one side.

"Elizabeth Weir," Elizabeth said. For the first time, the name didn't feel strange to her, but like a homecoming.

"Our first commander," Sheppard said. "We believed she was dead."

"A queen believed lost and found again." There was an odd expression on the queen's face, one Elizabeth couldn't read. "I am — you may call me Alabaster."

And was that an actual name, or a translation, or a word she had chosen for some other reason? Elizabeth nodded in acknowledgement.

"But this is a distraction," Guide said, with a flash of teeth. "However pleasant! The matter at hand is the Wolf."

"The commander is correct," Alabaster said. "Have you come to some decision?"

"We're not giving anyone to the Wraith," Lesko said.

"Then he is here." Guide took a step forward, and Sheppard's hand tightened on his P90.

"Easy, big guy, we don't want any misunderstandings."

"It seems to me that there have been too many 'misunderstandings' already," Guide snapped. "Your allies have admitted he is here. Hand him over, or suffer the consequences."

"To be murdered? Never." Lesko's fists were clenched.

"Has anyone asked the Wolf what he wants?" Elizabeth asked. There was a moment of silence, and she pressed her brief advantage. "Surely he has something to say about all of this."

"We won't turn anyone over to the Wraith," Lesko said again.

"Would he want others to die for him?" Elizabeth asked. "Particularly if no one is saved by that sacrifice? Surely that's a choice a man should make for himself."

She saw Yoran's gaze flicker, and Lesko's mouth tightened. Tallisk said, "That's a hell of a thing to ask of anyone."

"He knew what he was getting into when he started this," Yoran said.

"Let's at least talk to him," Elizabeth said. "No one wants a slaughter. Not even the Wraith."

"I see no reason to let you out of my sight," Alabaster said. "You will forgive me, Elizabeth Weir, but I cannot help thinking that this is some ploy to help the Wolf escape."

"I assure you it isn't," Elizabeth said. "But if it'll make you feel better, I'll stay here, and Colonel Sheppard and Teyla will talk to the Wolf."

"You and the Traveler captains will stay," Guide said, and Elizabeth nodded.

"Elizabeth," Sheppard said, his voice a warning, but Elizabeth ignored him, her attention on the Wraith.

"Do we have an agreement?"

Guide and Alabaster exchanged silent stares, and then Guide bared teeth in a nearly-silent snarl.

"We are agreed," Alabaster said.

"Thank you." Elizabeth turned away, and Sheppard caught her sleeve, drawing her close enough that a whisper might not be overheard.

"Do you really want me to talk this guy into giving himself up?"

"I want you to talk to him," Elizabeth answered. "I want you to find out what he wants, what he can offer, anything that will buy us time."

"Yoran is not easy with this," Teyla said. "And I do not think Alabaster wants to destroy these ships."

"Right." Elizabeth gave a brisk nod. "That's something we can build on." She only hoped it was true.

CHAPTER SEVEN

EMBER tapped his claws uneasily on the edge of the console, wishing that the Lanteans' machines would hurry up and complete the DNA analysis. Lorne's new, stricter quarantine seemed to be working, insofar as there had been no reports of plastic being destroyed outside the areas already affected. Ember would have thought that to be a good sign, if the destruction within those areas hadn't been accelerating. And if the threat of the 'little replicator' wasn't hanging over all their heads. Surely, surely, it was only a false positive. He looked up as Beckett emerged from his narrow office, and barely suppressed a hiss when he saw the expression on the human's face.

"Aye, you were right," Beckett said, and set a sheaf of paper on the console between them. "The DNA matches the pattern you gave us. I'm just waiting for the full results to transfer to the rest of the program."

Ember bared his teeth, saw the human recoil, and shook his head in apology. "I had hoped—but no matter. That is what it is."

"You said you knew this bug," Beckett said. "What do we do now?"

"We must stop it before it can mutate further." Ember reached for the papers, translating the Lantean terms to his own symbols, hoping that there would be some hint, some key that would let him give a better answer. "And that is not an easy thing to do."

"Do you mean to tell me you don't know how to kill it?"

"As I said, it's a danger to us as well as to humans," Ember said. "There is not always anything good we can do."

Beckett made a face. "How long do we have?"

"I don't know. Anything from a few hours to a few weeks." Ember stopped, cocking his head to one side. "Is the program ready?"

Beckett reached for the nearest keyboard, touched a series of keys. "The data's just loaded. You've got something?"

Ember swung the screen so that he could see more clearly, watching the model coil and unspool. "Possibly. This is not the most dangerous strain—it's relatively weak, not as quick to divide and spread as others I've heard about. And that means we have time before it can mutate, a week or more rather than hours. We breed a weakness into the solvent in case we need to destroy it quickly. If we can target that, we should be able to destroy it."

"Show me," Beckett said.

Ember edged to one side, calling up the original analysis. Together, he and Beckett worked through the first few screens, mapping out potential weak spots. The first could be targeted easily enough, but the most effective compound would damage the Lanteans' electronics; the second Beckett vetoed as harmful to the human respiratory system. The third, though... Ember tipped his head to one side, trying to transform the two-dimensional image into something more familiar. His feeding hand throbbed, a steady pulse that matched his heartbeat, and he closed his fingers tightly, digging his claws into the heel of his hand. "Here. The cell wall—this thing—" He pointed, unable to find an equivalent word.

"Peptidoglycan?" Beckett said. "That's the cell wall."

"Yes. That. In this, the bond here, between these sugars, is weaker, and can be disrupted." Ember touched the screen again. "You see? To do so will also slow the growth process, as it will inhibit cell division."

Beckett nodded slowly. "Aye, I see that. And this compound looks essentially harmless."

"It is slippery," Ember said. "We use a related compound to clean the hives. But it should not harm even human flesh."

"Let's try a test batch," Beckett said.

It took another two hours to create a sample large enough to experiment with, the process hampered by Ember's having to translate his own terms into language the Lanteans could follow. But at last it was done, and Beckett managed a tired grin.

"Well. It works on the samples, anyway."

"Yes." Ember studied the screen with satisfaction, admiring the way the cell walls were thinned and leaking. Even where there was resistance, the new compound was making good headway. And at worst it would help slow the mutation rate.

"Dr. Beckett." That was Lorne's voice again, and Beckett looked toward the nearest speaker.

"Aye?"

"We really need something to shut this down." Lorne's voice was tight with strain. "We're starting to lose key equipment, and I can't replace it if it's not going to last longer than this."

"We've made some progress," Beckett said. "We have a liquid that should at least slow it down."

"That would be great, Doc. We need it now."

"There's worse," Beckett said. "Ember says he believes this will mutate further, producing a strain that will prove infectious to humans."

There was a moment of silence before Lorne spoke. "How bad?"

"Potentially fatal to everyone on Atlantis," Beckett said. "The good news, such as it is — we've some time to find an answer."

"How long?" Lorne asked.

"A week, Ember says."

"Ok." Lorne paused. "Work on that. In the meantime, though, we need something up here to keep the systems running."

"It'll take us a couple of hours to make up another batch," Beckett said.

"We need something sooner than that," Lorne said.

"I can take the rest of what we have up to them now," Ember said. "I think it would be useful to see how the bacteria responds in a natural setting."

"If you cross the quarantine line," Beckett said, "you know you can't come back."

"I know." Ember nodded. "But there is research equipment there, is there not? And we can share files by network. I would like to be where I can see the results first hand. And I will be able to monitor any mutations more directly."

"All right." Beckett touched his earpiece. "Major, I'm going to send Ember to you with all the anti-bacterial wash we have made. We'll send a second batch as soon as it's finished."

There was a little silence, as though Lorne was stifling a first answer. "Ok, Doc. We'll be waiting for him."

Radek rose cautiously to his feet as Ember arrived in the gate room, flanked by a pair of nervous-looking Marines. He was carrying a glass jar that looked as though it would hold two liters of liquid, and attached to it were a short length of hose and a metal nozzle. Obviously Beckett was having just as much trouble as the rest of them coming up with non-plastic tools.

Lorne had risen, too. "Ember. This is the stuff?"

The Wraith dipped his head. "Yes. We should begin at once, if it is as bad as you say —"

"Hold on." Lorne raised a hand. "Side effects? Hazards?"

"As far as we can tell, none. It does not harm human skin, nor does the aerosolized version affect breathing." Ember bared teeth in what might have been an attempt at humor. "It is slippery under-foot. We would all be well advised to step carefully."

"Doc?" Lorne turned to Radek, who shrugged.

"That's good enough for me."

"Ok," Lorne said. "Start with the computers?"

Radek nodded. "Yes. Though what a liquid will do to them when the cases are already degraded —" He broke off, knowing it was a futile protest, and beckoned for Ember to follow him.

They had placed the worst-affected items in one of the side offices, and turned off the local ventilators, though so far it didn't seem to have done any good. Radek unlocked the door, and heard Ember hiss as he surveyed the miscellaneous array of equipment scattered across the table and stacked on the cabinets that ran along the sides of the room. There was everything from shapeless lumps that had been Air Force-issue ballpoint pens and travel mugs for coffee to laptops whose keyboards had nearly disappeared and tablets whose cases were deeply pitted and scored.

"The computers, you said?" Ember asked, after a moment. "Though I think that if I spray them directly I will do as much harm as good."

"We have removed the batteries on the laptops," Radek said, "and we can dry them out later if they survive. The tablets — we will have to take the chance."

"Very well." Ember lifted the nozzle and pumped twice. A fine spray drifted over the keyboards, settling like a fog. Radek waited, half expecting to see some sign that the disinfectant was working, but there was nothing. He turned the laptops so that Ember could spray the rest of the cases, then held the tablets for him as well.

"Should we bother with the rest? It's all destroyed."

Ember shook the container, cocking his head to one side as he judged how much liquid was left. "At some point we must, otherwise the bacteria will simply spread again. But right now I think it is more important to treat your most vulnerable objects."

"Right." Radek led him in a circuit of the gate room, spraying down the cases of those laptops that seemed least affected, then the Marines' weapons and a few more pieces of equipment before Ember shook his head.

"There is no more. At least—" He shook the jar again. "If there are sponges, there is perhaps enough to wipe down a few more things?"

"Our sponges are all plastic," Radek said, but Sindye nodded. "There are some cloths we can use."

Ember handed her the container, and she hurried off, grabbing one of the technicians as she went. Radek took a breath, and looked at Ember. "You really think this will work?"

"Yes." Ember leaned against the nearest pillar, his white hair hanging lank. "At least, it will slow the spread for now. It worked in the lab, and it will work here. And that will buy us time."

There was something not quite right about him, Radek thought. Did he know something about the bacteriophage that he wasn't sharing? No, he looked almost as though he was exhausted, but the Wraith did not tire the way humans did. They did get sick, though, they'd learned that much from Todd—Guide—and he cleared his throat. "Ember. Are you—?"

Ember turned, straightening, the momentary strangeness falling away. "Yes? Am I what?"

"I thought—" Radek shrugged. "Nothing, never mind."

"Dr. Zelenka!" That was Sindye, waving at them from the doorway of the room where they had sequestered the worst-damaged machine. "I think we are seeing results."

"That would be an excellent sign," Ember began, and Radek nodded.

"Yes."

Sindye had set aside a plastic cup and a length of plastic tubing from one of the assay machines, laying each one out on sheets of paper so that she could mark the bacteria's progress. The ink had run where Ember had sprayed them, but even so the meaning was clear. "You see how the effect was spreading faster and faster," she said, pointing to marks that came further apart each time. "I've been checking this every fifteen minutes since I started keeping the record, and this is the first time that there hasn't been any increase in the affected areas. I think this is working."

Ember nodded. "Yes. That's what I hoped to see."

"Tell me some good news," Lorne said, from the doorway, and Radek turned to face him.

"This time I can, yes. Ember's compound has stopped the spread of the bacteria."

Lorne gave a slow smile. "Dr. Beckett just let us know that the next batch is on its way. He got it done faster than he expected. Maybe we're finally getting a handle on this thing."

"Don't speak too soon," Radek said, but he felt a surge of optimism in spite of himself.

Ember was shaking his head. "This is a respite, not a victory. What we must do now is find something that will destroy the bacteria, and treat all of Atlantis at once, so that none of it can possibly survive."

"That's not possible," Sindye began, and stopped herself. "All right, assuming we can find something that is toxic to this bug that won't kill all of us as well — how can you possibly treat something the size of this city?"

Ember gave a wry smile. "I don't know. But if we can find something to kill the 'little replicator', we can find a way to deliver it."

"Surely," Radek said, and hoped it was true.

"Well," Joseph said. "It's not as bad as I thought."

Ronon eyed the still-open pedestal of the DHD, and refrained from saying that it looked bad enough to him. "Yeah?"

"Everything works — well, nothing's damaged," she amended. "All the crystals are intact, no cracks, no burnt-out wiring."

"So what's wrong with it?"

Joseph made a face. "It won't dial anywhere except Atlantis."

Ronon felt his eyebrows rise. Aulich swore under her breath, and Parrish said, "Why not? Do we know?"

"Not for sure." Joseph hauled herself to her feet and touched the first symbol of Sateda's gate address. Instead, an entirely different symbol lit. She pressed the second symbol, and again the wrong symbol lit. "You see the problem. I've tried a dozen different addresses, but the only one that shows up is Atlantis."

"Why?" Parrish asked again, and Joseph shrugged.

"I think it's — well, the equivalent of a software glitch. The energy bolt somehow screwed up the programming, and locked the DHD onto the last address dialed."

"Can you fix it?" Ronon asked.

Joseph shook her head. "No, sir. We don't entirely understand how the programming works in the first place, and even if I wanted to take the risk, I don't have the tools that would let me access it."

"So you're saying we're stuck."

"Yessir." Joseph paused. "Well, at least for now. And I think we can actually dial Atlantis successfully, though I don't want to try unless we have to, just in case completing the dialing process blows up any subtle damage I haven't found. But if it's just the software, there's a good chance that the updates will fix the problem."

"Updates," Ronon said.

"You know. The Stargate system regularly updates the gate programming. We don't know the exact intervals, but it's fairly frequent. The next update should restore the original programming and let us dial out normally again."

Ronon considered that. The Stargates were such a normal part of life — and a technology so far beyond anything Sateda or anyone was capable of building — that everyone tended to take their functioning entirely for granted. But it made sense that there would be some way to correct errors and keep the entire system aligned and functioning. "But you don't know how long it will take."

"No, sir. We've never been able to work out the interval here. Could be anything from a couple of hours to a whole day. The longest recorded interval was thirty hours."

So their choices were to stay here or to declare an emergency and insist that Atlantis let them through the quarantine. Ronon didn't like either option very much, but on balance, he thought they were reasonably safe here. At least as long as the botanists didn't do any more exploring. They had food; they could improvise shelter, and the conifers looked as though they'd burn nicely, if they had to stay through the planet's long night. The trick would be to find enough water, and at least there was a stream bed within walking distance, and that didn't involve going any closer to the plants. And there was a good chance that Atlantis would solve its own problems before the update came through anyway. "OK," he said. "I say we stay here for now."

Aulich nodded. "I agree, sir."

"That does give us a chance to look around a little more," Parrish began, and Ronon shook his head.

"No. I think we've done enough science for right now."

Parrish looked as though he wanted to protest, then winced as he moved his arm injudiciously. "Maybe so."

"How long till nightfall, captain?" Ronon shaded his eyes to look toward the setting sun. It didn't seem to have moved much, but the shadows were longer than they had been before.

Aulich consulted her watch. "About seven hours now."

Water, shelter, fire. Ronon said, "Dr. Parrish, can we cut and burn any of those conifers without setting off the pods?"

Parrish blinked. "I think — probably so? Dr. Hunt and I can find out."

"If you would," Ronon said. "And see if we can cut some bigger branches. Those clouds are getting thicker."

Both the botanists nodded.

"Sergeant, you and the captain scout around, see if you can find anything we can use to build shelter," Ronon went on. "Samara, come with me. We're going to see if we can dig a well."

The dry stream at the bottom of the hill was broad, the sandy soil carved and channeled by a recent flow of water. Ronon chose his spot carefully, a wide flat spot at the lowest part of the channel where there was room to scoop out a good-sized hole. The sand was soft enough to scoop bare-handed, and it was the work of minutes to dig a shallow pit as deep as his hand. The sand there was cool and damp; he dug deeper, and was rewarded with a slow upwelling of water. He tasted it cautiously, and was relieved to find it sweet, not brackish or tasting of mud. He dug a little deeper, and water rose in the new depression, perhaps as deep as the first joint of his little finger, and clear to the eye. He gave a grunt of satisfaction and Samara moved to help, wielding a folded piece of plastic as a shovel.

When they'd finished, they had a hole about as deep as Ronon's forearm, already half full of water. Samara stretched a piece of camouflage fabric over it to keep out insects and more dirt, and Ronon sat back on his heels, pleased with their success.

"It's going to take a while to fill," Samara said, "but it's coming along."

Ronon nodded. It wouldn't be a lot — there wouldn't be any extra for washing, for one thing — but by nightfall they ought to have enough to drink and to heat the MREs. "Got something to carry it in?"

Samara grinned, and flourished what looked like another piece of fabric. "Folding bucket."

"Nice."

"And I've got a full tube of water purification tablets."

"Good." Ronon remembered an unpleasant three days on Appar, back when he was a Runner, when the water had been tainted without him realizing it. He'd barely managed to get up enough strength to make it back to the Stargate and dial a more hospitable world. The Lanteans were lucky their drugs and filters meant that almost never happened to them. He pushed himself to his feet, scanning the ground on this side of the hill. There were more of the conifers, a low tangle on the far side of the stream, and still more of the succulents in a rising bank beyond them, their pods rising over the broad leaves. A couple of the smaller insects bumbled past them, following the line of the stream and staying well clear of the succulents. "Let's see what they've got back at the gate."

To his pleased surprise, Parrish and Hunt had gathered an enormous pile of branches and bark from the conifers, and stacked it on cleared ground beyond the DHD. They'd managed to collect a few longer, nearly straight branches, and were planning, Hunt said, to cut a few more once they'd had a breather. She flourished a survival saw, jagged wire with handles, and Ronon nodded again.

"Does that stuff burn safely?" He'd been on planets where trees that looked like that were full of a smelly resin that went up in an explosive whoosh once he put a spark to it.

"It burns fast and hot," Parrish said, and nodded to a smear of ash on the ground. "Or the bark does. If we strip that off, the wood beneath should burn more slowly."

"That'll work."

"What I'd really like to know is how these plants are generating all that power," Parrish said. "I'm sure some of those pods have fired twice, and I don't see how they can do that on a purely chemical reaction."

"Let's concentrate on getting more wood," Hunt said, and Parrish sighed, but followed her.

Ronon looked to the horizon again. The sun was definitely lower now, its light reddened and the shadows darker. If they had to stay through the planet's night — well, the question was how cold it was going to get, and what kind of shelter they could pull together. "Captain! How long does it stay dark?"

Aulich turned away from her equipment, her almost-invisible eyebrows drawn together in a frown. "About nineteen hours — nineteen hours ten minutes."

That was a long time to huddle in the dark by a fire. Ronon said, "How cold does it get?"

"I don't know for sure," Aulich said. "This is planetary summer, but we're some considerable distance from the equator. My calculations say it's likely to drop to ten degrees Celsius — that's 50 Fahrenheit."

The two scales were still strange to Ronon, but he'd learned a few benchmark temperatures, and that one was pretty chilly. "Not so nice."

"No." Aulich looked at her screens again, still frowning. "That may not be the worst of it, either. You know I'm a meteorologist?"

Ronon nodded. "Yeah."

"When we first came through the gate, we sent up a weather balloon — and, you know, I just realized how lucky we were that it went straight up and didn't cast any shadows on those damn plants."

"Go on."

"I'm still getting readings from the instruments, and I'm picking up some data that — I think there are storms coming. Maybe bad ones."

"How bad?"

"Electrical storms," Aulich said. "Lots of lightning, probably heavy rain in places, maybe wind. I think what's driving them is the mismatch between the temperatures in the daytime and at night — I think the storms are a way of equalizing the pressures that result. But if we're out here in the open, right under the Stargate..."

Her voice trailed off unhappily, and Ronon nodded. "Not good."

"Not good at all," she agreed.

"How long?"

"How long till they get here, or how long will they last?"

"Both." Ronon turned to look at the western sky. Was it his imagination, or was there a darker shadow on the horizon?

"I'd say we'll start to see the effects in about seven hours," Aulich said. "As for how long... It's not a deep front, and it's moving fast. A couple of hours, maybe? But that's a long time to wait."

Especially without shelter. Ronon surveyed the area again, wishing he'd missed something, but there were no convenient caves, nothing at all to break the force of a storm. Maybe among the conifers, except that the bark was, by Parrish's reckoning, thoroughly flammable. Better to get off the planet, if they possibly could. "Sergeant?"

Joseph looked up from where she was sitting by the pile of wood, methodically chipping the jagged bark away from the harder core. "Sir?"

"Anything new from Atlantis?"

She pushed herself to her feet, wiping her hands on her pants. "No, sir. They checked in an hour ago, and the quarantine is still in effect. I reported our problem, but they said to stay put if it was safe."

Safe. That was the real question. Ronon said, "Any idea if they're making progress?"

"They said they were locking it down, sir." Joseph's tone was flat, matter-of-fact, but a briefly cynical expression flickered across her face. Aulich grimaced, and Ronon nodded. He'd heard that kind of reassurance before, and was willing to bet that the Lanteans had no real idea what was going on.

"No time frame either?"

"No, sir."

"And I'm guessing the gate hasn't reset, either," Aulich said.

"No, ma'am," Joseph said. "I'll keep checking."

Ronon looked back at the horizon, where a thin line of cloud just touched the sun's lower limb. Probably those were the storms, or their first forerunners, but even a small thunderstorm could prove deadly if they were trapped in the open. And there was no time to build the kind of shelter that would keep them safe, even if they had the materials. If he pushed, he was sure Atlantis would let them through, but then they'd be trapped inside whatever quarantine line had been established, and in the long run that wasn't any better than where they were now. If he'd evacuated everyone to Sateda when the plants first started shooting —

He killed that thought. He hadn't done it, and there was no point thinking about might-have-beens. It was still some hours before the storms reached them, and there was always a chance that either Atlantis would fix their problem or the Stargate would reset. And it was also possible that they might miss the worst of the storms, in which case they needed shelter against the rain and cold, some way to protect the fire... "All right," he said. "Keep me updated, sergeant. And call me the next time Atlantis dials in. I want to talk to Major Lorne. Captain, can you keep tracking the weather?"

Aulich nodded. "As long as the balloon stays intact and in range."

"Good enough." Ronon turned slowly, surveying the clearing around the Stargate. "So. What do we have in the way of survival gear?"

John started up the steep ramp to *Osir's* hatch, Teyla at his heels. There were armed guards just inside the hatchway, two men and a teenage girl, all grimly determined, and from directly overhead came a whine of overstressed servos. The ship's guns, John guessed, trying to depress far enough to cover the party on the ground. He hoped to hell they didn't spark a firefight before he could get a word with the Wolf. And what the hell he was going to say...

"I'm not asking him to give himself up to be killed," he said, under his breath, and Teyla glanced up at him.

"No. But there must be some other way."

Damned if I see it. John swallowed the words, plastered a smile on his face as he came level with the guards. "We're here to talk to the Wolf."

The three exchanged glances, and the girl said, "No, you can't —"

"Let's see what the Lanteans can do to get us out of this," one of the men said, and put a hand on her shoulder.

The other man nodded. "This way."

He led them through a series of cramped corridors, passing through hatchways and down a set of narrow spiral stairs until they reached what seemed to be a mess hall or some sort of communal space. It was crowded, women and children and a few adult men packed into the seats and crammed into corners on the floor, and John frowned, unable to work out what was going on. Their guide glanced back and shrugged.

"Women and kids. And the vital crew."

The minimum crew needed to raise the ship. All huddled together in the safest part of the ship, in the hope that they could escape the first round of firing. John nodded.

"Through here." Their guide ducked through a narrow hatch into a corridor lined with closed doors: residential cabins, John guessed. "This one." He knocked on the metal without waiting for an answer. "Wolf! The Lanteans are here."

There was a moment of silence, or what passed for silence in the creaking ship, and the hatch slid back. "What do they want?"

The man in the door froze, and John caught his breath. That was a face he had never expected to see again, no matter what he'd told the man's family. Older now, his forehead higher, with a few early threads of gray in his close-cropped hair, the left eye still a black void, all pupil, from the Wraith enzyme: Aiden Ford, who he had last seen standing ready fight off an entire hive of Wraith. Aiden Ford, who had kidnapped him and McKay and Teyla and Ronon, drugged all of them except John himself with the Wraith enzyme and taken them on a suicide mission to destroy a Wraith hive. If McKay hadn't managed to use the enzyme to overpower his guards so that he could escape to Atlantis and bring *Daedalus* to the rescue, they might all have died on the hive. John had been almost positive Ford had died there, covering their retreat. But not entirely sure.

His eyes flicked over the still figure, dressed now in the Travelers' motley gear, looking for signs of the enzyme addiction. But Ford's hands were still, his good eye clear, his expression moving from concern to shock, not the anger goaded by the drug.

"Lieutenant," John said, and heard his own voice strange and harsh against the hum of the ship.

"Major." Ford's good eye shifted. "I mean, Colonel."

Old instincts died hard: John saw Ford's hand twitch toward the start of a salute, and then relax.

"Teyla?"

"It is I, indeed," Teyla said, her voice grim. "You are the Wolf?"

Ford took a shaky breath. "Yeah. That's me. I had to do something."

Like you did before, John thought, remembering the fear in his gut as he watched Teyla and Rodney and Ronon succumb to the enzyme, transformed to manic fighting machines and then caught by the agonies of withdrawal. They'd been warned from the very beginning that messing around with the Wraith enzyme was dangerous — the people of Pegasus weren't stupid, and their most sophisticated cultures were more than capable of isolating and extracting the enzyme, and of discovering both its advantages and its addictive properties. But Ford had never intended to take the enzyme, not at first. He'd been attacked by a Wraith, found half dead with its feeding hand locked to his chest. The only reason he'd survived at all was that the Wraith had pumped him full of the enzyme. John remembered seeing him lying motionless in the infirmary as Beckett worked on him, remembered how it had felt when he had known that Ford was going to survive. Their victories had been small and hard-won then; they'd lost too many people in that first year, before they'd known if any of them would ever see Earth again. Unbidden, the image of Ford's flight from Atlantis rose in memory: he could have killed Ford, should have killed him, but he hadn't been willing to do it. He hadn't even taken a lethal weapon with him, because Ford was one of his men, and you never left your own behind.

"This changes matters," Teyla said, still with that note of anger in her voice.

"How the hell —?" John began, then shook his head. "No. We can get to that later. What were you planning to do, Lieutenant? Fight a hive and a cruiser single-handed?"

He saw Ford flinch, but the lieutenant's voice was fairly steady. "We thought we could outrun them, sir. But they got in a couple of lucky shots. We didn't expect them to follow us here."

"You misjudged them," Teyla said.

"Yes, ma'am."

"Did you have a plan for getting out of this?" John asked. "Because we need to know what you were planning if we're going to get you out of this."

Ford shrugged. "I was going to try to hide on the ship. There's a shielded compartment, we don't think the Wraith can spot it. And there's no way they're going to let the Wraith actually board, not without a fight."

"I do not think that will work," Teyla said. "And there is also your family to consider. If the Wraith threaten them, or indeed any of your shipmates…"

Ford looked warily from one to the other. "How do you know about them?"

"Elizabeth told us," Teyla said, and stopped. "But you do not know her story."

"Dr. Weir?" Ford frowned in confusion. "How does she know?"

"It is a very long story," Teyla began, and John cleared his throat. "You've been missing a long time, Lieutenant. Short version, while you were gone, Dr. Weir was believed killed, Atlantis escaped to Earth and then returned to Pegasus and fought Queen Death, and while all that was going on, we found out that Elizabeth had ascended and then been unascended for saving McKay's life."

"Wow. You've been busy." Ford winced. "Sir."

John smiled in spite of himself. "Kind of, yeah." Teyla shot him a look, and he bit his lip. "But that's not the point."

Ford straightened, visibly bracing himself. "With respect, sir, what is the point? Are you going to hand me over?"

"We are not," John said, the words harder and sharper because he knew he could and suspected that maybe he should, one life for all the other people on board the three ships. Neither Guide nor

Alabaster was going to give him up willingly, and John couldn't entirely blame them. But Ford was one of his, and he wasn't going to leave anyone behind.

"What, then, do you intend us to do?" Teyla asked. "Understand, I agree and I will back you, but – Guide will not let this go."

"Guide's not in charge now," John pointed out.

"Alabaster is no less determined than her father," Teyla said, and John bit his lip again.

"Ok, we bring him back to Atlantis."

"I doubt that will be acceptable," Teyla said.

"We have to try." John shook his head. "No. We've got to make it happen."

"Sir," Ford said. "I – Can I go back? After everything? And there's Atelia to think about – my wife. And the baby."

"You're listed as missing," John said. That skated over a lot of things, but you could argue that Ford wasn't responsible for most of them. He'd certainly make that argument, and so would General Landry. So would General O'Neill.

"I didn't try to contact Atlantis," Ford said. "I mean, after I – after I got off the enzyme and took up with the Travelers."

"Everyone believed Atlantis had been destroyed," Teyla said, cocking her head to one side. "I am sure the Travelers were no exception."

John nodded, hoping Ford would take the excuse, but the lieutenant's expression was grave.

"After Queen Death was killed –"

"I expect the Travelers weren't going to rearrange their schedule for you," John interrupted. "Look, this is stuff we can work out later. Right now, we've got to figure out how to keep the Wraith from killing you or all these other people." He glanced at Teyla. "And I'm damned if I see how."

"We will think of something," she said, but her expression was doubtful. "And we had best return now and see what we can arrange."

"Sir," Ford said. "If it's me or them – I volunteer, sir."

"We're not going to do that," John said.

"What you want," Elizabeth said patiently, not for the first time, "is for the Wolf to be gone."

"I want him dead." Guide showed teeth in what was meant to be a parody of a human smile.

Elizabeth ignored him. "And you want to protect your people," she said, to Lesko, who spread his hands in frustration.

"I can't see how we can do both. The Wolf is of our people now, we owe him that."

"If he were to be removed from the equation," Elizabeth said. Her throat was scratchy from too much talking, and she wished she had thought to bring a bottle of water. It had been a long time since she'd had to spend this much time arguing with anyone. "If, for example, he were to agree to cease activities and place himself under house arrest."

"Not in Lantean custody," Guide said.

Alabaster nodded. "Nor on Atlantis. That could hardly be considered security for us. Rather, it's one more weapon you hold ready."

"Perhaps a third party," Elizabeth said. "Or a neutral world."

"There's no place we could leave him that the Wraith wouldn't come," Lesko said. "Except maybe Atlantis."

"A world without a Stargate," Yoran said. "Within the human sphere. That's assuming we can trust the Wraith not to attack him anyway."

"And that we would trust you not to retrieve him the moment our backs were turned," Guide said. "No. Not acceptable."

Elizabeth cleared her throat. "What if —" She saw movement at the corner of her eye, John and Teyla emerging from *Osir* to make their way down the ramp. Teyla's face was utterly serene, a sure sign of trouble, and John's face was grim.

"Elizabeth," he said. "We need a word. Urgently."

"You'll excuse me," she said, generally, and moved to join them. "What is it?"

"The Wolf," John said. "He's Ford."

Elizabeth's breath caught in her throat. Surely that was impossible; Ford was long dead, killed covering Sheppard's escape from a Wraith hiveship after Ford's attempt to destroy it had gone horribly wrong. "It can't be. Can it?"

"It is he," Teyla said. "Though we have not had time to hear all his story."

But I have, Elizabeth realized. The Wolf, Atelia's husband, Jordan's father — and that was one more proof, a human name, a name from the Milky Way, from Earth itself, the name she had almost recognized when she traveled on *Osir*. It made sense, everything made sense, all the pieces of the story: the Travelers had found the man who would become the Wolf sick to death from enzyme withdrawal. Dekaas had nursed him through it — she spared a moment to appreciate the irony there, Wraith worshipper, Wraith pet, using Wraith-learned skills to cure the Wraith's devoted enemy — and Ford had recovered, healed enough to take a wife and build a life, in between attacks on the Wraith. "This complicates things."

"No kidding," Sheppard said.

Elizabeth gave a wry smile, and turned back to the others. "Alabaster! It seems that the man you call the Wolf is one of our people, whom we believed to be dead."

"This changes things," Alabaster said, "and not for the better."

"No," Guide snarled. "No, it does not. They still have only to surrender him."

"We are not just going to turn him over," Sheppard said. "Put that out of your mind."

"He has caused the deaths not just of our people," Alabaster said, "but of his own. How many humans now lie dead, or wait in feeding cells because of his actions? This cannot continue."

"No," Elizabeth said. "It cannot." She cleared her throat again, all the pieces falling into place, a sudden insight as blinding as lightning. "There is a third path. The Wolf cannot remain with the Travelers, and he cannot be given over to you. Let us send him into exile — send him back to Earth, from which he cannot return."

There was an instant babble of objection, and Sheppard gave her a wild look. "Can we do that?"

"Can't we?" Elizabeth raised her hands. "Please, everyone, not all at once!"

There was an instant of shocked silence, and then Lesko said, "How can we be sure you won't just hand him over to the Wraith?"

"Because he's ours," Sheppard said. Guide bared teeth at that, and Sheppard matched him glare for glare. "Lieutenant Ford is one of my men, and — as you well know — we don't leave our people behind."

"And if he is yours, why should we trust you?" Alabaster asked, tilting her head to one side. Elizabeth couldn't read her expression, but thought she was less angry than Guide.

"Because we still have common ground here," Elizabeth answered. "The reasons for our agreement are still valid."

Alabaster inclined her head gravely.

"You are asking us to trust a great deal," Guide said. "We have no way of knowing for certain that he will be taken to Earth at all, much less kept under confinement there. I cannot recommend this bargain."

"The commander has a point," Alabaster said, mildly.

"You have our word," Sheppard said.

"You will forgive me if I find that — not entirely adequate," Guide answered.

"We have no reason to jeopardize our agreement," Elizabeth said, but her mind was busy with the problem. Proof that Ford was safe on Earth, and likely to remain so: from the Wraith point of view, that was reasonable. The only question was, what would they believe, and how could the SGC provide it?

"If I might offer a suggestion," Teyla said. "You know that both General O'Neill and Mr. Woolsey have returned to Earth. If we were to escort Lieutenant Ford on his return home, and returned with photographs of him and his family with one or both of them — would that not serve your purpose?"

Guide and Alabaster exchanged looks again, and Guide said, "What proof have we that he would stay there?"

"His war's over," Sheppard said. "We know it, he knows it. It's time for him to go home."

There was another exchange of glances, and Alabaster said, "I will agree to this. You have my cleverman, my Master of Sciences Biological, on Atlantis at present. We will accept your proofs when we collect him from you."

"That seems reasonable," Elizabeth said.

"We'll need to work out the details, of course," Sheppard interjected hastily, and Elizabeth nodded. She hadn't forgotten Atlantis's problems, or their own mission, currently under guard in the Vanir installation. But from here, the rest was all details.

CHAPTER EIGHT

EMBER flattened his feeding hand against the console, pressing the handmouth against the cold metal as though that pain would drive out the inward ache. He needed to feed. He could feel his heartbeat slowing, his blood moving sluggishly in his veins, the bitter pulse of need in the center of his chest that echoed in his hand. He remembered all too clearly what Zelenka's life-force tasted like, strong and salt-sweet; he could imagine Sindye's, clear and bright, but forced his mind away. Solve the problem, he told himself. Then you can leave Atlantis and drink your fill.

He blinked hard, focusing on the screens in front of him. They had linked to Beckett's computers, and could study both sets of results: this compound seemed to have promise, but that had been true of the last three as well. "Let's proceed," he said, and heard his voice harsh and croaking. Zelenka gave him a look and Ember glared back at him, then turned his attention to the screen, watching the numbers scroll past. They were heading in the right direction, climbing slowly toward a respectable peak — but did it cross the threshold? He closed his eyes for an instant, unable to make the calculation come steady in his mind, and he felt a hand on his sleeve.

"Ember. Are you all right?"

That was Zelenka's voice — Zelenka's life-force so close at hand, and Ember closed his feeding hand tight, digging his claws into the heel of his hand. The vein on the back of his hand was throbbing. Just a sip, just a taste, just enough to end the worst of the hunger... Zelenka had had the retrovirus, had permitted him to feed before —

"Ember?"

"I'm fine." Ember straightened his back, baring teeth, and Zelenka stepped quickly away. Ember's feeding hand rose without volition, the handmouth gaping, and behind him Sindye cried out.

"Major! Major Lorne!"

Ember froze, closing his fingers tight again, and heard the click of Marines arming their weapons. "There is no — I am —" He stopped, unable to continue.

Zelenka said, "Stand down! Wait, Major." He took one step closer, though still not quite into reach. "Ember. You need to feed?"

Ember snarled soundlessly. "I am in control—"

"Answer the question," Lorne said. He had his hand on his sidearm, and at that Ember bared teeth.

"If you shoot me, Major, I will not regenerate. Yes, I am starving, and I must feed very soon."

There was a little silence, a withdrawal, and then Zelenka shrugged. "Well. I have done it before—"

"But not this time," Lorne said grimly. "And we're not discussing it here. Everyone, back to the gate room."

"The readings," Ember began.

"I'll stay with the experiment," Sindye said, and Ember let himself be drawn away.

"And if I volunteer," Zelenka began, and Lorne shook his head again.

"Sorry, Doc. I know feeding won't kill you, but every evidence is that it knocks you out, and we can't afford to put you out of commission right now. You're not an option."

Zelenka said something under his breath. "Nonetheless—"

"Yeah, I know." Lorne glanced around the gate room, as though he were assessing who had taken the retrovirus and who he could best spare. Someone young and strong, Ember thought, shivering in spite of himself. Someone whose life-force sang with energy. He could feel a dozen of them here, every life worthy of tasting, each one enough to sustain him. He closed his hands into tight fists, ashamed and hungry.

"Excuse me, Major?" That was a woman's voice, one of the crew sitting mostly idle at the consoles that monitored the Stargate. "Are you looking for volunteers for, um, the Wraith?"

"He's got to feed," Lorne said, his voice still grim. "We need him if we're going to get rid of this damn bacteria."

"Yes, sir." The woman squared her shoulders. "Sir, I volunteer."

"Salawi?"

"I've had the retrovirus, sir. No side effects. And right now I'm not doing much of anything."

"You don't have to do this, Airman."

"Somebody has to," Salawi said.

There was a silence that seemed to stretch into infinity. She was close enough that Ember could sense her life-force, cool and sharp as electricity beneath her skin. She was strong enough that he could afford to drink deep, to take everything that he needed — the retrovirus would protect her from any serious harm.

"I do not think," Zelenka began, and Lorne shook his head.

"It's not going to be you, Doc. No way." He took a deep breath. "All right, Salawi. And — thank you."

"Yes, sir," Salawi said, and hesitated for the first time. "Sir, where —?"

"Somewhere private," Zelenka said sharply.

"My office," Lorne said, in the same moment, and Zelenka nodded. "Ember. This way."

The room Lorne called his office was small and warm, with another long narrow window looking out onto a platform between the city's towers. At the moment, it was full of sunlight, and Ember blinked, startled. He had lost track of the planet's cycle in his focus on the bacteria; he had thought it was night, if he had thought about it at all. Lorne crowded in behind him, followed by a woman with a medic's kit; Zelenka pushed in, too, and the two Marines took up their places just inside the door. Salawi seated herself cautiously in Lorne's well-padded chair, and gave Ember a wary glance.

"What do I need to do?"

"If you would unfasten your shirt. Just the top buttons. Please." Ember kept his voice steady with an effort that made him tremble. He was starving, wanted nothing more than to drive his hand against her chest and drain every drop of the energy he craved, but with the other humans watching, he was seized with a strange sense of shame. This was all wrong, he should not have to feed so publicly, not on this woman who bore herself like a young queen. He could feel the Marines at his back, knew that their weapons were cocked and ready. He took a shuddering breath, and then another, and saw Lorne frown.

"Is there a problem?"

Ember shook his head. This was wrong, it went against every

instinct, everything he had ever been taught; humans were kine, they were food, they could not give life, offer sustenance as Wraith did to Wraith... And if he did not feed, he would die. He went to his one knee beside her chair, suddenly unwilling to loom over her, and lifted his feeding hand. "Are you ready?"

"Yes, sir." Her voice was thin but determined.

Ember laid his hand against her chest, the skin hot against his handmouth. He flexed his claws, and saw her flinch, felt the enzyme begin to pulse in his vein and the life-force begin to flow, just as cool and sharp as he had imagined, like sparks fizzing beneath his skin. He wanted, oh, he wanted to drink it all, to rip and tear and finally be filled, but he controlled himself, drawing it from her as carefully as he would draw sustenance from a hivemate, a brother, from a lover. She closed her eyes, her mouth twisting, and still he drank, feeling his own flesh ease and soften. She winced again, and he slowed his pull, then fed a bit of the life-force back to her, as he would to another Wraith, as was only polite and kind and proper. And that was too much to understand, but he was fed at last. He relaxed his fingers, freeing his handmouth and loosing his claws, and sank back onto his heels. He heard her gasp and looked up warily to see her straightening herself in the chair.

"Airman?" Lorne said. "Chauncey, check her out."

"Yes, sir," the medic said, and dragged her kit to the other side of the chair.

"I'm... all right, sir." Salawi's voice was faint but definite. "Just really tired."

Ember rose to his feet, new strength coursing through him. Physically, he was restored, but mentally... If these were not kine, he did not know what they were; this was forbidden territory, the deepest taboo, and he refused to think about it. "I must get back to work."

"Yes, indeed," Zelenka said, his voice briskly matter-of-fact. "Come."

Ember followed him past the Marines, knowing that his own movements were more fluid than they had been in days.

"You look better," Zelenka said. "And — you did not hurt her."

"I am learning," Ember said, and flung his hair back over his shoulders. "Now. We have work to do."

Ford got to his feet when John opened the door of the common lounge on the Travelers' ship. "Colonel Sheppard."

"As you were." John glanced around the room, eyes falling on the electric pot warming in the corner. "Want some tea?"

"I don't drink tea," Ford said bemusedly.

"I do." John poured some into a stainless steel handleless cup, dark and sweet, smelling faintly of smoke. Did they dry the leaves over wood fires? He took his time, then came and sat down at the little table, motioning for Ford to sit opposite.

Ford was watching him warily, but he took his seat. "What do the Wraith say?"

"They're willing to offer a deal."

Ford snorted. "And you trust the Wraith."

"I trust these guys," John said. "They've been as good as their word before."

"You're going to turn me over to them." Ford shook his head. "Unbelievable."

"That's not what the deal is." John cupped his hands around the warm tea. He took a long sip. "The deal is that you leave the Pegasus Galaxy, go back to Earth, and never return. Atelia and Jordan can come with you."

Ford looked stunned. As he ought to, John thought. He took another sip of tea.

"I can't do that," Ford said slowly. "I can't just leave. This…" Words failed him.

John took another drink, marshaling his thoughts. "Let me tell you about this news story I read a little while ago. It was about this Japanese guy. He'd been a soldier in World War II and he got stranded on a tropical island. He was stuck there for a long time, forty years. And when people showed up, when they tried to rescue him, he didn't believe them. You see, he thought the war was still going on. He didn't believe it when they told him that it had been over since before they were born." He met Ford's eyes across the table. "Finally they had to go get his old CO who was like ninety to go tell him that the war was over."

Ford's face didn't change. "You think I'm like that guy."

"I think when you've been on a long deployment you get invested. But sooner or later, the deployment is over." He made his voice harder. "It's over, Lieutenant. It's time to go home."

Ford sat back in the chair, his eyes evading John's, his mouth twisting.

"You've got people waiting for you. Your cousin Sheri. Your grandparents. You've been MIA for four years."

"Grandma. Grandpa." He shook his head. "I don't know what to say to them."

Like he'd known them in some other life, John thought. That's what it was like. "They'll be so glad to hear you're alive they won't care what you say," John said. "They'll be thanking God that you're alive."

Ford bent his head. "Yeah. That's what Grandma would say." His voice sounded choked.

John dropped his voice. "Go home, Aiden. Take your wife and your son and go home. It's time."

He saw the moment of decision, the heartbeat where he gave in. Ford took a deep breath. "What happens here? What happens to all these people? The Travelers – I can't just…"

"They're going to have to work it out with the Wraith themselves. We can't make everybody get along and we can't solve everybody's problems for them. We've got them to the table. But they're going to have to make their own deals."

"And if they don't?" Ford challenged.

"Then people are going to keep right on dying, just like they have for thousands of years." John put the teacup down. "That's not up to us. If humans and Wraith are going to share this galaxy, they're going to have to come to some kind of terms everybody can live with."

Ford shook his head. "I'm not on board with sharing this galaxy with the Wraith. And neither are a lot of people. We'd be better off if they were all dead."

John shrugged. "That's not possible."

"What?"

John shrugged again. "I said, that's not possible. You can't kill them all. The Ancients couldn't kill them all. Nobody can. The Wraith exist. Arguing over whether they ought to is stupid. They do. You might as well argue that gravity shouldn't work. It does. This is the world we live in. And either people are going to keep on killing each other, or they're going to make peace. This isn't a winnable war."

Ford was looking at him intently, like he was actually seeing him for the first time. "You're different," he said. "You're not the same Major Sheppard who came out here."

"That's right," John said. "I'm not." The cup of tea was warm between his hands, just like the first one the Athosians had offered him on the first day. But he was different. He was happy. And that gave him a lot to lose. He'd been a guy with nothing to lose, who could risk everything on the flip of a coin and not care how it landed. And now – now it mattered. Maybe someday Ford would find that place too. "Your deployment's over," he said gently. "Today you're going home."

They thrashed out the outline of an agreement while the stars wheeled overhead, and as the sky paled so that only the brightest of the stars could still be seen, it seemed as though they had come to an agreement. It was, Teyla thought, workable. No one had everything they wanted, but no one lost everything, either. *Osir* and *Mirilies* would lift shortly, with *Durant* remaining behind to monitor and make sure that Alabaster's hive did not pursue. Two hours after they had entered hyperspace, Alabaster's hive would depart, leaving Guide and the cruiser to make sure the Lanteans kept their part of the bargain. Two hours after the hive left orbit, *Durant* would lift ship, and that would leave only the question of how they were going to get Ford back to Earth. Perhaps by then Lorne would have solved the problem with the plastic-eating bacteria. Perhaps by then they would have found time to decide what to do about Dis.

"Teyla!"

That was Lesko again, and Teyla turned, putting on her best trader's smile. "Yes?"

"You have my doctor, remember? We want him back before we leave here."

"Yes, of course." And that was one more problem to be dealt with, though most of that would be up to Dekaas himself. "He is within, still tending to the injured party."

"Will you send for him?" Lesko gave her a hard stare. "I want to get all my people together."

"I will see if he can leave his patient," Teyla said, and turned away before he could say anything more.

"Trouble?" John asked, falling into step beside her, and she gave him a quick smile.

"I do not think so. Captain Lesko wants his doctor back, that is all."

"I bet he does." John sighed. "I need to talk to Atlantis, see what their status is. But first I need to figure out what we're going to do with Dis. We can't just let him go around unascending people."

"You do not want to bring him back to Atlantis?" Teyla asked. "Once the bacteria is dealt with, I mean."

"I'd rather not. I don't want him getting too good a look at our technology — I really don't want him getting a look at what we don't know about it. But I'm having trouble thinking of anything better to do with him."

"We could keep him confined, as we did the Wraith," Teyla said.

"I'm not entirely sure we could. I mean, yeah, if everything works right, we can hold him, but if it doesn't — I really don't want him loose on Atlantis. And I also don't want any of his friends showing up to blast him free. You remember how well we held them off the last time."

Teyla winced. The Vanir ship had gone right through the city's shields; the Vanir had stolen the Ancient artifact — another of Janus's misbegotten creations, the Attero Device — and kidnapped Rodney and Daniel Jackson, all without apparent effort. And all without anyone being able to lift a finger to stop them. It had taken everything Atlantis had, plus Guide's cooperation, to destroy the device, and they'd nearly lost Daniel in the process. "I had not considered that. Do you think there are more of them left?"

John shrugged. "I think we have to assume there are. Though I'm hoping maybe there aren't too many."

"One can only hope." Teyla drew a deep breath. "I will fetch Dekaas. I assume you want to leave Rodney on guard? And Dr.

Jackson." And that was a thing she would not have said five years ago, or even three, but Rodney had proved himself a hundred times over.

"Yeah. And in the meantime, I'm going to talk to Atlantis."

John turned away, heading for the jumper. Telya saw that Elizabeth was deep in conversation with Alabaster, and stared for a moment, still amazed that Elizabeth was in fact alive and so very much herself. It seemed impossible — seemed so much more than impossible that a part of her screamed it must be a trap, some bizarre creation of the Asurans. And yet she trusted Dekaas to have the knowledge to rule that out. The nanites the Asurans had left in Elizabeth's blood before had been all too obvious; Dekaas's equipment had been better, more sophisticated, than Sateda's in its heyday, and that meant it should be reliable. Elizabeth was Elizabeth, unmistakably, the familiar negotiator and leader, the woman who had ascended and then chosen to save Rodney's life and paid for it by being unascended. And to find Ford as well, alive, and free of the enzyme — it was all almost unimaginably good news, and Teyla hoped she would have time to savor it sometime soon. But there were other things to deal with now. She made her way back into the dark of the installation, closing the doors behind her as she went.

The other three were waiting in the infirmary, Daniel staring at Dis as though he could read its history on its wrinkled skin, while Dekaas was stolidly finishing an MRE. Rodney was pacing, his hands resting on the butt of his P90, and from the expression on his face, he had been caught in mid-rant when she opened the door.

"News?" Daniel rose to his feet, his hand on his pistol. He was, Teyla reminded herself, an experienced member of a gate team, no matter how often he ignored orders.

"We have come to an agreement, thanks to Elizabeth," she said, and was rewarded by the sudden almost beatific smile on Rodney's face. She ran through it quickly, getting a thoughtful nod from Daniel and a wider grin from Rodney.

"I knew it was her," he said. "I knew she was all right. And if this doesn't prove it —"

"You know what the IOA is going to say about that," Daniel said.

"I can't help it if they're that stupid," Rodney answered. "Which, of course, I believe they're more than capable of being, since they haven't let me back into my old job."

"I can't imagine why," Daniel said.

Rodney glared. "Though of course it gives me more time to pursue my own research —"

"Rodney," Teyla said, and he subsided. She looked at Dekaas. "Captain Lesko has asked if you are ready to return to the *Durant*."

"Dis is stable and will, I think, recover completely," Dekaas answered. "So, I suppose — yes, I am." He paused. "You said that the hive was Alabaster's?"

"Yes." Teyla watched the emotions flicker across his face: yearning, regret, sorrow, certainly, and perhaps a weary sort of fear. For a moment, she thought he would say something, but he merely nodded, and reached for his jacket again.

"Yes. I'm ready."

"Then I will take you to *Durant*. Colonel Sheppard asks that the rest of you stay here." Both Rodney and Daniel nodded, but she fixed Rodney with a queen's stare. *Do not quarrel so much that Dis escapes.*

Rodney flushed, and shook his head. "No, no. We'll be fine."

"Good," Teyla said aloud, and let the door close again behind her and Dekaas.

"I've done the best I can for Dis," Dekaas said, as they made their way through the corridors. "I don't think the machine produced a complete recovery — I don't know if that's because Dis's injuries were so severe, or if the machine wasn't working at full capacity, but I don't much think it matters. Dis will heal in time, but for the moment there's still a considerable weakness."

"That can only work to our advantage," Teyla said frankly. "The Vanir are more powerful than — well, than we or any other people can handle."

"From what I've seen of their technology, I would have guessed as much," Dekaas answered. "If it's possible for us to get access to the infirmary — the Vanir have shown no interest in reclaiming the installation, and you know how much we could use it."

"They may show interest now," Teyla pointed out. "And if so, this world will no longer be safe for anyone. But I will speak to Colonel Sheppard."

"I'd appreciate it."

They had reached the entrance to the installation, and Teyla saw the medic brace himself as he stepped out onto the brightly-lit pavement. John was nowhere in sight, but Elizabeth was still talking to Alabaster, who had been joined by Guide. *Osir*'s hatch was closed, the crew presumably readying the ship for takeoff; the hatches on *Mirelies* and *Durant* were still open, but there were no Travelers in sight. She wondered for a moment where Ford and his wife had gone, and guessed they were on one of the other ships, or perhaps with John. Out of the corner of her eyes, she saw Dekaas's face for once unguarded, watching the Wraith with a mix of longing and regret, and she touched his sleeve.

"Do you wish to speak to them? You said you once knew Guide."

"It was a long time ago, and that queen is dead. I remember Alabaster as a child at her mother's knee. But, yes, I would like to speak to them, if I may." Dekaas gave her a wry smile. "If only to annoy Guide."

"I see no harm in it." Teyla glanced around again — still no Travelers in sight, and surely even if one saw them speaking to the Wraith, it would not betray Dekaas's past — and started toward the Wraith, opening her mind to them. *Guide. There is one who wishes speech with you.*

Guide turned, and she felt the surge of emotions as he recognized the man at her side, shock, surprise, something between displeasure and nostalgia. She caught the briefest glimpse of another Wraith, slender and elegant, and then Guide had himself under control again. *Seeker's — pet.*

"This is Dekaas," Teyla said aloud, and, looking sideways, saw tears in Dekaas's eyes. He had seen what she had seen, she realized; he had the Gift, the same ability to read the Wraith telepathy.

"Dekaas?" Alabaster said, surprise changing to uncomplicated pleasure.

Dekaas bowed sharply, the gesture encompassing both of them. "Lady."

I might have known he'd survive, Guide said.

I was sure you would, Dekaas answered. His tone was oddly uninflected, as though he hadn't used his Gift in a very long time, but his meaning was clear.

Guide showed his teeth in what Teyla thought was genuine amusement. *You are just as I remember.*

Dekaas bowed again. *Thank you.*

Elizabeth looked from one to the other, obviously aware that there was a conversation going on that she couldn't follow. "This — you were on Alabaster's hive?"

"Her mother's," Dekaas answered. "Though I remember the Lady when she was young."

"As I remember you," Alabaster said. "Should you wish — I would welcome you to return to us, on my hive."

My Queen, Guide began, and Alabaster stopped him with a look.

The Fair One would find him useful, I think. And he is our responsibility.

Pets, Teyla thought. Useful beasts. Creatures to be taken in by responsible persons. From Dekaas's expression, he could perceive the same nuances in Alabaster's mental voice, and yet she could feel his longing as well.

"Dekaas!"

Teyla turned, to see Lesko at the bottom of *Durant's* ramp.

"Dekaas, what the hell —?" Lesko stopped abruptly, his expression changing, and Dekaas's eyes flickered closed for an instant. "So it's true. I never would have believed it."

Dekaas straightened his back, his face setting into a cold mask. "I'm still myself."

"You're a worshipper." Lesko shook his head. "We trusted you."

"And when was that trust misplaced?" Elizabeth asked, her voice deceptively mild.

"Elizabeth." Dekaas shook his head. "It's not worth it." He looked back at Alabaster. "I will come with you, Lady. With thanks."

"You won't set foot on *Durant* again," Lesko said.

"There's nothing there I need," Dekaas said. "Keep the equipment — call it payment for my passage all these years. I will go with Alabaster."

Lesko looked startled, as though he'd expected protests, pleading. Or perhaps, Teyla thought, he'd just realized that he'd rid himself of his only doctor. "Very well," she said aloud.

"Tell me about the off world teams," Lorne said. He leaned back in his chair, and rubbed at the stubble on his chin. It had been too long since he'd slept, and there wasn't much chance of rest any time soon. He put that thought aside, and concentrated on the matter at hand. At least this was something useful he could do, instead of worrying about whether or not the *alflageolis* had mutated into something worse. "Banks?"

"At last check-in, everyone reported no changes, except Dr. Hue on PRG-881." There were dark shadows under Banks' eyes, and her hair hung lank in its loose tail. "She reports her party has evacuated to Sateda since they didn't come prepared for arctic camping. It's deep winter on PRG-881. Peters and Ramirez report that they've established camps, and are going to wait it out. Peters had planned a two-night stay anyway, and Ramirez — it was supposed to be a quick in and out to get her samples, but she always comes prepared to stay a while. And of course Colonel Sheppard's team has reported all well. Dr. Parrish's group, that's PGX-239, says the plants have stopped shooting at them, but the DHD is still out of commission. They're waiting for the system to re-set or for us to call off the quarantine."

"Right," Lorne said. Four of the five were fine, but the fifth... Plants that fired energy bolts and a damaged DHD were definitely major problems, but he didn't want to bring them back here when there was a chance the *alflageolis* would kill them all anyway. At least Ronon's team didn't seem to be in immediate danger. "When are we scheduled to check with them again?"

Banks glanced at her watch. "About twenty minutes, sir."

"I want to talk to them myself," Lorne said. "In the meantime, how are we doing for food?"

"We're all right, sir." That was Captain Kudela, who had taken charge of supplies after he'd been stuck in the gate room on his way back from PDG-313. "There are enough MREs in the jumper bay to last all of us for four days, and I've been talking to Sergeant

Pollard and Dr. Wu about ways to get more supplies through the quarantine if necessary. The biggest problem right now is that we have to keep the contaminated trash, but hopefully the scientists will fix that."

The biggest problem was the looming mutation, changing harmless bacteria into something that would kill everyone on Atlantis. Lorne swallowed the words, knowing he needed to present a positive front. If there was no cure, Ronon's team would be better off waiting for the DHD to reset and going to Sateda or just about anywhere else. But that was the absolute worst-case scenario, he told himself. Beckett was bound to find a solution. "All right, that's it — unless either of you has anything to raise?"

Banks and Kudela exchanged glances, and Kudela said, "No, sir."

"I'll let you know when we're about to call PGX-239," Banks said, and let herself out of the office, Kudela at her heels.

Left to himself, Lorne took another swallow of his cooling coffee — too cold, really, but he wasn't going to waste any. The scientists are doing their jobs, he told himself. Even the Wraith — even Ember is doing his part. They're going to find an answer. He leaned back in his chair, closing his eyes. He'd rest, just for a minute, and then get on with his day.

A knock woke him, and he jerked awake to see Banks peering sheepishly around the edge of the door. "Sorry, Major," she said, "but you said you wanted to talk to Ronon."

"Right." Lorne pressed the heels of his hands into his eye sockets until he saw sparks, then hauled himself out of his chair. "On my way."

The Stargate shimmered blue against the multi-colored glass. Lorne ignored it, focusing instead on the screen at Banks's station. "Ronon."

"Major." The image was flecked with static. Banks frowned and touched keys, and it steadied again.

"What's your situation?"

In the screen, Ronon shrugged. "We've figured out how to keep the plants from shooting at us, but we've got another problem. We're about five hours from sunset, and Captain Aulich says we're going to get a line of strong storms passing over us at that point. We don't have any decent shelter here, and we can't get away from the gate without running into more of the plants."

"How bad do these storms look?"

"She says they're strong. Lots of lightning."

Lorne swallowed a curse. "And there's no shelter at all?"

Ronon shrugged again. "We're working on a dugout in the side of the hill, but it's not going to be much good against a thunderstorm. It'll keep the rain off — mostly — but that's about it."

"We've run into a bigger problem," Lorne said. "There's a real possibility that this bacteria is going to mutate into something that's fatal to humans. I don't want to bring you through unless there's no other choice."

"Ok." Ronon paused. "Is there any chance you'll have the problem solved before our sunset?"

"We're working on it," Lorne said, and thought from Ronon's expression that he understood what was really being said.

"We should be fine until the storms hit," Ronon said. "And if we don't get hit directly, we should be able to hang on."

"Understood," Lorne said. "If you come back here, and we don't get this resolved — it's a death sentence."

Ronon nodded.

"I'm hoping it won't come to that," Lorne said, and tried not to see the doubt in Ronon's eyes. "Atlantis out." He tapped his fingers on the nearest console, trying to juggle the pieces into a new shape, but nothing seemed to fit. He scowled, and touched his radio. "Dr. Zelenka. Can I have a word?"

The little scientist appeared a few moments later, his hair disordered as though he'd been tugging on it. He looked dead tired, like everyone caught in the quarantine zone, his skin pasty and the skin under his eyes swollen and heavy. "Yes? Is it important?"

"Yeah. You heard about the problems on PGX-239?"

Zelenka paused. "I thought they were to evacuate to Sateda?"

"There's a problem with the DHD." Lorne ran down the situation, watching Zelenka's expression change from annoyed to concerned. "What I want to know is, is there anything we can do for them from here?"

Zelenka jammed his fingers into his hair, disarranging it even further. "Are they sure it's a software problem? Not the DHD itself?"

"They're pretty convinced."

"Who is the technician?"

"Sergeant Joseph. Claire Joseph. She was on SG-5 and then a gate tech at the SGC before she was assigned here."

"I know her." Zelenka nodded. "She knows her business. If she says there's nothing wrong with the DHD itself, I believe her. And that — if it's not a cracked crystal, a bad connection, something physical like that, there's not much we can do. Not only did the Ancients do everything they could to make the programming inaccessible — if in fact it's really a program as we understand programming, and not something far more complex — but we have never unraveled much more than the addressing system. It's not as though I could somehow go through and reinstall the dialing program."

"Ok." Lorne hadn't really expected any better. Not even Carter had actually reprogrammed the system, just used it to transmit the codes that destroyed the Replicators. "Joseph tells me the system will reboot automatically at some point. Is there any way we can trigger that from here? Make it happen sooner?"

"Maybe? I will look into it, though I'm needed in the lab — but at least this is something that is actually in my field." Zelenka gave a wry smile. "But I'm not hopeful."

"Could McKay do it?" Lorne winced, wishing he'd been more tactful, but Zelenka didn't seem offended.

"Rodney is a genius. If anyone could, it would be him. I would ask him, the next time they call in. The problem is that this is a sealed system. We have no access to the workings of what we are calling the programming, and we have never been able to find that access except once on Datara."

"Do what you can," Lorne said, and to his embarrassment, his voice cracked. "We've got six people we need to bring home."

"I will do my best," Zelenka answered, and turned away.

Parrish sprawled full length in the grass of the hill, grateful for the break. His arm was burning in spite of the field dressing — it would probably hurt less if he hadn't spent so much time cutting branches from the conifers, and then figuring out how to harvest the largest leaves from the succulents without setting off the plants' offensive reflex. He was actually quite pleased that they'd managed to get enough of the big leaves to make a roof for Ronon's low-lying shelter without triggering more than a couple of bolts. And it was pretty ingenious how Ronon had shaved pointy slivers from the chunks of bark so that he and Samara could use them as improvised nails to fasten the leaves to each other and to the frame in overlapping "shingles." If it was just rain they had to worry about, he'd have given them pretty good odds, not just of surviving, but of surviving in a certain amount of comfort.

The Stargate closed again, and he watched Ronon walk away from the DHD. It didn't look as though they'd be leaving any time soon, and that was the real problem. He sat up and reached for his water bottle, pulling out the survival filter that he carried and sucking the water through it like a straw. It had an odd, not unpleasant taste, as though it were colder than it actually was, but he put the bottle aside after the first few swallows. The stream would probably fill overnight, if Aulich was right about the oncoming weather, but just in case there was no point in being wasteful. In the west, the sun was sinking into a rising bank of cloud, its disk glowing cherry-red, like molten iron. Surely the people on Atlantis would get this whatever-it-was under control before the storms got here.

From his vantage point on the hillside, the patch of succulents seemed to extend for several hundred meters, maybe even a thousand meters, the plants growing larger and blending into a thicker jungle. He took out his binoculars and scanned slowly along the line. Yes, it looked as though there were another, larger succulent further away; it also had a central pod, but its leaves grew in pairs rather than a staggered spiral. The pod itself was different, too, standing further out of the nest of leaves, and its top was more pointed. Some of them were more than a meter tall, a few perhaps as much as two meters, though it was hard to judge size at this distance. But that made them the tallest objects in the area by some considerable margin, except for the Stargate itself, and that meant that those pointed pods were more likely than not to attract the lightning.

He frowned, a vague idea taking shape, but before he could put it together, Ronon called his name. "Dr. Parrish! All of you! We need to talk."

Parrish pushed himself to his feet and started down the hill, falling in with the others as they gathered around the stack of meteorological equipment. Ronon's face was grim, and Parrish felt a thread of fear worm its way down his spine. "What's up?"

"Bad news," Ronon answered. "The problems on Atlantis are worse than they thought. Apparently this bug is going to mutate into something lethal — not right away, they've got some time, but they really don't want anybody coming through the gate now."

There was an instant of silence, and then a babble of questions, but Parrish barely heard them. That was bad news, all right, pretty much the worst he'd heard in all the time he'd been on Atlantis. If that was the case, then no, there was no way they should risk going back, no matter how bad the weather got. They'd have to hope that either the Stargate reset itself or the people on Atlantis found a cure. He shivered in spite of the sunlight. That was the joker in the pack, the fear of some deadly disease that could run like wildfire through an unprotected population. That had happened twice already on Atlantis; each time, the medical staff had beaten the bugs, but it had been too close for comfort. The second time, the disease had destroyed memories, and only the fact that Teyla and Ronon had each had kirsan fever as children had bought them a chance to save the city. But they had found a cure both times, he reminded himself. The medical staff was good — was the best in Pegasus. They'd find an answer.

CHAPTER NINE

THE CAR from Peterson Air Force Base pulled up at the Cheyenne Mountain gate, and Richard Woolsey saw the airman on duty come to attention when he recognized General O'Neill in the backseat. It only took a moment for them to be waved through.

"Convenient to hitch a ride with me, huh?" O'Neill asked as he leaned back. "First class service all the way from DC."

"Yes," Woolsey said. It had definitely registered that all of the usual little irritations of traveling as the IOA's representative had somehow been whisked away when traveling with O'Neill instead. Not only were three stars magic, but everybody liked O'Neill. He seemed to know everybody in the Air Force. Or maybe it was just everybody in the Air Force in Colorado. Or maybe it was that everybody in the Air Force wanted to claim that they knew O'Neill.

General Landry was waiting for them in the conference room on level 26, beside the vast windows that looked out on the Stargate. He looked pleased to see O'Neill – less so to see Woolsey.

"I brought a friend," O'Neill said jauntily. He was kidding – probably. Or maybe he was reminding Landry that Woolsey was supposed to be on their side, and that he had been when the chips were down and Atlantis was stuck on Earth.

"Mr. Woolsey," Landry said, shaking hands. "Good to see you."

"It's good to see you too," Woolsey said. And because he was concerned, he cut the rest of the pleasantries. "Any word from Atlantis on this latest problem? The bacterial – or is it viral – contamination?" He of all people didn't envy the folks who were working on the problem. An alien infestation was bad news, and potentially terrible news, if this latest report about potential mutation was accurate. Part of him wished he were there, taking reports from Beckett and Zelenka, trying to work the problem himself rather than being stuck here.

"Yes, any word on our little infection?" O'Neill asked. He was probably as worried as Woolsey, and he probably wished he were in the field just as much. And that was something to bring Woolsey up short – he wished he were in the field as much as O'Neill did.

Before Landry could reply there was the hooting of an alarm and the sound of the gate beginning to dial. Instead of replying to O'Neill, Landry picked up the phone and pressed a button, no doubt calling down to the control room below. He glanced up. "It's Atlantis. Come down and you can talk to Major Lorne yourself."

"On my way," O'Neill said, no humor in his voice now as he led the way quickly down the metal staircase. Woolsey followed.

The monitor below lit with a close up of Major Lorne's face. "Major, what's the situation?" O'Neill asked.

If Lorne was surprised to see O'Neill instead of Landry, he didn't let it show. "Dr. Beckett says we're making good progress on finding a formula that will kill this thing, sir," he said. "Their models are looking promising, but he wants to tweak it to achieve a higher kill rate before we use it."

O'Neill nodded. "And our off-world teams?"

"Sitting tight. Ronon's team is having some weather-related trouble, and they may have to come back if it gets too hairy. We're trying not to do that for obvious reasons, but if we have to, we will."

"Understood," O'Neill said.

"Ronon has good judgment," Woolsey said. "He'll make the right call."

"Is that you, Mr. Woolsey?" Lorne asked.

Woolsey moved into camera range. "Yes. Good to see you, Major. I have every confidence you'll get this thing worked out." And there was a time he wouldn't have said that. But that was before he'd known Atlantis so well.

Lorne nodded, the corners of his eyes crinkling. "There's something else important. Dr. Weir is alive."

"What?" O'Neill said.

Woolsey drew a deep breath. "It was true then. The rumors Dr. McKay wanted to follow. It didn't seem possible." Improbable, impossible, wishful thinking – and yet. His throat closed. And yet.

"Dr. Weir was on Sateda," Lorne said. "We found her. She walked right up and said, 'Major Lorne, it's good to see you.' It's her."

"Are you certain?" Woolsey asked.

"How did she get there?" O'Neill asked at the same time.

"She had been Ascended," Lorne said. "Apparently she got kicked out for helping us."

"As Dr. McKay theorized," Woolsey said. He was proud his voice didn't shake a bit.

O'Neill nodded. "Where is she now?"

"Still off-world with the team because of the quarantine. Also we've put our protocols for Formerly Ascended Personnel into effect."

"We have protocols for Formerly Ascended Personnel?" Woolsey blurted. "Really?"

"General O'Neill wrote them," Lorne said.

"First, find them some clothes," O'Neill said.

"Dr. Weir had already taken care of that herself," Major Lorne said. "But per protocol she is remaining off-site until we have done a complete battery of tests."

"You've seen her." Woolsey knew Lorne had already said he had, but he had to ask again. To confirm. To be sure, as sure as he could be until he saw her himself.

Lorne nodded. "Yes."

"And?" O'Neill prompted.

"I think she's Dr. Weir." Lorne's voice was firm. "And Dr. Jackson thought so too. He was ascended himself."

"If Daniel thought she checked out, that's good enough for me." O'Neill nodded. "Ok. Run the tests as soon as you can. And I'd like to talk to her as soon as possible."

"As soon as we get this quarantine situation cleared up," Major Lorne said. "We'll have Dr. Beckett go out and run the tests."

Or they could send someone via spaceship from Earth if Atlantis fell to the infection, but there was no need to say that. There were a few more instructions exchanged, and Lorne disconnected from his end. Woolsey looked at O'Neill in amazement as the wormhole disengaged. "Dr. Weir," he said. "I don't believe it."

O'Neill's eyes were alight as he clapped Woolsey on the shoulder. "Believe it. Stranger things have happened."

Radek leaned against the edge of the table, watching as Ember touched keys, his claws loud on the metal. In the screen, the symbols that represented the bacteria and the bacteriophage faded and reformed.

"Aye, that's better," Beckett said, from the speaker, and Ember bared teeth.

"I'm not sure it's enough," Sindye said, frowning at her own results. "I still show nearly ten percent survival rate."

The light changed, and Radek looked over his shoulder to see Lorne standing in the doorway. Lorne beckoned, and Radek came to join him, wishing he knew more about experimental biology.

"How's it going, Doc?"

"Progress, I think." Radek shrugged. "How's Airman Salawi?"

"Sound asleep, but unharmed," Lorne answered. "She'll get a medal for that, once I figure out how to recommend it."

"I expect that this does not come up so often," Radek agreed.

"Well, you know how it goes, Doc. It's all uncharted territory here." Lorne sobered quickly. "When you say progress —?"

"I mean it is going fairly well," Radek said. "They have not found the exact compound they wish to use, but they think they are close. And the disinfectant seems to have slowed the bacteria's effects considerably."

"Yeah. That's what I thought — things didn't seem to be falling apart quite so quickly — only I didn't want to mention it for fear of jinxing things." Lorne paused. "Why can't we just keep spraying it around? Isn't it killing the stuff?"

"It kills much of it, and weakens the rest," Radek answered. "Understand, I'm not a biologist, but that's what both Beckett and Ember say. The problem is, anything it doesn't kill will still mutate. And we will have the same problem."

"And we can't risk spreading it here in Pegasus or, worse, back to Earth," Lorne said. "So we're stuck with a time bomb until they find something that'll destroy it completely."

"Pretty much so, yes."

Lorne jerked his head toward the door. "That wasn't the only thing I wanted to ask. If you don't mind, Doc?"

Radek followed warily, wondering what new disaster was looming. "Yes? I will be needed —"

"Ember. He wasn't — you know, faking it? Because Salawi doesn't seem all that hurt."

And why am I the one who has to defend the Wraith? Radek shook his head. "I don't think so. He was — I had noticed he was not right. Perhaps he was just being careful?"

"I guess." Lorne didn't sound convinced, and Radek didn't really blame him. Dealing with the Wraith was... confusing. For everyone.

"I must get back," he said, and Lorne nodded.

"Keep me posted, Doc."

"Of course." Radek turned back into the lab just as Sindye straightened from her screen. A moment later, Ember did the same, flexing his fingers, and Radek looked form one to the other. "Results?"

"The next test is running," Sindye answered, "and the simulation."

"It looks promising," Ember said. "But if it works — I am considering the best way to deliver it to all the affected areas."

"You said it had to be done all at once," Radek said.

Ember nodded. "That is best. Then there is no chance of anything being overlooked, or of anything escaping."

"Then it can't be applied as a liquid or even as a spray," Radek said.

"An aerosol?" Sindye asked.

"Through the ventilation system?" Radek considered that. It might work, and it would certainly spread the compound widely enough. "We would need to be sure it wouldn't be so heavy that it damaged exposed equipment."

"Or affected people's breathing," Sindye said. "But at the same time, it would need to be heavy enough to coat everything, and do it evenly."

"I think we can create an aerosol that meets those criteria," Ember said thoughtfully. "A fine mist, very like the mists that hydrate our ships — yes, I think we can do that with this compound. It will leave a residue, but it will be almost intangible."

"Just creating an aerosol doesn't mean that it will reach everywhere at the same time," Sindye said.

"No, certainly not," Radek said. "But if we use the ventilation system, and give it a push — it will be very close." He looked at Ember. "Will that be enough?"

The Wraith considered. "Yes, I think — Yes. It should be."

So it would have to be in the ventilators. Radek reached for his laptop, wincing at the roughness of the plastic case. If he'd needed a reminder that the *alflageolis* had merely been slowed, not stopped, that would have been more than enough. He put that aside, and called up the plans of the local ventilation systems, angling the screen so that Ember couldn't see. The Wraith bared teeth in what might have been wry amusement, but did not pursue the question. There were three key junctions, Radek saw, three places where an injection of aerosol would spread quickly and evenly throughout the city. Two were easily accessible from within the quarantine area; the third could be reached, but it would be easier to get to the junction from an access passage on the tower's third level. They would have to reprogram the city's protocols to allow the aerosol to spread without Atlantis's automatic defenses attempting to scrub it out of the air, but he thought he could manage that. McKay would do it more quickly, of course, and possibly better — but McKay wasn't here. It was his job.

"What do we have that we can adapt to produce the aerosol?" he asked.

"Here?" Sindye looked momentarily nonplused. "I don't know, I'll have to take an inventory."

"If you would, please." Radek reached for a stool, setting the laptop on the console in front of him, and touched keys to enter the maintenance subroutines. If he could piggy-back on one of the scrubber routines, that should surely allow him to tag the aerosol as harmless... He scrolled through the system, found the section he wanted, and brought it to the foregrounded window. If he altered these parameters, just here, added an exception? He shook his head, annoyed at himself for failing to see the obvious. That would open the system to other outside hazards, ones that he wanted the system to continue to reject. Of course, he would be removing the patch as soon as it had worked, but — it would be better not to take the chance at all. There was bound to be another way.

He flipped back to the main window, began scrolling again through the list of system routines. If not maintenance, what? The health screens were unlikely to be helpful, designed as they were to keep things out rather than to introduce them, and he scanned down the rest of the list without finding anything more promising. He scrolled up again, more slowly, making himself pay attention to each section heading, but saw nothing until he reached the health screens again. He studied them more carefully, and touched the keys that opened up the test subroutines. Perhaps he could adjust one of the system tests to let him release the aerosol. He could worry about the push later.

But, no, there was a secondary test procedure that was intended to send a blast of air throughout the ventilators. If he could adapt that, disable the filters for the duration of the test — yes, that would be possible with only a minor revision of the code. He typed the new commands into the simulator, watched as the ventilation pumped a solid volume of air through the system. That part would work, though he would need to refine the code a little. And if they could get the aerosols into position, once they had the final compound —

And that was the trick, of course: they had to have a compound that would actually destroy the *alflageolis* once and for all. He saved his work and closed the laptop, then came to stand at Ember's shoulder. "Any luck?"

"The analysis is nearly finished." Ember glared at the screen as though he could force it to produce results more quickly. "It is… promising. I don't want to say more."

Were the Wraith superstitious, Radek wondered. Before he could say anything, he heard Sindye swear. "Trouble?"

"Yeah." She straightened from the sample boxes where they were monitoring the degradation. "I don't like to say it, but I think our disinfectant is losing its effect."

Radek swore in turn, and Ember swung around, moving for the first time at his full Wraith speed. He checked himself with an effort, and bent over the boxes, hissing softly.

"I think you're right. And — its DNA is changing."

"So what do we do?" Radek asked. "I have a way to disperse the aerosol, but it is not yet made, nor do we have the dispensers."

"We have some time," Ember said. He had himself under control again. "This is not yet out of control, just beginning to grow again. We have time."

"Enough time?" Radek couldn't stop himself from asking, and was unsurprised when the Wraith shrugged.

"Let us hope so."

Osir was the first to lift, rising into the now-lightening sky with a whine of engines. John watched from inside the jumper, Elizabeth and Dekaas standing silent beside him. Teyla had returned to the installation to check on Rodney and Daniel, which was probably a smart thing to do, but he missed both her common sense and her ability to talk to the Wraith. Though from what she had said, Dekaas also had the Gift. Presumably he could translate if necessary, though John wasn't sure if he ought to trust a returning Wraith worshipper. Pet. Whatever. Neither one seemed like a term he'd choose if it was him, but he couldn't think of anything better.

The jumper's screens showed that *Osir* had reached orbit, the hiveship staying well out of range, and he toggled the jumper's radio. "*Mirilies*. You're go for launch."

"Thanks," Yoran said, his voice crackling in the speakers, and a moment later *Mirilies* rose from the pavement, dust whipping in sudden spirals as the antigravity took hold. It shot into the sky, faster than *Osir*, and John checked the jumper's screens again.

"I show both *Osir* and *Mirilies* in orbit," he said, on the channel they had agreed to share. "Guide, your cruiser may land."

He saw flecks of red as *Durant*'s guns went hot, but the Wraith had agreed to allow that — mostly, John thought, because there wasn't much *Durant*'s weapons could do if the Wraith decided to attack. He saw the dot that was the cruiser change course, angling well away from the two Traveler ships, and then drop into the atmosphere. They could all see it then, a streak of fire and smoke high in the twilight sky, and then at last hovering at the end of the field as agreed. It was too big for the landing area, but the ground beyond it to the north was level enough, and the Wraith pilot brought it gently to a stop.

John glanced over his shoulder. "Ok. What happens next?"

"In two hours, the hive can break orbit," Elizabeth answered. "I suspect it may take a bit longer than that, but I don't think that's a problem. Two hours after they're gone, *Durant* can leave. And then — we need to decide what to do with Dis."

"I don't want to bring him to Atlantis," John said. "Too risky."

"I agree." Elizabeth rested her folded arms on the back of the empty co-pilot's chair. "I wonder... It's a real problem for them, and they're not going to stop hunting until they find a way to get Ran back."

"I don't know that that's our problem," John said.

"Well, it's likely to remain mine," Elizabeth said, with a wry smile, and John nodded.

"Ok, yeah. We can't take him back to Atlantis, we can't keep him prisoner here — and I really don't think it's a good idea to hand him that Vanir scout we found and send him on his way. Got any better ideas?"

"I'm thinking," Elizabeth said. "It's possible..." She shook her head. "Let me think about it some more, please."

"Ok," John said again. "But we don't have a lot of time."

"Understood."

The radio hissed, and Guide's voice sounded in the speakers. "Sheppard. Our cruiser has landed. We will be exchanging some of our people, and then returning them to the hive with our queen. If anyone is coming with us, they should be ready."

John looked over his shoulder at Dekaas. "That would be you."

The medic nodded.

"Copy that," John said. "He'll be ready." He glanced back again. "As long as you're sure you want to. You can still back out."

"And do what?" Dekaas smiled. "My bridges are burned. And — this is what I want."

John swallowed the first two things that came to mind. "Whatever you say. But if you decide differently —"

"Thanks," Dekaas said. "I appreciate that."

"I want to talk to Daniel," Elizabeth said abruptly. "And I think Dekaas should take another look at Dis while we have him."

"Go ahead," John said. It was like old times, like it had been at the beginning of the mission, and though he knew he probably shouldn't let himself fall back into the old habits, it was almost impossible not to. This was Elizabeth, unmistakably herself and unmistakably unharmed — the SGC had trusted Jackson twice after he'd been ascended; they could trust Elizabeth Weir. "Tell Rodney I want to talk to him."

"I'll send him back," Elizabeth said, and led Dekaas down the ramp. As they crossed the pavement, someone appeared in *Durant's* hatch, waving. John couldn't hear the words, but both Elizabeth and the medic paused, and a teenage girl came running down the ramp, a bulging satchel banging at her hip. She said something more, and Dekaas took the satchel. He slung it over his shoulder, and the girl ran back up the ramp. Dekaas gave another of his wry smiles and he and Elizabeth disappeared into the installation. And surely that was a good sign, too, John thought. Dekaas had been prepared to walk away with nothing, but at least someone on *Durant* didn't think that was fair. Both Teyla and Elizabeth believed in those little victories.

He looked back at his controls, considering his options. He needed to find out what was happening on Atlantis — surely they had the bacteria under control by now — and at his thought, symbols flickered across the communications display. A few moments later, the screen lit, and Lorne looked out at him. He looked like hell, badly shaved and puffy-eyed, and John frowned.

"Major. What's your status?"

"Making progress, sir." Lorne looked distinctly wary.

"Have you got the thing knocked down?" John asked.

Lorne sighed. "Dr. Zelenka has figured out a way to disperse an aerosolized compound throughout the quarantine area, which should take out the *alflageolis*. Dr. Beckett and the others are still working on the necessary compound."

John considered that for a minute. "So you've figure out how to kill it, except you don't have anything to kill it with?"

"Pretty much, sir." Lorne paused. "Dr. Beckett is confident they'll have a compound that's at least 95 percent effective."

"Except somebody doesn't think that's going to be enough."

"I think everyone would like it to be closer to one hundred percent," Lorne said carefully.

John bit his lip. There was no point in blaming Lorne, who was doing everything he could to get the outbreak under control, and who wasn't a scientist in the first place. "Does anyone have an estimate of how long it's likely to take?"

"Hours rather than days," Lorne said. It sounded as though he was trying hard to be optimistic about that. "And the *alflageolis* is still a long way from turning into a killer. But no one's willing to be more precise than that."

"Ok." John tapped his fingers on the console. "What about the teams that were off-world — Parrish's team? Ronon get through all right?"

"Ah. Yes, sir, Ronon joined them, and it turns out that what looked like an attack was actually a local plant that apparently fires energy bolts as a defense mechanism."

"Par for the course," John said, after a moment. "Are they going to stay, or evacuate to Sateda?"

There was another little pause, and then Lorne said, reluctantly, "Actually, sir, they've run into a problem. One of the plant's energy bolts clipped the DHD and now it will only dial Atlantis."

"That sounds like kind of a significant problem, Major. Especially if those plants are shooting at them."

"Apparently the plants are no longer shooting in their direction," Lorne said. "But there's another problem. There's a line of bad storms moving toward them — something to do with the temperature differential between day and night. I don't want to bring them through unless their lives are at serious risk."

Great, John thought. Just great. And if it was me, I'd rather take my chances with a storm than with some weird disease. "Do they know what's wrong with the DHD?"

"Sort of?" Lorne paused, marshaling his thoughts. "It doesn't seem to be a problem with the device itself — none of the crystals are cracked or anything like that. It's more as though the bolt scrambled the software. Zelenka tells me that the system will re-set on its own, but nobody knows when."

Well, that was better than it could have been, John thought. There were actually some decent options there. "I'll talk to McKay, see if he's got any ideas. Don't bring them back unless there's no other choice, Major."

"Yes sir," Lorne said. "Colonel, is there anything more on Dr. Weir?"

"It's definitely her, and she's definitely not a Replicator." John grinned in spite of himself, and saw the same smile spread across Lorne's tired face. "And I've got more good news. We've found Lieutenant Ford."

"What?" Lorne blinked, and his grin widened. "Ford's alive?"

"Yep." John quickly ran down the events of the last few hours, and saw Lorne shake his head.

"Wow. Sir, that's excellent news. Alive and well?"

"We've made a deal with the Wraith to take him back to Earth," John said. "The only question is how we're going to do it, and what we're going to do with Dis while we do it — that's the Vanir, Major."

"Are we going to be able to take him back, sir?" Lorne asked.

"We'd better be." John heard the edge in his own voice, and made himself relax. "He was missing in action, and was taken in by local friendlies and got stranded there. That ought to be enough for the SGC."

"Yes, sir." Lorne nodded. "You want me to pass the word to General Landry?"

"That'd be a help," John answered. "Tell them — well, I don't know when we'll be arriving, but they can be expecting him. And a wife and child."

"I'll tell them that." Lorne shook his head, the smile breaking out again. "Damn good news."

"Yeah." John matched the smile. "Yeah, it is."

Elizabeth made her way back to the Vanir infirmary, Dekaas trailing silently in her wake. Teyla had opened another MRE and was methodically assembling its components into a meal while Daniel sat on one of the infirmary platforms, his pistol ready to hand. Dis seemed not to have moved from when she had left, still sitting almost primly on the edge of its platform, and Dekaas frowned.

"If you'll allow me to look you over," he said, and the Vanir turned the full force of its stare on him.

"If you wish."

"Thank you." Dekaas moved closer, running his fingers cautiously over Dis's scalp, and then testing pulse and respiration.

"No trouble?" Daniel asked, and Elizabeth shook her head.

"The first two Traveler ships have left. The Wraith cruiser has landed, and they're swapping crews between it and the scout that landed first."

"I expect Guide and Alabaster are arguing about who will stay behind, and who will go," Teyla said, with a small, rather cat-like smile. Elizabeth glanced at Dekaas, and saw a similar smile flicker across his face: telepathic communication, or did they simply both have the same opinion of the Wraith in question? "Are you hungry? There are more MREs."

"Yes, thanks," Elizabeth said, abruptly aware that she was, in fact, quite hungry. She tore open the bag and began putting together the meal, wolfing down the cheese and crackers while the chili-mac heated.

"Any idea what Sheppard plans to do about Dis?" Daniel asked.

Elizabeth shook her head. "The Colonel hasn't said."

"You would be best advised to let me go," Dis said.

"Would you agree to stop trying to make Ran unascend?" Elizabeth asked, and the Vanir shook its head.

"We cannot. We have been through this before. I am prepared to agree not to pursue you further, however."

"Sorry," Eliabeth said. "No deal."

"You cannot stop us. Nor, I think, do you wish to see my people driven to extinction." Dis tipped its head to one side, and Dekaas retreated, seating himself beside Teyla.

"I'm not entirely sure I'd have a problem with that," Daniel said. "Your presence in this galaxy has hardly been an unmitigated good."

"I also do not see why we should help you," Teyla said.

"I am not asking for help," Dis answered. "I am merely suggesting that you release me."

"Well, I for one might consider releasing you," Daniel said, "or at least encouraging Colonel Sheppard and Dr. Weir to release you, if you turned over the unascension device to us. It wasn't yours anyway."

"I do not think you would be wise to raise the question of original ownership," Dis pointed out. "You did not build Atlantis, either."

"We are the descendants of the Ancestors," Teyla said heavily, "and that has its burdens as well as its benefits."

Elizabeth said, "What would you consider reasonable, Dis?"

Dis blinked slowly again. "We must have Ran's genetic material. We must have her eggs, or our species will die. We are not prepared to sacrifice ourselves needlessly. Our lives and our worth have not ended, though we are damaged. I am prepared to refrain from studying you, as the price of my release, but I cannot offer more."

"There are other alternatives," Daniel said, with a meaningful smile, and Elizabeth sighed.

"We can't just kill him."

"He's tried to kill us," Daniel pointed out.

"He was trying to examine an unascended person," Elizabeth said, reluctantly.

"Which seems to have involved killing you, or at the very least some extremely questionable medical examinations," Daniel answered. "Not to mention that they invaded Atlantis and nearly got both me and McKay killed. And nearly destroyed all the Stargates in the Pegasus Galaxy, which would have been a disaster of monumental proportions."

"That," Dis said, "was the fault of the Attero Device, not us. We did not build a flawed machine."

"Maybe not, but you sure didn't care what happened." Daniel glared at the Vanir over the top of his glasses.

"And again, I must agree with you," Teyla said, sounding faintly surprised.

"We cannot simply kill him," Elizabeth repeated firmly. Though what they should do with him — what they could do with him... She turned her attention to the remains of her meal, hoping that she could come up with something.

Rodney left Elizabeth and Daniel to argue with the Vanir while Teyla watched it as though debating how much trouble it would be simply to kill it now, and made his way back out through the installation. The landing field was mostly empty now, just the Wraith cruiser with a pair of blades standing guard at the base of its ramp, matched by *Durant* and its guards waiting just inside the hatchway. The jumper was sitting where they had left it, the rear ramp lowered and the lights on inside the cabin. He could just make out Sheppard in the pilot's seat, and at that moment Sheppard looked up and waved impatiently for him to hurry. Rodney sighed, and started up the ramp.

"Elizabeth said you wanted me."

"Yeah. Lorne says they've got a problem with the DHD on PGX-239."

Rodney slouched in the co-pilot's seat in the jumper's cockpit, dividing his glare equally between Sheppard and the controls while Sheppard ran down the problem in depth. It was fully in the planet's day— probably getting close to noon — but the heavy twilight made him feel suddenly vulnerable. The windows opaqued themselves in response, and Sheppard jumped.

"Hey. You might give me some warning."

"I don't like the idea of someone shooting in at us,"Rodney said.

"Nobody on this planet has anything that'll punch through Ancient glass."

"Then let's say I don't like people watching me." Rodney turned the full force of his glare on Sheppard, who ignored it. "You realize that this is impossible, don't you?"

"Reprogramming the DHD?" Sheppard gave an elaborate shrug. "I assumed that was why Lorne wanted me to ask you."

"I admit that I've made something of a career of doing the apparently-impossible, and usually stretching the limits of our theoretical knowledge in the process —"

"You see?"

"But this — and you don't know how much it pains me to say it — this really is impossible."

"C'mon."

"No, listen. Just listen." Rodney took a deep breath, controlling the irritation that he knew was born of frustration at being unable to help. "What Lorne's calling 'software' — you know it really isn't any such thing, right? We don't really know what it is, and we don't have any real handle on how it works. We've been able to make the entire Stargate system do things for us —" Or at least Sam Carter has. "— but we've never actually been able to access the 'program' that makes it all go. Not 'we haven't figured it out,' but 'we haven't ever seen it.' Haven't gotten our hands on it. We don't know anything about it. We've never been able to take apart a DHD and read whatever it is that's inside it. And it's not anywhere in the Atlantis libraries, either, and believe me, we've been looking."

"You'd think there'd at least be notes," Sheppard said.

"You would. But, no, nothing." Rodney shook his head. "Sometimes I wonder if the Ancients wiped a few files when they kicked us all off Atlantis that time. But, anyway. No information. So, no, there's no way I can reprogram the DHD on PGX-239, not even if I was there with them with all the lab equipment I needed and Atlantis's libraries to back me up. And I most certainly can't talk Zelenka through a procedure that nobody's even invented yet."

"Ok." Sheppard nodded thoughtfully. "So what if you —"

"Sheppard. John. I *can't*." Rodney leaned forward, the anger gone. "If you gave me a spare DHD, one that I could destroy if I had to, and a solid year of doing nothing else — maybe then. Maybe. Now? In time to get them off PGX-239? I can't do it. No one can. We need to do something else."

Sheppard sighed. "Ok. So do you have any idea when the DHD will re-set itself? Will it re-set itself? I'm this close to telling Lorne to bring them through and to hell with the quarantine."

"That would be a really bad idea," Rodney said. "Look, the periodic reboot is one of the few things we do know a little about. It happens fairly often — apparently on some kind of regular schedule, though we've never really figured out the actual intervals involved. It might be related to pulsar signals, or maybe the alignment of the entire system with the galactic center, and certainly it takes into account local conditions within the network —"

"Rodney?"

Rodney stopped, blinking.

"What's the longest the system has gone without resetting itself?"

Rodney paused. "Thirty hours, give or take an hour. Once in the Milky Way it went seventy-eight hours. We don't know why. And of course we don't know when the last reset happened."

"We probably ought to keep track of that," Sheppard said.

"Yeah. Believe me, I'm putting it on my list."

"Damn it." Sheppard squinted as though he could see the Wraith ships through the opaque windscreen. "If Guide wasn't waiting for us to get Ford out of his hair, we could take the jumper and go get them."

"I could take it," Rodney said. "You'd still have the Vanir ship, assuming it flies."

"Won't work." Sheppard gave a little smile. "I already asked. He thought it was an excuse to get out of the deal. Not to mention we don't know if the Vanir ship actually works or not."

"It probably does —" Rodney stopped, seeing Sheppard's expression. "Ok, no, I haven't actually tested anything."

Sheppard nodded. "Yeah. So we wait it out."

"There's nothing else we can do," Rodney said, and wished fiercely that there was.

Ember stared at his screen, his teeth bared as he considered the latest result. So close, so very close, but not good enough, not yet. Each tiny change they made brought them closer to the target, but so far nothing had gained them the necessary level of effectiveness. They needed 100 per cent.

He switched screens, calling up an unaltered model of the bacterium. Maybe they were going about it wrong. Maybe there was another way to attack, some other weakness he had missed the first time — the first ten times. He shook that thought away, and made himself work his way through the cell's structure, and then through the genetic material of both bacterium and bacteriophage. Certainly the latter was distinctive, and dangerous, a compact bundle of molecules with no obvious weakness and deadly potential. Or was he looking at the wrong thing? He tipped his head to one side, considering the pattern. They had been targeting the most obvious points, but perhaps a more subtle approach might be equally effective.

He called up a new protein, adjusting its structure to fit like a key into the *alflageolis's* receptors. That was the easy part; the bacteria would take it up without difficulty. The question now was payload. What if he used the protein to insert a more voracious bacteriophage, one that would destroy host and existing parasite? Could that be done without creating something worse? Yes, if he could adjust the genes that governed its reproduction, create a kill switch that would inactivate the cell when it tried to divide.

These were all familiar tools in his lab. Here on Atlantis, he had to create each one from the raw materials, a tedious and time-consuming process, but at last he was finished. He spun the model in the screen, but could find no weak spots, and transferred it to the simulation. That would show if he had found something useful, or if he'd wasted his time. But there was nothing else he would do until Beckett's latest simulation finished, he thought, and straightened from his workbench.

Zelenka looked up from his own computer at the same moment. "Anything?"

"Nothing from Beckett. I have set another simulation to run." Ember came to join him, ignoring the Marines at the door. "And you?"

Zelenka shrugged, and adjusted his glasses. "I can see how to create vapor cloud that will blanket the contaminated area in less than thirty seconds and cover the entire city in slightly more than three minutes. I am working to reduce that time, though I am somewhat hopeful that even *alflageolis* won't be able to respond that quickly to the attack."

"It should not," Ember agreed. "But faster is better, just in case one or two have already achieved a useful mutation."

A chime sounded from the main console, and he swung back to check the screens. Beckett's simulation was finished, and he hissed at the result. Still only 97 per cent success.

"Aye," Beckett's voice said, from the speakers, and in the secondary screen his image nodded. "I don't think we're going to get any better."

"And I think we must," Ember answered.

"We're running out of time." That was Sindye, looking up from her sample boxes. "The rate of deterioration is starting to accelerate again, and I'm seeing more anomalous DNA. And there are the off-world teams to think about."

"There is nothing you can do about them," Ember said. In fact, the only thing that would help them was to destroy the *alfalgeolis*, but the Lanteans seemed incapable of accepting that answer.

"How long do we have?" Zelenka asked.

"With the mutation, there's no telling," Sindye said.

"It may happen now, or tomorrow, or ten days from now," Ember said. "The timing cannot be predicted, only that it will happen."

"Which means we have to choose now," Beckett said. "It'll take at least three hours to manufacture enough of the stuff to make a difference, and probably more like four."

"And the aerosols cannot be placed in an instant," Zelenka said. "I'll need an hour and a half. Two hours would be better."

"Then I say we go with this one," Sindye said. "It's the best of the bunch, 97.36 per cent kill rate, and we'll buy enough time to attack again if anything does survive."

"It's not good enough," Ember said.

"But we don't have anything better," Beckett said. "And we're out of time."

"I had an idea," Ember said. "I tried it in the models, and the simulation is running."

"Let me look at it," Beckett said.

Ember's claws clicked against the keys as he forwarded the files to Beckett's machine.

"That's a different approach," Beckett said, after a moment. "I see what you've done, but we can't just go at it blind."

Sindye leaned cautiously over Ember's shoulder, and he moved back to let her see. "What if we make up both compounds? By the time we've finished, we'll know if this works."

"We don't have the equipment," Beckett said. "If we tried it, we wouldn't end up with enough of either one."

"I am right," Ember said. He took a deep breath, groping for the words that would convince the Lanteans. "You are out of time, not just for us, here on this station, but for your people off-world. This is my craft, my art, and I know this will work better than the other compound that we have developed. I have spent my life making such things — I am Master of Sciences Biological, and I would, I do, stake my life on it."

There was a silence, and then Zelenka said, "You're that sure?"

Ember nodded. "I am."

He heard Zelenka take a breath. "Then I say we do it. One thing we know about the Wraith, they know how to manipulate living matter."

"Dr. Sindye?" Beckett asked.

"I don't —" She stopped, shaking her head. "Yes. Yes, let's do it."

"And I agree," Beckett said softly. "It's a hell of a risk, but —"

"I am right," Ember said. "And it will destroy the *alflageolis*."

"It had better," Beckett said, and cut the connection.

CHAPTER TEN

THE SUN was setting behind a rising bank of clouds, the disk hidden entirely while the tops of the clouds were spread with scarlet light. The air was thicker, growing cooler and more damp as the sun was withdrawn, and a tendril of breeze caressed Ronon's bare arms. He'd felt all these things before, on a dozen other worlds, and wasn't surprised to see a flash of light in the sky to the west. Aulich's thunderstorms must be on the way. He realized he was counting, automatically, following the old Satedan rule that counting the time between flash and thunder and dividing by seven would give a rough distance to the strike, but there was no answering sound. Another flash split the air, and he realized it was a distant plant, firing straight up into the air.

"I wondered if any of the insects would swarm," Dr. Hunt said. She was rolling her sleeves down against the breeze, hat jammed firmly on her head to control her fine hair. "It looks like they're starting."

"So those plants are feeding?" Ronon shaded his eyes to try to see more clearly, but detail was drowned in the blinding scarlet light.

"I think so. Of course, we'll be able to see more clearly as they get closer."

She sounded surprisingly cheerful about the idea, and Ronon barely stopped himself from shaking his head. The scientists' priorities sometimes seemed a little skewed. "I'm sure that will be interesting."

"Fascinating," Hunt agreed, and then looked faintly embarrassed. "I mean, yes, I see that it's also a problem, but…"

Ronon clapped her on the shoulder. "You can always take notes from the shelter," he said, and turned away.

Aulich was still working on her array of equipment, but as he approached, she closed the lid of her laptop and began unplugging one of the peripheral components. "I want to keep scanning for as long as possible," she said, "but once the storms get closer, all of this, this pile of stuff, is going to be a lightning hazard."

Ronon eyed the stack warily. It was nearly up to his shoulders, a

generator at the bottom and various bits of sensor equipment and
computer gear piled apparently haphazardly on top of each other.
"More like a lightning rod."

"Yeah." Aulich grimaced. "Though I've been wondering if I
could use it to deflect strikes from the shelter? Though of course
the Stargate itself is the biggest thing around."

Ronon looked over his shoulder at the shallow shelter they had
scraped into the side of the hill, the leaf-shingled roof tilted to
shed the rain. The team would just fit beneath it, jammed shoulder to shoulder: not particularly comfortable, but it would help
conserve warmth until the storms passed and they could get a
fire going. At least the resinous bark would make lighting damp
wood easier. "Anything new?"

"I'm definitely picking up two lines of storms." Aulich lifted the
laptop's lid again, turning it so that Ronon could see the screen.
In a black box, a line of yellow flecked with red stretched from
one edge to the next; behind it was another, wider band, and
between them were thin strands of green. Aulich touched a key,
and white symbols popped into view, almost obscuring the lines.
"That's the lightning. You can see it's about the same in both lines,
though the second line is a little dryer. Not a lot of fun, though."

"No." Ronon studied the screen. "How big are these? I mean,
how long will it take for these to pass over us — I assume they
will pass over us?"

Aulich nodded. "It looks to me as though these storms are
essentially a feature of twilight on this planet. The ground cools
off really quickly once the sun goes down, and that fuels these
big lines of thunderstorms. They're not entirely solid —" She
touched the laptop again, making the lightning disappear and
then zooming in on the closer line of storms. The band of yellow resolved into a broken, jagged pattern, each section of yellow
narrowly fringed in green, many with cores of red. She was right,
there were gaps between the sections, not big ones, but spaces that
showed no color at all. "And they're moving fast. About seven-
ty-five kilometers per hour. The first band is only about ten kilometers wide, so it won't take long to pass us. If we get lucky, and
hit a gap, or even the fringes of a storm, rather than the heart, it

may not be that bad."

"What are the chance of that?"

"Hard to tell. The lines are stable, but the storms in them shift in size." Aulich shrugged. "At the moment, this is the section that would hit us." She pointed to the edge of one of the larger yellow sections. "At least I'm not picking up any hail. Or any kind of rotation that would give us tornadoes. This is just straight-line wind and rain and a lot of lightning."

Just a lot of lightning. Ronon glanced involuntarily at the Stargate, towering over everything else in sight, and Aulich gave a grunt of amusement.

"Well, yes, that does constitute a hazard."

"Yeah."

"Although, like my equipment, it might decrease the chance of a strike on us. But there's ground conductivity to worry about. Lightning's weird, it can travel through the ground sometimes. I think we're far enough away, but — it's unpredictable."

Ronon nodded, feeling the breeze on his arms again, a soft, testing touch, promising more to come. The sky had darkened further, and in the east he could see a single bright star low on the horizon. A second winked into view as he watched. He looked back to the west just in time to catch another volley of bolts from the pod-plants. This one was closer, clearly plants rather than lightning, but behind the flashes, the horizon was blue-black with cloud. "How long till it hits?"

"Just under six hours."

"How long do you need to dismantle all of this?"

"An hour, hour and a half." Aulich considered the question. "I can pull off the non-essential stuff now, try to stack it out of harm's way — or, more likely, where it's not going to harm us. I wish to hell we could get things back to Atlantis. I hate the idea of losing so much equipment."

"If you sent it back to Atlantis, it would be destroyed, too," Ronon said. "There's a lot of plastic here."

"Yeah." Aulich didn't sound entirely convinced, and Ronon didn't blame her. Something buzzed past his face, and he lifted a hand to swat it away.

"Let's get your non-essentials unhooked before the plants start feeding here."

The uneasy truce was still holding. The Travelers had mostly retreated to *Durant*, waiting for Alabaster's hive to leave orbit. A few of the younger crew hung around in the hatchway, watching the Wraith who had taken possession of the secondary building between the spots where their cruiser and scout had landed. Ford and his wife and son were down in the Vanir installation, waiting for Sheppard to figure out how they were all going to get back to Earth, since Atlantis still didn't seem to have fixed its contamination problem. Guide had announced that the scout would be leaving in two hours to take passengers back to the hiveship, though the cruiser would remain to see that Sheppard kept his promise. And that meant, Rodney thought, that this was his first, last, and only chance to see if Jennifer was traveling aboard Guide's ship. He hurried across the pavement, not stopping until the blade guarding the entrance hissed and lowered his staff.

"I'm — well, you know who I am," Rodney said. "I'm looking for Jennifer. Did she come with you?"

The blade looked wary, but a new shape loomed behind him, resolved to Guide, eyebrows raised. "As it happened, she insisted, though I told her she could not influence the outcome. But, yes, she is here."

"I'd like to see her."

"Would she like to see you?"

"You could always ask her," Rodney snapped.

Guide showed teeth. "Perhaps. Wait here."

"Oh, for — it's cold out here!" Rodney wrapped his arms around his chest, scowling. "Can't I at least get out of the wind?"

"He said, wait here," the blade answered, and Rodney sighed.

"If I come down with pneumonia…"

The blade ignored him, his eyes traveling to something beyond Rodney's left shoulder. Rodney turned to see Dekaas walking toward them, a small bag slung over his shoulder. He looked tired, wary but hopeful.

"Halt." The blade lowered his weapon again, and Dekaas lifted both hands, showing them empty.

"The Queen has permitted me to join the hive."

"I will consult," the blade said, and took a step backward into the shadows.

Rodney looked uncertainly at the other man, not knowing what to say. Dekaas seemed to take the silence for criticism, and his shoulders tightened.

"And are you going to try to convince me to stay? When everyone now knows I served the Wraith, and no one is happy with this new treaty? That it would be better to stay with my own kind, even if I will never be trusted?"

Rodney shook his head. "No, that wasn't — I wasn't even thinking that. I've lived with the Wraith myself, I know what it's like. That it's not all…" He stuck there, not knowing what word he actually meant, and settled for, "not all bad."

"You're no worshipper," Dekaas said.

"No. Look, it's a long and complicated story, but, short version, I was kidnapped and turned into a Wraith — I actually thought I was a Wraith — and —" Rodney stopped, shrugging, not wanting to remember everything he'd done when he'd believed he was Quicksilver. "Well. I thought I was one, anyway."

"And the Lanteans let you back." Dekaas's voice was flat.

"It was different —" Rodney stopped, abruptly aware of the pit opening up in front of him. All he could say was that the Atlantis team knew him, that it hadn't been exactly his fault or his choice, and none of that was actually going to make the other man feel any better. Dekaas's mouth twisted as though he'd tasted something bitter, and Rodney turned in relief as a familiar voice called his name.

"Rodney!" Jennifer came hurrying out of the shadows, her blonde hair pulled back in a long loose tail. "Guide said you were here."

"Yes, I just wanted to, you know, say hi. Before you left." Rodney made himself stop. "This is Dekaas, by the way. He's going to join you."

"I heard about that," Jennifer said, with her ready smile. She held out her hand. "Welcome. Alabaster said I could borrow you to help with the retrovirus trials."

Dekaas blinked, but accepted the handshake. "Thank you."

"Guide said something about your speaking Wraith? Or I guess it's more like being able to hear them?"

"I am Tainted," Dekaas said. Rodney thought he braced himself as he spoke. "I can't always make myself heard, but as long as I'm addressed directly, I can understand them."

"Telepathy," Rodney said aloud, and concentrated. *Can you hear me?*

Dekaas whirled to face him, eyes wide. "You also—"

"I told you, I was turned into a Wraith. Apparently this telepathy thing is lasting."

"That's what Teyla called the Gift," Jennifer said. "Being able to understand Wraith telepathy. Among the Athosians, it's used to warn of impending attacks."

"Among my people," Dekaas said, "it was a guarantee that you'd be part of the tribute. The Wraith came every three years, and took a hundred from among us all. The Tainted are the first to be chosen, only if there aren't enough of us do they draw lots among the normal ones."

"But the Wraith didn't eat you," Rodney said.

Jennifer glared at him, but Dekaas shrugged. "There was an old woman among the tribute, she taught three of us how to speak. When the Wraith came, their Master of Sciences Biological was curious about us. He kept me as a... pet, and taught me what I know."

"You know the Wraith equipment, then," Jennifer said, determinedly cheerful. "That will be very helpful. As will your being able to act as a translator. I know I'm missing a great deal of nuance."

"I expect you will find him useful." That was Guide, reappearing abruptly behind Jennifer. Rodney jumped, but Jennifer didn't move, merely favoring him with a quick smile. "Seeker trained him well."

Dekaas grimaced at that, though Rodney wasn't sure if it was because of the choice of verb or because of the mention of the long-dead cleverman. He remembered Daniel on *Durant*, probing heedlessly: *was Seeker your friend?* Captor, teacher, friend... It was a conundrum Rodney remembered all too well.

"I'll be very glad to work with you," Jennifer said, to Dekaas. "I'm sure I'll learn a great deal from you."

The medic managed a smile. "As will I."

"This way," Guide said, showing teeth, and Dekaas followed him into the shadows.

"Will he be all right?" Jennifer asked, lowering her voice. "I mean, he doesn't have to come back if he doesn't want to."

"He can't exactly stay with the Travelers now," Rodney said.

"Well, no, but Colonel Sheppard — Teyla — surely they could help him find someplace where he wouldn't be outcast?"

"From what Elizabeth said, the hive, Guide's hive before his queen was killed, that was as close to home as Dekaas had after his people basically gave him to the Wraith." Rodney paused, considering. "This is his choice. I — well, I can see how he'd do it."

Jennifer sighed, but her voice was determined. "And having someone on board who's lived with the Wraith, who had a place in their culture — he can at least tell us more ways to make life possible on a hive."

"So you're still staying?" Rodney hadn't meant to say that, and felt the blood rising in his face.

"You know I am." Jennifer smiled. "There's so much to be done."

Rodney nodded. "Well. Be careful."

"I will." She reached out abruptly, drew him into a quick, fierce embrace. "I have to go now. But you be careful, too."

"I always am!" Rodney began, indignantly, but she had turned and was walking away into the shadows. "Mostly. About as much as you are."

She didn't answer, of course. She was too far away, and moving further. He took a breath, and turned away himself, starting back toward the Vanir installation.

The scout had returned to *Just Fortune* two hours ago, and the hive had made its way out of orbit. Teyla had watched from the co-pilot's seat of the jumper as it made the leap to hyperspace, and now *Durant* was ready to lift, Lesko's face framed in the communications screen.

"You'll attack if they try to stop us, right?" Lesko asked, and John heaved a sigh.

"Yes, I will attack. But they're not going to try to stop you."

"That's what you say." Lesko looked over his shoulder, and nodded to someone out of the camera's sight. "All right. We're ready to lift."

"Copy that," John said, and the jumper's weapons came to life. "Guide, *Durant* is ready to lift. We've gone hot as a precaution."

He didn't say against what. Teyla smiled, and heard and felt the amusement in Guide's answer.

"Very well."

Teyla could hear *Durant*'s engines wailing as they rose toward full power, the sound only attenuated by the jumper's hull. "What will we do next?"

John glanced at the communications console, presumably making sure their microphones were turned off. "We have to figure out what to do with Dis. And then we need to get Ford back to Earth, assuming that Atlantis has fixed its little problem. But right now, Dis is the bigger problem."

"Dr. Jackson has suggested killing him," Teyla said. "I do not know if he is serious."

"They did nearly kill him," John said. "So I suppose I can't blame him. But I guess we really can't."

"Probably not." Teyla watched as *Durant* climbed away from the field, slowly at first, and then steadily faster, the white heart of its propulsion field glowing at its stern. It rose into the night, the field's light dwindling until it was lost among the crowding stars.

"In orbit," John said. He was watching the jumper's sensor display. "No sign of any Wraith, not that I expected any. Ok, they're breaking orbit — and entering hyperspace."

Teyla craned her neck, but couldn't be sure if she'd seen the flash of light or if it was just an illusion, a trick born of the star-filled sky.

"Guide," John said. "*Durant* has jumped to hyperspace. We're standing down."

"That is good news," Guide answered. "And next I presume we will see you lifting for Earth, to remove the Wolf from our galaxy?"

"You will," John said, "but not before we've had a chance to catch our breath. We need to rest before we can leave."

"If you must," Guide said. "But I would not take too long if I were you. I might grow impatient."

"We had a deal," John said.

"We did indeed," Guide said, "and that deal was that you would rid us of the Wolf."

"And we are going to take him home," John said. "Just not until we've rested."

"Very well," Guide said again, and his presence was abruptly gone from the edges of Teyla's mind. He was still there, if she made the effort, but even the general tone of his thoughts was closed to her.

She looked at John. "And now?"

"And now we rest," John answered.

They made their way back to the Vanir infirmary, to find Rodney hunched over his laptop and Daniel heating what looked like yet another round of instant coffee. Ford's wife and baby were asleep on one of the corner beds, a display unit wheeled to screen them and give them at least the illusion of privacy, while Ford and Elizabeth were deep in a low-voiced conversation. Dis was still sitting on the edge of its bed, its pointed face completely expressionless — almost, Teyla thought, as though it had not moved at all since she had left.

Elizabeth looked up at their entrance, her face breaking into a wide smile. "Colonel! The lieutenant and I have been catching up on a few things."

"Glad to hear it," John said, without much sincerity. "*Durant's* away, so all that remains is to get Ford back to Atlantis. The problem is, we've got to figure out what to do about this guy first." He nodded toward Dis, who blinked gravely.

"I have made an offer," the Vanir said. "Release me, and I will guarantee that no one will hunt Dr. Weir any further."

"I'm not sure we can do that," John said, riding over a snort from Daniel and the start of an indignant comment from Rodney.

"You know, Colonel, something has occurred to me," Elizabeth said. "Would it be all right if I asked Dis a question?"

John waved a hand. "Be my guest."

"You're determined to force Ran to unascend," Elizabeth said. "Is that because she's refused to help you? Or have you even asked?"

There was a silence that seemed to stretch forever. Teyla's breath caught in her throat, and she could hear her own heartbeat suddenly loud in the quiet. Surely the answer could not be that simple — surely the Vanir would have tried to contact their own kin. Or would they?

Could they? One did not contact the Ancestors, after all...

Dis blinked slowly, its great eyes blank. "We did not ask. How could we? Besides, it is well known that the Ascended are not permitted to meddle in the affairs of lesser beings."

"That's actually — well, somewhat debatable," Daniel said. "It's against the rules, yes, but any number of ascended beings do in fact interfere with ordinary mortals. That's how I got ascended in the first place. And the second place, for that matter."

"Me, too," Elizabeth said. "And it was Ran who helped me."

"And I'd bet it was Ran who arranged for you to be unascended where you were," Daniel said. "Where you could be found, and find your way back to Atlantis."

Elizabeth nodded. "Which argues that she might be willing to help her own people. Maybe even more so, since they are her kin."

"To help others ascend is one thing," Dis said. "To save us, she would have to unascend. What being would do that voluntarily?"

"We don't in fact know that, do we?" Rodney asked, looking up from his laptop. "I mean, we don't know what the limits of an ascended being's power is, only that it's amazing. Or at least it was pretty amazing when I was on my way to being ascended, and if it was that good without getting all the way there, you have to think that Ran might be able to do something for them without having to go all the way to unascending."

"Well, possibly," Daniel said. "Morgan le Fay was allowed to give us the names of two planets where we might find the Sangraal, and though the others stopped her from telling us which one we should look on, we don't know what happened to her after that, whether she was punished or not. Oma Desala was given multiple chances, and used them to help multiple people ascend. Though I do have to point out that both Elizabeth and I were forcibly unascended for saving people."

"We interfered very directly," Elizabeth said. A smile flickered across her face as she glanced at Rodney. "And I hasten to say that I'd do it again. But it seems to me that it's possible that providing genetic material, or even information that would allow for the repair of damaged genetic material — I could make a case for that being a much less direct action. Oh, I wish I could remember more."

It was tempting, very tempting indeed, but Teyla shook her head. "I would like to believe this, but I cannot help thinking that this is the splitting of hairs."

"That's one thing I do know," Daniel said. "Hair-splitting was a very popular pastime among the Ascended."

"Very well," Dis said slowly. "I will accept the premise for the moment. What if we ask Ran, and she refuses us?"

"Then you're no worse off than you were before," Elizabeth answered. "And you can proceed according to your conscience."

"But if she says yes," Teyla said, "then the Vanir have achieved their great need without loss to anyone. Including themselves."

Dis raised its hands in what looked like frustration. "But this proceeds from a false assumption. There is no known way to contact an ascended being."

"Actually, that's not entirely true," Daniel said. "Everywhere that the Ancients seeded populations, they also created so-called shrines, some of which contained sources of hidden knowledge, some of which contained healing devices, and some of which, yes, let the newly-settled populations contact their mentors. There are just as many shrines in the Pegasus Galaxy as there are in the Milky Way."

"That is so," Teyla said. "There are indeed many shrines, and many offer great gifts. Though I have never known anyone who received an answer directly from the Ancestors."

"But there must be ones that were meant for establishing contact," Rodney said, reaching for his laptop. "They'll be in the Atlantis database, all we have to do is find one that looks likely —" He grimaced. "Except, of course, that Atlantis is locked down, which means I can't do a search. Damn it."

"We'll have to wait until Lorne says we're clear," John said. "He said they were getting close."

"Guide will not want to wait much longer," Teyla said. "He is already unsure of our intentions."

"He's got to be the most suspicious Wraith I've ever met," John said, with a sidelong look that made her smile in spite of herself.

"I am serious, John."

"So am I."

"Um. There's — I don't know where there are shrines in this galaxy," Daniel said, "but I know where there are half a dozen in the Milky Way. In fact, I know where there's one on Earth."

"You do?" John asked, and in the same moment Rodney said, "Of course you do."

"And we've got that ship up there," Daniel went on. "There's no chance the Wraith can keep up with it. We can take that to Earth, see if Ran will help, and take Ford and his family home at the same time."

"Guide will try to follow us," Teyla said.

"But there's no way he can keep up with an Asgard ship," Rodney said. "I hate to say it, Sheppard, but this makes sense."

"Where is this shrine you're thinking of?" John asked.

"Scotland. The Outer Hebrides, in fact." Daniel was looking faintly smug, Teyla saw with annoyance. "It's on Eilean Mhure, which is one of the Shiant, or holy — or perhaps charmed — islands. Our UK members did some investigating there, and there's some evidence that the so-called Castle Rock was actually a landing site for either the Asgard or the Ancients."

It was, Teyla thought, essentially a good idea. She looked at John, who was nodding slowly, as though he'd come to the same conclusion.

"Well, Dis?" he asked, and the Vanir nodded slowly.

"Yes. I am willing to try this."

"Ok." John gave a lop-sided smiled. "So now all we have to do is convince General Landry that this is a good plan."

Aulich had stripped her tower of machines down to the last, largest console, a black box that was as wide as Ronon's forearm, and reached a bit higher than his waist. She and Joseph had cached the other machines on the far side of the Stargate, and had tied a ground sheet over them. They'd used the few metal stakes they'd brought with them from Atlantis to fasten the corners, and added more slivers of wood and a net of interlaced bungee cords to hold it all down, but Ronon couldn't think it looked very secure. Or very dry.

And that was going to be a problem soon. The clouds had nearly reached the zenith, blotting out the light; the air felt heavy, and every sound seemed magnified. The breeze had died to the merest whisper, but it had a chill edge, warning of the storms to come. He could see lightning flickering along the horizon, though it was still too far off for them to hear thunder. At least the insects seemed to have stopped swarming; a few plants were still firing, but they were on the far side of the hill.

"How's it looking?" he asked, and Aulich looked up from her laptop.

"Better than before. It looks as though we're in a gap between two storm cells." She turned the laptop so that Ronon could see, and pointed to the screen. "We're here, and the storms are coming on steadily at 75 kilometers per hour. They haven't changed their movement since I started tracking them, which means that this gap here —" She pointed again. "Is what's going to pass over us."

"Does that mean we won't get any rain?" Ronon stared at the screen, trying to make sense of the images.

"Some, probably. My instruments aren't going to pick up anything too light. But not much." She called up the white marks that indicated the lightning strikes. They lay thickly over the two yellow blobs, but there were only three in the gap between them. "The better news is that there is a lot less lightning. A lot less."

"Enough less to make it safe to stay in the shelter?" Ronon asked.

Aulich shrugged. "I think? At least as safe as it ever is to be outside in a storm."

Ronon considered that. The Lanteans were more concerned about weather than his officers on Sateda had been, but then, the Lanteans both knew more about how lightning worked and had more places to hide from it. He'd lived through more than one big thunderstorm during training, and still more when he was a Runner. He wasn't exactly eager to test himself against the storms, but he wasn't as sure that they needed to break Atlantis's quarantine. Especially if they were in a gap between the storms.

"Excuse me, Ronon?" Joseph called from the DHD. "It's time for Atlantis's check-in."

The Stargate's symbols were already lighting as he moved to join her. A moment later, the wormhole whooshed and then stabilized, and a window opened on Joseph's laptop. Lorne looked out at them, his chin unshaven and his eyes heavy with exhaustion.

"Ronon. How's it going?"

"Same as before." From the look on Lorne's face, nothing had changed for the better, but Ronon asked anyway. "Can we come back yet?"

"No progress with the DHD?" Lorne countered.

Ronon looked at Joseph, who shook her head. "Sorry, sir. I've been over the hardware half a dozen times, and I can't find anything wrong. I've been waiting on a re-set, but so far we haven't gotten one."

Lorne grimaced. "We're still in quarantine here. The biologists are making progress, but we're still contaminated. I'm reluctant to bring you through unless there's absolutely no other alternative."

Ronon looked back at the rising storm. Lightning flickered in its base, giving brief glimpses of towering shapes among the uniform purple-black, but it was heaviest to the north and south, visual evidence of the gap Aulich had promised. "Captain Aulich's been tracking the first line of storms, and it looks as though the big ones are going to pass to either side of us. Most likely the Stargate will draw any lightning we have. I think we can stay here safely enough."

"The Stargates can withstand a direct lightning strike," Lorne said. "When do you expect the storms to hit?"

"Captain?" Ronon looked over his shoulder, and Aulich came to join him.

"Sir?"

"When do you expect the storms to hit?" Lorne repeated.

"About an hour, sir." Aulich glanced at Ronon. "I was going to get the last system under cover, and set it up for a quick shut down."

Lorne's mouth tightened. He didn't like this much, Ronon thought, and, to be fair, he himself wouldn't like it at all if he were in Lorne's position. But on balance, he'd rather risk the storm than find himself trapped on Atlantis at the mercy of a fatal disease.

"How long will it take for the storms to pass?" Lorne asked.

"They've been very consistent in both speed and heading," Aulich said. "We'll be in rain for about forty minutes, but the worst of it — not more than fifteen minutes. Probably closer to ten."

"And we're between cells," Ronon said.

Lorne nodded slowly. "All right. We'll make contact again in two hours."

"Better make it two and a half, sir," Aulich said, and Lorne nodded again.

"All right, two and a half. Good luck."

"Thanks," Ronon said, and the image disappeared from Joseph's screen. A moment later, the Stargate closed. He hoped they wouldn't need too much luck after all.

CHAPTER ELEVEN

DIS PRONOUNCED the Vanir scout serviceable, and John set Teyla to keep an eye on the Vanir while the rest of them finished stripping away the stiff cocoons that covered the ship's interior. To John's relief, there was a cargo compartment, just large enough to contain the puddlejumper, as well as enough narrow cabins for everyone and enough of the inert base material that fed the ship's nutrition consoles, according to Dis, to supply a trip three times as long. John checked the MREs anyway, and was relieved to see that there would be enough to get them all to Earth. He didn't like the idea of being dependent on the Vanir for everything. For a moment, he wished he could lie down, just for an hour or two, but told himself he could rest once they were in hyperspace. Finally, though, everything was ready, and he and Rodney headed back to the jumper, emerging onto the pavement to find the cruiser readied for lift-off, only a single blade on duty at the open ramp.

"Presumably that's a good sign," Rodney said, settling himself into the co-pilot's seat. "As long as it's not because he's, you know, getting ready to blast us out of existence."

John scanned the displays as they came to life. "Doesn't seem to be. I assume you're not picking up anything that would suggest otherwise?"

Rodney shook his head. "You have to remember, though, I'm not Teyla. It's not like I can pick up what they're thinking when they're not thinking more or less in my direction."

John considered that for a moment, then nodded. "I'll take it." He touched the controls, extending the sensors' reach — empty, all the way to the next planet's orbit, no sign of Wraith or Travelers — and then turned his attention to communications. "Atlantis, this is Sheppard."

There was a long pause before Banks answered, and another long wait before Lorne appeared, looking if anything more tired and less shaven than the last time they'd spoken.

"Colonel. Everything all right?"

"We're fine here," John said. "What's your status?"

"We're making progress." Lorne glanced over his shoulder at something out of camera range. "Dr. Beckett and his team have just finished synthesizing the aerosol disinfectant, and we're getting ready to place the canisters. We expect to be clear in about four hours."

Assuming the aerosol worked. John heard the words as clearly as if they'd been spoken aloud, but nodded. "That's good news. What about Dr. Parrish's team?"

"Waiting out a storm. We're not risking bringing them through until we get this cleared."

"All right."

"Will you be returning to Atlantis then, too, sir?"

John shook his head. "We can't wait that long. Guide's getting impatient. And we've managed to make a deal with the Vanir. We're going to take the Vanir ship to Earth and bring Ford home that way. Since we can't contact the SGC directly from here, I need you to inform General Landry that we're on our way."

Lorne couldn't suppress a martyred look, but his voice was even. "Yes, sir."

"I take full responsibility, of course," John said.

"Yes, sir," Lorne said again. "Do you have an ETA?"

John looked at Rodney, who shrugged. "Given that the Asgard hyperdrive is a whole lot more efficient than anything we have — and I'm really hoping to get a good look at it while we're on board, by the way — I'd say we should be there in a couple of days. Fifty hours, give or take."

"You heard Dr. McKay," John said, and Lorne nodded.

"Fifty hours. I'll notify the SGC, sir."

"Thanks, Major. Sheppard out." John looked at Rodney. "You're sure you've got that door working?"

"Of course I'm sure. Besides, if I wasn't sure, how would we get the Vanir ship out of there?"

"That would be the problem," John said. "Guide."

"Sheppard. I thought you were resting."

"Change of plans. We'll rest while we travel."

"That is, of course, your business." Guide paused. "I dislike mentioning this, but our sensors show only you and Dr. McKay aboard."

"That's right. We've got another ride." John activated the engines, and saw the cruiser's guns flash to life. "Hold your horses! Like I said, we're taking a different ship. McKay, open the hangar."

"Working on it." Rodney did something with the controls, and above them the side of the mountain cracked open, showing a thin line of light that slowly widened as the massive doors began to inch apart.

"What is this?" Guide demanded, and the cruiser's guns swung to cover the opening.

"We've got a better ride," John said again. "No offense, but I want to be sure you're not going to try to follow us."

The hangar door was fully open now, spilling light onto the field. John raised the puddlejumper, turning it on its axis to arrow straight between the doors. The Vanir ship was waiting, the cargo hatch open, and Teyla's voice spoke in his ear.

"John. We see you. Dis says you are coming in high."

John frowned, adjusting his altitude, and a light flashed on his own sensors: too low. He corrected, and the warning vanished.

"You are good," Teyla said in the same moment.

John didn't answer, concentrating on bringing the jumper into the bay. There was less than a meter's clearance on both sides, and proximity warnings flashed yellow as he eased into the opening, cutting power as he went. The jumper slowed, kissed the interior wall, and settled onto its skids.

"Status report?" John demanded, and the jumper flashed an instant answer: no harm done.

"Dis says there is no structural damage," Teyla reported.

"Great." John was already out of his seat. "Shut her down, McKay! I'm going up top."

"Why me?" Rodney demanded, but the jumper was already shutting down under his command.

John ignored him and sprinted for the control room. He arrived just in time to see the scout slide out of the hangar, Dis at the controls. On the landing field below, the Wraith cruiser had pulled in its ramp, and was obviously scrambling to launch.

"They're going to come after us," he said, but Dis didn't even blink.

"It will not avail them."

The scout had fully cleared the hangar. Dis moved one hand, and it shot straight up into the atmosphere, the installation falling away beneath them. There was no sensation of movement, but just watching the ground recede was enough to make John catch his breath. Far below, he could see the cruiser laboring after them, and said, "Let him scan us."

"Why?" Dis asked. "I can prevent it easily."

"I want him to know we have Ford on board," John said. "Hold us in orbit until he's done it."

"That is wise," Teyla said.

"Very well." It was hard to read any expression on Dis's face, but John thought the Vanir was mildly annoyed.

They flashed through a layer of cloud, thin wisps past in an instant, rising into the greater dark of the upper atmosphere. Over the limb of the horizon, the distant sun appeared, tiny and diamond-bright; Dis adjusted the sensors, and the screen split between the stars ahead and the cruiser following in their wake.

"They are scanning us," Dis reported. "As you requested, I have not blocked their probes."

"Thanks." John watched as the cruiser continued to gain altitude, growing more graceful in its movements as it reached microgravity.

"Do you wish me to continue to wait for it?" Dis tilted its oversized head to one side.

John looked at Teyla. "You think they've got enough?"

"I believe so." She had the distant look that suggested she was eavesdropping on the cruiser, and John nodded.

"Let's not wait any more, then."

"I believe that would be sensible," Dis said. It adjusted the controls, and the scout leaped forward, the planet receding at an impossible rate. Ahead, the stars seemed to blur slightly, as though the sensors could not quite compensate for the sudden burst of speed.

"Whoa." That was Rodney, appearing in the control room door. "That's — we must be making at least .75C. Three-quarters the speed of light."

"Better than that," Dis answered. It bent its head to study something on a smaller screen, then looked up again. "We will be ready to enter hyperspace in five of your minutes."

"Wait, aren't we too close —" Rodney looked at the secondary screen, the planet they had just left indistinguishable from the starfield around it. "Ok. Never mind. Look, Dis, I'd really like to take a long look at your engines."

"We can discuss an exchange of technical information once we have spoken with Ran," Dis answered. "Not before."

"Just a look —"

"McKay," John said, and Rodney subsided.

"Oh, all right. But you'll regret it later."

"I do not think I will," Dis answered, and for the first time John wondered if the Vanir had a sense of humor.

"What about the Wraith?" he asked.

"They are too far away to get a good fix on our precise coordinates," Dis answered, "and once we are in hyperspace we will easily outrun them. They will not be able to track this ship through hyperspace."

"Best news I've had all day." John leaned on the edge of an unoccupied console, suddenly aware of just how long it had been since he'd had anything like rest. It was easy to lose track, traveling from world to world, but it had to be pushing twenty-four hours. The desire for sleep clawed at him, a weight that dragged at his very bones. At this point, even the stark Vanir sleeping cubicles looked inviting.

"Stand by for the transition to hyperspace," Dis said.

John started to brace himself, and the screens were abruptly filled with flowing light. "That's it?"

"We are in hyperspace," Dis said. It scanned its screens. "I show no indication that the Wraith ship has tried to follow us."

"That's —" John shook his head. He had expected something more spectacular, or at least more elaborate; the rougher transition of an Air Force ship or the enormous building power of Atlantis herself. This stepping from the normal universe to hyperspace in the flip of a switch, the blink of an eye. Efficient, he thought, but anticlimactic. "Right. Ok."

"I estimate that it will take about forty-nine of your hours to reach the destination provided by Dr. Jackson," Dis went on. "I have engaged the autopilot. I would recommend that you refresh yourselves as needed."

Sleep, John thought. Sleep would feel so good. But someone

needed to keep an eye on Dis, and he'd already told the others to take a break, so —

"Get some sleep, Sheppard," Rodney said. He grinned. "I want to hang out with Dis for a while anyway."

"Of course you do," John said. Maybe it was just that he was tired enough not to care, but he really didn't see anything wrong with the plan.

"I will stay with him for a little while also," Teyla said.

John nodded. "Right," he said again. "I'm going to get some sleep."

The cruiser keened as it rose through the atmosphere, a high, grating noise just at the edge of hearing. Guide could feel the Hivemaster's unease, the faint flutter in the laboring engines, but forced it all to the back of his mind, concentrating instead on the Vanir ship as it rose into open space. *Thrice Bold* could go no faster; the engines were at their full capacity and more, and he bared teeth in a snarl.

Keep the sensors locked on that ship.

Yes, commander. The cleverman Sky bent over his station, tuning the sensors to their optimum frequencies. *They are drawing away rapidly.*

I can see that, Guide snapped.

Commander, they're still in range of our cannon. That was Tempest, at the fire control station. *Let me take a shot.*

There's not enough power, his companion protested. He glanced over his shoulder. *Divert from the engines?*

No. Not yet. Guide controlled his temper with an effort. *Hivemaster!*

We are at maximum output, the Hivemaster answered. *And everything is going to propulsion. Once we leave the atmosphere, there will be less drag, but until then —*

He did not finish the thought, but he did not need to. Guide snarled again, but kept his hands gentle on the flight controls. He could feel the pressure on the hull easing as they rose into the thinner air of the mesosphere, felt the hull relax into the familiar cold, but the Vanir ship was already at the edge of their range. *Tempest?*

The blade shook his head. *They're at extreme range, Commander.*

To have any chance of hitting them, I'd have to take three-tenths of our power output, and even then they'd probably just outrun the bolts.*

And leave *Thrice Bold* falling further behind. *Hold your fire,* Guide said. He caressed the flight controls, urging the cruiser to give him every bit of its best performance. *If we can track them to Earth—*

He didn't need to finish the thought: if they could find the way to Earth, they would have the best of all bargaining chips for dealing with the Lanteans. Even Alabaster would recognize the utility of such information, though he suspected she would prefer not to use it. As indeed would he, but it would be foolish—dangerous—not to gain the information if they could.

Thrice Bold cleared the atmosphere at last, a surge of new power against his palms. The Vanir ship was invisible to the naked eye, one more point of light amid the crowded field of stars, but on the sensors' readout, her track was clear, a fading line that ended in a red dot. It was still pulling away, acceleration increasing at an incredible rate. It was no wonder hives in the past had warned each other to give these beings a wide berth.

Hivemaster...

We're still at maximum output, the Hivemaster said.

I need more.

There is nothing more to give you. There is already too much strain on the hull. We can't continue at this pace.

Guide could feel the flight controls shivering against his fingers, underlining the Hivemaster's warning. *Keep them on the sensors.*

I have a fix, Sky answered, and Guide allowed himself to hope. If they could just get a bearing on where and at what angle the Vanir entered hyperspace, at least they would have a clue to Earth's location.

It was still pulling away, *Thrice Bold* straining to follow, and then, abruptly, it was gone, too far ahead for them even to catch the flash of its translation. Guide hissed his frustration, but eased the cruiser's speed, feeling the controls settle under his touch. *Did you get it?*

Yes... Sky's tone was less certain than the word. *I have a fix, anyway.*

Extrapolate their course, Guide ordered. *If you can.*

There was a long silence, Sky bent over his console as he monitored the calculations. Guide slowed the cruiser's speed again, watching as the signs of strain eased back to something more like normal.

Sky lifted his head, his tone abject. *Commander, I'm sorry. I've got a general heading, but nothing more.*

Guide gave the ship its head and came to look over the cleverman's shoulder. The display showed a cone of possibility, widening rapidly, and he shook his head. *We can't follow that.*

No, Commander. To give Sky credit, he didn't duck away. *But it's possible — we know that the Lanteans came from another galaxy.*

So they claim, Tempest muttered.

Guide ignored him. *Go on.*

If I project a hyperspace course using this as the point of origin, we can see if it intersects any galaxies, Sky said. *It's a long shot, Commander, and very likely there will be more than one. But it's better than nothing.*

Guide nodded slowly. It was a very long shot, certainly, but he, and all the Wraith, were committed to a very long game. The Lanteans had bargained in good faith, he was willing to admit that, was even prepared to concede that Weir and Sheppard at least — and Teyla, though she was different, being in some sense kin — intended to keep their word and leave the Wraith in peace in their share of the galaxy. But Weir and Sheppard would not rule forever. They were human, and therefore mortal, and someday others would take their place. And still others would follow them, down the centuries, and there was no reason to think that their goals would stay the same, or that the same promises would carry the same advantages. They needed to know the location of the Lanteans' home, because some day they would be enemies again. *Do what you can,* he said. *In the meantime — we will rejoin our queen.*

Ronon crouched just outside the shelter, the first solid winds whipping at hair and skin. Beside the DHD, Aulich and Joseph drove two final stakes into the tarp that covered the last piece of their equipment, and stood for a minute with their heads together, staring at the western horizon. The clouds boiled up behind them, blue-black and jagged, lightning flickering in their depths. Overhead, pale shapes whipped past on the rising wind, rags of cloud blowing past at a lower level than the darker billows of the main storm. The air was filled with a low mutter of thunder, punctuated with the occasional louder blast, and the snap of the succulents firing either at the sound or at invisible insects. Behind him, the others were already crowded into the shelter, Parrish and Hunt and Samara pressed shoulder to shoulder into the dirt. Ronon had suggested they open up some MREs, more to give them a distraction than because he thought anyone was likely to be hungry, but he didn't look to see if they'd done it. In the distance, lightning split the air, a jagged, forked bolt running from cloud to ground. He counted silently, reached twenty-one. Three Satedan leagues, which worked out to something like two and a half Lantean kilometers. Close enough that they all ought to take shelter now, and he rose to his feet.

"Lieutenant! Sergeant! Come on back now!"

"On my way," Aulich called. She closed her laptop and started back up the hill, but Joseph lifted a hand.

"Hang on, I just want to check the DHD —" She turned to the pedestal as she spoke, pressing symbols. Ronon held his breath, but the first symbol that lit was not the one she pressed. She pressed the second one anyway, shaking her head, and turned away. "Sorry, sir, no go."

"Come back," Ronon repeated, and she started toward them. The air smelled strange, sharp and cold, as if ice had a smell; the hairs on his arms tickled, lifting. He'd felt that before, and dropped to a crouch. "Get down!"

Aulich had felt it too, skimmed her laptop away from her as she dropped to her knees. Joseph did the same, covering her head, just as a bolt of lightning slammed into the stand of conifers thirty meters beyond the Stargate. Ronon blinked, blinded, light beyond white searing his retinas, and the thunder struck, the sound buffeting his skin. Beyond the ringing in his ears, he heard Parrish swear, but the smell and the tickling were both gone.

"You all right?" He pushed himself upright, ready to go to either of them, but first Joseph and then Aulich straightened.

"All right, sir," Joseph said, and hurried toward the shelter.

"Good," Aulich answered, and stooped to retrieve her laptop. "No damage here either."

"Get inside," Ronon said, and waited while they fitted themselves into the narrow space. He took the end, his shoulders wedged against Aulich's on one side and the peeled wood of the roof support on the other. It was dark inside, and almost as dark outside, the clouds pressing down like a weight, bringing an instant midnight. Aulich worked her laptop open, the screen throwing sudden light as she checked the screen. "Well?"

"So far, so good," she answered. "We're still in the clear corridor, and everything's holding steady."

"How long before we're really in it?" Parrish asked.

"About twenty minutes." Aulich touched keys, and Ronon looked over her shoulder to see the clean lines and colors slowly dissolving into a sea of blue-green static. "And then about ten minutes before it passes over us. I'm going to have to shut down soon. It's too dangerous, and I'm not getting any good readings—"

There was another massive crack of lightning, flash and sound almost on top of each other. Ronon felt the others jump, and this time it was Samara who cursed and then apologized. It wasn't nearly as close as before, though, and he made himself take a careful breath.

"Hey, Doc, you got my rations?" He wasn't really all that hungry, and he could almost feel the surprise, transmitted shoulder to shoulder down the line.

"Yes," Parrish said, with only the slightest hesitation. "Yes, right—right here." He produced the woven carrier and handed it along.

Ronon took it, unwound the clasp, and pulled out the first thing that came to hand. It was a strip of dried meat, coated with the sweet-sharp pepper sauce that helped preserve it, and he broke off a piece, tucking it into his cheek to let it soften. "Thanks." He shifted the piece so that he could speak more distinctly, raised his voice to be heard over the thunder. "Like I said, if you want to eat, now would be a good time."

He could feel the resistance, and then felt it break, first Hunt, then Joseph reaching for MREs. A moment later, Parrish did the same. Samara produced one of the little battery-powered lamps and set it on the dirt between his toes. It wasn't as comforting as a good fire, Ronon thought, but it served the same purpose, light and hope against the dark. More lightning flashed, filling the sky, and for a moment he caught a glimpse of the roiling clouds. Thunder rolled, a steady rumble punctuated by louder roars like an avalanche. At the other end of the shelter, Parrish produced a water bottle, and he and Hunt carefully filled their cookers, propping up the pouches to let them heat without spillage. Samara was eating his cold, slurping whatever it was directly from the pouch. Only Aulich still bent over her laptop, squinting as though she could force the image to come clear.

"Captain," Ronon began — hadn't someone said that electronics could draw the lightning? — and she looked up with a wincing grin.

"Shutting down." She touched keys as she spoke, the screen going dark, then closed the computer and tucked it behind her back. Joseph touched her shoulder, handing her an MRE, then began to open her own.

The western sky was full of fire, sheets of lightning that threw the clouds' tortured shapes into sharp relief, punctuated by bolts that stabbed to the ground like twisted, barren trees of light. The noise was constant, deafening, as much felt as heard. Ronon made himself break off another piece of the dried meat, and then another; when it was finished, he grabbed the next piece, but he barely tasted the vegetable leather. Another bolt struck somewhere behind them, light and sound almost simultaneous, and some of the pod plants let off a salvo in answer. Their bolts seemed pale by comparison.

Parrish leaned forward. "I think maybe that hit some of the pointed pods?"

"Careful." Hunt put a hand on his sleeve and he subsided.

Something was moving in the dark, and with the movement came a rushing drone. Ronon tensed, bracing himself for wind, but instead it was rain, a sheet of it so heavy that it looked like fog. It swept toward them, dulling the lightning and blurring even the Stargate's massive shape, and the first downpour hit the shelter like a blow. Everyone instinctively pulled their feet back, and Ronon glanced quickly at the leafy ceiling. There were leaks, but the construction held. And then it was past, as quickly as it had appeared, and he felt the relief travel down the line.

"Wow," Samara said. "Man, you couldn't even breathe in that."

"I don't think you'd actually drown," Aulich said, though her tone wasn't as certain as her words, "but, yeah, not nice at all."

As the noise of the rain receded, it seemed as though the thunder was louder. Ronon made himself eat another strip of the dried meat, knowing he would need the energy, but he couldn't help watching the horizon. Was the lightning brighter? It seemed as though there were more bolts reaching the ground, and that they were marching steadily toward the Stargate clearing. Beside him, Aulich glanced at her watch.

"About fifteen minutes."

Ronon opened his mouth to ask whether that was until the worst hit or until it was over, and the words were drowned by another roaring wall of rain. It swept over the shelter, and behind it the air was suddenly chill and strange. He felt the hairs on his arms lift and saw Aulich look up in sudden alarm.

A bolt of lightning stabbed down into the clearing, slamming into the Stargate. The ring seemed to glow for an instant, caught in a light no longer white but weirdly blue-purple, and then the thunder slammed down on them. Ronon's vision was full of blurred lights, jagged afterimages. Light seemed to run along the ring, long sparks crackling as they spanned the gap and vanished into the dark.

Joseph started to get to her feet, but Aulich grabbed her arm, forcing her back down. "You'll get yourself killed."

The sergeant took a breath, shaking herself. "Yes. Sorry, ma'am."

"It hit the Stargate," Samara said. "Oh, man. We are so screwed."

"The Ancestors built the Rings to withstand storms," Ronon said. "The Stargate's the biggest structure around on most worlds. It has to be able to take getting hit by lightning."

Joseph nodded vehemently. "Yeah. Yes, sir. We've seen this before. It'll be all right."

"But the DHD was already damaged—" Hunt broke off with a gasp. Ronon thought Parrish might have nudged her.

"It's a software problem," Aulich said. "Not hardware. The hardware should be fine."

Ronon hoped she was as certain as she sounded. His skin was

still tingling, hairs stirring against his skin. Two more bolts struck in quick succession, one among the succulents and the other further off, at the edge of the stand of conifers.

"Not much longer," Aulich said, half under her breath. "Not much longer now."

Ronon took a deep breath, bracing himself for more, but the worst of the storm seemed to have passed. There was still thunder, but it seemed to come from behind them now, and he thought he saw breaks in the clouds overhead. Aulich checked her watch again.

"Permission to boot up the computer? We should be past the worst now."

"Go ahead." Ronon waited while the machine cycled and the screen lit, revealing more lines and blobs of green.

"Yeah," Aulich said. "Ok, I think we're good." She angled the laptop so that Ronon could see, pointing to a space between two broad yellow line. "That's us, here. The first line of storms has passed us."

A crack of thunder punctuated her words, but it was clearly behind them. Ronon uncoiled himself and took a cautious step outside the shelter. The air was much colder, and he hunched his shoulders against the wind.

"Ma'am, sir, I got to take a look at the DHD." Joseph scooted forward, her toolkit already in hand. Ronon looked at Aulich, who shrugged and nodded.

"I think it's as safe as we're going to get, sir."

"Go ahead," Ronon said, and Joseph hurried away. "The rest of us — let's get a fire started."

They had collected wood before the storms hit, and stashed it under one of the smaller tarps. That had blown partly loose, and the wood was damp, but Parrish had kept several handfuls of the resinous bark in the shelter with them. Ronon and Samara stacked the wood in front of the shelter, and then Ronon tucked the bark into the driest crevices and applied a lighter. The bark spat and popped, throwing out sparks and a hot, green-toned flame; the branches smoked heavily for a few minutes, and then caught fire. Ronon fed it more bark, and more of the damp wood, and sat back onto his heels, satisfied with the result.

"That feels good," Hunt said, and held out her hands to the blaze.

The shelter would capture at least some of the fire's heat, Ronon thought. The fire might not survive the next round of storms — almost certainly wouldn't, if the rain was as hard as the first bands — but they could rekindle it afterward if they had to. It wouldn't be precisely pleasant, but they would certainly survive until the planet's sunrise. None of them were looking at the DHD, he noticed. But even if the DHD was unusable, Atlantis knew where they were. If worst came to worst, they'd send one of the Taur'i warships to rescue them, or they could even ask the Genii for help. Ladon Radim owed them that much. Atlantis did not abandon its people. It would just be a matter of surviving long enough for the ships to reach them. Unless Atlantis itself was overtaken by disease before they could send for help... He killed that thought. The Stargate was undamaged, and surely Atlantis had told its off-world teams and the SGC about this problem; they could get supplies that way, from Sateda and the alpha site and any of half a dozen other worlds, both food and shelter, and they could make it if they had to. He wasn't going to admit that there were any other options.

He made himself walk toward the DHD. Joseph was crouching by an open panel, headlight shining into the interior, and she looked up at his approach, the beam of light flashing across his face and chest.

"So far, so good, sir. The lightning doesn't seem to have done any physical damage."

"Ok."

"I suppose there's a chance the shock caused the system to reboot." Joseph closed the panel and came to her feet, the beam of her headlight now playing across the top of the DHD. "Permission to test it?"

"Go ahead." Ronon heard her take a deep breath, then press firmly on the first symbol in Sateda's address. There was a momentary pause, and then a different symbol lit: the first in Atlantis's address. She pressed a second, but again Atlantis's address lit.

"Damn." Joseph shook her head.

"At least it still works," Ronon said. "When's our next check-in with Atlantis?"

Joseph consulted her watch. "Half an hour, sir."

"Go back up to the fire and get warm," Ronon said. "There's nothing we can do until we find out what their status is."

They all trailed back to the DHD half an hour later to watch the Stargate open and stabilize. Lorne's image took shape in the screen, and Ronon could see the look of relief cross his face as he registered that everyone was present and unharmed.

"Dr. Beckett assures me they've come up with a workable solution to kill the bacteria," Lorne said. "The next step is to apply it."

"Do you have any kind of time frame on that?" Ronon asked, and thought he saw Lorne wince.

"Dr. Beckett is hoping to be ready to decontaminate in about three hours."

And then they would need to be sure that it had worked. Ronon wouldn't bet on that taking less than a couple of hours. He looked at Aulich, saw the same calculations in her eyes. "That's going to cut it close for us, Major. The next line of storms will be here in about five hours."

"Can you ride it out like you did this time?" Lorne asked.

Ronon considered. It had been bad, but not as bad as he'd feared. The shelter wouldn't protect them from a direct strike, of course, but there wasn't much out there that would. "If the storms aren't any worse. And we were in a gap."

There was a little pause. "Understood," Lorne said at last. "We'll try to hurry things up."

"That would be good," Ronon said.

"We'll check back with you once the decontamination process starts," Lorne said. "Atlantis out."

The Stargate winked out, leaving only the night sky and the distant flicker of lightning visible through its circle.

"What now?" Parrish asked, after a moment.

"We hunker down and wait," Ronon answered.

Parrish nodded, though Ronon couldn't entirely read his expression, and put an arm around Hunt's shoulders. "Come on, Gina. At least we got a look at how those plants absorb power."

"I'm not sure I entirely agree with you," Hunt answered, but let herself be drawn away.

"Sammy. How are we doing for wood?" Ronon asked.

Samara looked at the pile. "I could cut some more."

"Yeah. Do that." Ronon surveyed the clearing again, the dark thick beyond the circle of firelight and the lights of headlamps and flashlights. Someone had switched the generator back on, and a couple of standing lamps added their light to the area by the fire. Overhead, the clouds were shredding in a fierce wind. PGX-239 lay in a particularly dense stellar neighborhood; the sky was filled with points and swirls of light, thrown in generous handfuls only partly veiled by the scudding clouds. On the western horizon, though, a solid bank of cloud was rising again, and there were faint flickers of lightning in its depths. It was still too far away for them to hear thunder, and he allowed himself a sigh of relief. At least they had this respite.

"Ronon?" That was Aulich, straightening from the largest piece of her equipment. "Can I have a word?"

"Sure." Ronon waited, and when she didn't move toward him, came to join her. "What's up?"

"Now that the generator's running again, I've got the radar and the other scanners working, so I'm starting to get a good look at the next line of storms."

"Ok."

"The good news is, I don't think we're going to see too many of those incredibly heavy rain bands."

"And the bad news?"

"I don't think we're going to be in a gap this time." In the light of her laptop, Aulich's face was very grave. "Unless there's a significant change in the wind direction, we're going to have a heavy cell pass directly over us."

That wasn't good. The lightning had been too close for comfort even in a gap. "No sign that the storms are weakening? Or even that there's less lightning?"

"No, sir." Aulich shook her head. "I'm afraid not."

"How long?"

"Like I said before. About five hours."

About when Atlantis said they'd be able to lift the quarantine. "Cutting it close," he said, and Aulich nodded.

"Yes, sir."

Ronon considered the problem. Lorne said they were ready to decontaminate, and that they were pretty much certain the process would work. If he was right, there was no point in taking the risk of waiting — except that if he was wrong, they'd be risking not quarantine but an unpleasant death. "Back to the shelter."

The others were gathered there, standing close to the fire as the wind swirled sparks from the blaze, and Ronon winced at their relieved expressions. "All right. I've got some news."

He laid out the situation as clearly as he could, watching the faces change from relief to renewed concern. "We could go through now," he finished, "but that's taking a chance that this bacteria will still mutate. And if it does, it's fatal."

There was a little silence, no one willing to be the first to speak, and at last Parrish shrugged. "We're all right for now. I say hold off a little longer. No point in risking it until we absolutely have to."

There was a murmur of agreement, and Ronon nodded. "Right. For now, we stay."

Radek looked around the conference room, making sure everyone was there. Lorne leaned on his elbows at the head of the table while Sindye fiddled with the connections, attaching her failing laptop to the projector one last time. One of the Air Force technicians — Shalcross, Radek remembered — was helping, a roll of electrical tape in hand. Ember was there as well, seated carefully three seats from the nearest human, his hands folded politely on the table. The rest were the volunteers who would help place the cylinders, an Air Force lieutenant named Casson, Spitzer and Hernandez, both Marines, and Dr. Koninsky, who as an astrophysicist had been useless for the research, but was an expert rock-climber.

Sindye gave a grunt of satisfaction, and the big screen lit. It fuzzed with static for a moment, but then the connection held. The image faded into focus: a schematic of Atlantis's ventilation system, carefully edited to show no more detail than was absolutely necessary. Three spots were marked with green dots, and Lorne straightened.

"All right, gentlemen, ladies. What's the plan?"

"We have synthesized the neutralizing compound and placed it in fifteen aerosol containers," Radek began. "Those are they, on the cart by the door." There was a rustle as everyone turned to look, but he ignored them. "Each cylinder is, as you can see, about sixty centimeters long — approximately two feet — but weighs fifteen kilograms. That's a bit more than thirty pounds. As you see from the diagram, there are three spots where the neutralizing compound must be introduced into the ventilation system, and five cylinders must be placed in each spot. Each cylinder has been fitted with a radio trigger that will release the gas, and that trigger will be released by a program run from the control room. That program will also simultaneously initiate what we might call a pulse of air that will ensure the even and near-instantaneous dispersal of the gas throughout the quarantine area."

"And we're sure that this gas is harmless to humans?" Lorne asked.

"Yes." Radek nodded firmly, and Ember lifted his head, his hair slithering across his leather coat.

"It was a necessary parameter."

Was that a joke? Radek thought. Lorne gave the Wraith an equally doubtful glance, and turned his attention back to the screen.

"What if the radio trigger fails on some of these? Will it still work?"

"It will not," Sindye said. "It'll take the full amount to fill the entire contaminated volume. But we have to do it soon."

Lorne nodded. "Aside from anything else, the team on PGX-239 needs to be evacuated as soon as possible. In less than four hours, they're going to be hit by a line of storms —" He broke off before he finished the sentence, but he thought everyone knew what would have come next: *a line of storms they may not survive.* "We are not leaving them there. If the *alflageolis* isn't neutralized, we're going to bring them through anyway."

"If we haven't got this under control by then," Sindye said, "we're putting them at potentially worse risk."

"I'm well aware of that, Doctor," Lorne said. "Which is why this needs to work, first try."

"We have collected gas masks from the jumpers," Radek said. "The gas itself may be harmless, but the aerosol blast could cause eye or lung damage to the person right on top of it. One person will stay with the cylinders and if any fail to release on signal, they will trigger them manually."

"It is not ideal," Ember said, "but it will be within the parameters."

Lorne nodded. "All right."

"Casson and Hernandez, you'll take the western node, here."
Radek touched the screen. "Your best access is through the corridor below, on level twelve. There's a maintenance hatch here, and if you follow the shaft to the west, you're only twenty meters from the node."

The lieutenant nodded. "And we can just put the cylinders on the floor of the shaft?"

"That's correct," Radek answered. "Dr. Sindye, you and Spitzer will take the southeast node, accessed through the jumper bay. Dr. Koninsky and I will take the north node."

"That's the one that doesn't have ladders," Lorne said.

"That's the one that we don't know about," Radek corrected. "It was not intended to be accessed for any maintenance purposes, and we have not explored it since our arrival. However, other isolated sections of the internal systems have turned out to be fitted with handholds, so —" He shrugged.

"Maybe we should take that one, sir?" Casson said. "Hernandez and me, we've done mountain training."

"You have the farthest to carry your cylinders," Radek answered. "And they are heavy. That's why I assigned that to you. Dr. Koninsky is an experienced climber."

Koninsky nodded. "It's not very far."

Casson was still looking at Lorne, who nodded. "We'll go with the plan as laid out. And — good luck, all of you."

CHAPTER TWELVE

IT WASN'T far to the entrance point, even dragging the heavy cylinders. Radek checked each one a final time, making sure the release system was securely closed, then looked up at the hatch set at the top of the wall. A band of decorative carving rose beside it, forming an unexpectedly easy ladder. Beyond that lay a secondary ventilator, and twenty meters to the left was the entrance to the connecting shaft. Up that, Radek thought, and with luck there would be some sort of handhold, and then they would be at the node. Or at least that was the plan. And always assuming that the compound worked. Beckett had rushed the simulation to its conclusion, but the results had been — uncertain. Ember's analysis had been confirmed, but the simulation itself only claimed 88 per cent accuracy. Simulations weren't everything, of course, Radek reminded himself, and it remained true that Ember knew more about this sort of thing than any of the humans. But if this went wrong, they weren't likely to get a second chance.

"This is it?" Koninsky asked, squinting up at the hatch.

Radek nodded. "Let me get it open."

He hauled himself up the ladder without waiting for an answer, and entered the code that would unlatch the cover. It sighed softly and sagged outward, and Radek slid it back, feeling the air suddenly stronger on his face. He was tempted to hurry ahead and see whether there were any supports in the connecting shaft, but made himself climb back down instead. Koninsky had already donned a headlamp and slung the coil of rope around his shoulder, ready to climb, and Radek gave an approving nod.

"Yes. You first, and then we will bring up the cylinders."

"Right." Koninsky swung himself easily up the ladder and disappeared into the opening. A moment later, he stuck his head back out and dropped the end of the rope. "Ok. Ready to go."

Radek tied the rope to the net that held the first two cylinders, and steadied them as Koninsky hauled them up into the dark. He did the same with the next two, and then the last, and followed it up the ladder, sliding carefully into the ventilator. Koninsky had already dragged the cylinders some way along the passage, and Radek switched on his own headlamp and followed him.

Together they hauled the cylinders further down the ventilator to the connecting shaft. It was covered by a wire grill, but the ventilator was narrow enough that it took less than a minute to remove the fasteners that held it in place. Radek tipped his head back to survey the shaft, hoping to find handholds, and a moment later a second beam joined him as Koninsky did the same. The metal walls stretched slick and bare, and Radek swore under his breath.

"No, wait," Koninsky said. "I think — isn't that a rung, about two, maybe three meters up?"

"Maybe?" Radek stared up into the dark. "According to the schematics, the entire shaft should be only five meters."

"If you can give me a boost up," Koninsky said, "I can definitely get to that rung — and all the way up, if I have to."

"Take the rope," Radek said, and braced himself to take the other's weight. Koninsky scrambled from bent knee to shoulders, and Radek felt his weight shift as he groped for purchase inside the shaft.

"The metal's not that slick," Koninsky said. "I think — yeah, I've got it."

Radek felt the pressure on his shoulders ease, and looked up to see Koninsky bracing himself in the narrow shaft, back against one wall, feet against the other, arms outstretched. As Radek watched, he hitched himself up the walls, moving with careful precision.

"Yeah, there's a ladder." His voice floated down, breathless with exertion. "Just rungs, but it goes all the way to the top."

"Good." Radek stared after him, holding his breath as Koninsky reached the level of the ladder and groped for something above his head. For an instant, he hung by both hands, and then his feet found a lower rung, and he straightened carefully, the light of his headlamp sweeping ahead of him up the shaft.

"I'm good! I'm heading up."

"Yes, go ahead," Radek answered, and bit back the instinctive 'be careful.' This was not really a time for caution.

His radio buzzed, and Lorne spoke in his ear. "Dr. Zelenka. Report your progress, please."

"We have reached the shaft below the node, and Dr. Koninsky is on his way up." Radek glanced at his watch, and winced: forty minutes to go. "We will be in place in time."

"Roger that," Lorne said. "Let me know when you've placed the cylinders."

"I will do so," Radek said, and peered back up the shaft. Koninsky was climbing quickly, making good use of the ladder, and even as Radek watched, he reached the top and pulled himself out onto an invisible platform. A moment later, he leaned back over the edge, his headlamp shining down the shaft.

"I'm secure, but we've got a problem. There's a door in the way, looks like some sort of shutter or something. It's between us and the node."

Radek swore. "Can you see fasteners?"

"Maybe?" Koninsky pulled back, and Radek swore again. That was all they needed, a barrier that wasn't listed on any of the schematics he'd consulted. Why the Ancients couldn't document their changes —

"I can see hinges and some fastenings," Koninsky reported. "It looks as though it was secured from the other side, though."

"Damn it." Radek closed his eyes, trying to remember similar things he'd seen in Atlantis's working spaces. "Where are the hinges? Top and bottom, or to the sides?"

"Just at the top," Koninsky answered. "Wait a minute, I can see some fasteners along the lower edge. They look pretty common. Atlantis's standard. Give me a second." He vanished from the top of the shaft, and there was a distant scraping sound. "I can't quite get them, but I think maybe two of us —"

"All right." Radek took a deep breath, trying not to think of the time ticking away. "Let's get the gas up first. Then if you can help me up to the ladder, we can work on them together."

They managed to haul the cylinders up, Radek wincing each time they slammed against the walls of the shaft, and then the rope snaked down again. Radek took it warily, fastening it around himself in a makeshift harness, then tucked his toolkit into the front of his jacket. Koninsky leaned over the opening.

"Ok, that looks good. I can't lift you very far, but I think I can get you into the shaft. There's a rim inside the opening — if you can reach that, I can help you the rest of the way. Then I can belay you while you walk up."

"Yes." Radek eyed the opening dubiously — this was not what he had expected when he had gone into the sciences — but stretched until he could just reach the opening. Yes, there, it was, a rounded ridge big enough to wrap his fingers over, and he looked back to Koninsky. "Yes, ok, I have found the ridge."

"Pull," Koninsky called, and Radek felt the harness tug at him. He heaved himself up at the same time, and came scrambling into the shaft, bracing himself as he'd seen Koninsky do.

"Good. Now walk yourself up."

Radek could no longer see Koninsky, but the steady pressure on the rope was reassuring. He bent his knee, slid one foot up the shaft, and pressed hard, feeling his back slide along the rough metal. The ladder's lowest rung was a little closer. Six years in the doctorate program, six years as a post-doc, and then teaching, and all for this? He swore under his breath, and made himself move again.

Finally he reached the ladder, managed to get first one hand and then the other onto a rung. He freed one foot, resting it on the lowest rung, and swore again. He was going to have to release his other leg, lean forward, step up, and pull up all in the same movement, and for a second he wasn't sure he could do it.

Koninsky's voice floated down. "Are you ok?"

"Yes." Radek glared at the ladder. "Yes, I am fine." He lunged for the ladder, feeling the rope take his weight for a heart-stopping moment, and then he'd made it, stood clinging to the rungs with both hands, his feet securely planted. "I'm fine," he said again, and began to climb.

He hauled himself out onto the narrow platform, breathing hard, and began unwinding himself from the rope. Koninsky coiled it neatly into a corner, out of the way of the cylinders of gas. Radek extracted the toolkit from his jacket. "Where are these fasteners?"

"Along the bottom edge." Koninsky pointed. "Looks like it's hinged along the top?"

Radek tilted his head, letting the light from his headlamp play over the metal of the shutter. It looked newer than some of the other components, which might explain why it wasn't on the schematic. As Koninsky had said, there was a raised line along the top of the shutter that was surely a hinge, and a line of dimpled dots along the lower edge and halfway up the sides that were the familiar Lantean fasteners. He reached into the toolkit for the Ancient driver that would fit those dots, and swore as it skidded free. The Ancients had plugged these fasteners for some reason. He had the correct tool to remove them — yes, there it was — but it would all take time. He glanced at his watch and winced. They would need to hurry if they were going to get the cylinders placed in time. He handed the screwdriver to Koninsky. "Here. I will remove the plugs, you take care of the fasteners."

"Ok."

Radek inserted the tool into the slight depression, turning the shaped head until he felt it catch and lock. He removed the first plug, and then the next, setting them aside. Obviously the Ancients had meant the ventilation shaft to stay blocked at this point, though he could see no reason for the change. Was he causing more problems by removing the shutter? He closed his eyes, trying to remember the schematic's smallest details, but he could see no reason. The tool slipped, and he cursed, made himself pay closer attention. There was no time left; they had to do it this way.

He removed the last plug, and a moment later Koninsky twisted out the last fastener. Radek felt along the lower edge of the shutter, but there were no handholds. The toolkit contained a thin-bladed chisel; he worked that into the gap and pried gently upward. "Quick—"

Koninsky reached into the widening gap and pulled up. The hinge groaned, and Radek quickly grabbed the edge as well. For a moment it resisted, the hinge clogged by rust or paint, and then it reached a tipping point. An invisible counterweight engaged, and the shutter folded itself neatly against the ceiling. Radek eyed it dubiously, and saw his doubt reflected on Koninsky's face.

"Do you think it will hold?"

"We might as well assume it will," Radek answered, and ducked through the opening. They were almost on top of the node, and he allowed himself a sigh of relief. "All right, start handing the cylinders through."

Koninsky did as he was told, passing the heavy bottles through the gap. Radek positioned them at the node, turning each one so that the nozzle was pointed down the corridor. As he placed the fourth cylinder, his radio buzzed.

"Dr. Zelenka. Are you in position?"

"Almost," Radek answered, and reached for the final cylinder. "Yes, we are ready."

"Stand by," Lorne said.

"Zelenka!"

Radek glanced back, and saw Koninsky waving the gas mask in his direction. He jerked off his glasses and reached for it just as Lorne spoke again.

"Transmission in three, two, one..."

The nozzles hissed in concert, and Radek closed his eyes and mouth, dragging the mask up over his face. He could feel the gas cool on his skin, could smell flowers as well as the rubber of the mask, and held his breath, settling the mask into place. The first blast of air struck back and shoulders, driving the gas to its destination. He blinked hard, opening his eyes, and saw that one of the cylinders hadn't fired. He hit the manual release, saw the gas billow out in a pale cloud just as the second booster hit, and backed down the ventilator toward the shutter. Koninsky caught his shoulder.

"Careful."

Radek let himself be steered to a sitting position against the side wall, and Koninsky touched his radio.

"Gate room, Dr. Koninsky here. All cylinders released."

"Confirmed," Lorne said. "We have full release in all three areas."

Radek nodded. The gas was thinning out, he could no longer feel it cool against his skin, and he pulled off the gas mask, blinking hard. No burning, no discomfort; he coughed experimentally, and his throat felt normal as well.

"You dropped your glasses," Koninsky said, and held them out.

Radek frowned, focusing with an effort, and slipped them on. The world slid into sharpness, and he allowed himself to relax again. He touched his radio. "Gate room, this is Dr. Zelenka. What are the dispersal reports?"

"They are within the planned limits," Ember answered. "You

have achieved 90 per cent dispersal in the quarantine area in the first fifteen seconds, 100 per cent at thirty, and complete dispersal throughout the city in seventy-one seconds. We are waiting on the sample results now."

Radek let his head fall back against the wall of the ventilator, and saw Koninsky grin, holding up crossed fingers.

"The first samples indicate that the coverage is complete, and within acceptable limits." Ember paused. "We are seeing an even deposit throughout the contaminated area."

"Good," Radek said. "That's good."

"We'll still have to run tests to be sure we've gotten it all," Sindye said. She sounded out of breath, but satisfied. "But if we have —"

"Then we can lift the quarantine," Lorne said. "And get our people back."

"If it has worked," Radek said, and pushed himself to his feet. He looked at Koninsky. "We must get back to the gate room."

Ronon nudged more wood into the blazing fire, hunching his shoulders as another scatter of raindrops blew across the clearing. The fire hissed and leaped up as the wind caught it and the three people inside the shelter drew in their feet as a few embers fell close to their toes. Thunder rolled steadily in the distance, and the lightning was creeping closer. At least the plants seemed to have stopped shooting — maybe they were concentrating on collecting a charge, Parrish had said, or maybe there was some sort of natural overload switch, that stopped them from shooting once noise or vibration became too great. He had spent nearly an hour prodding carefully at the edges of the stand of succulents, and then retreated to the shelter to warm up again. The stars had vanished two hours ago, and in the flashes of lightning, the clouds roiled and tumbled.

Aulich came up the hill, laptop in the crook of her arm, the light from its screen illuminated her face. Ronon went to meet her, careful to stay out of earshot of the people in the shelter.

"Well?"

"No change," she said. "It still looks as though one of the strongest cells is going to pass right over us."

Ronon looked at the screen, the image centered on a blob of yellow and red. Its core was white, and at the very center, a thin line pulsed in and out. "What does that mean?"

Aulich didn't pretend to misunderstand. "The part that's flashing is off our scales. Lightning, atmospheric pressure, rainfall rates — we never see anything that high, so we don't have a color to represent it."

"And that's what's going to hit us?" Ronon stared at the screen. "How much worse than what we had before?"

"A lot worse," Aulich said. Her voice was grim. "There's less rain than in the first line, but we're going to be right in its path. And when we do get rain, it's going to fall harder than last time."

Ronon grunted, not sure he could imagine that. It would almost be like being underwater, more rain than air.

"And there's more lightning. A lot more." Aulich touched keys, and the familiar symbols appeared, almost obliterating the colors behind them. "We can count on at least six times as many close strikes we had before."

"What are you counting as close?"

"Within thirty meters of the clearing."

Ronon nodded. That meant — if Aulich was right – they'd be facing eighteen or twenty bolts, and the odds against one of them hitting the shelter just went way up. "That's a problem."

"Yeah." Aulich looked away, concentrating on her keyboard as she removed the overlay and zoomed out to show a more distant view of the storms.

"How long before it hits us?"

"Three hours, maybe three and a half before we're in the worst of it. But there's going to be enough lightning and rain to keep us from using the Stargate before that — two hours at most."

"Right." Ronon took a deep breath to steady himself. "We'll evacuate to Atlantis before then. And hope they've solved their problem by then."

The symbols on the Stargate lit, Atlantis dialing in as promised, and Ronon made his way down the hill. He reached the DHD just as the unstable wormhole billowed and steadied, and Lorne's face appeared in the screen of Joseph's laptop.

"Good news. The release of the gas has been successful. We've got teams checking the quarantine area to be sure it worked, but we should be able to open the gate very soon."

"How soon?"

Lorne's mouth tightened. "An hour, they tell me. Maybe a little longer. They need to take samples and then run the tests —"

"We've got about two hours before we have to evacuate," Ronon said. "We're right in the path of the biggest storm yet."

"How bad?"

"Bad. Worse than last time."

"Damn it." Lorne shook his head. "You know the risk."

"We've got two hours before we have to move," Ronon said. "Then we're coming through."

"Understood," Lorne answered, and Ronon cut the connection.

Joseph fiddled with her laptop, and gave him a sidelong glance. "That bad, sir?"

"I'm afraid so." Ronon took another deep breath. He needed to tell everyone, make sure that there was a single general plan that covered everything, in case he or Aulich or any of the others were hit by lightning. "No luck with the DHD?"

"No, sir." Joseph shook her head.

"Right." Ronon lifted his voice. "Everybody! Back to the shelter, I've got something you need to hear."

They gathered around the fire, backs to the wind, sparks spiraling up with every new gust. Ronon looked them over, impressed again by the Lanteans' sheer doggedness. No one here had expected to risk their lives when they came through the Stargate; this was supposed to have been an ordinary scientific mission, nothing particularly dangerous or even particularly important. Except of course that every person on Atlantis, from its officers down to the cooks and lowliest technicians, had chosen to step through a Stargate, knowing that there were dangers in Pegasus that had never existed on their homeworld. He was proud to stand with them, prouder still that they accepted his leadership. He cleared his throat.

"Ok. Some good news, some bad news. The good news is that Atlantis says they've treated the quarantine area and it seems to have been successful. They're running tests to be sure, and as soon as that's done, they'll open the Stargate. The bad news... We're currently in the path of storms that are a lot bigger than the ones we went through. Captain Aulich gives us about two hours before we have to dial out. We'll wait as long as we can to see if Atlantis can't finish clearing their area, but if they haven't, we are going back anyway."

There was a little silence, and then Parrish lifted his head. "There's no chance we could ride it out here?"

"There's too much lightning," Aulich said. "It's — No. It's not going to be survivable."

"How convinced is Atlantis that they've got this thing under control?" Parrish asked. "Because if they've done an all-out push, and it hasn't worked, we still might be better off taking our chances here and waiting for the DHD to reset."

"What part of 'not survivable' didn't you get?" Hunt asked.

"Let's face it," Parrish retorted, "if Atlantis can't get this bug under control, that's not survivable, either."

"Ok," Ronon said, loudly. "This is not a debate."

"No," Parrish said. "Sorry."

He was right, Ronon knew, and a part of him was tempted by that very plan. Better to take their chances here and eventually dial out to somewhere besides Atlantis than to be trapped on Atlantis waiting to die of a plague. But he had seen the first line of storms, and he trusted Aulich's readings. And he trusted Atlantis's scientists. "We're going to leave the equipment," he said. "Take what you can carry easily — what you can run with. We can come back for the rest of it." He thought Hunt looked doubtful, but she said nothing. "Two hours. In the meantime, get packed, and get rested. This is likely to be hairy."

They kept the fire going, more for the reassurance than for the warmth, though the wind that blew in ahead of the storms was perceptibly colder than before. Hunt and Samara pooled supplies to come up with a thermos's worth of coffee, and shared it out in their few cups. Ronon accepted one with the others, though he wasn't particularly fond of the bitter taste. It was more important that they share this warmth, physical and emotional, than that he enjoy the drink, and besides, the caffeine was likely to come in handy.

"Atlantis will contact us, right?" Parrish asked, both hands wrapped around his cup.

"As soon as they've cleared the gate room," Ronon said. It was the fourth time he'd said it, but he managed to keep his voice calm. "Or we'll dial them if the storm gets too close."

A crack of thunder punctuated his words, louder than the steady distant rumbling, and he glanced over his shoulder to see the eastern horizon flashing like a chain of signal beacons. Against the flashing clouds, he could see three bolts of lightning, white-hot forks stabbing from cloud to ground.

"It's getting too close for comfort," Samara muttered.

"We're all right for now," Ronon said, and hoped he was right.

Aulich set her empty cup aside and opened her laptop. "I'm losing the signal, but as far as I can tell — yeah, we've still got some time."

Ronon managed not to look at the Stargate. Staring at it wouldn't make Atlantis call any more quickly. Instead, he slid another piece of wood into the fire, pushing into the heart of the coals so that one of the branches above it collapsed in a shower of sparks. Another gust of rain blew past, a sudden spattering of cold water on back and shoulders. He'd been through worse as a Runner, but he hadn't been responsible for anyone else then, either.

He looked around the shelter, seeing the day packs set ready for departure. They'd done what he'd told them, gathered up only the most necessary items — well, there was a leaf from one of the succulents sticking out of Parrish's pack, and probably more in Hunt's pack, but that was what they'd come to get. He didn't grudge them their samples as long as it didn't keep them from moving fast when the time came.

There was another crack of lighting, an instant of pure white light that threw everything in the clearing into sharp relief, and then thunder loud enough to drown out conversation. He had counted to two before it sounded: too close for comfort. "Sergeant. What's the time?"

Joseph consulted her watch. "Been an hour and forty since Atlantis called."

Twenty minutes before he had to decide. Twenty minutes before things got too dangerous, though that last strike seemed to indicate that the storm had speeded up. He looked at Aulich. "What's your radar tell you?"

She shook her head. "I'm losing the signal. Everything is — it's all static, sir. Sorry." Her eyes widened. "Or else it's rain. It might be rain."

"Like the rain that hit us before?" Ronon asked sharply. They'd been lucky the shelter had held up under it; he had no desire to experience it without some protection.

"Or worse. But I think what's messing me up is rain."

"Can you tell if it's moving any faster?"

Aulich shook her head. "I'm sorry, sir. I just can't tell."

Another blast of lightning lit the clouds, followed instantly by thunder. Too close, Ronon thought. It was time to go. "Sergeant! Dial Atlantis. Everybody else, get what you're bringing and move out. We're going through."

The thunder was growing louder as they huddled by the DHD, packs in hand. Joseph dialed the Stargate, and Ronon braced himself in case it failed. They hadn't let the DHD run its course since it had been hit; they'd always let Atlantis dial them. There was no knowing how much damage the bolt had done. Ronon looked to the horizon again as the symbols lit and circled. Lightning flared above a lowering shelf of cloud, and beneath it he could see a solid gray wall advancing across the fields of succulents. It was coming quickly; in the next series of strikes, he could see the plants swallowed by the wall of water. He could hear it, too, a heavy hissing that swelled rapidly toward a dull drumming almost as loud as the thunder. The last symbol lit, and the wormhole erupted into the clearing. He heard Parrish let out his great in a sigh of relief, and Hunt grinned broadly.

"Atlantis, this is Dr. Parrish's team," Joseph said. "Are we clear to come through?"

"Stand by," Banks' familiar voice answered. "Ok, clear!"

"Move!" Ronon raised his voice to be heard above the sudden roar of water. He could see it clearly now, a gray wall that looked nearly solid in their lights. Hunt was staring at it, open-mouthed, and he caught her shoulder turning her bodily toward the Stargate. "Go, go, go!"

Aulich sprinted toward the Stargate, Samara at her heels. Parrish and Hunt followed, Parrish laboring under the weight of his pack. Hunt made it up the stairs at the first enormous drops of rain hit them, and vanished though the wormhole. Parrish stumbled on the stair, and Samara caught his arm, dragging him upright again.

"Go," Ronon said, to Joseph, and the sergeant ducked her head and started for the Stargate. Ronon followed, counting. Hunt was through, and Parrish, and Samara… Something struck his back, hard and cold as though someone had thrown a bucket over him; behind him, another enormous drop hit the fire, extinguishing it in a hiss and a cloud of steam. He was at the stairs, Joseph a step ahead of him, and the wall of water swept over them, a weight that drenched them both instantly. He stumbled, and Joseph went to one knee, coughing and sputtering. There was no air, nothing to breathe, just the roar of the water dragging him down. He reached out blindly, found Joseph's shoulder and hauled her upright. She staggered, still choking, but found her feet. Just ahead was the hazy blue of the wormhole. Ronon cupped his hand over mouth and nose, and shoved Joseph ahead of him into it, then staggered after her.

Just as suddenly, he was in Atlantis's gate room, gasping for air as water streamed down his face and body. The others were there ahead of him, Parrish, Hunt, Aulich, Samara, Joseph, and he gasped with relief as the Stargate winked out behind them. All back, all safe, even if they were leaving enormous puddles on the gateroom floor.

"Everyone all right?" Lorne called from the control room, Zelenka at his side looking more than usually disheveled.

Ronon glanced at the others, received nods and small smiles in answer. "We're good."

"That was cutting things a little too close for comfort," Zelenka said. "I am sorry we took so long."

Ronon shook his head, saw the nearest Marine duck as the water splattered across the floor. "We made it. That's the main thing."

"And presumably the quarantine is lifted?" Parrish asked. "Because if it is — I, for one, really want some dry clothes."

Ronon laughed with the others, knowing that it was at least

partly sheer relief. But they'd made it, he'd gotten everyone through the first storm, and brought them all home. He was, he thought, allowed to be satisfied.

The Vanir ship was stark and empty, every surface planed smooth, with a dull gray coating that didn't soften the solidity of the metal underneath. Teyla had thought the Lantean ships coldly utilitarian, until she came aboard this scout. Compared to it, *Daedalus* and the *General Hammond* were as warmly inviting as the tents of her people. She had been given one of the eight identical berthing spaces, with a niche carved into the bulkhead for sleeping and a pair of cubes, one protruding from the wall and the other from the floor, that could be converted into various items of furniture, and she had played with them for a while, looking for some shape that was less severe than the rest. The light that diffused from the ceiling threw no shadows, and she shivered and palmed open the compartment door.

The corridors were just as plain and featureless, the light just as dull, with none of the visual cues that the Lanteans used to direct traffic in their ships. And also none of the decoration the Ancestors put everywhere, the careful use of proportion and color and elaborate, delicate abstraction. The Vanir had nothing, revealed nothing, their spaces as featureless as their skin.

At the first cross-corridor, she turned left, and was relieved to hear voices in the distance. In the room that was apparently the ship's kitchen and common room, Daniel and Elizabeth had configured more of the cubes into a table and awkward-looking chairs, and somewhere they had acquired coffee. Elizabeth looked up as Teyla came through the door, a smile of welcome spreading across her face.

"Teyla. There's coffee and food if you want some."

"The coffee's real," Daniel said. "How the Vanir acquired it, or why, I'm not even going to ask. The meals are MREs, though."

"I will have coffee, thank you." Teyla found the pot, an incongruously shiny bulb tucked into a niche in the wall, a set of Lantean-style mugs ranked in a second niche next to it. She filled herself a cup and came to join the others, perching cautiously on another of the configured cube-chairs. "Has Dis said how long it will take us to reach Earth?"

"Another ten hours," Elizabeth answered. "Assuming the estimates were right in the first place. Dis wasn't sure how efficient the engines were going to be. This ship was moth-balled for a long time."

Ten hours. A long time to spend in this uncongenial space. Teyla made herself smile as though it didn't bother her. "Do you think Ran will answer? She has been badly treated in all of this."

"I think she'll at least listen," Elizabeth said. "She was — she struck me as both wise and compassionate."

"And she may have some ideas that none of us have thought of," Daniel said. "That's the thing about being ascended, you know — so much more. Impossibly more. There may be half a dozen solutions right in front of us, only we don't have the ability, the simple knowledge, to see them."

There was a definite touch of frustration in his voice, and Teyla tipped her head to one side. "You must regret losing that, after you were forced to unascend."

To her surprise, Elizabeth gave a fleeting smile, and Daniel grimaced. "Well of course I miss the knowledge," he said. "Or at least I think I do. Since I can't even remember what it was that I knew, it's hard to be absolutely sure. I miss the idea, I suppose?" His expression hardened. "What I didn't like was the price."

Elizabeth nodded. "Yes. I am sure that what I knew, what I had, was wonderful, but... To be forever forbidden from interfering, even to save lives — no, I couldn't live with that, either."

"The Ancients would say we can't interfere because as a species we lack the maturity to assess and understand the consequences of our actions," Daniel said bitterly. "Though I can't say I've been particularly impressed by their ability to grasp consequences."

Teyla nodded, thinking of the Wraith. Though of course those had been the Ancestors who had chosen not to make the sacrifices necessary to ascend — but, no, that was not the whole story. The Ancestors had seen themselves as infallible, standing above other beings like the only adults in a universe populated by children. "They were powerful and full of knowledge," she said slowly, "but I cannot think they were always wise."

"Certainly not as wise as they thought they were," Daniel said.

There was a note in his voice that made Teyla wonder if he was talking about himself as well.

She turned at a footstep in the corridor, to see Atelia peering cautiously into the compartment, the baby Jordan nestled comfortably on her shoulder.

"Come in," Elizabeth said, smiling, and Daniel rose to drag another cube into the 'chair' configuration.

Atelia eyed it uncertainly, but sat, settling Jordan more comfortably on her lap. "I'm still getting used to those things."

"So are we all," Teyla said. She rose from her place to sort through the stack of MREs. "I am sure you must be hungry, after you have slept."

"I am," Atelia admitted. "And so is Jordan — aren't you, baby?"

The boy gave a shy smile, then buried his head against his mother's shoulder as Daniel smiled back at him.

"This one is a Lantean breakfast," Teyla said, setting the package on the table. "Or there is one with stew?" That would be her personal choice — she had never really understood the Lantean preference for sweet things in the mornings — but Atelia reached for the first one.

"Want me to heat it up for you?" Daniel asked. "You've kind of got your hands full."

Jordan squirmed as he spoke, and Atelia laughed. "Sit still, baby! Mama's getting you something." She smiled at Daniel. "Thank you, that'd be a help."

Teyla watched as Daniel quickly opened the meal and began sorting out the various packets. "Ok, here's a muffin top and some apple butter and crackers, that looks likely. And — granola? And a Pop-Tart — sorry, toaster pastry. And I'll heat the sausage."

Atelia took the muffin top, breaking off pieces for Jordan to cram into his mouth, scattering them both with crumbs. Daniel squeezed lines of apple butter onto the crackers and passed them over as well, then opened the other packets and fitted the package of sausage into the heater. Teyla couldn't help remembering the first time she'd watched John assemble a meal out of what she had thought were remarkably unpromising ingredients. She still preferred Athosian rations, the cakes of dried fruit and meat bound with lard and the bags of parched grains and berries, but she had to admit that the Lanteans' supplies kept better and were far more varied. If you had to spend weeks on the march, Athosian rations grew tedious indeed. These days, she knew, Lantean rations were traded far and wide, as desirable as the Lanteans' medical supplies.

"Is it true that Dekaas was a Wraith worshipper?" Atelia asked. She and Jordan had finished the muffin top, and were sharing the toaster pastry now.

"Yes," Teyla said. This was a hurdle they would all have to cross, each one at their own pace.

Atelia sighed. "That—I liked him. He was a good doctor."

"Yes," Teyla said again.

"He took good care of Jordan when he had the Ulari fever. He's cared for nearly everyone on *Osir.*" Atelia shook her head. "And—he went with them, didn't he? With the Wraith?"

"He had been found out," Elizabeth said, gently. "I don't think he felt safe anymore. And he believed he could do some good among Alabaster's people."

Daniel looked up from his coffee. "Back in the Milky Way, back on Earth, we have a remarkably persistent legend about vampires. Nearly every culture has some version of it: monsters that haunt the night, that appear out of the dark to drain the blood, the life force, from of innocent people and leave them withered husks — or turning them into monsters in their turn. The origins of the monster, the vampire, are varied — some are devils or demons, some are unfortunates who died in ways that left them vulnerable to the taint. In one culture, if a cat or dog jumps over a dead body, it will become a vampire; in another, failure to perform the correct funeral rites dooms the dead to rise and prey on the living. But one thing remains constant: the vampire feeds on the living."

"The Wraith," Atelia said. "Those stories are about the Wraith."

"I think so," Daniel said. "I think that when humans were evacuated back to the Milky Way after the Ancients were defeated by the Wraith, they told their children and grandchildren about the horrible monsters they were fleeing from. And there was enough remembered truth in those stories that they survived, and were passed down through the millennia. Somewhere out there, beyond night, there are monsters who will drain your life for food." He paused. "But that's not the only piece of the story. Vampires come back for their families, not out of hate but out of misplaced love. Some vampires sought immortality, heedless of what they had to do to achieve it. Some were humans who fell in love with a vampire who courted them in the night, and accepted the change willingly. Some of the most terrible vampire stories are about parents who must destroy their children, siblings who must destroy each other, rather than see them transformed, no matter how much they love the lost one. There are tales of entire villages that were forced to unearth all their dead, dismember their bodies one by one, violating all custom and all the proper rites and rituals in respect of death, to find the vampire, or vampires, and destroy them."

The tale had come around in a suspiciously neat fashion, and Teyla gave him a sharp look. Atelia said, "That is how my husband hunted the Wraith. And yet…" She looked away, shaking her head.

And yet it had done as much harm as good, Teyla thought. And both Atelia and Ford had known that in the end. She said, "We have no such tales among my people. Nor among any folk that I have known."

"You have the Wraith," Elizabeth said. "You don't need stories."

"And do your stories offer any hope besides kill or be killed?" Teyla knew her voice was sharp, but she didn't care. The Wraith had not chosen to become what they were.

"People still tell vampire stories," Daniel said. "As I said, it's an amazingly persistent legend. The most recent versions tell of vampires, who hide in the corners of the world, dangerous, yes, and still hungry, but who follow their own codes of ethics, who feed without killing and who make more vampires only with the consent of the changed. It's the same story, but from a different perspective."

Teyla let out a long breath. That was where he had been heading all along, through all this rambling story: change is imaginable because it has been imagined. She couldn't argue with that. Atelia fed Jordan a cracker, her face startled and thoughtful, and Teyla thought the idea had sunk home. And that was enough for now. "Here," she said, "will he let me take him? Then you can eat."

"Are you sure?" Atelia asked.

"My son is only a little older," Teyla answered. "And I miss him."

As she had expected, that was enough. She took Jordan onto her own lap, settling him so that he could see his mother, and offered him another cracker before he had a chance to think of crying. Atelia reached for the packet of sausage, eating quickly now that she was able, and Teyla relaxed into her chair. It would not be an easy homecoming, but it was a better ending than any of them had believed possible.

Lorne ran a hand through his hair, thinking wistfully of his own room, his own bed. He'd been sleeping on a cot in the back of his office since the outbreak, and he was thoroughly sick of it, though at least tonight he could, with luck, return to his proper quarters. He was tired of MREs, too, and of the same clothes, and ready to drink something besides the coffee brewed in the 48-cup urn that lived in the larger conference room. More importantly, Atlantis was all but out of fresh food. There was still plenty to eat, but it was all canned or frozen or powdered, and Sgt. Patterson reported that he had reserved the last few dozen eggs for cooking. Not to mention that there were still teams off-world: they'd gotten Dr. Parrish's team back safely—and from all accounts it was a damn good thing they'd had Ronon with them—but there were still a couple of teams waiting for the final all-clear before they could come through.

His tablet chirped and he touched the screen, scanning the latest report from the team tasked with tracking down any remaining traces of contamination. This was the second sweep, and so far it had all come back clean. And if that didn't mean they could resume normal operations, he thought, he wanted to know why. The main computer beeped at him, and he looked up to see Beckett's face framed in the screen.

"Major. I see you've received the report."

"It's looking good," Lorne said. "Unless you're going to tell me that there's something you've missed?"

"It's certainly looking promising," Beckett answered.

"What more do you want us to do?" Lorne asked, controlling his tone with an effort. "We need to resume gate travel—we've got people off-world who need to come home and we're running out of fresh food. Not to mention that we've already brought people and equipment through the gate room without any signs of harm."

"I know that." Beckett looked annoyed himself. "But we also can't risk this getting loose anywhere else."

Lorne took a deep breath, controlling his own irritation. He'd definitely spent too many nights sleeping in his office. "I'm absolutely with you on that, Doc. So what else do you suggest we do?"

Before Beckett could answer, there was a knock at the door. Lorne looked up to see Zelenka and Ember standing in the doorway, and waved them in. "I got your report. Dr. Beckett and I were just discussing it." He turned the screen so that they could see as well, Ember staying carefully out of reach of either human.

"I think we are clean," Zelenka said, and Ember nodded.

"We can't resume travel through the Stargate until we're absolutely certain the *alflageolis* is eradicated," Beckett said. "I'm proposing to send a team into the corridors around the quarantine zone with some of our more sensitive equipment, so that we can do one more sweep and be positive that we haven't missed a trace amount."

"At some point, we are going to have to start believing our instruments," Zelenka said.

"We need to take the time," Beckett said. "If we're wrong, we can't exactly go back and do it over."

Yes, but is this next test going to be good enough, Lorne wondered, or is it just going to make you want to do it one more time? They had to be careful, yes, but there was a time when you had to take a chance. He curbed his impatience. Beckett was the expert; he ought to have the last word. He looked at Zelenka, though, who shrugged.

"We have been over this three times, each time with more sensitive equipment," Zelenka said. "And this last time we also used UV light to test for anything we might have missed with the other scanners. Not to mention that we've seen no sign that the degradation of plastics has resumed."

"Any remaining bacteria would have fluoresced under that light," Ember said. "We saw none such. And our examination was exacting."

"Aye." Beckett drew a deep breath. "And I know we're running low on supplies. I suppose we can resume gate travel."

"That would be helpful," Lorne said. He made himself stop and continue more carefully, "But I need to be sure it's safe. As you say, we won't get a second chance."

"I still want to have some of my technicians do a final scan," Beckett said, "mostly of hard-to-reach places, but — yes, I think we've got it."

"Thanks, Doc," Lorne said. "I'll keep gate travel to a minimum until you've finished."

"That's probably a useful precaution," Beckett said, and the screen went dark.

Lorne looked from Ember to Zelenka, Wraith to human, wondering how it was they'd managed to adjust to Ember's presence. The same way they'd gotten used to Todd's — Guide's, he supposed: both sides had remained very clear on the terms of their relationship. And yet he was not, precisely, afraid of Ember. He shoved the thought away. "Well, what do you think? Should I hold off a little longer?"

Zelenka spread his hands. "We must be sure, yes, but we also need to get supplies. It's a risk worth taking."

"I think we are free of this," Ember said, "but Dr. Beckett's technique will make certain. Send only a few teams through, yes, but if this comes back clean, I think you are safe."

Lorne nodded. "Thanks, gentlemen. I appreciate all your hard work."

Ember bowed his head gracefully, his hair whispering across the shoulders of his leather coat, but Zelenka shrugged. "Yes, well, what I want most of all just now is a night's sleep in my own bed. If I'm no longer needed?"

"Go for it," Lorne said, and waved them away.

It took another couple of hours to bring back the last of the gate teams and send out Pollard and his people to trade with the usual suspects. Sateda, at least, had reported no signs of the infection, and Lorne allowed himself to relax as the last of the Marines who had been working there came through. That was the last thing he had to deal with, at least until Sheppard and his people returned from Earth, and he closed his eyes, letting his head fall back against the chair's battered headrest. Just a little rest, that was all he wanted...

"Incoming wormhole," Banks called from the gate room, and he pushed himself to his feet.

"Trouble?"

"No, sir." That was Salawi, back on duty and seemingly none the worse for having been fed upon. "It's the SGC."

Crap. Lorne swallowed the word, and did his best to look noncommittal as the image formed on the console screen. General Landry looked out at him.

"Major. Can I assume you have your problem under control?"

"Yes, sir." Lorne automatically straightened his spine. "We've resumed limited gate travel pending one final check."

"And that's why Colonel Sheppard is on his way to Earth? In a Vanir ship, I might add. To talk to an ascended Vanir? Or is she an Asgard?"

"I honestly don't know, sir."

"With Dr. Weir. Who has been presumed a Replicator and dead for the last three years."

"We believe she was ascended and then unascended, sir. By the Vanir. The ascended one."

Landry's eyes narrowed. "And on top of that — well, it's a damn good thing he's found Lieutenant Ford, and his brand-new family, but what's this about needing proof that he's back on Earth to give to the Wraith?"

"As I understand it, sir, that was our best way to preserve the current agreement," Lorne said. "The one that says the Wraith don't eat us."

For a second, he thought he'd gone too far, but Landry just shook his head. "Do you have an ETA for me, Major?"

Lorne glanced sideways, to see that Salawi had pulled the information up on her screen. "Should be about ten hours, sir. Though they may be going directly to the site Dr. Jackson identified."

"They'd better not be," Landry said. "Not without contacting us first."

There was nothing Lorne could say to that, and Landry's scowl deepened.

"Right. Consider yourself lucky that this wasn't your idea, Major. SGC out."

The wormhole winked out. Lorne took a deep breath, and then another, thinking all the things he'd like to say to Sheppard when Sheppard returned, then put that firmly aside. Time enough for that after he'd gotten some sleep.

The Vanir ship bored on through hyperspace. Dis said they were about eight hours from Earth orbit, sending Rodney into paroxysms of frustrated curiosity, rocketing back and forth from bridge to engine room while Dis ignored his questions. After half an hour of that, John retreated to the little common room, only to find Ford carefully pouring himself a cup of coffee. The lieutenant looked up, startled, and John gave a careful nod.

"Lieutenant. How's the kid taking the trip?"

"Better than I am, sir," Ford answered. "But then, he's always lived on a spaceship."

"Yeah." And that was one more piece of weird for Pegasus, John thought, and nodded when Ford held up the pot in mute question. He wondered what Jordan would make of it when he was older, whether he would remember anything of babyhood – if, when he was finally old enough to be told the truth, it would come as a total shock or as confirmation of his strangest dreams. He pulled two of the cubes into a 'chair' configuration and settled himself at the table, wrapping his fingers around the cup. "I've been wanting to ask, how the hell did you get off that hive?"

Ford gave a wry smile. "Luck, mostly. And a lot of it's not real clear. After you guys got away, I kept fighting, and then I got knocked off one of the catwalks and got clear of pursuit. After that, when the other hive started shooting – or was that you, sir?"

John nodded. "A little of both. I got 'em started, but they didn't trust each other in the first place."

"Wraith," Ford said, and shook his head. "Anyway, in the confusion, I managed to steal a Dart, but I couldn't really fly it, and ended up crashing on the planet." He shrugged. "It's not real clear after that. I was running low on the enzyme, starting to really hurt, and the next thing I remember is being on *Durant*, with their doctor looking after me." He looked away, his face closed and unhappy. "That – wasn't fun. He pulled me through, but it had to have been a solid year before I was anything like back to normal. Atelia said – she told me he knew what to do because he was a Wraith worshipper?"

John nodded again.

"That – it's weird, that's all. He seemed like a decent guy."

"It's complicated." John refrained from adding anything more. Everybody was going to have to figure this one out for themselves. There was nothing more he could do or say that was going to change anyone's mind, any more than he was ever going to convince Ronon that this was a good plan. He and Ronon had settled for 'it's the best plan we've got.' At least on Earth Ford wouldn't have to deal with the consequences of that choice every day. "What happened then?"

Ford shrugged. "The Travelers didn't know where Atlantis was — half of them thought you'd blown it up rather than let the Wraith get it — and most of them didn't really trust you enough to want to make contact. From some things Dr. McKay said, I had the idea you'd moved the city anyway, so there wasn't much point trying to find you. And then *Durant* offered me the chance to transfer to *Osir*, because they tended to trade in areas that were under heavy Wraith pressure, and they thought my skills would be more use there. So I thought, well, I'll still be fighting Wraith, and I did some training and worked with some guys to improve their weapons to get a rate of fire that would actually take down a Wraith…"

"And you met Atelia," John said, and Ford nodded.

"Yeah. And I started thinking about ways to really stick it to the Wraith, and came up with the Wolf. But we never managed to do as much as I wanted. Most people only wanted to do one, maybe two missions, and then go home. And we couldn't avoid collateral damage. We killed a lot of Wraith, though, sir. We had them worried."

"You did," John said. It was no one's fault, least of all Ford's, that that answer had proved unsustainable. "You absolutely did."

"Colonel." Ford leaned forward, resting his elbows on the table. "What's going to happen to me? What are my options?"

"As far as I'm concerned, you're a missing man and we're lucky to have you back," John said.

"Thank you, sir." Ford paused. "Is that how the SGC will see it?"

"You were taken prisoner, escaped, and took refuge with friendlies," John said. "That's how I see it, and that's how the SGC's going to see it. Do you really think General Landry's going to do anything different?"

"I – you could see it as desertion," Ford said. "Stealing the puddle jumper and running like that. Threatening to shoot a superior officer."

"You weren't in your right mind," John said. "We didn't know what the enzyme would do to you, but that's an explanation, not an excuse. We should have kept you under tighter watch so that you couldn't do something crazy. That's our fault – my fault, as the officer in charge." He leaned forward, willing Ford to believe him. "We failed, Aiden. Not you. We failed you."

They sat in silence for a long moment, Ford's expression blank, the look of a man contemplating visions only he could see. Dead Wraith, John guessed, remembering Afghanistan. Dead friends. And then, slowly, Ford's face eased, and he gave a small, wry smile.

"I hope Atelia likes Earth."

And that his family liked Atelia, John thought, and that he and they would be able to adjust, one presentable worry standing in for all the ones you couldn't say. "She's a Traveler, she's used to strange cultures. And you'll have all the support you can handle. Landry and O'Neill will see to that."

"Thanks." Ford shook his head. "I thought – I was sure I'd never come home."

"You'll get used to the idea eventually," John said.

CHAPTER THIRTEEN

THEY CAME out of hyperspace into high Earth orbit, chasing the dawn line around the planet. John watched the image in the main view screen, orienting himself by glimpses of the planet and the altitude markings displayed in Dis's smaller screen. They were well clear of the ISS and most satellites, though he could see them on another secondary screen, flecks of green and orange forming a chaotic-seeming swarm around the planet.

"We have achieved orbit," Dis said. "Where is this shrine of which you spoke?"

Jackson looked up from the console where he'd been studying something, but John held up his hand. "I need to contact the SGC first. Otherwise there's a chance someone will get irritated and take a shot at us."

"That does not concern me," Dis said.

"I grant you that they probably can't touch this ship," John said, "but that doesn't mean getting shot at wouldn't be annoying."

Dis blinked once, and then again, as though it was trying to understand the comment. "That is so," it said, after a moment. "You may use the communications console. It is now adjusted to function in a way you will understand."

"Thanks," John said. Behind him, the door opened, admitting Rodney and Teyla, but he ignored them, concentrating on the console. As Dis had promised, he recognized the Asgard symbols, and was able to find the SGC's 'safe contact' frequency on the second try. "SGC, this is Lieutenant Colonel John Sheppard. Come in, please."

He had to repeat the call twice more before he got an answer, but at last the board sprang to life. "Colonel Sheppard. General Landry advised us we should expect your call."

"Thanks. We are inbound from Pegasus in a Vanir ship — looks just like an Asgard scout, but it's a Vanir."

The SGC's response was reassuringly prompt. "Copy that, Colonel. We have you on our scanners. Plan has you headed for an island in the Outer Hebrides."

"Eilean Mhuire," Jackson interposed, politely enough by his standards, and John nodded.

"That's correct."

"You're cleared for Scotland," the SGC answered. "Please inform us at once if there are any changes in plan. Oh, and General Landry would like a word with you once you're back."

"Copy that," John said, and knew his voice sounded grim. He forced a smile, knowing it probably didn't look sincere. "We'll check in once we've resolved this question."

"Thank you, Colonel. Good luck!"

"Thanks," John said, and broke the connection.

"Oh, please," Rodney said. "Landry's going to call you on the carpet for fixing everything?"

"You'll be lucky if General O'Neill doesn't join him," Jackson said.

"If you will give me the coordinates for this Eilean Mhuire," Dis said, "I will begin our descent."

The Vanir ship descended into the dawn above Eilean Mhuire, cloaked and shielded against visual and electronic scanning. They were coming in from the west, skimming the foam-tipped waves, the island looming green and shadowed ahead of them. The rising light just caught the top of the headland, leaving the stony beach below in shadow.

"This is where we are to land?" Dis sounded doubtful.

"Yes." Jackson leaned closer to the screen. "There are caves in those cliffs, see there? To the right — south — of the broader beach."

Dis brought the scout lower still, barely thirty feet above the water. It looked as though it were a calm day, quiet, and it took John a moment to remember that it was late winter here, far north in Earth's northern hemisphere. The headlands were brown grass patched with snow, and in Colorado at the SGC the snow would be deep, hanging heavy on the fir trees — ski season. But it would be spring soon, just as it was in Atlantis, turning toward their first summer on their new world.

There was a narrow strip of rocky beach visible at the base of the cliff, just barely wide enough to allow the scout to land. Dis brought it down with slow care, proximity alarms flashing as the port side nearly scraped the cliff, and hovered for a long moment before letting the ship settle gently onto the rocks. John felt the ship shift under him as the landing gear adjusted to the uneven ground. Dis turned away from the controls without a backward glance.

"Which way?"

Despite Dis's care, the scout's starboard edge was in the water, so that they had to wade through the shallows to reach dry land. The waves were cold enough to make John's breath catch in his chest, and he was glad of his heavy boots. It didn't seem to bother Dis, though; the Vanir made its way over the rounded rocks as easily as if they were level ground. John offered a steadying hand to Teyla as she splashed through the water — her smile as she took it was amused — and then to Elizabeth, who nodded her thanks and turned back to survey the ship.

"Should we be worrying about the tide?"

"I wouldn't think so." John surveyed the beach. It was all rock, not the sandy beaches of his childhood, but he could see strands of seaweed and debris just beyond the reach of the furthest waves. "That's the tide line, there. It's either just before or just after high tide, and either way, the ship should be fine."

"If you can call this a beach," Rodney said. "Did I ever tell you about my friend who collected sand from every beach he ever visited? He went to Maine once, and all he could find to bring back was a big rock. Just like these."

"Where's Ford?" John interrupted.

"He said he wanted to stay on the ship with Atelia," Elizabeth said.

John gave her a sharp look. "Do you think that's a good idea?"

"I think it is well," Teyla said. "I do not think he wants to cause trouble, not here where there are no Wraith. Or where it would endanger his wife and child."

"And if you're worrying about him stealing the ship," Rodney said, "the Asgard were always able to lock down their technology pretty well. Even I couldn't get into it."

"That wasn't what I was thinking," John said, though in fact it was. But both Rodney and Teyla were right, and that let him relax a little. The truth was, he still wasn't quite sure what to say to Ford, any more than anyone had known quite what to say to him after Afghanistan. He had found his way back; he would have to believe that Ford could do the same.

Jackson had moved ahead of them, into the shadow of the cliff, and was playing a flashlight along the deeply fissured rocks. The air was chill, and smelled of wet rock and seaweed and, beneath that, the pervasive smell of the ocean. John licked his lips and tasted salt.

"Over here!" Jackson waved a hand, and the others converged on him. He was standing close to the foot of the cliff, shining his light into one of the many vertical fissures. From even a few yards away, it looked like all the others, but then John realized that what he had thought was simply shadow was actually a narrow opening that led into the cliff itself.

"This is the place?" Dis tipped its head to one side.

Jackson nodded. "This is it. The entrance is pretty narrow, but it widens out a couple of meters in."

The entrance looked more than just narrow, John thought. They'd all have to turn sideways and wriggle through, and it was maybe a good thing Ronon wasn't with them, because there was no way he would have fit through that opening. He pulled out his flashlight and flicked it on. "Ok. Let's go."

They wedged themselves one by one through the gap. It wasn't so bad for Dis and Teyla, John thought, or even for Elizabeth and Rodney, but Jackson had to struggle, and John himself had an awkward moment when his jacket caught on a projecting rock and he wasn't able to free himself immediately. And it was long, a good six feet of scraping between rocks until at last the entrance opened out into a stone-floored tunnel that bored on into the rock. The walls were bare, John thought, but Jackson played his light over the right-hand wall for a moment, and settled on a shape like a capital T carved into the wall.

"Thor's Hammer," he said. "If you look close, you can see it was painted — looks like the kind of interlacing patterns you see in medieval Celtic manuscripts. There's, or there was, a shrine to the Virgin Mary on the headland directly above the final chamber."

"Wasn't Thor one of the Asgard?" John let his light play over the carved hammer. Sure enough, if you looked hard, there were traces of pigment, reds and blues and ochre yellows, all faded so that they almost blended with the rocks.

"He was." Jackson nodded. "We've seen a couple of his shrines off-world, although we don't think this one was specifically his."

"Don't these things usually have lights?" Rodney turned his light on the ceiling, letting its beam explore the rough-hewn stone. "Are we sure this is stable?"

"Yes," Jackson said. "And we don't get lights until we reach the inner chamber."

The tunnel led on into the hill, the air dry and cold and clean-smelling. There had to be some kind of ventilation shaft, John thought, but any openings were hidden in the shadows. They'd gone maybe a hundred meters when the tunnel abruptly ended, opening out into a cylindrical space. The floor and walls were smoothed, almost polished, and as they stepped into the room, light flared from the ceiling, as though a clouded sky had suddenly appeared above their heads. There was a circular platform in the exact center of the floor, its surface carved with interwoven lines that seemed to tangle when you looked at them. John reached for his P90, and stopped himself with an effort. This was an Asgard shrine, he reminded himself; Jackson promised it was, if not harmless, at least not actively hostile. Maybe even friendly.

"*Astan edhal*," Dis said, for the first time shaken out of its composure. "A — place of passage, you might say? I had heard of such, but did not believe —"

"What do we do now?" Rodney asked. He turned in a slow circle, scanning the walls. "I thought these things were more, I don't know, decorated. Full of technology. Something."

Jackson cocked his head as though listening to something only he could hear. "Wait. Just… wait."

Elizabeth's head lifted, and then John heard it, too, a faint, soft humming, steady and growing louder. It was like bees in a hive, or a box of kittens, definite but somehow unthreatening, and Teyla took a step back so that she was at his side.

"The Ancestors?"

"I don't know." John kept his hands on his P90, in spite of being fairly sure that whatever was making that sound probably wasn't hostile, and almost certainly had better weapons at its disposal.

Welcome, seekers, you who are of the people.

The words came from everywhere and nowhere, filling the air without vibration.

What do you wish from the Ancient Ones?

The people, John thought. Did that mean all of them, or people with the ATA gene — or maybe just Dis? He looked at Jackson, who was looking at Elizabeth, and swallowed a curse. He'd fantasized about catching Jackson without something to say, but this wasn't what he'd had in mind.

"I seek my foremother," Dis said, stepping forward so that it was almost at the edge of the platform. "Millennia ago, one of our people Ascended, stepping outside of time and space and all our knowledge. Since then, we continued to progress, and as we did so, we remade ourselves over and over again. When we could no longer reproduce sexually even with assistive technology, we began to clone ourselves, transferring our consciousness from body to body until those bodies in their turn could no longer be duplicated. Our species is dying, slowly and terribly. Each life lost takes with it knowledge, experiences, consciousness, that will never be again. In this galaxy, our people chose to end their lives as a species rather than risk what remained of their knowledge falling into the hands of peoples who would inevitably use it for destruction, but we in the Pegasus Galaxy are determined to live instead. These bodies cannot be saved, but if we had the eggs of a female born before the cloning began, we could restore ourselves to what we once were. If we could obtain a sample of undamaged DNA — even a scan, a reading — we could, with great effort, rebuild our species. It is for that reason we seek Ran: so that we do not perish utterly from this universe."

Ran. The word was a whisper than ran round the edges of the chamber, echoless and yet ever-present, the word repeating as though it chased its own tail. *Ran.*

Light bloomed above the platform, a pale and watery globe that swelled to perhaps a meter in diameter. In its depths, a storm churned, and at the heart of the storm was a shifting figure, wrapped in strands of wave and cloud and rain. For a moment, she seemed human, with a grim face and hair dark and lank as seaweed, a net wrapped around her and clenched in both hands. Then she was a mermaid, noseless and flat-chested, fangs and claws bared, and then a grinning skeletal creature wound with gold like coiling serpents, her net crowded with ships. And then she changed again, the storm fading around her, until she was at once familiar and strange, an Asgard, enormous black eyes blinking slowly in a pointed face, and yet not, an Asgard taller and distinctly female. The sphere began to descend, its edges dissolving while the shape within it grew more and more solid, until as her feet touched the stone of the platform, the sphere faded into wisps of light and shadow.

"Ran," Elizabeth whispered. "I remember…"

"I am Ran," the being said, and her tiny mouth curved into what was unmistakably a gentle smile. "I have chosen to assist you in this endeavor, Dis. We have argued long and hard among us, and I have said I will not let the last of my kindred vanish from the universe. Extinction is an evil that overrides many other rules. I may or may not be permitted to return, but I will not be hindered in this."

Dis stared, eyes wide, mouth slack. "Lady…"

"I cannot promise success," she said. "It has been a long time, and you have done so very much to yourselves in all these centuries. And I certainly cannot promise that you will be either what you were, or what you most wish to be. But I will attempt to help you live."

"That…" Dis stopped, and John wondered if and how the Asgard wept. "That is more hope than we have had in a thousand years. We will take that chance."

"Then I will go with you." Ran stepped down off the platform. She was a good head taller than Dis, and more sturdily-built, her skin less wrinkled. And she was certainly female, where all the other Asgard had been completely sexless. "Elizabeth. I am so very pleased to see you well."

"And I to see you," Elizabeth said. Ran held out her hand, and Elizabeth took it in both of hers, ten fingers encompassing four, pale skin and dark. "I owe you so much."

Ran smiled again, turning so that she could take them all in a single glance. "You have chosen as I expected. You are not for Ascension, Elizabeth, not yet."

"No." Elizabeth released her, tears running unashamed down her cheeks.

"We must go," Ran said, and took Dis's hand.

John shook himself, made himself clear his throat. "Um, we have a puddle jumper on board. And some of our people are still there."

Ran blinked, then nodded. "Your own craft. That was wise of you to bring it. We will unload it for you, and then depart."

They followed her out, along the tunnel and then back through the narrow gap. The tide had receded, leaving the Vanir ship still tucked against the cliff, but with enough bare beach to land the jumper as well. It was the work of a few minutes to get Ford and Atelia and the baby onto the jumper, and then John brought it carefully out of the hatch, parking it on the stones as clear of the scout as he could manage. He lowered the back hatch and scrambled out to join the others, Ford and his family following more slowly.

"I bid you farewell," Ran said, from the scout's ramp. "Do not look for us any time soon. We have much work to do."

"We won't bother you if you don't bother us," John said.

"I think I can promise you that," Ran said, and the hatch slid closed behind her. A few moments later, the scout rose silently from the stony beach. It hovered for an instant, balancing on invisible force fields, and then shot up into the air, vanishing with impossible speed.

"We should have asked for more," Rodney said. "I barely got a chance to look at those engines—"

"Rodney," John said, and the scientist stopped abruptly. "Let's go home."

It was still early morning when they landed in Colorado Springs, the puddle jumper chasing the sunrise around the curve of the planet. Elizabeth had napped for most of the way across the Atlantic, the old habits that let her sleep whenever the chance arose kicking in efficiently, but as John brought them down onto the hidden landing space, she found herself wide awake, and strangely nervous. What if Dekaas had gotten it wrong? What if she really were some weird Replicator time-bomb, programmed to believe herself to be Elizabeth Weir at such a deep level that even people who had known her well would be fooled? She shook herself, annoyed. Ran had saved her — Ran had helped her Ascend, and when she had unascended, she had done so in her own body and as herself. Those worries were pointless.

Jordan was awake, too, and starting to fuss as Atelia and Ford tried to gather their belongings, clearly feeling their nervousness.

"Let me take him," Daniel said, and swung the boy into his lap, dangling what looked like a particularly complicated key ring in front of him.

"Thanks," Ford said, hoisting a heavy bag onto his shoulder, and Atelia closed her own satchel with a sigh of relief.

"Yes, thank you."

"I'll carry him, if you'd like," Daniel said, and settled Jordan on his hip with unexpected competence. They trailed out one by one into the bright morning, the mountain soaring above them into a vivid sky crossed by a single contrail. Atelia looked up at it, shading her eyes, and Ford touched her shoulder, saying something Elizabeth couldn't hear. Rodney and Teyla followed them, and Elizabeth glanced back to see John bringing up the rear, a pair of dark sunglasses hiding his eyes. He saw her looking, though, and smiled. The expression looked odd somehow, and then she realized she had never before seen him smile without reserve.

"It's good to be home, huh?"

"Very good." Elizabeth nodded, and then, because he of all people would understand, added, "And more than a little strange."

"A lot of changes." John nodded back, and lengthened his stride to catch up with the others, taking his place in the lead. "General Landry!"

There were Marines waiting at the edge of the field, of course, as well as Landry and a knot of officers. Elizabeth found herself hanging back a little, unsure what she wanted to say about everything that had happened, and found herself next to Daniel and Atelia. Jordan was beginning to fuss again, and Atelia reached for him.

"Here, I can take him now. Come to Mama, big boy."

Daniel made the transfer easily. "Can I carry your bag?"

"No, I've got it," Atelia said. And indeed, she seemed to be balancing everything with the ease of long practice. "Thank you. You're very good with him. Do you have children of your own?"

A shadow crossed Daniel's face. "No."

Atelia winced. "Oh. I am sorry. The Wraith —?"

"No." Daniel shook his head, managing a smile that seemed almost genuine. "My wife was killed. Not by the Wraith, but by an enemy from our own galaxy, one we eventually defeated. But it was many years ago."

And that, Elizabeth thought, was a fair summary of his life, even if it left out many of the important things. But it was a story Atelia would recognize, and probably that was what Daniel had meant.

"When Aiden first told me of his world," Atelia said, "I thought it must be a paradise. But I soon realized it was not so."

"There is nothing like the Wraith," Daniel said. "Which I hope you'll find an advantage."

Atelia smiled as he'd meant, but her eyes were still shadowed.

Elizabeth said, "Earth is like most other worlds, good and bad alike. The greatest difference is that most people can't walk through a Stargate to get away from their troubles."

Atelia's eyes widened at that, as though it were a thought she had never before imagined. And probably she hadn't, Elizabeth thought. There were very few worlds in Pegasus that didn't have an accessible Stargate; even the Travelers were raised with the certainty that if they lost their ship or were left behind, they could dial a new world and escape there. One more thing Atelia would have to adjust to, here on Earth.

"It might be better if they could," Daniel said, under his breath, and she couldn't entirely disagree.

John and General Landry were talking, she realized, with additions from Rodney and, once, Teyla. And then she heard her own name, and Ford's, and she stepped forward to take Landry's outstretched hand.

"Dr. Weir. Quite frankly, we never expected to see you again. It's good to be surprised."

"Thank you."

"I gather you're in competition with Dr. Jackson for number of times Ascended and Unascended."

Elizabeth smiled in spite of herself. "I sincerely hope not, General. Once was quite enough for me."

"Lieutenant." Landry returned Ford's salute, then held out his hand. "Welcome home, son."

"Thank you, sir." Ford's voice didn't break, but he was blinking furiously.

Landry looked away. "Right. Let's get inside. Colonel, I hope you understand that you're leaving us that puddlejumper. There's no way we're getting it down to the gate room in one piece, and frankly we could use a spare."

"Yes, sir," John said.

The next few hours passed in a blur, as they were passed from one department to another, from debriefing to medical to another debriefing and another medical and a conference with Landry and several staff members who were new since her time. Sometime in the middle of the afternoon, she was assigned a suite in the guest quarters and promised clean clothes and a few hours' rest, and dropped onto the narrow bunk and slept before she had even thought of taking off more than her shoes.

She woke again to polite but insistent knocking, and opened her door to a quartermaster sergeant who arrived with a change of clothes and a second set of towels, and the polite reminder that it was getting late and the mess hall would be going to late-night service in an hour or two. She rubbed her eyes, disoriented — somewhere around eight o'clock here, and her body thought it was very early morning — and John loomed up behind the sergeant.

"Oh, good, I caught you. General O'Neill wants a word with all of us."

"Certainly." Elizabeth let the sergeant set her burden on the nearest table, and smoothed her hair into something like reasonable order. "Do I have time for a shower?"

"Better get it over with," John answered, with his familiar flinching smile, and she nodded.

"All right. But there needs to be food."

"I've been promised sandwiches," John said.

There were sandwiches, three big trays of them sitting on the credenza to one side of the big table, as well as salads and chips and an enormous plate of cookies: Earth food, American food, the sort Elizabeth hadn't seen since long before she'd awakened without memory. Her body remembered, though, and she filled her plate without shame. Ford was doing the same, and he met her look with a sheepish smile.

"It's funny, you don't think you've missed something until it's there."

Elizabeth nodded. "I know. Roast beef with cheddar…"

"Tuna salad. Who'd ever miss tuna salad?" Ford added a third wedge to his plate and turned back to his wife. She already had a plate, Elizabeth saw, and she was distracting Jordan from the cookies with a piece of bread.

"I don't know why they always put this stuff — this, kale, whatever it is — on every single plate everywhere," Rodney said. "Nobody eats it. I don't think it's even edible."

"It's better than lemon slices," John said, coming up to snag another couple of cookies. Rodney glared at him, but before he could respond, General Landry tapped on the table.

"All right, folks, if everyone has had a chance to get something, I'd like to get started."

Elizabeth obediently took her place at the table, sliding into a seat between Teyla and Daniel. Atelia had one end of the table, where she and Ford could corral the baby — currently being bribed with a chocolate chip cookie, which he seemed to be regarding with some doubt — and Landry had the other, with O'Neill next to him.

"I thought we'd wait to get started until we were all here," O'Neill began, and the door opened. Elizabeth turned, to see Richard Woolsey framed in the doorway, his suit slightly rumpled, as though he'd been on his feet all day.

"Gentlemen. Ladies. I apologize for the delay."

"Glad you could make it," Landry said, and gestured to a chair.

Woolsey smiled and nodded, but filled a plate before he sat down.

"I see you missed dinner," O'Neill remarked.

"I've been on a conference call," Woolsey answered, unperturbed, and Landry cleared his throat.

"I wanted us to get together tonight so that no one was left wondering what the next steps were going to be. Lieutenant, your next steps are up to you — and I expect you to take as much time as you need to decide what that's going to be — but I want to assure you and your wife that she will be accorded all assistance as you adjust to life back here on Earth. We'll arrange for all the paperwork she'll need, and we also have a team working on a cover story for all of you. I assume you've discussed the position of the SGC with her?"

Atelia said, "Aiden has said that your Stargate is kept secret, and that therefore I must seem to be from a war zone on this planet. I am willing to pretend to be so, though I don't understand how you've kept such a secret."

"With great difficulty," O'Neill said.

Landry ignored him. "Excellent. I think that takes care of the Lieutenant for now. Mr. Woolsey?"

"Yes." Woolsey put down his sandwich. His tie was unspotted, Elizabeth saw, and there wasn't even an errant crumb on his plate. "Dr. McKay, the IOA wishes me to express their displeasure at your returning to Earth against their express orders."

"Hey! It's not like I had a choice, except maybe to stay behind on a freezing, night-time planet. Which, yes, had a Stargate, but it was on another continent, and I couldn't dial Atlantis anyway." Rodney stopped abruptly, as though he'd wandered into a mine-field. "Though I'll be more than happy to head back just as soon as possible —"

Woolsey nodded. "Quite so. Consider their displeasure expressed."

Rodney opened his mouth and shut it again. "Oh. Ok. Right."

"Dr. Weir." Woolsey's thin mouth curved into an unexpected smile. "And Lieutenant Ford. First, I'd like to say both personally and on behalf of the President — and of course of the IOA — how very glad we are to have you back. The President was briefed yesterday on your situation, and asked me to convey a greeting on his behalf, a welcome home, and, for Mrs. Ford, a welcome to what he hopes will become her home."

That was unexpected, and unexpectedly moving. Elizabeth felt tears prick at the corners of her eyes, and looked down to hide them. There was an awkward murmur of agreement, and then O'Neill said, "There'd better not be a catch to that."

"Ah."

O'Neill's eyes narrowed. "Lieutenant Ford and his family are purely a US military issue."

"Indeed they are," Woolsey said. "I'm happy to say that the IOA has no argument there, nor any claim to jurisdiction. But —"

"Me," Elizabeth said.

Woolsey dipped his head. "Dr. Weir. The IOA feels that your status is somewhat ambiguous. Certainly they feel that you cannot be considered to still be the leader of the Atlantis Expedition —"

"Not unreasonable," Elizabeth said. "Nor do I expect to be treated as such."

"Noted. However, they are also concerned that this might be a trick by some surviving faction among the Replicators, and they do not wish to let you stay on Earth until that has been disproved to their satisfaction."

"Oh, come on," O'Neill said.

Daniel looked up from his plate. "You know, the same point could have been made about me the last time."

"Except that you showed up naked in my office," O'Neill said. "Which seems to have meant something to someone. Come on, Woolsey, this is bull. Dr. Weir was helped to ascend by one of the Asgard, and was then unascended for interfering in human affairs. This — I hate to say it, but it's practically SOP."

"She was unascended for saving my life," Rodney said. "I knew when it happened, when she saved me, that it was her, and I knew she was going to get into trouble for it. And here she is. You're going to kick her off Earth for that?"

"She's already here," John said. "Already on Earth. Nothing's happened, and nothing's going to happen."

"The IOA is unwilling to concede on the matter," Woolsey said. "Believe me, I've tried."

"What do they want me to do?" Elizabeth asked. *My mother,* she thought. *Have they already told her? Is she expecting me, and then I can't come home after all? That would be worse than thinking she was dead.*

"The IOA would like you to return either to the Alpha site or to Atlantis and submit to further testing — specifically to be sure there are no nanites in your bloodstream — before they rule on the question again."

Elizabeth took a deep breath. That wasn't as bad as she'd expected, and certainly better than it could have been. To return to Atlantis, an Atlantis mostly at peace with the Wraith, an Atlantis where things had moved forward rather than back — the idea filled her with unexpected excitement. "I'm willing to go back to Atlantis. What level of evidence is the IOA willing to accept to prove that I'm not a Replicator?"

"A reasonable one," Woolsey said firmly, riding over something profane from O'Neill. "It may take some months to convince them of that, but I expect — I am determined to see it happen."

"All right." Elizabeth nodded. "I will want to discuss what's to be done about my family."

"Absolutely," Woolsey said, and Landry leaned forward.

"We're happy to put our support teams at your disposal, Doctor."

"If that's settled, then…" Woolsey brushed an invisible speck from his lapel. "I believe that a photograph was required?"

"That's right," John said. "You and General O'Neill and Lieutenant Ford. To prove that he's back on Earth with you."

"It's a shame Sam isn't here," Daniel said. "The Wraith are matriarchal, they'd probably react better to having her in the picture, since they seem to think of you two as her consorts…"

"Daniel," O'Neill said. "Right. Let's get this over with."

Elizabeth refilled her plate while the pictures were being taken, not so much because she was still hungry but because the long unfamiliar flavors seemed so astonishing. She was debating one last cookie — chocolate chip or sugar? — When she looked up to find O'Neill at her shoulder.

"Are you all right with this?" His voice was soft enough not to carry to the others. "I'll go to the mat on this if it's not. And win."

Elizabeth blinked, surprised and touched, but slowly shook her head. "It's not worth spending that capital, General. I'm not a Replicator, and it's easy enough to prove it. And — I'd like to see Atlantis again. Even if it's just to say goodbye, I need that."

"All right." O'Neill nodded. "Let me know if you change your mind."

"I will," she said, and knew she would not.

Four days later, she stood in the gate room with the others while high above them technicians in the control room dialed Atlantis. For a moment, the room was filled with the memory of all the others who had waited there with her that first time, packs in hand, ready to cross to another galaxy where no one knew what might be waiting. She could remember the excitement, the ball of nerves in the pit of her stomach, but this time she felt only relief. She'd bought time to figure out how to break the news to her mother, and she'd gotten the time to say goodbye. Those were both rare gifts.

"Time to go," John said.

Elizabeth nodded. "You're staying?"

"We're seeing Ford home," John said.

"Just for a few more days," Teyla said. "General Landry thinks I might be helpful to Atelia as she settles in to her new life."

"I expect you will be," Elizabeth said. "And I'll see you soon."

"You shall," Teyla said, with a warm smile, and they embraced, forehead against forehead in the Athosian way.

When Teyla released her, John held out his hand, but Elizabeth shook her head. He smiled, and allowed her to embrace him as well. Behind him, the Stargate began to turn, the symbols lighting, six and then the vital seventh. The wormhole exploded out into the room, and stabilized to the familiar shimmering pool of blue light. Like water, Elizabeth thought again, and lifted her new carryall.

"Gentlemen," she said, to Rodney and Daniel. "Shall we?"

"After you," Daniel said, and she walked up the ramp and into the wormhole without a backward glance.

She emerged into Atlantis's gate room, the light dim behind the glass so that for a moment it was as though she was arriving for the first time. It was still beautiful, still the soaring city, walls of glass and light and glory, and suddenly the room was full of the sound of applause. She looked up to see the control consoles jammed full, two or three people at every station and every one of them clapping and cheering, and her eyes filled with tears. Rodney and Daniel were clapping, too, backing away so that she stood unaccompanied, caught in the moment. She spread her hands in helpless wonder, and Lorne came down the steps to greet her, limping slightly.

"Doc. Welcome back."

"Thank you." Her voice broke, and she tried again. "Thank you. All of you."

Something rattled on the floor behind her, and the clapping

was overtaken by a wave of sudden laughter. Something nudged her foot, and she looked down to see a champagne bottle tied with a bow. There was a card taped to it, and she stooped to pick it up. *This one's for you*, it read. It was signed simply, *O'Neill*.

Daniel settled back into a comfortable routine once he'd gotten himself reestablished on Atlantis. Beckett and the rest of the medical personnel were busy running tests on Elizabeth — tests that station rumor said proved conclusively that she was entirely human — and the rest of the science staff was busy either with Rodney's notes on the Vanir ship or with routine maintenance or projects of their own. For once, he had free rein in the Ancient database, and no particular research agenda at the top of his list. He spent several days tracking down obscure questions that had perplexed him on his first visit, but at the end of the first week, he had to admit to himself that his real curiosity was about the Wraith. Ember would be going back to Guide's hive — Alabaster's hive, Daniel reminded himself — as soon as Sheppard and Teyla returned from Earth, and that didn't leave much time. Of course, he could have asked McKay — as McKay would have been happy to point out — but he wanted to talk to an actual Wraith. And that meant Ember.

The Wraith scientist was housed in what was practically his own tower, a slender spire with no transfer chambers of its own and only a single, easily guarded exit. Daniel waited until the middle of Atlantis's morning, well aware that he was avoiding McKay's eye, and made his way across, talking his way past the Marines on guard without difficulty. Though of course, he reminded himself, there was no reason they should have been told to keep him from talking to anyone. He found the Wraith — Ember — in the lower chamber, where the windows ran from floor to ceiling, broken only by a dozen slender pillars. At the top and bottom of the windows, the glass was faceted into bands of prisms, and the space was flecked with hundreds of shards of rainbow. Ember stood at the far end, facing out toward the city's edge and the vivid blues of sea and sky beyond, his black coat a sharp contrast to the brilliance. His long white hair was bound up in an elaborate double fall — personal display seemed to be extremely important to the Wraith, Daniel thought, presumably because of the competition for the queen's attention. He wondered where Ember fell in the Wraith canon of beauty, and if and how he would compete for Alabaster's favor.

Those were all questions for which he had hoped to find answers, and he cleared his throat. "Ember?"

The Wraith turned astonishingly quickly, his coat swirling, though Daniel suspected he had actually slowed the movement. "Dr. Jackson?"

"Yes. I know you're due to leave shortly, and I wondered if I might ask you some questions."

"Since there is no longer any need to search for Vanir sites, there is no reason for me to stay," Ember said. "What sort of questions?"

"We know very little about the Wraith, about your people and your culture." Daniel spread his hands. "I'd like to know more."

Ember showed teeth in what Daniel hoped was a smile. "You should be careful, you may find out things you do not wish to know." He shrugged, and waved toward one of the benches that were the room's main furniture. "But, certainly, you may ask. I will not promise to answer anything that might compromise my queen or my people."

"Fair enough." Daniel seated himself, and Ember circled him to take a seat opposite him. Just out of reach, Daniel noticed. Was that courtesy, and was the circling an expression of social dominance? Ember's eyes were hard yellow-green, the pupils contracted to hairline slits, the sensor pits bracketing his nose starkly visible in the harsh light. "Doesn't the sunlight bother you?"

Ember tilted his head to one side. "I, too, am trying to learn things."

"About humans?"

"Yes."

"And you'll put yourself through a certain amount of discomfort in order to do so?"

"Would you not do the same?"

Daniel paused. "Well, yes. But probably not when there's no one else around, unless I'm missing your reason."

"This place, Atlantis." Ember waved his hand — not his feeding hand, Daniel noticed — in a circle that encompassed the room and the view beyond the enormous windows. More flecks of rainbow fell across him, bright against the dark leather. "It is to you what our hives are to us: home, yes, but also a living symbol of what you desire a home to be. I am trying to understand it, as well."

There was some truth to that, Daniel thought. Atlantis contained much of the best, and some of the worst, of the Ancients' aspirations; the towers reached to the stars, but there were labs and hidden chambers that contained some very bad ideas. "I would like to see a hiveship myself. Now that things are more — settled — between our people."

"You would not like most of them," Ember said. "The feeding cells are... utilitarian. For us to use."

Daniel ignored the chill that ran up his spine. "I thought some hives had humans on board, as worshippers?"

"That's what other humans call them. They do not think us gods, nor would we wish them to."

Which makes a change from the Goa'uld. Daniel swallowed those words as too revealing of things the SGC would probably prefer to keep obscured. "What do you call them, you Wraith, I mean?"

"Pets."

That had been the term the Wraith had used in the alternate universe, though Daniel suspected that the relationships were a bit more complicated. And probably were more complicated here, too. "Have you... kept pets?"

"I have not!" Ember's voice was sharp, and Daniel spread his hands.

"Sorry, I didn't mean to offend. I don't understand."

Ember took a breath. "It is a matter of some disagreement among us. Some lineages accept the practice, and some do not. My first queen did not, nor did Guide after I joined him. I do not yet know what Alabaster will do."

"Why did they disapprove?"

Ember's mouth curved into another teeth-baring smile. "It's never wise to become too friendly with one's food."

Fair enough, Daniel thought. "All right, why do other people, other queens, approve of it?"

"I don't know."

That was not entirely true, Daniel thought, looking at the sudden stiffness in Ember's stance, but he didn't know how to pursue the question without offending further.

Ember said, into the silence, "We all know that humans are intelligent beings. Most people prefer not to think about it too closely."

Most humans didn't like to think too hard about where their food came from, either. But there was more to it than that. Daniel nodded slowly. "Among humans, to eat together, to share a meal, is a particular kind of intimacy. It joins people together — among our ancestors, to break bread, to share food, was to create a truce even between the bitterest enemies; sharing food, sharing a meal, is part of our ceremonies of marriage and birth and death. Even today, diplomacy is accompanied by state dinners, a meal between heads of state to show that they are meeting in friendship. On the individual level, nearly every human culture on Earth and off it has some rule that says you must offer food to a guest — when you go to somebody's room even here on Atlantis, they're probably going to offer you a cookie or some chips or a cup of tea. It's not just about nourishment, but about connection. And it's even more about that with the Wraith, isn't it? Because the same process that nourishes you can be reversed — you can take the life from humans, or you can give it back. That has to have tremendous meaning."

Ember blinked once, then made a sound that might have been laughter. "You are indeed a clever man. No wonder Carter values you."

"So to feed from a human and restore him or her —"

"That is the Gift," Ember said. "And the Gift may be made between Wraith as well — any blade, any cleverman, would gladly bare his chest for the queen's hand. In old-fashioned hives, the queen tastes the life of any man she allows to serve her — Death did so — but she always has the right, in any hive anywhere. Our lives are hers. And so it is, to a lesser degree, with the lords of the zenana, the officers of the hive. In an emergency, the superior may claim the life of the inferior, and the inferior should give it gladly, though that's not always the case. I am Master of Sciences Biological, and I would think it shameful to feed from my men when I should have prevented the emergency in the first place."

Daniel nodded again. "And is the Gift ever given between equals?"

"Between the closest of friends," Ember said. "Between brothers. Between lovers. And that — this is why the retrovirus frightens me. We must go from thinking of humans as kine to people worthy of our most intimate attentions."

"That's why some queens don't allow pets," Daniel said. "Your biology's not that different."

"That intimacy is forbidden," Ember said flatly. "Clevermen are killed for that."

But not always, Daniel thought. Or maybe they're just not all caught. Or maybe some queens care less. "Not blades?"

Ember hissed. "I have never heard of a blade choosing to do so. It's us clevermen who have access to humans anyway."

"It's not actually the same," Daniel began, and Ember laughed again, his feeding hand clenching tight.

"The act is exactly the same, and if it is not to be mere food, then —" He shook his head, the pale hair bright in the sun. "I have fed on Zelenka, who is a colleague and a comrade, we shared the experience of working with Quicksilver — with McKay. That wasn't so strange. But this young woman, Salawi — she is brave and generous as any blade and therefore I, in honor, owe her what I would owe a blade who had rescued me. And I am not ready for such a bond."

Daniel let out his breath in a silent whistle. That was complicated, all right. If Ember was right, the Wraith were having to change not merely from hunter to herder but to accept humans into their closest and most complicated relationships. And that was a hell of a change, for both sides. On the other hand... It was a new path for both, and there would be a chance to make new rules.

Ember nodded as though he had read the thought. "I think this is what Guide knew would happen. And somehow —somehow we must find our way through." He lifted his head, the alien lines of his face suddenly very marked. "But we are Wraith. We will survive."

"I believe you will," Daniel said.

Radek made his way to the mess hall for an early dinner, enjoying the feeling of having nothing more to worry about than Atlantis's routine maintenance and an interesting theoretical problem involving the aurora. Rodney had declined to get involved with the latter, too, which left him with research he enjoyed and no pressing reason to solve the problem immediately. No one would die — nothing would even break if he and Sommer and Joyce Han didn't come up with a provable theory about the observed color shifts. When you added that to almost a week of sleeping in his own bed, with as many showers as he wanted, he felt definitely content with the world.

There was fresh food back on the buffet line, local legumes and new-picked vegetables and cutlets of a Behranin bird that tasted like chicken, and he filled his tray contentedly. The only thing missing was a nice glass of wine — perhaps a vino verdhe? But if he wanted alcohol, he was restricted to the brandy he'd brought from Earth, or the moonshine the Marines brewed in the depths of the South Tower. He fixed himself a cup of coffee instead, and turned toward the tables.

It was early evening, and the sky beyond the long windows had hazed to twilight purple, the first threads of the aurora flickering on the horizon. They seemed to be blue tonight, and he steered for a table where he would have a decent view, only to have to stop short to keep from colliding with Elizabeth.

"I'm sorry," he said, checking his tray to be sure he hadn't spilled his coffee, and she gave an apologetic smile.

"No, I should apologize. Is this your table?"

"Not at all." Radek shook his head to emphasize the words. "Perhaps you would join me?"

"I'd like that."

They settled themselves, laying out silverware and plates and adjusting the trays, and Elizabeth gestured at her plate. "I see Sergeant Pollard is still the expert at getting local supplies."

"He is a genius," Radek said, with perfect sincerity. "He had the idea of trading Tupperware to the Athosians, and the Athosians connected him with all their suppliers."

"I guess the IOA relaxed some of the strictures on trading after I was gone?"

"After we returned," Radek said. "When we were forced to land here, we lost all possibility of getting supplies from the local planet. And we have a lot of things that people here need."

"Including Tupperware." Elizabeth smiled.

Radek shrugged. "Lightweight, waterproof, and hard to crush. For a nomadic people, it has some obvious advantages."

"True enough."

"Speaking of trade with other worlds, however..." Radek gave her a sidelong glance. "There's a rumor that Colonel Hocken will be retiring, and that she's planning to take a job on Sateda. Bringing an airplane kit with her."

Elizabeth hesitated, then shrugged. "I don't know that it's a secret. She's discussed it with the Air Force, anyway, but I don't know if she's decided to take the job yet."

"She will," Radek said. "Or at least I think so."

"Have you thought about staying? If you don't mind my asking."

"I don't mind." Radek smiled, buying time to consider just how honest he wanted his answer to be. It was not that he didn't trust her, but that there were so many contingencies, so many possibilities still to consider. And he had time, of course, plenty of time to work out exactly what it was he wanted. "I've thought about it, yes. Atlantis is — amazing. Impossible. I am — I have been, in spite of everything, very happy here. If things could be worked out, I would certainly consider it." He paused, but there was something about the mess hall, the way it was communal and yet private enough, that invited confidences. "And you? When you came back, when we saw you, we all —" He shook his head, unwilling to go further. "You could certainly stay."

"That's kind," she said, "and I do thank you. But — I expect I'll go home eventually? Probably sooner, rather than later. I needed to come back, to say goodbye properly, but now — someone else should have my old job, and there are things I want to do back on Earth."

That made sense. Radek nodded, but before he could say anything more, Ronon loomed over the table, his tray piled high with the leaf-wrapped chopped chicken-and-vegetables that Pollard had adapted from a Satedan recipe. "Mind if I join you?"

"Not at all," Elizabeth said, warmly. "I was hoping I'd get a chance to sit down with you. I'm so amazed at everything that's being done on Sateda."

"Yeah." Ronon settled himself, began to eat with quick, neat movements. He never spilled the filling out the end of the rolled leaf,

Radek thought, and allowed himself a sigh. "Cai's done a good job."

"He has," Elizabeth agreed.

"He's asked me to come back," Ronon said, and Radek realized that this was no chance conversation. "Maybe not right away, but in time. Once they start having elections again, and a real government."

"It would be our loss," Elizabeth said, "but you'd be excellent for them."

"I don't want to be a figurehead," Ronon said. "Not just the guy who was a Runner and lived."

"You've already moved far beyond that," Elizabeth said. "You'd proved you were more than that before I died."

"And I can't be Lantean — can't be your representative. Not the way things are with the Wraith. I mean, I'm going to put up with it. Do what I have to, and, yeah, I'm glad Sateda's in the protected sphere for as long as that lasts." Ronon shook his head. "I just think it's going to come back to bite us in the end. And we have to be ready for that."

Elizabeth gave a slow nod. "That's not unreasonable. You may even be right. There may be a break later between us and Sateda. But let's hold on to what we have for as long as we can."

"Fair enough." Ronon nodded in turn, tension leaving his shoulders. "What's this I hear about Colonel Hocken retiring to Sateda?"

"That seems to be everywhere," Radek said. "I heard the Marines have a pool on when she's going to get here."

"I'd forgotten about the Atlantis grapevine." Elizabeth looked faintly dismayed.

"Working better than ever," Ronon said.

"Radek!"

Radek turned to see William Lynn and Eva Robinson coming toward them with laden trays.

"Mind if we join you?"

"Not at all." Radek shifted his chair to make room, and then made the introductions, letting the conversation turn to more general things.

EPILOGUE

"DELTA 2538 arriving from Denver, bags on carousel D," John said, pointing at the overhead sign.

Ford glanced back at him, a smile replacing the worried look he'd worn the entire flight. "I know my way around Hartsfield pretty well, Colonel. Remember, I'm from Atlanta. I can find the baggage claim."

John shrugged. "I figure it's been a long time."

Ford's smile faded. "Yeah. It has."

"Where is…" Atelia began. Her brow was furrowed, Jordan riding high on her shoulder, a black baseball cap with a yellowjacket on it proclaiming that he was a Georgia Tech fan.

"It's this way," Ford said, and put his arm around her back, steering her through the press of passengers crowding into the atrium. John and Teyla followed with carryon bags. John figured they had enough to handle with the baby and diaper bag.

At least Jordan wasn't crying. He'd been good through the whole flight, too little to understand the momentous step he was making. Atelia did. She looked scared. Teyla was good moral support, though, explaining how she'd found Earth intimidating at first too, when Atlantis had been grounded in San Francisco a year ago. Two weeks of debriefing in Colorado Springs hadn't prepared her for the crowds, for the sheer number of new things all over the place all at once. But since her cover story was that she'd grown up in a remote, war torn country, hopefully people would cut her some slack. And Jordan – Jordan would never remember a time when he lived in another galaxy.

The Atrium was crowded. People hurried to make their flights or stopped to get something to eat on their way out. Visitors got their bearings. Arrivals looked for ground transportation or directions to the parking lots. And people waited.

There – out of the corner of his eye John saw the movement, a young woman putting her hands to her mouth suddenly – Ford's cousin Sheri. Behind her was an old couple, the man in a brown

STARGATE ATLANTIS: THIRD PATH   273

cardigan, the woman leaning on a cane. John caught the moment when they saw.

The old woman took one heaving breath, and then Ford turned. He crossed the patterned floor in three steps, and then she was in his arms, her head on his shoulder, her hands clenching on his jacket. "Grandma," he said. "Grandma." And again, disbelievingly. "Grandma." He bent his head over hers.

Sheri put her arms around him from behind, holding him tight between them. Atelia stopped uncertainly just behind.

The old man looked at her, his face as solemn as the baby's, tears running down his still face. He reached one hand out, touching the baby's hand. "You must be Jordan." Jordan looked back, held high on his mother's shoulder. "And you must be Atelia."

"I am," Atelia said, and her voice faltered a little.

"I hear you've taken good care of the boy."

"I have tried to, sir," she said.

Ford turned, pulling away and reaching back for her hand. "Grandma, I want you to meet Atelia. And Jordan." Sheri pressed her hands to her lips again as Ford's grandmother drew them into her embrace.

Teyla made a noise suspiciously like a sniffle, and John looked at her sideways. "There is something in my eye," Teyla said sharply.

"Mine too," John said.

Sheri ducked around the hug and came toward him. "Colonel Sheppard," she said. "I don't know how to thank you. When we talked a few years ago and you said you hadn't given up…" She stopped, then began again. "I thought you were just giving our grandparents false hope. I thought it would be kinder to just say that Aiden was dead rather than to keep listing him missing in action and saying that he might be found. I never thought… I never thought he'd come home."

"He's home," John said, and found he couldn't say anymore.

Sheri smiled at Teyla. "I don't believe we've met."

"This is Teyla Emmagen," John said. "She's one of our civilian contractors who has been instrumental in hunting for Ford."

"Then I should thank you too," Sheri said. "You have no idea how much this means to us."

"I do," Teyla said. "It is always our prayer that our lost ones may somehow be returned to us."

Ford's grandfather had taken baby Jordan in his arms, pressing his rough cheek against the baby's smooth one, whispering in his ear.

"Will you stay?" Sheri asked. "We'd love to have you for dinner and thank you."

"I'm afraid we've got another flight to catch," John said. "We just wanted to see Ford home. But I expect you can take it from here."

"I'll never forget what you've done," Sheri said.

"We don't leave our people behind," John said, and shook her hand. He and Teyla walked away, leaving Ford and Atelia in his grandmother's arms while Sheri corralled the carryon luggage. They made their way across the Atrium, around the potted plants and the business travelers with their rolling bags and the benches full of people talking on their phones. They stopped behind a huge palm tree at the edge, looking back. Ford's grandfather was thumping him on the back while Ford explained something. His grandmother was taking the baby carefully, Atelia supporting her elbow.

"He's going to be ok," John said.

"Yes," Teyla said.

"Really ok."

"Yes," she said. "In time. Aiden will be ok." She looked at him. "And will this day come for you? Will your deployment end as well? Will there be the day when you come home to Earth and never look back?"

John shook his head, feeling free and light and utterly at peace. "No," he said. "I have a home. Atlantis is home. And when I get back there, that's when I've come home. That's where my family is." He opened the channel on his radio. "Hammond, this is Sheppard. Mission accomplished. We're ready when you are."

"You've got it, Sheppard," Sam Carter's voice said cheerfully. "Stand by for transport."

"We're going home," John said, taking a long look around the atrium of the Atlanta airport. They were back in a corner, Ford and his family wrapped up in each other.

Nobody noticed when they disappeared in a faint shimmer of light.

Stay in touch...
Follow us on Twitter
@StargateNovels

Find us on Facebook at
facebook.com/StargateNovels

Sign up for our newsletter
at StargateNovels.com

THANKS!

STARGATE SG·1.   STARGATE ATLANTIS™

Original novels based on the hit
TV shows **STARGATE SG-1** and
STARGATE ATLANTIS

Available as e-books from leading online
retailers

Paperback editions available from
Amazon and **IngramSpark**

If you liked this book, please tell your
friends and leave a review on a
bookstore website. Thanks!

Milton Keynes UK
Ingram Content Group UK Ltd.
UKHW041243240424
441691UK00054B/1136

9 781905 586707